This is a work of fiction. All characters and events are either a product of the author's imagination or used fictitiously, and any resemblance to real people or events is entirely coincidental.

SERPENT'S CROWN

Copyright © 2021 by Beth Alvarez

All rights reserved.

Cover art by Beth Alvarez

Edited by Amanda Dimer Silva

No part of this book may be reproduced in any form or by any electronic or mechanical means, including information storage and retrieval systems, without written permission from the author, except for the use of brief quotations in a book review.

First Edition: February 2021

ISBN-13: 978-1-952145-13-1

SERPENT'S CROWN

BOOK FIVE OF THE SNAKESBLOOD SAGA

BETH ALVAREZ

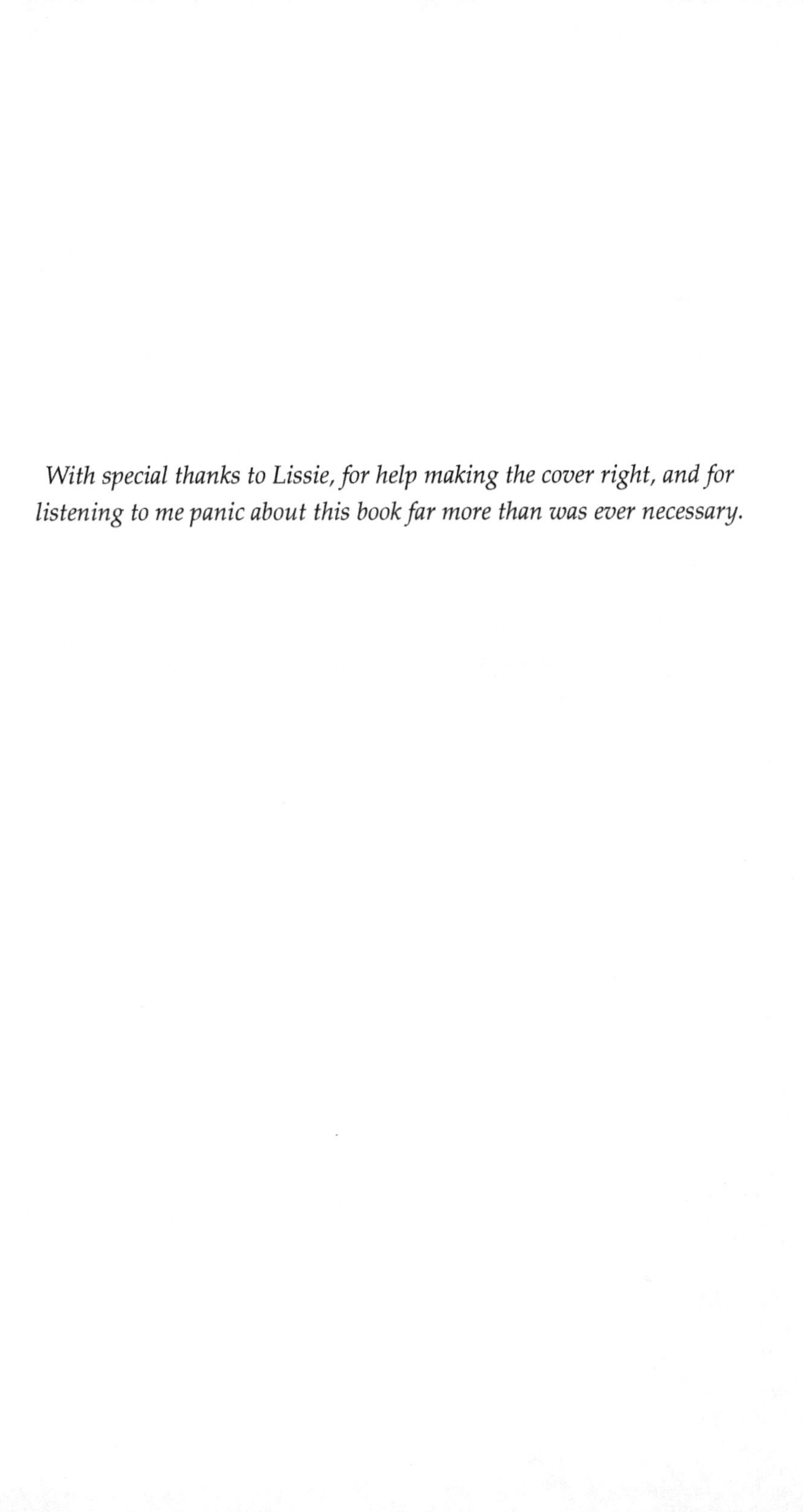

With special thanks to Lissie, for help making the cover right, and for listening to me panic about this book far more than was ever necessary.

Elenhiise Island

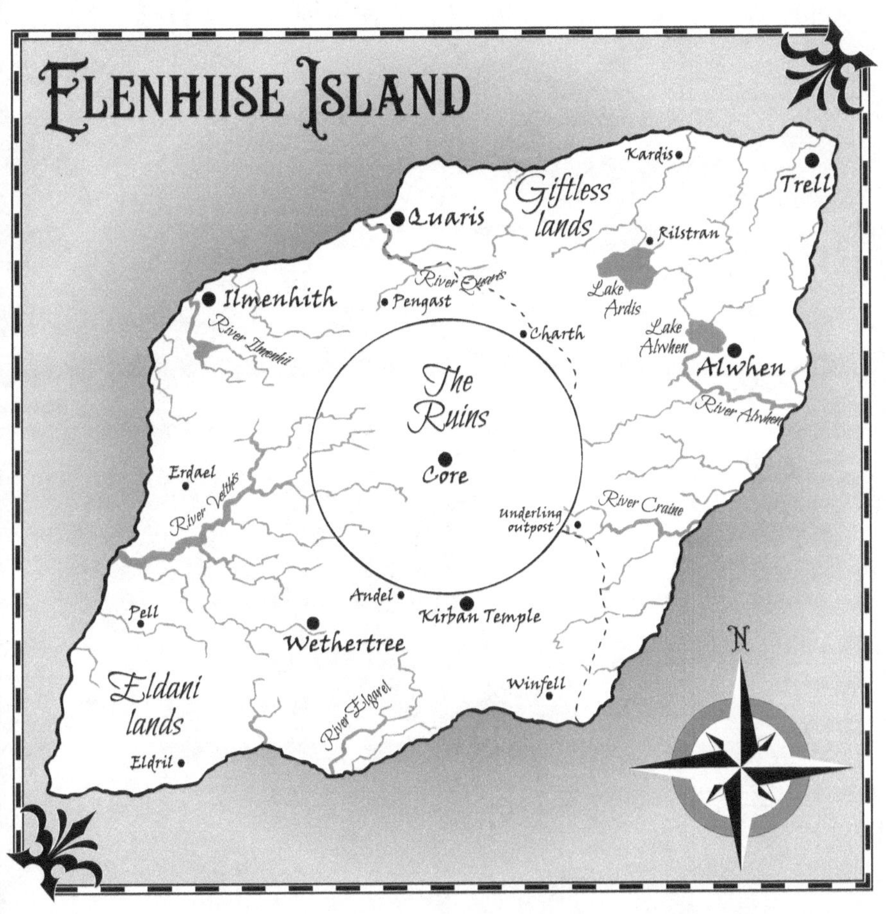

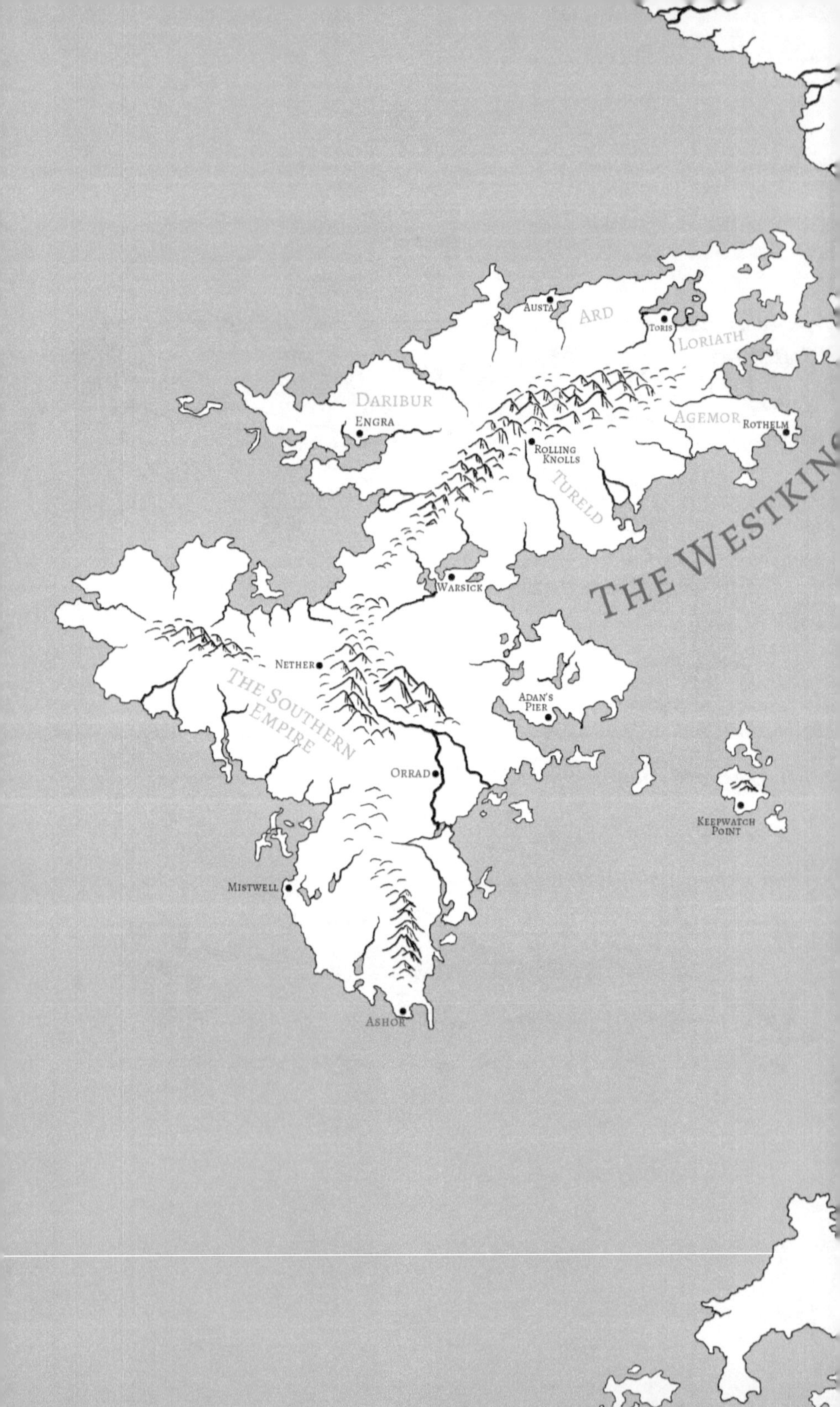

AUSTA
ARD
TORIS
LORIATH
DARIBUR
ENGRA
AGEMOR
ROTHELM
ROLLING
KNOLLS
TURELD
THE WESTKIN
WARSICK
NETHER
ADAN'S
PIER
THE SOUTHERN
EMPIRE
ORRAD
KEEPWATCH
POINT
MISTWELL
ASHOR

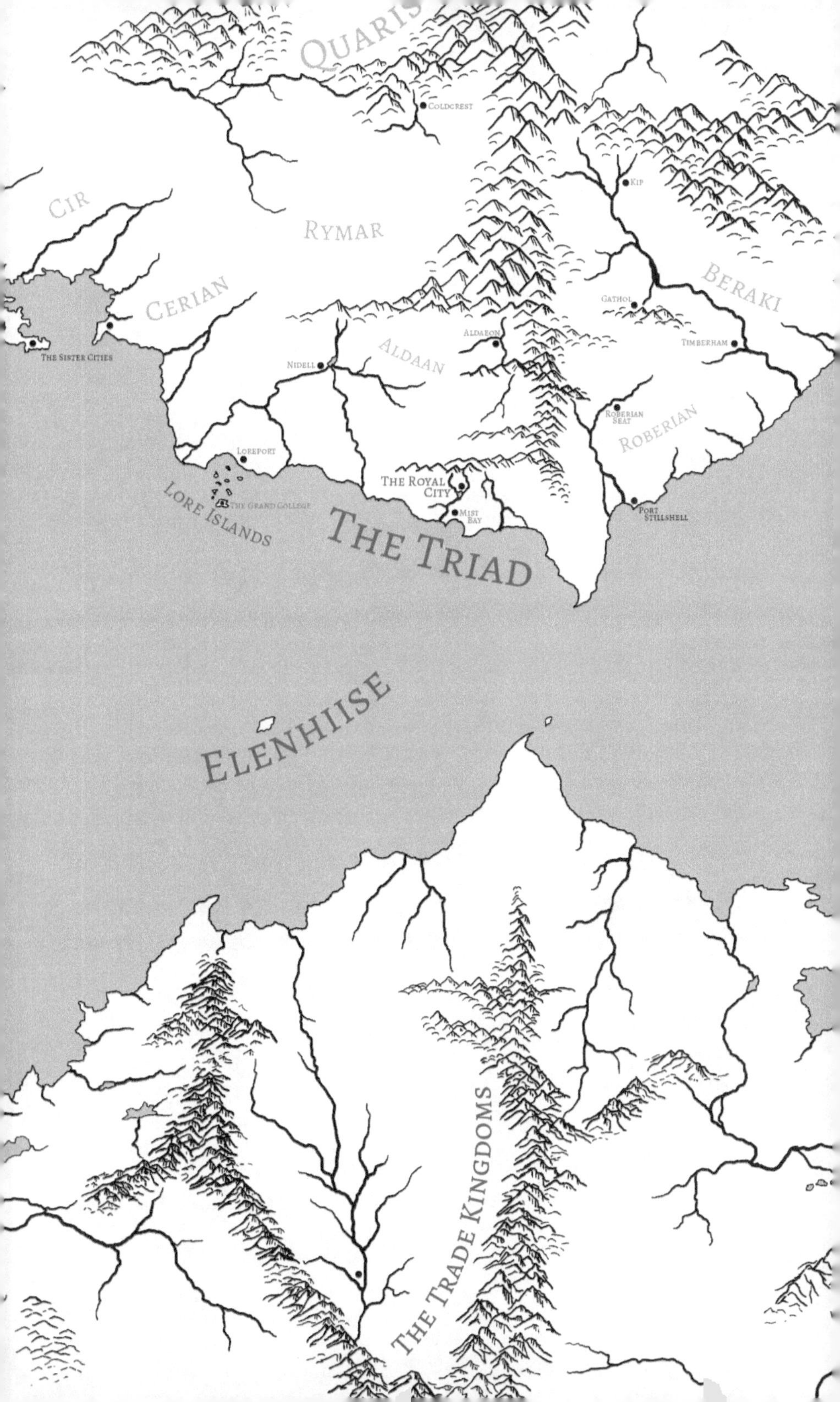

QUARIS
CIR
RYMAR
COLDCREST
KIP
CERIAN
BERAKI
GATHOL
ALDAEON
THE SISTER CITIES
TIMBERHAM
NIDELL
ALDAAN
ROBERIAN SEAT
LOREPORT
ROBERIAN
THE ROYAL CITY
LORE ISLANDS
THE GRAND COLLEGE
MIST BAY
PORT STILLSHELL
THE TRIAD
ELENHIISE
THE TRADE KINGDOMS

CONTENTS

FOREWORD

At the end of book 4, Serpent's Wake, I stood at a difficult split in the road. There were more adventures to write, more things that happened in the linear timeline, that were things I wanted to explore. But that meant two, maybe three books where it was more like Rune being along for the ride in other people's journeys than him actually resolving his own problems, and Firal… nothing of note happened to her at all, and she wouldn't have been in those stories. Those are stories that are still going to be told, but ultimately, I decided their place was not in the core Snakesblood Saga.

This story is about the forces that interact between Rune and Firal, bringing their lives together and pulling them apart, which meant the real place the story should resume was here: some six pents—thirty years—after the events in Wake. That's a lot of time for humans like you and I, but not so much for the Eldani.

Those other stories? They're coming, but they'll be on their own, a separate series that can be read by itself. If you're curious to see how things pan out, you can always read those before tackling this, but it's definitely not necessary to read them before starting here, with Serpent's Crown.

Let's get started, shall we?

OLD FRIENDS

"SHE IS NOT HIS CHILD." ENNIL TANRYS STUDIED THE TEACUP IN HIS hands. It was not a good brew, bitter beyond what honey could save. The tea was too dark, obscuring the fine porcelain, and its surface swam with oils that promised to stain. It was unworthy of his attention, but he stared at it anyway. Anything to keep from looking at the monster that sat in his parlor. He took a sip and grimaced at the taste. He'd sent his staff away as soon as she'd appeared in his study. In the future, he'd wait for one of them to make a pot of tea before he dismissed them.

Unwilling to drink the rest, Ennil put his tea aside. "I never expected my family line would end like this. My brothers dead before they could sire children, me unable to sire more than one. My son married to a queen for decades, and the only child in the house isn't even his."

"A tragic tale," his companion said, her tone dry. "But what makes you think I care?"

This time, he made himself look at her.

There was a time she might have been beautiful, with her high cheekbones and fine brows, but magic had spoiled her long ago. Her hair fell in snowy ringlets around her shoulders and her eyes shone a frigid, shocking blue. All mages ended up as cold and colorless eventually, and Envesi had been Archmage, the first leader of Kirban Temple.

Ennil could look past the lack of color in her flesh and features. He had for years. It was the new changes that bothered him; he didn't understand what could drive someone to such madness. She'd experimented on others first for a reason. She should have known what to expect.

Yet there she was, her legs crossed and her reptilian feet exposed. She cradled a teacup in her white-scaled hands and tapped a rhythm of impatience against it with one clawed finger.

It was all he could do not to shudder.

"Don't forget that I was one of your first supporters, Archmage." The title hadn't been hers in nearly thirty years, but it rolled off his tongue before he could catch it. He glanced down as he took the small ewer of cream from the tea tray. "I don't always like your methods, but I have always stood by your cause. You founded the temple with a single intent. Judging by your appearance now, I'd say nothing has changed."

Envesi sipped her bitter tea without so much as a flinch. "Go on."

"They call her the Everchild." Ennil watched the cream swirl into his tea and offered her the ewer. She didn't move. He put it down. "You'd have to see her to understand. I know it's not uncommon for the children of mages to grow slowly, but if I didn't know better, I'd think her no more than a handful of years in age."

She raised a brow, the most vivid expression he'd seen her wear since her arrival. "And she is not?"

"She was born not a full year after they wed, which happened immediately after your... departure." Ennil didn't know a more sensitive way to reference her exile from the island. He expected she'd be irritated by its mention, but she didn't seem to care.

"If I didn't know you, Lord Tanrys," she all but spat his title, "I'd think you were exaggerating." She peered at him over the rim of her teacup. Her snake-slitted eyes gave him chills. "Does the girl speak?"

"A few words. As many as can be expected, for her rate of aging. I do not exaggerate when I say she is small. Hardly more than a babe."

Envesi pursed her lips. "And the mages? Have they evaluated her yet?"

"That, I can't say." He sighed and slouched in his chair. "My connections in the temple are all but nonexistent, these days. I expect you'd have more luck prying that sort of information from the mages yourself." His lack of connections with mages didn't bother him, but he was unlikely to tell her as much. Ennil had never liked mages, but he wasn't foolish enough to let them take his dislike as disrespect.

She snorted softly, amused. "Why, Ennil, what makes you think I've kept any foothold in the temple?"

"Because you've kept a foothold with me," he said.

She smiled.

"Were circumstances different, I'd think it no more than an oddity. But Firal is your blood, and the girl's father was..." He trailed off and his eyes drifted back to her hands. He couldn't bring himself to say what he meant, but he couldn't hide his distaste, either. He'd spent years stifling it for Kifel's benefit, but Kifel had been a friend. Envesi was not. And Lomithrandel, of course, was responsible for the mess Ennil's son had landed in to begin with.

Envesi lifted her tea once more. "Are you certain?"

"If you saw her, Archmage," he said, "there wouldn't be a doubt in your mind."

"Very well." She drained her cup and set it aside, then smiled again. "Shall we begin?"

Unwilling to disrupt the peace of the queen's office, Medreal lingered in the doorway with a tea tray balanced on one arm.

Firal sat behind her desk, her chair turned toward the high arched windows that overlooked the palace gardens. She hummed quietly, rocking the dark-haired girl in her arms. The child chewed on her fingers, her big eyes trained on her mother's face.

It wasn't often the stewardess saw the queen content. Too often, Firal's duties kept her from mothering the girl the way she wanted. Lulu, of course, always wanted time with her mother. Neither cared how unconventional their relationship was. Normal queens didn't feed or fuss over their own children, but Firal was hardly a normal queen.

Medreal was loath to disturb them, but if she didn't, the council would. She cleared her throat as she stepped inside and closed the office door with her heel.

Firal glanced up, shifting the baby in her arms. She sat the girl upright and pressed a kiss to her forehead. "You don't need to wait by the door, Medreal. If you stood watching as long as you wanted, the tea would grow cold."

The stewardess chuckled. She should have known she couldn't sneak up on them. The queen was a mage, after all. Though their powers were different, they could still sense one another. "I apologize, Majesty. I enjoy seeing you together. Goodness knows it doesn't happen as often as we'd like."

Making a small sound of displeasure in her throat, Firal moved papers on her desk to create room for the tea. "No, it never does. I appreciate your respect for our privacy."

Medreal glided across the room to deposit the tray on the edge of the desk and fill a teacup. She added sugar and cream, but did not stir it before she placed the cup in front of Firal with a spoon on the saucer. "I understand the need. I've held this job a long time, my queen. I have watched many of your predecessors struggle to strike a balance between kingdom and family."

Firal stirred her tea, watching absently as the cream blended into the drink. "Did they succeed?"

"Not often." Medreal tried to smile as she looked down at the baby on the queen's lap. Lulu gazed back with thoughtful violet eyes. Her father's eyes, in more ways than one. Even now, seeing them in the girl's sweet face put a lump in Medreal's throat. She had loved Ran as if he were her own, though she doubted he ever knew it. It wasn't that he was ignorant of other people's feelings. He was simply too distracted with his own ambitions to notice. To have his daughter in the palace was a blessing, but often bittersweet.

The queen tucked a wayward ebony curl behind her pointed ear and sighed as she lifted her cup. "I suppose the council will expect me soon?"

Medreal nodded. "I thought it best you have some tea to clear your head before you meet with them."

"I wish I could clear my head," Firal said. "I can't imagine what they want to fuss over this time. The state of the kingdom is the best it's ever been, but I suppose there's always something more to fuss over."

The stewardess laughed. "Oh, there always is." She held out her hands to Lulu in invitation. The girl wiggled on her mother's lap and reached for her. Stewardess to the queen was only one of Medreal's titles, and the less important, in her mind. Playing nursemaid to the royal children had always been her favorite role. "I'm sure you're ready to eat, aren't you, little one? Let's sneak off to your room, then. Your mother will come for you when she's done."

Firal forced a laugh and lifted the babe into Medreal's arms. "If I'm ever done." She leaned forward to kiss one of the girl's round, rosy cheeks. "I love you, precious girl. Be good for Nana."

Smiling, Medreal shifted the child onto her hip. "Don't worry. We'll be waiting when you're finished."

"Of course. Thank you, Medreal." Firal bowed her head and settled back in her chair to finish her tea.

Medreal left the tray and smoothed Lulu's dark hair as she toted her out of the office and up the hall.

In truth, there was little left for Medreal to do around the palace. Her involvement in matters of politics was still welcome, but often unnecessary. Firal had come into her own through the years, and with Vahnil at her side to help manage the kingdom, the only thing that truly required the stewardess's attention was the baby in her arms. It wasn't that there were no other nursemaids qualified for the duty; Firal simply trusted her best. And with the girl's peculiarities, it made sense for Medreal to fill the role.

Lumia—Lulu, as those close to the girl knew her—took after her father in more ways than just her eyes. Born a free mage, she was unrestricted by element, more powerful than most could imagine. Medreal didn't know why Lulu had been born unbound, but she was certain it had something to do with the chaotic power the child's father bore. That, too, made Medreal the best choice for nursemaid.

After all, she was the only other free mage on the island.

Firal was strong enough in her own Gift; her mother had been Archmage, and magic ran deep in her blood. But the power that flowed through the child was different, slowing her growth beyond what even the most powerful Eldani mages experienced. Some thought it meant the girl would be a burden. What the queen herself thought, Medreal didn't know.

Brushing away the worry for another time, the stewardess bounced the baby on her hip and pushed open the door to the royal quarters. "Here we are," she said in a sing-song voice, easing Lulu to the floor and directing the girl toward her nursery. Eager, the child toddled ahead.

A tray of fruits, rolls, and a sweet or two waited inside, with a pair of cups and a pitcher of fruit juice beside it on the low table. Delivered only moments before they arrived, Medreal supposed. The wedges of apple on the silver plate hadn't begun to brown.

"Bite?" Lulu held up a slice she gripped tight in her chubby fist, her eyes bright as she offered the treat to her nursemaid.

Medreal chuckled. "Thank you, love." She leaned forward to take it and paused when she heard the large door to the royal quarters creak open.

That wasn't right. She would have sensed Firal coming, and Vahnil was meeting with the master of docks at the river. No one else would have entered without knocking.

It wasn't Firal, but Medreal sensed *something*. A muddied feeling of power, like the swimming confusion of a mageling first coming into their Gift. No, that wasn't it. It was something else, something familiar. Something she hadn't felt since...

Her eyes widened and Medreal sent a thrust of energy to the queen, a Call relating panic and urgency. The message no more than left before something invisible slammed against her and wrestled the flows of power out of her grasp.

Free magic.

It shot through the room like a shockwave, spilling dishes across the floor.

Gritting her teeth, Medreal pushed with her own energy and snared a thread of power from the air before her unseen opponent could stop her. She spun it into a blade of raw energy and cut at the magic that held her Gift at bay.

The wild power spun around her, muddling her senses. She retreated, turning to look for Lumia.

A mistake. The door opened and she couldn't turn back quickly enough. Her shoulder caught against a man's chest just as his dagger sank between her ribs.

Her breath escaped with her grasp of the energy around her, magic abandoning her as crimson bloomed across the bodice of her dress.

Lulu whimpered and opened her arms.

Medreal couldn't reach her. Her knees buckled, spilling her

onto the floor. The man brushed past her and bent toward the dark-haired girl beside the low table. Lulu turned toward him, reaching up, wanting comfort from the man she thought was her grandfather.

"This wasn't a part of our agreement," Ennil growled, cradling the baby to his chest and glaring toward the doorway.

"I never gave you promises in writing, Lord Tanrys," a woman replied.

Medreal choked on her breath and struggled to grasp power again. She couldn't heal herself. No mage could. But if she could only reach magic... She had to do *something*.

Clawed feet bearing white scales slipped past her. Medreal reached for the hem of the white robe as it brushed by, clutched it with a gnarled hand that was rapidly losing strength.

Envesi arched a brow and spared her a single glance. Then she jerked her robes away and waved a hand, splitting the air with the crackling power of a Gate as if it were little more than a thought. "Now come along, unless you mean to join her."

Ennil hesitated, looking at Medreal on the floor.

Anger bubbled inside her and tears brimmed in her dark eyes as he met her gaze. She'd never liked the man. Now she hated him.

"Ennil," Envesi prompted sharply, lingering beside the Gate.

He tore his eyes away and kissed Lulu's temple as he cradled her close. With the girl secure in his arms, he strode through the portal alongside the one-time Archmage.

The Gate closed and no matter how Medreal tried, magic still escaped her. Of all her duties, looking after Lumia was the only one that mattered, and she had failed. She squeezed her eyes closed, pressed a hand to the wound in her side and curled up on the floor.

With her last breath, she wept.

2

RESPONSE

With the thirtieth anniversary of Firal's coronation fast approaching, it was hard to believe there had been a time the capital city rebelled against her. Still, no matter how long she held the title, Firal didn't think she would ever be comfortable being a queen.

Her father had ruled for nearly three hundred years and had accomplished much in those thirty decades. Though his rule had been cut short, his was a tall shadow to escape.

But if the people of Elenhiise didn't love her, at least they respected her. Their loyalty had been hard-won; she often forgot just how young her rule was. It was not uncommon for Ilmenhith's throne to be held seven or eight hundred years. Some still called her the Girl Queen.

The island of Elenhiise was split into two kingdoms, but dominated by the Eldani. Like most with mage blood in them, Firal expected a long life. She hoped comfort in a leadership position would come with time.

Her skirts swirled around her ankles as she made her way from her comfortable office to the less comfortable council meeting that awaited. Her council managed most things, though they still required oversight and permission to act. In that

9

respect, it seemed a great deal of being a leader was merely keeping everything organized. Even as a mageling, Firal had excelled with organization. She'd had plenty of opportunities to practice in the temple, helping manage Nondar's office and classroom and volunteering in the temple library. Organizing people was little different from organizing things, it was simply less comfortable. Things didn't protest being managed.

On the whole, her kingdom ran smoothly. There were always problems, but none so severe as the starvation and riots that had punctuated her first year on the throne. She hoped everything would *remain* trivial, when compared to those first days.

Pausing outside the stuffy formal parlor where her council always met, Firal sighed and smoothed her dress. It wasn't often she attended council without Vahn by her side. Her husband claimed to have no mind for politics, but he was good with people, and his time as part of the guard—however brief it may have been—had taught him how to stand his ground. But he was overseeing a problem that couldn't be managed from the palace, which meant she had to put on her best queenly air and push into the parlor alone.

The councilors at the table stood as she entered, and all of them bowed in respect. There were a few chairs empty, but she paid them little mind. She already knew Vahn and the harbormaster were out, tending matters she only hoped were going smoothly. Strange, though, that Ennil wasn't present. He never missed meetings.

"Good morning." Firal graced them with a smile as she strode toward the table in the center of the room.

Despite their deference, Temar was the only one of the councilors who returned her smile. "Good morning, Majesty." The white-robed woman glanced to the door as she spoke, as if she expected someone else to join them. As the leader of Firal's court mages, Temar had assisted in opening the Gate for Vahn's departure, so she couldn't have expected him. Was she looking for Ennil?

Firal restrained a frown and drew a breath to address the council. A wash of energy struck her before she could speak. The sensation of power that came with Medreal's Call raced over her skin like a thousand jabbing needles, stealing her air, and the emotions hit her like an avalanche. Surprise. Panic. Fear.

"Majesty?" Temar stepped forward, her brow knit with concern.

Firal spun on her heel. "Something is wrong." Nothing rattled Medreal. For the woman to be afraid...

Fear clawed at her heart, and Firal gripped her skirts and ran.

She didn't think to call for help, though she heard councilors and the pair of guards from the parlor running after her.

The door to her quarters stood open a crack. She flung it open so forcefully that the door banged against the wall. "Medreal!"

No reply.

Opening her senses, she felt for the woman's Gift. It should have been a beacon, lighting the way. Instead, she felt nothing.

"Brant's roots," one of the guards murmured as he pushed past her.

Firal followed his gaze and her stomach dropped.

The nursery door stood halfway open. Silver dishes lay scattered across the floor behind it. Among them, a plain blue skirt was just visible through the doorway.

"Summon the king at once. Send the other mages to retrieve him by Gate." Temar's firm voice was a muted drone, all but drowned out by the sound of Firal's heartbeat in her ears.

Step by step, Firal dragged herself toward the nursery. The other guard moved forward and slid into the nursery after his partner with his sword ready. Behind her, the voices of the councilors blended together into a sickening cocktail of speculation.

Blood filled the plush carpet underfoot. The guardsmen's boots left tracks as they checked every corner of the room. Firal froze, staring at the body on the floor. Not even half an hour past, Medreal had filled her cup with tea. Now her stewardess

—her friend—lay curled in death with tears still wet on her face.

"Where is she?" Firal didn't recognize her own voice. It was calm, steady, strong—everything she wasn't.

"There's no one—" one of the guards began.

Firal spun on him. "Where is she?" she screamed.

The guard shrank back.

Tears filled her eyes until she couldn't see. "Shut down the palace, post guards at every door—"

"Majesty," Temar said before she could finish. "Do you feel that?"

Firal glared at the court Master as the other councilors turned from the room to carry out her orders. She couldn't feel anything clearly. Already more guards clustered in the next room and serving staff peered in from the hallway, their presence clouding her senses. She tried to focus, squeezing her eyes closed, willing herself to feel what the other mage had found so easily.

Something prickled nearby. A tingling remnant of energy left behind.

"Whoever did this, they departed through a Gate," Temar said. It took Firal a moment to realize the mage was speaking to the guards, not her. "They can't have come in through one. There's only one signature."

"Impossible. A group of mages entering the royal quarters would have drawn too much attention. To open a Gate without them, they'd have to be—" Firal stopped short.

The stewardess had been strong, one of the most powerful mages Firal had ever known. For anyone to make it past her after that frantic Call could only mean one thing. Cold dread settled in her stomach.

"Majesty," a guard called from the other room.

She turned, mindful not to look as a white-robed mage drew a sheet over her friend's body. Firal couldn't bear to look again. The vision of Medreal's tear-stained face was already burned into her mind.

The guard met her at the door. "I spoke to the serving staff. They saw two people enter. One was a woman in white. The other..." His voice hitched as he met her eye. He drew a breath and went on. "They swear it was Lord Tanrys."

Firal couldn't keep her brows from rising. Ennil? Why would he have been there? "The woman, what did she look like?"

The guard shook his head. "None of them got a clear look. She wore long robes and a cloak with the hood drawn. They did see white hair, my queen, but no one seems to recall her face."

Sniffing back tears she didn't have time for, Firal drew herself up. "Summon Archmage Kytenia immediately." She clenched her fists at her sides to keep her hands from shaking. "And send the mages to retrieve Lord Tanrys from his estate the moment they return with Vahn."

A handful of guards peeled away with a mage to carry orders.

"My queen," Temar said, moving closer. "May we speak in private?"

"Now is not the time, Temar."

The white-robed woman shifted uneasily, glancing at the crowd in the other room. She frowned and lowered her voice. "But I feel it is important, Your Majesty. Are there any mages familiar enough with your quarters to open a Gate to here from somewhere else?"

"They wouldn't need to," Firal said curtly. "If this had been normal mages, Medreal would have been able to handle it."

The Master mage pursed her lips. "I know she was a wild mage, but—"

"If that's all you know, you know very little." Firal swallowed against the lump in her throat and the icy queasiness in her stomach. Part of her wanted to fall to the floor and sob, but a greater part simmered with an anger and hurt so deep she thought she might burn up. Neither emotion could be given precedence. Her child was missing, kidnapped, but she was a queen. A ransom was most likely to follow, though who wanted it, she couldn't imagine.

She strode on through her quarters. "If you are not assisting the mages or cleaning my quarters, remove yourself immediately. I want a handful of guards outside my door and no more than a pair inside. And I will speak to the Captain of the Guard. Fetch him at once!" Her voice was steel, though unshed tears stood in her eyes. She would weep for Medreal and scream for her daughter in time, but right now, she was a queen.

Her quarters began to empty and Temar moved close behind her again.

"Majesty, if you know something..." the woman started.

"Don't pretend you don't know there are mages more powerful than us, Temar." Firal watched the flow of people moving into the hallway, listened to the whispers that rose among them. There would be a thousand rumors by the end of the hour. The entire city would know Lulu had been taken. She couldn't decide if that was a problem or not. "One resided in the palace for many years."

Temar started to speak, then seemed to think better of it and returned to the nursery to assist the mages there.

A new cluster of people moved up the hall, against the flow of people.

"What's happened?" Vahn all but shoved aside the guards at the door. He panted for breath. Doubtlessly he'd run all the way from the Gating parlor. His blond hair was a disheveled mess and his cape hung lopsided over his blue finery.

Firal moved to meet him. It would have been easy to throw herself in her husband's arms, but she made herself remain calm as she righted his clothing and smoothed his hair. "Treason," she said. "Someone has taken our daughter. Her nursemaid is dead." Despite the strength of her will, her voice cracked.

Vahn gaped and looked past her to the nursery. "How? Where have they gone? How did they escape?"

"Through a Gate opened in the nursery. I don't know how

they opened it. There were only two." She shook her head, frustrated. A Gate-stone would have allowed such an escape, but they were rare enough that even Ennil wouldn't have had access to one. But would the white-haired woman who had been seen with him?

Vahn's expression grew dark. "And nobody stopped them in the palace?"

Firal scoffed. "Why would they, when one of them was your father?"

His mouth fell open and his brow furrowed as he worked to close it again. He didn't speak, but she saw the unspoken question in his blue eyes. Ennil Tanrys was father of the king-consort, and as far as the man knew, his family was set to inherit the throne. Why would he kidnap his own granddaughter?

"I don't know," Firal murmured, though she saw the shadow of concern that crept into his expression.

"I passed Ordin on the way up," Vahn said with a sigh. "I assume you called for him, but he was speaking to some of his men."

"They've already told him what's happened, no doubt," Firal said. "He'll probably be a moment." Ordin Straes was a capable man and as good a Captain of the Guard as she could have asked for, but Firal sometimes wished he were a little less proactive. He wouldn't believe the kidnappers had escaped through a Gate until he heard it from Temar or from Firal herself, which meant he'd have men stationed at every path out of the city before she had a chance to speak to him. It wasn't a bad thing, she had to admit; they had no way of knowing where the Gate led, and if the guards carried everything they'd heard to him, he'd already have men on their way to watch the Tanrys estate.

"Do we wait for him here?" Vahn asked.

Firal shook her head. "We will go to my office. Temar, dispense directions among the others and then attend us. Leave the other mages to their work and let them oversee the staff.

Have someone send for the coroner." Again, her throat felt thick. She swallowed hard and went on. "When Captain Straes and the Archmage arrive, send them to my office."

"And Lord Tanrys?" Temar asked.

The order to put him in chains leaped to the tip of her tongue, but Firal hesitated. She couldn't have him arrested based on the word of servants she hadn't spoken to herself. It wasn't that she didn't trust them, but Ennil was her father-in-law and a member of her council. Rash decisions had hard consequences. "Bring him to me."

The Master mage bowed and turned to distribute orders as Firal swept out of the room.

Vahn hurried to her side. He said nothing, though he reached for her hand. She took it gladly. His grip was strong, comforting and warm. She needed it.

"It will be okay," he murmured.

She wished she had his confidence.

The tea tray still sat on her office desk, just where Medreal had left it. Blood and earth, she should have asked her to stay!

For what? a quiet voice asked in the back of her mind. Firal knew it wouldn't have changed anything. The stewardess was a free mage, and she'd faced the intruder and lost. Firal was skilled in her Gift, but she was not strong. She'd never even reached the rank of blue mageling. If she had been present, the only thing that would be different was that she would be dead, too.

"Should I ask them to bring more chairs?" Vahn asked. There were only a few, one behind her desk and two before it.

Firal shook her head. "There are enough for us and the Archmage. Anyone else can stand." She let go of his hand and dropped into the chair behind her desk. Her head spun. Now that she had a moment to sit, she felt too dazed for tears. For a moment, she wasn't sure it was happening at all. Perhaps it was a dream. A nightmare. Perhaps she was still asleep.

"Your Majesty?" A guard appeared at the open door.

Perhaps not.

Tired, she waved him in. Her fatigue vanished as soon as she saw the man behind him. She surged to her feet.

"My queen," Ennil began before she could speak. He lowered his hand from his head. Whatever curse had been ready on the tip of her tongue died when she saw the blood that streaked his face. He held a rag in one hand. He glanced down at it, grimaced, and put it back to his temple to stanch the blood flow. "I believe we have a problem."

His wife slipped in behind him, quietly scolding and reaching for his arm. Ennil obliged, bending so Vivenne could look at his injury.

"What is the meaning of this?" Firal braced herself against her desk.

"A handful of us went to the Tanrys estate to, ah, apprehend Lord Tanrys as you requested," the guard with them said. He looked uncomfortable. "When we arrived, we found him like this."

"Resting in Vivenne's favorite flower bed," Ennil said dryly. He scowled as Vivenne rearranged his grayed hair and put the rag to his temple again. He took it from her and strode closer. Aside from the gash at his temple and a split at the corner of his brow, the whole right half of his face appeared to have been skinned by stone. "Though it seems I traveled across the walkway, first."

"My people saw you in the palace," Firal said. "Entering my quarters just before Lumia was taken."

Vahn laid a hand on her shoulder. Whether he was trying to calm her or offer support, she wasn't sure.

"Yes," Ennil sighed.

She raised a brow. She'd expected him to deny it.

"A curious situation arose this morning." Ennil dropped into one of the chairs before her desk with a groan. "I found myself unexpectedly entertaining a woman I never thought I would see again. Vivenne was out. I sent the rest of my staff away, assuming their presence would put them at risk."

"The woman in white they saw you with?" Firal asked.

He nodded, then winced and adjusted the rag at his temple. "One of my stablehands was to retrieve members of the guard. He was found dead in the alleyway behind my house just after they found me. I don't know who killed him or how, but I suppose it doesn't matter."

"We don't have time for long-winded discussion, Father," Vahn growled, his words uncharacteristically sharp.

Again, Ennil nodded. "Of course, forgive me. The deposed Archmage, my queen. She wanted to know about your daughter."

Every inch of her went cold.

"I assume it's because the girl is her grandchild. She wanted to know if the girl was Gifted. I had few choices but to be cooperative, my queen. I am just a man. Without a sword in my hands, I'm powerless. And even with one, what can I do against a mage that powerful?" The corners of Ennil's mouth twitched with the admission. He had been Captain of the Guard before Ordin Straes. Admitting weakness couldn't be easy. "After we spoke, she insisted we see the girl."

"And you took her?" Vahn almost snarled. He lurched forward, like a beast ready to strike.

Firal laid a hand on his arm to stop him. "Letting her kill him wouldn't have stopped anything. If Envesi wanted into the palace, she would have found a way."

Ennil nodded. "I knew Lulu wouldn't be without protection, but I didn't expect..." He trailed off and released a frustrated sigh. "She has changed, Your Majesty. And I don't mean her personality."

The cold grip of fear squeezed her body tighter. It was all Firal could do to keep from shivering. "What has happened?" she asked quietly, though a part of her already knew.

Vivenne rubbed his shoulders and Ennil reached to touch her hand. "Your Majesty," he began slowly, as if testing his words. "What do you know of unbound mages?"

"I am a temple-trained mage, Ennil." Firal stifled a prickle of irritation. As if there was anything she could learn about magic from someone who couldn't even feel it. That he asked at all was an affront. "My education has been robust." That wasn't entirely true, of course, but he didn't need to know that. If not for Rune, Firal wouldn't have known it was possible for mages to exist without the bonds of affinity. But he'd been different, special. A child without parents, birthed by magic itself. Until she'd learned of Medreal's Gift, she'd always thought he was alone.

"Of course, I apologize." He bowed his head with a hint of shame. "I knew what had happened as soon as I saw her. I thought putting her in a situation where she would face another mage was the best chance I had."

"How did Medreal die?" Vahn asked.

Firal narrowed her eyes. It was a sound question. The woman had bled out, obviously stabbed, though no weapon was found.

Ennil met his son's stare without wavering. "A dagger, Your Majesty. Envesi overpowered her."

Vahn frowned. "Why not kill her with magic?"

"I don't know. I don't know why she wanted the girl, either." Ennil shook his head. "What I do know is that she opened a Gate by herself. I'm not positive, but I believe the location on the other end was a mage outpost abandoned when the temple fractured before her exile."

"That doesn't tell us much," Firal muttered. "There are dozens of them."

"And even if you knew which one held her, there's little you can do without the backing of temple Masters," a sweet voice added from the door.

Kytenia's arrival was a small relief. Firal expected to see the heads of the Houses of affinity behind her, but she was alone.

As graceful as ever, the white-robed woman glided into the room. Kytenia's face still looked too young for her to hold the title of Archmage, but her russet hair had begun to change. White wings at her temples and a sprinkling of white throughout the rest made her appear older. It was strange to envision her as white-haired like the other Masters. Each mage's transition was different, but it happened to all of them eventually. Kytenia's hair had changed first, meaning she'd stretched beyond every plateau and reached the pinnacle of her strength. Her eyes would change next, paling to the cold too-blue that symbolized full understanding of her Gift. Both were changes Firal had once looked forward to, herself. Now, having been outside the temple and without training since she'd taken the crown, she recognized that for her, those changes would probably never come.

Firal straightened behind her desk and bowed her head in greeting. "Thank you for joining us, Archmage Kytenia."

Kytenia returned the nod, though hers was ever so slightly deeper. Kytenia was second in power only to Firal herself. Well, Firal and Vahn. They had declared him as her equal in rulership years ago, one of many uncustomary actions taken to soothe the tensions that followed the death of Firal's father.

Ennil rose from his chair, though he looked unsteady. Vivenne supported him and they bowed to the Archmage together.

Kytenia waved a hand in dismissal, barely noticing them. "I encountered your Captain of the Guard in the hallway," she said. "I asked him to divide my mages into his ranks before meeting with us. That will give us time to determine where forces should be sent and when."

"Thank you, Kytenia. Please, sit." Had it been anyone else, Firal might have been irritated to hear they'd given orders to her men. But Kytenia was her dearest friend, and the two of them were used to working together. The comfort and familiarity they shared made both their jobs easier. "How much of that did you hear?"

"Enough," Kytenia said with a frown. She took the other chair in front of Firal's desk and her eyes skirted over Vahn. Often, when the Archmage looked at him, Firal felt a pang of sadness. Vahn had been Kytenia's betrothed, his marriage to Firal one of both convenience and political necessity. The Archmage was good at tempering her emotions, though there was often a gleam of sorrow in her hazel eyes when she saw him. Today, her eyes showed nothing. "Though if what Ennil says is the truth, the mages I brought with me today won't be nearly enough."

Firal nodded slowly and finally allowed herself to ease into her chair. She felt weaker as she sank into the cushions. They had never discussed unbound magic where anyone else could hear. As far as Firal knew, it was an official secret to be held between the crown and the Masters of the Houses of affinity. And for good reason; if Ennil truly was suggesting Envesi had found a way to unravel her affinity, it meant they were facing something new. "What numbers are we looking at, Kytenia? Five Master mages to equal one of her?"

The Archmage grimaced. "Likely more. Linking Masters of the five major Houses still leaves us with outlying talents uncovered. And at best, letting them tie their Gifts together gives the lead mage access to more draw points for energy. Greater sway over the elements means nothing if they aren't well versed in how to handle them."

"And the Archmage—former Archmage, forgive me." Ennil grimaced at his blunder and avoided Kytenia's eye. "She has likely had a great deal of time to practice her new skills. She seemed comfortable, despite the changes she's obviously experienced."

"Comfortable enough to defeat Medreal," Firal said.

"Which means what?" Ennil asked, reaching up to clasp Vivenne's hand. She still hovered behind him, pale as a ghost. She'd always been a soft-spoken woman, but she'd said nothing at all while the others spoke. Was it fear or something else that kept her silent?

"That if we are going to stand a chance at storming her

bastion and getting your granddaughter back, we will need mages on her level." Kytenia shook her head, disgruntled.

"And where do we find those?" Firal asked.

"The mages in Lore," Vahn said. "If anyone knows where to find mages with that sort of power, it'll be them."

The Archmage hesitated. "In years past, I would have thought that. But you're forgetting the civil war they had just before the treaty was signed. I work with Headmaster Arrick often and he's never mentioned having mages that strong in the Triad. I can send a missive, but..."

"Let me help," Vahn said, determined. "Trust me, they'll find one."

3

TRUST AND TURBULENCE

Kytenia slid a finger down the page as she skimmed the list of names. She couldn't think of a worse time to be handed paperwork, but she didn't dare put it off. Though she had served as Archmage of Kirban Temple since the beginning of Firal's reign, there were still some Masters who sought to take matters into their own hands. She had little time to prepare for departure, but eliminating one thing from her never-ending list of duties couldn't hurt.

"This is fine," she said at last, pushing the paper back across her desk. There were several more notes she had to find before she could leave, and she didn't appreciate the addition of more clutter to sort through. "Accept them all."

"All?" Anaide repeated. The look on her face was nothing short of horrified. "We've never accepted all applicants before!"

"Well, it was bound to happen sooner or later. We receive fewer applicants every year, and with the Grand College breathing down our necks in hopes they can snatch our mages away, we'd better do our best to keep the dormitory occupied. We can't stave them off forever. I see no reason to refuse any of these." There had been a list of exchange program negotiation points somewhere on her desk, and Kytenia was determined to deliver it while she was there. Her chest tightened and her stomach turned at the very notion of attending something so frivolous when her best friend's child was missing, but an Archmage was expected to be composed and prepared for duty at all times. She'd been sent back to the temple specifically to retrieve any documents the headmaster of the Grand College might expect during one of their visits. Their request for assistance, she understood, bore a chance of ruffling some feathers, and it was best to proceed as if nothing was out of the ordinary.

Anaide huffed and took the paper back. She examined it as if she expected to find fault in Kytenia's decision, but there was none. Her withered lips pursed, adding ever more wrinkles to her already ancient face. Did the woman ever look anything other than sour?

Kytenia didn't give her a chance to think of any more objections. "Are the others coming or not? I'm sure I don't need to remind you I am short on time."

"The Masters have been summoned, yes." Anaide narrowed her eyes and lowered the paper. "Really, though, I see no reason you shouldn't be leaving now."

It took effort not to snap. "I will leave when I have issued orders," Kytenia said. "I don't know how long this will take, and if things go poorly, I will not have the temple left without direction."

The pinched look on the Master of Water's face said more than her protests ever would. It wasn't that she thought Kytenia should leave without giving directions, it was that she expected those directions should be given to *her*.

Kytenia tried to keep what she thought of that from showing in her expression. Some part of her still suspected Anaide was bitter about having been overlooked. Edagan had always been more amicable—or diplomatic, at least—but Anaide never did anything but sneer or fuss over every choice Kytenia made. There was value in having critics to keep one grounded, but after so many years as Archmage, she wished the title granted her a little more respect.

Just when Anaide opened her mouth with what was sure to be another complaint, the door to Kytenia's office opened.

"I'm here, I'm sorry," Shymin announced in a hurry. Her hair was mussed and she brushed at her sleeves as if she'd just changed into her white Master's robes, but that was nothing unusual. Since Shymin had taken over as Master of the House of Healing, she'd proven herself a determined and hands-on teacher, which meant she was often elbow-deep in noxious herbal concoctions or giving firsthand demonstrations on how to properly suture wounds. Neither activity was well-suited to wearing white.

She hooked a finger in the sleeve of her robe to turn the hem right side out, then gave Kytenia an apologetic smile. "Have I missed anything? I was told you're going somewhere."

"Yes," Kytenia said, grateful for her sister's interruption. Anaide glowered, but the old woman stayed quiet, which was a blessing Kytenia was grateful to receive. "An emergency. I am to escort King Vahnil to the Grand College for a meeting with the headmaster. I'll explain more when I can, but I've been asked not to speak of the matter until we return."

Shymin's brows shot up, but she nodded. "I wondered why your entourage was still waiting downstairs. I suppose you'll need to Gate back to Ilmenhith right away?"

"Yes, so I need to keep this brief. Is Rikka coming?" Kytenia gave her sister a hopeful glance, but tempered her disappointment when Shymin shook her head.

"She's out running errands, I believe. If you have orders for her, I'll be happy to make sure she gets them."

Kytenia nodded. "I hope to return within a few hours, but if I am held up, please hold any correspondence and I will see to it when I'm back. The temple should continue to function as normal until further notice. Is Edagan here, by any chance?"

"She has been doing drills with magelings of late," Anaide said. "I can ensure she receives orders, if necessary."

Of course she could. "See to it she continues classes as usual," Kytenia said. "I will have more specific tasks for them later. For now, Shymin, I'd like you to keep an eye out for messengers, and if there is anything urgent, summon me by Calling and I will do my best to return. Anaide, I'd like for you to begin compiling a list."

The older Master straightened. "A list, Archmage? Of... students?" She glanced at the paper still in her hand, which Kytenia had almost forgotten.

"Outposts," Kytenia said. "A full list of all mage outposts on Elenhiise that have been held in the last hundred years, whether abandoned or currently occupied."

Anaide's brow furrowed. "Whatever for?"

"I'll explain more later." Where had that negotiation sheet gone? Kytenia stepped back and surveyed her desk with her hands on her hips. "Shymin, help me sort all this, please. I had a letter addressed to Headmaster Ortath and I can't seem to find it."

Without a word, Shymin swept forward and began gathering papers, sorting them with a quick eye and a practiced hand. "Here, Kyt." She lifted a page with smudged ink and frowned at the lack of legibility. "Should I rewrite this?"

Kytenia snatched it from her fingertips. "No time. Tell the Masters waiting downstairs to prepare a Gate back to Ilmenhith for me. I have to go."

"Don't worry," her sister offered with a smile, answering Kytenia's unspoken question. "We know what we're doing by now. We'll keep everything running until you return."

"Thank you," Kytenia said with a sigh as Shymin disappeared. She couldn't spare more than a moment, now. The mages farther down the tower would be waiting with a Gate ready.

"Is there something more I should do?" Anaide asked, her tone almost a lament. "Gathering information on outposts is—"

"Of utmost importance right now," Kytenia finished for her as she rolled the paper in her hands and jammed it into one of the hidden pockets of her white robes. She hadn't been in her office even ten minutes, but it still felt like she'd dallied too long. "Please, focus on gathering that information, and I will call a formal meeting to explain more once this errand is complete."

The Master of Water frowned as if she wanted to say more, but Kytenia gave her no chance. She hurried down the tower, smoothing her white-streaked hair as she walked. Neither Anaide nor Shymin had said anything to make her think she appeared frazzled, but she still felt as if she looked like a spooked cat, with all its fur on end.

Several floors below her office, a handful of mages waited around a Gate they'd begun to open the moment they sensed her coming. The crackle of power in the air made Kytenia shiver, but she couldn't hide and wait for it to grow steady. As Archmage, she should have been assisting.

Shymin met her just in front of the Gate as the image within it stabilized. Ilmenhith's Gating parlor waited on the other side, with court mages in blue-trimmed white milling around the edges of the room.

"I hope everything's all right," Shymin remarked softly as she righted one of Kytenia's curls.

"It's not, but it will be." Or at least, Kytenia hoped. She clasped her sister's arm for a moment, then pressed on. The Gate's power sizzled against her skin as she stepped through to the palace. Though she'd expected the party destined for the Grand College to be waiting for her, the court mages were the only ones in the room.

Kytenia stopped one of them. "Where is Vahn?" She regretted the familiarity the moment it left her mouth, for the mage frowned at her.

"His Majesty is coming," Temar answered her from the other

side of the room. "He is still in his office, but will be here shortly."

"Thank you, Temar." Kytenia spared a stern look for the mage she'd addressed first, but thought better of trying to reprimand the woman. The tension in the air was already thick without her dressing down a court mage. She needed as many cooperative mages as possible for when the time came to comb mage outposts.

The court Master gave a slight incline of her head, and then the room grew still.

Kytenia tried not to fidget; Archmages did not fidget. Or at least, she assumed they didn't. The temple had only known two before her, and she couldn't picture either one being overtaken by nerves.

By some small stroke of luck, she did not have to wait or fidget long. Vahn strode through the doorway with purpose in his step and guards at his back, though he motioned for the armored men to halt beside the door. "Ready the Gate," he commanded, more firm, more powerful than she was used to hearing from him. Vahn was not weak, but he was gentle. That gentleness was what had drawn her to him, so many years ago, before fate had pulled them in different directions.

There was none of that gentleness in him now. His blue eyes were like cold steel, his jaw set and his brows drawn together in such a stern look, he hardly seemed the same man.

"Yes, Majesty," Temar replied. A flick of her fingers put all the court mages into motion, and no more than a breath later, the air hummed with power once again.

Kytenia straightened as the king approached her.

"You have what you need?" he asked. He stopped before her, but did not look her in the eye. Instead, he gazed toward the archway where the mages wove their power into a portal that would take them to the mainland.

"Yes," she replied, though she couldn't help the touch of

uncertainty that colored her voice as the Gate beside them stabilized.

The palace hosted a permanent Gate to the Grand College of Lore, but it emptied into a large courtyard where dozens of other Gates stood, and business made the way crowded. Instead of using that one, Temar led the opening of a Gate that led directly to the large auditorium in the college.

Vahn motioned for her to accompany him. The guards beside the door started forward, but he lifted a hand. "Stay here," he ordered. "The Archmage and I will go alone."

The men shifted, unsettled, as he strode through the portal without another word.

After a deep breath with which to compose herself, Kytenia followed.

Moving through a second Gate so quickly after the first gave her a shudder, but another breath was enough to steady her.

As she expected, the auditorium was not empty. A handful of magelings gaped at them from the seats that curved around the speaking stage they now shared with a flustered man in Master white.

"Excuse me," Kytenia began, offering a sweet smile as she sorted out the words in her head. She had learned enough of the trade tongue to make herself useful, but the language still took more concentration than she liked. "I am Kytenia, Archmage of Kirban Temple, escort to King Vahnil of Elenhiise."

"I am in the middle of a class," the man protested when he finally found his voice.

"I can see that." She skimmed the audience with another small smile, this time an apologetic one. "Forgive us for interrupting, but we require the assistance of Headmaster Ortath at once."

The man turned to Vahn and his face fell. "In the middle of my class?" His voice cracked with defeat even before he finished, his thoughts clear in the way the corners of his mouth drew down. Who was he to argue with a king?

"Summon him immediately," Vahn said, an uncharacteristic gruff edge in his tone.

The Master's shoulders slumped, but he nodded.

Kytenia turned toward the seated magelings. "Your class must be rescheduled," she called. "I apologize for the inconvenience, but this cannot wait."

Before she'd finished the last word, the magelings rose and gathered their things in a hurry.

The aggrieved Master sighed, but bowed toward Vahn and Kytenia, then shuffled toward the main aisle.

"Oh!" Kytenia hurried after him and pulled the rolled paper from her pocket. "Please see that this is delivered to the head of your admissions office, as well."

The man's shoulders sagged more, but he took the paper and muttered an agreement.

Vahn raised a brow when she returned to his side. "What was that for?" he asked in a whisper.

She did her best to look cheerful. "So he doesn't come back."

A soft, humorless laugh escaped him.

Unsettled by the sound, Kytenia turned toward the doorway and waited, heavy thoughts of free magic on her mind.

4

SECRETS TO KEEP

ARRICK ORTATH, ARCHMAGE AND HEADMASTER OF THE GRAND College of Lore, smoothed his white sleeves as he hurried into the auditorium.

The Grand College was a school, first and foremost, and while his private offices were acceptable for hosting honored guests, there were no parlors in which said guests could wait. He'd considered commissioning the addition of parlors more than once, but the college's coffers were not as deep as they once had been. He tried not to let it bother him. The first time he'd received visitors from Elenhiise, he'd met them in the auditorium as well. If nothing else, at least it was consistent.

"Welcome," Arrick called in greeting. He slowed to catch his breath, hoping his accent wasn't too thick. The alliance with Kirban Temple had required most of the college's Masters— himself included—to learn a new language. Likewise, Kirban's Masters and monarchs had agreed to learn the trade tongue commonly spoken in the Triad, but it would have been presumptuous to greet visitors in his own language. Especially when one of them was a king.

"You look well, Archmage Arrick." Kytenia Silaron was Archmage of Kirban, though with her eyes still hazel and her hair only just beginning to turn white at the temples, Arrick thought her too young for the part. He wasn't foolish enough to say it out loud, though.

Arrick inclined his head in a gracious response before he dipped in a bow to King Vahnil. "As do both of you, Archmage, Majesty, given the circumstances. My steward told me little about the purpose of your visit, but it was enough to divine it isn't for pleasure."

"Would that it were." Vahn, too, appeared too young to be king—at least, to Arrick's eyes. The Eldani aged slowly compared to the humans, and the old blood was rich on Elenhiise. The king had matured since their first meeting, but his face was still boyish and his figure slim. His blue eyes—natural blue, not the sharp blue of mages—normally had a snapping, mischievous light in them, but today they were somber. It made him seem older, somehow.

"We have need of mages," Kytenia said, her gaze traveling around the auditorium. Her posture was stiff and wary, and she kept her voice low, as if she feared being overheard by the wrong person.

Arrick frowned. The number of mages residing in the Grand College had dwindled until the place no longer justified its pretentious name. His ranks paled in comparison to the number of students in Kirban. Why would they come to him instead of relying on Kytenia's own mages at the temple?

"Not your mages," Vahn added, guessing his thoughts. "The Aldaanan mages. Can you help us contact them?"

The *Aldaanan*? Arrick's frown deepened and he gave his head a twitch. "Why would you need the mages of Aldaan?"

"They have power we do not," Kytenia didn't even try to soften her words. "We face an emergency in Elenhiise that will require such power."

Surely she wasn't suggesting that they were fighting a free mage. If that were the case, it was no wonder they hadn't tried to count on Kirban. Arrick had seen what free mages could do, though not firsthand. The college's ranks had been decimated by a single free mage during the civil war some six pents before. Until now, he'd thought it a relief that the civil war had also been the last time the Aldaanan were seen.

"Walk with me," Arrick said softly.

They fell in step alongside him, one on either side. He hadn't realized until that moment that the king brought no entourage. That he felt so safe in the Grand College should have made Arrick swell with pride. Instead, it made his stomach turn.

"What you ask may well be impossible," Arrick began, keeping his voice low. "After Tolmarni's War, we spent a great deal of time and energy trying to make amends with the Aldaanan mages. Despite our efforts, it's never come to fruition."

"They won't have peace?" Vahn asked.

"We can't find them," Arrick replied. "They vanished after the war. We found traces of their travels. Villages where people had seen them pass through. Places where works of great magic had been done. But it became something like chasing ghosts."

"I don't understand," Kytenia said. "Where would they have gone?"

"I couldn't say. As you may know, during Tolmarni's War, the Royal City sent an army led by Captain Garam Kaith to strike against the college mages. According to Kaith, the Aldaanan never intended to abandon their capital city. They sought refuge for their families and intended to return to Aldaeon after things settled. But they never did."

Vahn made a small sound of displeasure. "Do you think they're in hiding?"

Arrick shrugged. "If they are, it's nowhere the Grand College or its allies have sway."

None of them said any more until they reached their destination. The office he'd chosen was not where he regularly held audiences. It was reserved for his private study. A small room, too cramped and informal for receiving guests of such stature, but the slow, mindful way they both spoke made it clear they'd be more comfortable in private. Arrick only hoped they would be more forthcoming, as well.

As he expected, Kytenia lifted a hand and spun a ward against eavesdropping the moment the door was closed.

"If my mages are able to assist you, I am happy to offer them." Arrick moved a pile of books from the low couch against the wall and gestured for them to seat themselves.

"Your mages and mine are both at a disadvantage in the situation we face." Kytenia sat primly on the edge of the couch. Vahn remained standing.

"My daughter was taken this morning." The king's eyes hardened until they glinted like cut gems. "Stolen from her quarters by a mage outside the bonds of affinity. Her nursemaid —a mage herself, mind you—was overpowered and killed."

"Brant's roots," Arrick murmured, dropping into a chair. Papers crunched beneath him, forgotten. "You don't think the Aldaanan are—"

"I am sure they are not involved," Kytenia said before he could finish. "But you see how without their assistance, we won't be able to do anything. A single free mage on our side, however, will give us the strength we need to face our opponent and bring Princess Lumia home."

That hardly made sense. A single free mage wouldn't be enough to overpower another unless one was inexperienced. *No, he told himself, rubbing his chin to hide his frown. A free mage needs only serve as an access point.* If Kytenia's mages were skilled and powerful enough, they could link and draw endless power through a free mage to augment their own strength. A single mage tapping a free mage's Gift would burn themselves to cinders, but a group of mages with their power tied together could handle the load. If the group were large enough, it could mimic the force of the finest Aldaanan mages.

"Surely you know of someone who can help us." A strange note of suggestion tinged Vahn's tone.

Arrick's skin prickled and suddenly, he understood. There

was someone, and both he and the young king knew who. "Perhaps," the Archmage said slowly. "There is one..."

Confused, Kytenia glanced between them. "I thought you said the Aldaanan mages were gone?"

"They are," Arrick said. "But there is a mage, one in servitude to King Vicamros, who may—"

"Then see he is summoned." Vahn drew an envelope from his pocket, a dark square sealed with blue wax. He pressed it into Arrick's hand, his already hard eyes growing steely. "Present that to the king and I am sure you will have no trouble."

Arrick's mouth worked a while before he formed words. "Yes, Majesty. I will see it delivered at once."

Vahn nodded and turned toward the door. He motioned for Kytenia to follow. "Thank you, Archmage. We shall leave this matter in your capable hands."

Turning the envelope in his hand as the pair vanished through the doorway, Arrick stared after them with a growing sense of dread.

He did not need to read the letter to know it held the beginning of the greatest turmoil since Tolmarni's War.

HAD they been anywhere but the Grand College, Kytenia might have worried about walking alone. Vahn's insistence that they go without a guard escort unsettled her, but she knew she was in no position to argue with the king. She had no doubt he would have gone without her if she'd objected.

She watched him from the corner of her eye as they walked. Part of her had assumed he would be calmer after this meeting was over. He wasn't; instead, he moved with a long stride, his face stony. His booted steps echoed in the empty hall, crisp and commanding, a sign of the inner turmoil he had to be facing. His cold exterior made her heart sink. When she'd given him up to help her best friend, she'd never imagined he would someday fit his role as king.

She sensed other mages around them, but they skirted the hallway and kept out of sight. The Grand College kept odd rules, like expecting magelings to stay out of the way. No doubt they were intimidated by the feeling of her power. She wasn't as strong as Nondar had been, and nowhere near as powerful as the first Archmage of Kirban Temple, but she held enough might to deserve the title of Archmage.

"What was in that letter?" she asked, her eyes trained on the end of the hallway. The hall spilled out into the auditorium the college mages used for Gating, still empty after their disruption of the morning's lesson. Part of her felt bad for having interrupted a lecture, but their choice to use the lecture hall for Gates was not her fault.

"A message for their king." Even his voice was cold.

Kytenia raised a brow. She'd assumed that much when he'd ordered the Archmage to deliver it. "You expected Arrick wouldn't be able to help us?"

"I was uncertain, but I feared as much. Firal and I do a great deal of business with the Triad. We hear things now and then." He frowned. "I had two letters prepared. Just in case the rumors we'd heard about the Aldaanan mages were wrong."

She eyed him again, fighting a rising wave of concern. She didn't expect him to spill secrets, even if she was Kirban's Archmage, second in power after the crown. But knowing the Aldaanan were gone, knowing there was another option, being prepared to seek both—it showed the complicated workings of politics, a shadowed world of half-truths she never thought Vahn would be comfortable in. She'd always thought him honest.

"How did you know there was someone else?" She struggled to keep it from sounding accusatory, but he still grimaced.

"As I said," he murmured, "I've heard things. I am not positive this will get us anywhere, but it's better than nothing.

The island is vital to the Triad now. If the mage I've heard about really exists, Vicamros won't refuse to aid us. Judging by Arrick's response, he does."

Kytenia nodded. Striking up an alliance with the Triad was one of the greatest decisions Firal could have made at the beginning of her rule. The connection between the Grand College and the temple allowed the installation of permanent Gates, which created an advantage no one else had. Instead of a waypoint for small trade and resupply between the northern and southern continents, Elenhiise became the sole gateway to trade. Ships need sail only half as far, and traverse just the southern seas to offload at the island for goods to be transported by Gate to and from the north. The extra cost of the taxes levied was easily outweighed by the value of time saved, meaning there was more trade than ever, and all of it trickled money into Ilmenhith's coffers. The island had never been richer, and now the Triad controlled nearly all trade in the north.

All the more reason for someone to seek a way to dig into their wealth.

"How do we know she won't demand ransom, Vahn?" Kytenia asked quietly as they passed into the auditorium. It was empty, save a single Master, who jumped to her feet and hurried to fetch the others needed for a Gate.

Vahn watched the Master vanish around a corner and sighed. "She once had the opportunity to be queen. She threw it away to pursue her cause. There won't be a ransom."

"Then why take a child?"

Vahn snorted. "You're the Archmage, Kytenia. You should know more about what she wants than I do."

She shivered. She knew more about the former Archmage's ambitions than she wanted, and she did see one connection. Lumia's Gift was special, something never recorded in the history of the temple. A natural-born free mage, an asset like no other. But she was only a child. Her Gift had not yet come to fruition, unusable and undetectable, save through the way it slowed her aging. Unless Envesi knew how to set it free. Another chill rolled through her and Kytenia rubbed her arms.

"Vahn," she murmured. "Will one mage be enough?"

The Master returned with a cluster of mages at her heels. They formed a practiced semicircle and the air hummed with energy as they began to open a Gate.

Vahn gave her a searching look, his face grim. "If they send the one I've asked for, one will be plenty."

The Gate opened, and he stepped through.

5

HOME

NO MATTER HOW HE SHIFTED, GARAM COULDN'T MAKE HIMSELF comfortable. In years past, he wouldn't have noticed the carriage rocking and jolting as it lurched up hills and bumped back down them. The seats were padded enough they wouldn't leave bruises, but he'd be sore when the ride was over. One more sign he was getting old.

He didn't travel often anymore. Everything he needed was in the Royal City. His home, his family, the Spiral Palace where he offered service as part of the king's council. His friends were kind enough to visit his estate instead of expecting he'd come to them. Under normal circumstances, he was content with that. This time, he couldn't afford to wait.

The ride grew smoother as the carriage turned onto a narrow avenue lined by trees dressed in rich early summer foliage. Sweet fragrances from manicured flower beds drifted on the breeze, accompanied by birdsong. If not for the protests of his aching body, Garam thought the peace might lull him to sleep.

The carriage slowed to a halt in the circle before the manor house and the driver called soft reassurances to his horses. The footman offered his arm when he opened the door, but Garam waved him away. Instead he took his cane from the floor, eased himself out of the carriage, and pressed a hand to his back as he stood.

There had been a time when Garam Kaith was powerful, both in appearance and political position. The Captain of the Royal City Guard, tall and broad-shouldered, dark-skinned and stony-faced, with his black hair and beard shorn close and kept perfectly edged. Now he felt a shell of that man. He walked stooped with a cane, his hair and beard white, his muscles soft and the skin of his face slackened with age.

"Do you need a hand to the door, Lord Kaith?" the footman asked.

Garam snorted and waved him away. "Leave a man a little pride. You just worry about the horses. There's a stable and yard around back. Park the carriage there, tend the horses and wait for me."

The footman nodded and clambered onto the driver's seat for the short ride. Garam paid them no mind. The brass-capped end of his cane clicked against the cobbles of the walkway that led to the front doors, the bright sound a pleasant addition to the cheery birdsong.

The house was grand, two and a half stories high and hidden away in a garden surrounded by a grove of trees. Most of the land holdings were leased to nearby farmers. Only the wooded part in the middle of the property was fenced and private. It was all they needed, Garam supposed. Two curved steps led him to a pair of ornately carved doors with dark iron fittings, and he shifted his cane to his left hand so he could knock.

A moment passed before one of the doors creaked open and a round, boyish face peeked out. The youth peered at Garam and blinked. Then he grinned and threw the door wide. "Lord Kaith! You're not who I expected."

Garam chuckled and lurched up the last step as the boy motioned him into the house. "Sorry to disappoint you. I take it your brother's not in yet?"

Rhyllyn flashed him a smile and pushed the door closed behind them. "No, but he should be here soon."

The young man was an oddity, though no stranger than the owner of the estate. Twisted by uncontrollable magic, Rhyllyn sported drab olive scales on his arms and legs below the elbow and knee, as well as claws on his four-fingered hands and three-toed, too-reptilian feet. His bright blue eyes were slitted in the center, like those of a cat or a venomous snake, but the rest of him was human enough. He had mousy brown hair and a pleasant smile, which was really all he had in his favor, trapped in the middle of awkward teenage years as he was. Strange to think the boy had grown so little in the thirty years Garam had known him.

"Please, make yourself comfortable. Would you like a drink?" Rhyllyn started toward the doorway between the grand, sweeping staircases in the foyer. The youth didn't live there all the time. Instead, he bounced between the estate and the chapter house of mages stationed in Roberian's capital. If he was at the estate, his mentor likely was, too.

"No, thank you. Is Alira present?" Garam took a step toward the parlor. The clack of his cane echoed loudly around them and he paused, glancing down at the fine parquet flooring and the brass tip on his cane. He put it down more carefully with the next stride.

"No, sir. She was called back to the capital last night." Rhyllyn walked to the couches with him, then glanced over his shoulder.

Garam raised a brow. "Did I interrupt something?"

"Oh, I just started something for supper. Will you be staying with us to eat?"

"Not likely. Don't let me keep you, though. I'll just sit here and wait." As if to punctuate the statement, Garam dropped onto one of the couches and heaved a sigh of relief as he sank into the plush blue upholstery.

"With those boots on my rug?" The front door slammed shut and both Garam and Rhyllyn jumped.

"You're home!" Rhyllyn laughed and ran to greet his brother.

Rune scooped him into a bear hug and ruffled the boy's hair with one hand. Then he shoved him back and dropped his bags to the floor with little regard for the parquetry. "Didn't burn the house down yet, I see. Alira here?"

"No, just us." Rhyllyn dragged the bags to the foot of one staircase while his brother strode into the parlor.

There was no blood shared between the two of them. Their snakelike eyes, scales and claws were all they had in common, but even those differed. Rune's scales were a rich emerald green, his eyes bright violet—the most unnatural color Garam had ever seen. But a lot about him seemed unnatural, both in power and appearance. Garam had always found the man's features unsettling. Too graceful, too symmetrical, like the face of a fine sculpture by a master artist. Only the man's tangled, chin-length brown hair seemed normal.

"Figures you'd come in now," Garam said with a grunt as he labored back to his feet. "Just as soon as I get comfortable."

"It's good to see you too, Garam." Rune met him at the couch to share a quick embrace. Then he stepped back, his hands on Garam's shoulders. "Look at you. Finally gave up and started using a cane, I see. I can't believe how much you've changed."

Chuckling, Garam shrugged away. "And how much you haven't. You're barely any older than the day I met you. Still couldn't grow a beard to save your life."

"Ah," Rune sighed, rubbing the patchy stubble that lined his jaw with a smirk. "Something to thank my maker for, I suppose. Never was fond of how stern yours made you look."

"Wasn't wearing it to impress you. My wife is still fond of it. That's good enough for me." Garam sank back to the couch, unable to suppress a sigh of relief. He was tempted to borrow a cushion for the carriage ride home. "How was the trip? Did you find what you were looking for?"

Rune hesitated, then shrugged. "It's been a long time. I'm starting to think what I'm looking for doesn't exist." He unstrapped his sword from his side and leaned it against the couch opposite from where Garam sat. The fine blade looked like it belonged in the rich manor, its twisted black hilt polished to a shine. It had appeared out of place on its wielder's hip, but Rune rarely went anywhere without it. After the ordeal the man had gone through to keep it in his possession, Garam hardly blamed him.

Rhyllyn put a pair of goblets and a bottle of wine on the low table between them. Garam hadn't even seen the boy leave to fetch them. He nodded in silent appreciation. "They have to be somewhere. Where else is there to look?"

"Not many places. Not without crossing the sea and delving into the hinterlands. And we both know what happened last time I tried that." Rune scooped the bottle from the table and turned it over in hand. His brows lifted. "Good choice. You haven't been drinking out of my stash while I was gone, have you, Rhyllyn?"

"Anything is a better choice than what you drink on your own," Garam muttered.

"And less likely to ease my frustrations." Rune filled both goblets and pushed one across the table. Rhyllyn's shadow crossed over them and Rune lifted his head. "Where are you going?"

Rhyllyn paused at the door. "Kitchen. Bread needs me. You two go ahead, we'll talk when you're done."

Garam picked up his goblet as he watched the youth excuse himself. "He's a good boy. You're fortunate to have him here."

"Missing yours?" Rune smirked over the rim of his cup as he sat.

"Ah, they're moving on. The children are all grown now, most have started families of their own. We just welcomed our sixth grandchild, you know. That's the way it is with families. They tend to grow."

Rune nodded slightly. "And Sera?"

Garam narrowed his eyes and took a slow draw from his cup. "She doesn't like it when you ask about her."

"I've never let what other people like dictate what I do," Rune said.

"I've noticed." Garam paused, glancing into his cup. It was a good choice, a fine red wine like nothing he'd tasted before. Brought back from afar, no doubt. "Either way, she's doing well. Little ones aren't so little any more, but they have another on the way. She and her husband are happy, that's what matters."

Rune frowned and sipped his wine.

Garam raised one white brow. "What?"

"I'm sure you heard from Rhyllyn when I would be coming home. I appreciate your visit, Garam. I don't see friends often enough these days." He leaned forward and put his goblet on the table. "Which is why I wonder why you're here."

Swirling the wine in his cup, Garam stared at the ripples and eddies and avoided his friend's eye. "That easy to see through me, huh?" He hesitated, tracing the rim of the goblet with a fingertip. They were good cups; fine silver with delicate etching, though the pattern was unfamiliar. He studied it as he spoke. "Three days ago, a missive arrived from one of our allies, accusing you of treason and demanding that you be arrested and returned to them."

Rune rested his elbows on his knees, laced his green-scaled fingers together and closed his eyes. He wasn't surprised. A bad sign.

Garam wet his lips and went on. "Under normal circumstances, I think Vicamros would have laughed at them. But they're too valuable for him to dismiss something like this, and their letter was rather hostile. The council demanded a hearing on the matter."

"After all I've done for them," Rune murmured. He took his wine again and drained it in a few swallows.

"It was a difficult meeting. I was there. Vicamros appreciates everything you've done for him, and for his father, but he's trapped in a bad position. He resisted, but the council put a lot of pressure on him. We can't lose Elenhiise, Rune. Not after they've become the most vital port of trade in the civilized world."

His friend said nothing, merely refilled his goblet.

Garam sighed. "I'm sorry. Offering a warning ahead of the guards' arrival was the best I could do. I got a bit of a head start, maybe an hour, though I'm sure they've gained on me. It's all the time I can give you."

Snorting, Rune leaned back in his seat. "Time to do what? Pack my bags and get back on the road? Try to make it out of the Triad before every farmhand and mercenary finds out there might be a price on my head?"

"I didn't say it was a good option," Garam said, "but your choices are slim."

Rune shook his head. "I'm not running. Not this time." There was an edge in his voice. A note of determination, frustration, rather than resignation or surrender. The choice of words, however, made Garam pause.

Slowly, Garam reached for the bottle on the table to refill his goblet. "I've made a point of never prying, you know. But the council is... speculating. You know how they are. If any part of this accusation is untrue—"

"There are a dozen different things they can claim to have me hung, Garam. If I deny one, they'll still have me on others. And it seems their reach has grown long. Where else can I go?" Shaking his head again, Rune took the bottle back and filled his cup to the brim. "I fled execution. It doesn't matter that they violated law and custom to see me hang. I still ran. Knowing what happened won't make any of the council want to support me in this. I suppose it was foolish for me to think I'd escaped."

Garam nodded slowly. "So what now?"

"What else?" Rune stifled a humorless laugh. "We drink. The guards come, and they cart me off to Elenhiise so Her Royal Fickleness can get a noose around my neck."

"And Rhyllyn?" Garam asked in a hushed tone.

Rune turned his head toward the kitchen. For a moment, something else replaced the agitation on his face. Wistfulness. Regret. "I'll need a favor."

"He'll be taken care of," Garam assured him. "He'll always have a place with my family, and I'll fight the council to make sure your lands and title aren't stripped, no matter what happens. As long as my family lives, House Kaith will stand with him."

Nodding, Rune looked down at his wine. "Thank you."

"You're going to need to tell him."

"I think he'll figure it out as soon as the guards show up to arrest me."

"We'll see if he appreciates the dramatics." Garam chuckled and lifted his cup.

Rune smirked and raised his to meet the toast.

They finished in a few swallows. A shame, really. It was a good wine.

Outside, the sound of horses and men in armor drove the birdsong to silence.

6

OLD WOUNDS

"You did *what*?" Firal's voice cracked and she fell back into her chair.

"It's the only choice we have." Vahn paced in front of the tall windows lining her office, one hand on his sword, his knuckles white. "Kytenia said as much herself. We can't do anything without a free mage, and if there's anyone in the world who might help us..." He sighed and paused to look out across the city.

Firal felt weak. Days had crawled by without so much as a whisper from her daughter's kidnapper. No demands—though somehow she knew there would be none—and no hints as to where they might be. She'd cried herself dry each night and worked through the days without rest.

Though she wasn't sure her child was still on the island, she'd ordered the guard and army to action. Men assembled in the courtyard below, preparing to scour the countryside and collect every mage available while they were at it. Many of the chapter houses across Elenhiise were empty now, the mages largely contained in Ilmenhith and the temple. Only a few Masters were still scattered across the island to serve as healers and a voice for the queen. Sending a party to collect them would soothe her nerves for a while, at least. If this came to a fight, every mage they could find would be necessary.

But this? And without so much as asking her? Firal squeezed her eyes closed, suddenly sick to her stomach.

"This is asking a great deal of Vicamros." Her voice quavered. She'd pretended to be calm and sure in front of courtiers and soldiers, managed to keep herself together in front of her friends. Now her strength was spent and she teetered on the verge of tears. After all she'd been through, this struck too close to betrayal.

It had been ages since her first husband had disappeared into the ether and never returned. The very notion they might find him now, that they could comb the world for him after hope had been long abandoned, made her ill. She couldn't fathom their chances. She'd almost given up on the thought he was alive.

"I haven't asked Vicamros to search, just to watch. That's not overstepping our bounds. He needs us too much now. Considering how easy it would be for us to strike up an alliance with someone else, he won't risk our connection. If Ran is there, Vicamros will give him to us. It's the best chance we have."

She didn't want to admit he was right.

Vahn glanced at her over his shoulder. "I'm planning to ride with my father to collect mages. I think if word comes, it would be best if I'm not here."

Firal tried not to frown. There was a deeper meaning in those words, something that made the uneasy churning of her stomach worse. *Do what you have to*, the undercurrent whispered. His eyes said it, instead of his voice. *Just don't make me watch.*

She pushed herself from her chair and crossed the office to slide her arms around his middle. Her cheek rested against his back and he tensed in her arms.

They'd married out of necessity, barely friends, certainly not lovers. He'd spent the first year sleeping on the floor beside her bed, more of a bodyguard than a husband. Building a relationship that was any more than that had been difficult, sometimes forced, but she had come to love him.

"It was thirty years this spring," she murmured. "And besides, he was your friend, too."

"He was." Vahn put his hands atop hers to hug her arms to his chest. "And if he comes, I'll speak to him when I'm ready. Until then, as I said, it would be best."

Firal nodded against his back and squeezed him tighter.

She wasn't the only one hurt by Rune's departure, though she knew it was better than his death. He'd been her first love, Vahn's best friend, and a traitor to the crown. She'd done her best to address her feelings, forced herself to move on and make the most of what she had. But after she'd done so, they'd simply never spoken of him again. It was clear Vahn still struggled, and the relationship they had now made things more complicated. He expected trouble. He expected to be hurt.

"Just remember," she said, and swallowed hard when her voice cracked. "You're my husband now."

"Yes." Vahn laced his fingers with hers, and all his hidden uncertainties spilled out in a single word. "Now."

A TEAM of mages waited in the courtyard. They stood to one side, idly watching as the grooms checked saddles and hooves while the men prepared for departure. Vahn was grateful for the mages, though he regretted the half-circle of Masters wasn't coming with them. Only one was to ride as part of their group, a woman named Kepha, who Vahn didn't know. Kytenia had chosen her to represent the mages, which was good enough, but he still would have preferred a Master he knew well.

The woman waited beside his father, excluded from the half-circle of mages meant to open a Gate. She was cold and neutral, white-haired, blue-eyed, and clothed in white robes like every other Master he'd ever seen. All mages looked the same, after a while. Perhaps that was what they intended. A unified front, where one was indistinguishable from the rest. He imagined the solidarity was beneficial.

Ennil met him a short distance away from the gathering company. He wore his dress armor, gleaming silver enameled with Ilmenhith's royal blue. His graying hair was slicked back and his face freshly shaven. The side of his face was still healing, which must have made the task difficult, but Ennil had refused to have a mage heal him. No sense in using magic, he said, when a man's body could do the same work on its own. A stubborn viewpoint, but one the man had held for as long as Vahn could remember.

"Are you ready?" his father asked, giving him a look-over.

Vahn wore the plain armor of a cavalryman. Only the silver circlet on his brow set him apart from the other soldiers. Odd, he thought, how his father would stand out instead of the king. "As I can be." Vahn wasn't eager to leave Firal, but he didn't like feeling powerless, either. He was just a man. One of Eldani blood, but diluted enough that he knew his wife would far outlive him. He had no Gift, no power, no way to fight the forces that had taken his daughter. He couldn't understand the challenges the mages would face in trying to retrieve her. But riding to collect mages, sending them back to serve beneath Kytenia—that was something he could do.

Better still that it kept him out of Ilmenhith, should an answer come from the mainland.

A small part of him thought he should stay. To comfort and support Firal, but also to see his friend if the summons was answered. But that part was drowned by a sense of resentment, a bitter grudge he hadn't realized he'd allowed to grow.

Ran had been his friend once, but Vahn wasn't sure he could still call him that. Vahn had made sacrifices on Ran's behalf. Given up his life, his aspirations, his future. He'd grown content in what he had, but it had taken a great deal of work. Work to make Firal love him, work to build a relationship between the two of them, work to be a good father to a child who could never be wholly his. Some part of him resented that most. He was the only father Lulu had ever known, and he loved her dearly, but there was a voice inside him—a small, sour, angry voice he hated—that lamented the color of her eyes. The girl was beautiful, so like her mother. But those eyes were a snare laid around her mother's heart, a small reminder of what could have been. Love had always seemed to come so naturally to Ran.

Just like everything else.

Ennil passed directions to the soldiers while the groomsmen gave the horses' girth straps one more tug and handed off the reins. The only thing left for Vahn to do was ride.

He tried to focus on what waited ahead, taking his horse's reins without acknowledging the groom. He needed to be busy. Surely he'd feel better once he was on the road. Riding always helped clear his head, and traversing the countryside could only help more. Or so he hoped. It could just as easily make things worse.

What *would* happen in Ilmenhith after he left? The thought was unsettling and Vahn frowned as he swung into the saddle. He knew he couldn't stay if things were to go smoothly. He didn't doubt Firal's fidelity. If Ran had stayed the person Vahn knew, he'd never need to. But he didn't know how negotiations would happen, if it would be private or put before the council, and either method could be disastrous.

"Where first?" asked one of the mages.

"Wethertree," Vahn replied absently. "Theirs is the only remaining full chapter house outside Ilmenhith. We'll speak to them first, make arrangements for Gates as necessary, then round up the mages in that area."

The mage nodded and retreated to rejoin the others, a few steps back. They spoke a moment in low voices and then began whatever it was they did to open Gates.

Vahn stared at the crackling edges of light that opened in the air before them and drew his mount's reins tight.

Perhaps he was worried about the wrong things. The longer he stewed over it, the more he unraveled the tangled knot of concerns that weighted his heart. It wasn't Ran's return that bothered him. It was that Ran could do things he couldn't. That after so many years of effort, of working to be the father Lulu deserved, he could do nothing to save her. That three full decades after his departure, Ran was the only one who could.

Protecting a child was what a father was supposed to do. What Vahn had failed to do.

The Gate sizzled as it opened to the cool shade of Wethertree's woods. Vahn clicked to his mount as he moved forward and waved for the cavalcade to follow.

Replacement. That was what he feared.

"Everyone through and get that Gate closed," Vahn called. "The fewer people who know where we are, the better."

Ennil nodded, a subtle display of approval. Vahn barely noticed as he settled back into his brooding thoughts.

When he returned to Ilmenhith, would he still have a place?

***

CRACKLING power filled the archway in front of them. Rune flinched and averted his eyes. A handful of guards clustered at his sides and a ring of mages stood behind them. Rhyllyn and Garam brought up the rear. They shifted bags in their hands and rocked on their feet as they waited for the procession to move.

The trip to Roberian's capital city had been uneventful. If Rune hadn't already been exhausted from hours on the road, he might have thought it nice to travel somewhere by carriage. Not that the carriage was comfortable. Garam hadn't appreciated his jokes about the hard seats and jouncing ride, which dampened what spirits he'd tried to feign.

The men who'd come to collect him had expected a fight. They arrived at the door with their weapons drawn. But they hadn't been eager to carry out their orders, and when Rune made it clear he didn't intend to resist them, they seemed relieved. He couldn't imagine their position was much easier than his. He'd served as part of the Royal City Guard alongside some of their fathers, if not with the men who stood beside him now. That kinship made them seem more like an honor escort than the party responsible for his arrest.

Magic surged around them as the mages worked to open a Gate to the Royal City. Among the mages was Alira, looking older than Rune recalled, though it could have just been the way worry pinched her face. If he felt sorry for the men, he felt worse for her. They'd both come from Elenhiise. Wars had shredded their lives and then forced them together as friends. But Alira knew he'd manage. It was the burden he left her that made him pity her position.

Despite their lack of blood ties, Rune had declared Rhyllyn his next of kin. When he was away, Alira was the boy's custodian. Looking after the lad was difficult enough without her added responsibilities as a mage on top.

More than once Alira glanced toward Rhyllyn, her worry obvious. Rune caught her eye and nodded slightly as the Gate opened. It was all the reassurance he could offer, but it seemed to be enough. She swallowed and nodded back. Then the Gate opened and the guards moved, forcing him through the portal.

Rune blinked against the sunlight as he stepped into the courtyard at the forefront of the Spiral Palace. Behind him, the city roared. He dared a glance over his shoulder, keeping his expression as neutral as he could. A line of men in gleaming armor held the city at bay. The crowds beyond seethed with fury. He didn't know whether they were angry over his arrest or angry at him for what they now believed he'd done, but it didn't matter. It didn't change anything.

He'd expected the mages to take him somewhere more private, but the only other safe area for Gating was in the mage quarters, halfway up the twisting spire that towered over the heart of the Triad. It made sense to choose the courtyard instead. From there, they could walk him directly to the throne.

Six mages strode through the Gate after his escort, then more guards, along with Garam and Rhyllyn. The Gate fell out of existence behind them. He couldn't see it from this side, of course; Gates without an anchor on both sides only worked in one direction. But he could feel it, in spite of the seal that kept him from using magic on his own. He felt everything around him, every delicate flow of power, energy he still hadn't learned to shut out completely. Magic didn't avoid him. It simply no longer answered his call.

Not that it would have answered him in the Royal City anyway; not without his access stone. A barrier surrounded the city, keeping mages from touching power. Only mages with an access stone were able to bypass it, but the king was tight-fisted with the gems. Rune possessed one and it had come hard earned. Given the circumstances he'd landed in, he'd chosen to leave it behind. The last thing he wanted to do was make the guards or mages think he might try to use it when he was under arrest.

The guards started forward, and Rune moved along with them. The palace doors stood wide, but weren't welcoming. Inside, clustered around the columns that lined the great hall, nobles and councilors watched and murmured amongst themselves. Some sneered. Most didn't even look at them. Rune searched the faces of those who did. Some turned away.

Redoram Parthanus was among those present; Rune's first friend in the Royal City and one of his closest allies. The old mage held his cap, wringing it between his hands. He met Rune's eyes and then turned away, shaking his head. As a councilor, Redoram had a say in matters like this. No matter how hard he must have fought in his friend's favor, it seemed he'd been overruled.

"You have to reconsider," Rhyllyn said.

Rune frowned and turned back. The guards shoved the youth

back behind their line, but Rhyllyn seemed undeterred. He pushed close again, glaring at the men who kept him from reaching his brother.

"You can't just let this happen!"

"Enough," was all Rune said.

The guards led him to the edge of the white marble dais and fell into a half-circle formation behind him, two men deep. The mages arranged themselves with three to either side, and Garam led Rhyllyn to join one of their groups. They stood back, Rhyllyn worried, Garam solemn. The former captain leaned on his cane, but didn't seem burdened by the bag of belongings that hung from his shoulder. They were Rune's things, instead of his own. The guards had forbidden Rune from carrying the bag himself.

The mages and guardsmen bowed, and the king stood.

Tall and broad-shouldered, Vicamros II was the perfect image of a king. His blond hair was gray at the temples, his close-trimmed beard streaked with white at the corners of his chin. His hands were scarred and callused from years wielding a sword, and his blue eyes sparked with experience. It was strange to recall him as the boy Rune had saved years ago. He'd changed a great deal.

Their friendship had changed very little.

"Would that we were meeting under better circumstances." Vicamros stepped down from his dais and moved forward with open arms. He wore fine clothing in the green, blue, and amber hues that represented the Triad. No armor, and only a ceremonial jeweled sword at his side. His appearance made it obvious he harbored no fear. No matter the accusations, he did not see Rune as a criminal—or a threat.

"We have a history of meeting in uncomfortable situations, if you'll recall." Rune forced a smile as he accepted his friend's embrace.

Vicamros frowned and stepped back. "Yes, though often because of my folly."

"Folly this time, perhaps, but not yours. You've grown into a wise man and a good leader for your people." Rune clapped a hand to the king's shoulder.

Vicamros only sighed. There was a glassy sheen in his eyes and an odd set to the corners of his mouth.

He's saying goodbye, Rune reminded himself. Or saying it as best as he could, with so many people watching. "You've done what you had to, Cam. I don't blame you for this."

"I am sorry," Vicamros murmured. "You have been a good friend to me. Whether or not you blame me for it, the order came from my mouth, and it's a poor way to repay you for the service you've done my kingdom."

Rune hesitated. The land he'd been given was a reward for that service. He glanced over his shoulder, searching for Rhyllyn.

The king followed his gaze and his eyes narrowed. "Is he—?"

"Staying here," Rune said. "This is my business, not his."

Vicamros nodded. "You've built a strong legacy for him. I will see he has guidance."

"I've entrusted my holdings to Lord Kaith and his family, until Rhyllyn comes of age."

"A sound choice." Vicamros paused and lowered his voice so that only the guards nearest to them would hear. "Before you go, I had hoped to ask a final favor from you, my friend."

Rune raised a brow and looked down at himself, then back to the king. "What?"

"Truth." A hint of regret crept over his features, and Vicamros lowered his eyes. "I'm sure you've been informed of the accusation against you. If I have condemned an innocent man, then I wish to know. If only to be aware of what I've sacrificed for the sake of politics."

A difficult request. Rune couldn't deny it, but it wasn't what the proclamation from Elenhiise made it sound like, either. "I wish I had a simple answer for you," he said. "But if the question is whether or not I killed their king, then the answer is yes."

Disappointment filled the king's eyes and his shoulders sagged.

Rune raised a clawed finger and continued. "But it isn't what they say. I have never killed a man outside honest combat, where both parties entered knowing what the outcome may be. They say I murdered him, and they're wrong. In truth, it was... an accident." His voice quavered with the word, his throat thick. "It wasn't supposed to happen. Not like that. I wanted answers, not his death. I begged the mages to heal him, but it was already too late. And no one hates me for it as much as I hate myself."

Vicamros studied him, his brow furrowed. "He was an important man to you."

Rune gave the slightest of nods. "The most."

"Then my heart is heavier for this." Vicamros stood straighter and lifted his chin. "But the mages must prepare to open your Gate, and I cannot delay you any longer. Simply know that the people of the Triad mourn you, my friend, but few so deeply as I."

To Rune's surprise, one of the guards stepped forward with shackles for his wrists. Chuckling, he held out his arms to accept them. "Everything catches up with you eventually. I'll remember this day if I'm presented the opportunity to haunt somebody."

Choking back a laugh, Vicamros waved him away. He returned to the throne and watched as the guards and mages began the slow, shuffling procession to the Gating parlor halfway up the tower.

"I still can't believe you're going to your death so willingly," Garam said once the group escaped the great hall.

Rune looked at Rhyllyn out of the corner of his eye and shrugged. "Better to be cooperative and leave a legacy," he said. "Besides, I never said I wasn't going to fight. I'm just not fighting you."

The corners of Garam's mouth twitched with a suspicious frown. Good; let him wonder. The air of mystery would just make his plans for escape that much more impressive.

Now all he had to do was think up what they were.

The guards remained silent as they trekked up the curving walkways that led higher into the Spiral Palace. Halfway to the parlor where the mages would open the Gate, the procession slowed without comment to accommodate Garam's flagging pace.

One of the mages met them at the door. "We aren't ready yet," the woman announced, her tone disinterested, for all that her eyes wandered over the group with great curiosity. "There are a handful of dignitaries waiting for transport and you will have to wait your turn."

"The king himself ordered us up here," Garam protested.

"And the king ordered the dignitaries to go home," the mage replied. "Sit and wait in the front room. We shall call you back to the Gating parlor when it is your turn."

"We'll wait, thank you," Rune said.

The mage eyed his shackles and raised a brow, but motioned for the group to enter.

They filed into the waiting room. The guards posted themselves near the doors and near the couch where Rune made himself comfortable, but the mages moved past them to enter the Gating parlor ahead of the party.

"You don't look like a man marching to your death," Garam remarked as he and Rhyllyn found seats of their own.

Rune shrugged. "Who knows what the future holds?"

"Nothing good," Rhyllyn murmured sullenly.

"That," Rune said with the smallest of smirks, "is probably the truth."

The boy sniffed and turned away. "How can you do this? Just go like it doesn't matter? People here need you. The Triad needs you. You're a war hero, someone the people look up to—"

"I'm a lot of things, but a hero isn't one of them. I am a soldier who did what was needed when I was needed there." Rune fought back a sigh. "Alira wanted me to be a good example for you, and sometimes setting an example means taking responsibility for your actions."

"But it's not fair," Rhyllyn protested.

"No, it's not, but when are things ever? Fair isn't me not going or me not being called back, Rhyllyn. Fair is me never having to leave home in the first place and the two of us never crossing paths."

Sulking, the youth slouched in his seat.

"He's right, you know," Garam said. "And I don't think your brother would be as calm as he is if he knew this was the end of the road."

Rhyllyn frowned, doubtful.

A mage appeared in the doorway. "Your Gate is ready."

Garam leveraged himself up with his cane. "That was fast."

"We are efficient, Lord Kaith," the Master replied, her tone flat.

Rune stood and the guards fell in around him as he turned to follow the mage. Rhyllyn moved to follow, too, but the mage raised a hand to stop him.

"Our orders include only the Champion and Lord Kaith." Her blue eyes were cold, emotionless. They bore no sympathy for the boy who would be left behind.

Before Rune could say a word, Rhyllyn closed the distance between them and wrapped him in a hug. With his hands still shackled, Rune wiggled his arms free and lifted his hands over the youth's head to squeeze him close. Rhyllyn made no sound, but his shoulders trembled and hot tears dampened the shoulder of Rune's shirt.

"Alira will come for you soon," Rune said. "Within a few days, you'll have Garam, too. You won't be alone."

Rhyllyn's arms tightened around his ribs.

"We must depart," the mage said.

Slowly, Rune raised his hands and Rhyllyn let go. Before he could slip away, Rune caught his shoulder.

"Remember," he murmured, catching the boy's gaze. "We aren't the monsters they've made us."

Tears brimmed on his dark lashes and Rhyllyn tore his eyes away.

"Let's go," Garam said softly.

Rune nodded and leaned forward to press a kiss to his brother's temple. Then he turned with his head high and followed the mage into the Gating parlor.

"You are destined first for the Grand College of Lore," the mage announced as the portal stabilized. The college often bustled with merchants and sailors coming and going, but today, a group of white-robed mages waited on the other side, ready to intercept them.

Garam leaned close as they waited for permission to pass through. "What kind of monster are you supposed to be?" he mused softly.

Rune's eyes darkened and he chuckled. "Just wait and see."

NEW WARS

THOUGH IT WAS TOO LATE TO DO ANYTHING, FIRAL INSPECTED THE map spread across her desk one last time. She'd done her best to help ensure every mage outpost was marked. Temar had helped fill in the ones she forgot. The court Master worked more closely with the temple than Firal did. In some ways it was a relief to have someone else look after the affairs of mages and only bring her the important matters. In others, it seemed a bad idea.

Now more than ever, Firal was isolated. It had been bad enough when she was expelled from the temple and landed among the Underlings, forced to make a new home. It had been worse when she was named queen, pulled from the wilds and placed upon the throne. She hadn't known anyone in Ilmenhith, save the temple Masters present in the city at the time. Now she didn't deal with the mages at all. Her chief court Master handled mage relations so Firal was free to tend other things.

She'd done a poor job of maintaining friendships with her comrades in the temple. She regretted it, but couldn't see how it could have been different. Being queen meant great demands on her time, and though her rule had been stable for years, there were always whispers behind her back.

That she'd been raised in the temple and trained as a mage

was a point against her in the eyes of some. Mages were meant to serve everyone in need, not only their own people. Some thought that made her untrustworthy and too sympathetic to potential enemies. Others thought her too lax with the mages, liable to let the temple run over the kingdom roughshod, the way her father had. So she had tried to distance herself from the mages, the only thing she knew to do, and as a result even her relationship with Kytenia had grown cool and formal.

The isolation had been tolerable when Medreal was present, or when Vahn was there. But now they were gone—one forever —and for the first time in her life, she felt truly alone.

And so the letter on her desk couldn't have come at a better time. Cross-referencing Anaide's list of outposts with the one Temar had helped her put together was exactly the sort of busywork she needed. It was progress, useful, yet mind-numbing at the same time. She picked up the letter to look it over again.

Firal read and re-read the names of cities and outposts on the map until she was sure they had remembered every active station, hoping the task would distract her from the thoughts of Lulu that clouded her mind. Was her daughter crying? Frightened? Cared for? Would they harm her? Why couldn't Envesi simply make demands? Firal would have given half the kingdom—Lifetree's mercy, the whole kingdom—to have her back.

There was a time she'd felt the same way about Rune.

She squeezed her eyes closed as thoughts of him joined her worries. She'd fought so hard to keep them at bay, but in the wake of Vahn's request that the rest of the world be scoured to find him, they'd been difficult to restrain. He'd been so confident Rune would be found alive. But he'd never answered her Calling, and after the last time she'd seen him had ended with Anaide demanding he hang, she struggled to believe he still lived.

A knock at the door made her jump, but she sighed in relief. Another distraction. Exactly what she needed.

"Your Majesty?" Timid, the servant girl did little more than peek into the office. Medreal had always been the one to carry messages through the castle. Without supervision from the stewardess, no one seemed to know how to approach her. "Begging your pardon for interrupting."

"It's all right." Firal smoothed her blue gown and turned to face the girl. She tried to look serene and queenly. The nervous look plastered on the girl's face made her doubt she was successful.

"There's someone here to see you," the girl said. "The Chief Overseer of Core. He says he was summoned, Majesty."

More relief. Firal smiled and nodded. "See him in at once."

Requesting the Overseer's presence had been Vahn's idea. Firal regretted she hadn't thought of it on her own. The underground city of Core was extensive, most of it now uninhabited. If the woman who took her child was still on the island, Core presented an ideal hiding place.

On top of that, Core held one of two permanent, anchored Gates. The other was in Ilmenhith. Both led to the Grand College in Lore, far to the north. With Envesi being a free mage, it was unlikely she'd need an anchored Gate. But it was an easy escape route, and one that wouldn't leave behind any traces of power for other mages to find. The Gate in Ilmenhith was used for politics and closely supervised trade, guarded by her own mages, but the Gate in Core was used for the transport of goods to and from the mines. Mages would have to be assigned to watch it.

All this depended on the idea that the woman was still on the island, of course. Firal couldn't imagine where else they might be. According to Kytenia, the former Archmage hadn't been seen by anyone connected to the Grand College in years. Firal tried not to think of that little problem, much like she tried not to think of the woman seen in the palace with Ennil at all.

Firal had never reconciled with the knowledge that the former Archmage was her mother. For all those years, her lonely upbringing in the temple made her long for a mother who had been there the entire time.

The door opened again, this time without a knock. The same servant girl led two people into the office, gave a curtsy and ducked out as soon as they were through the doorway. At the front was a man in his middle years, with bronzed skin and sleek black hair, though it was graying at the temples and more gray was sprinkled throughout. He had a squared jaw and a hard look to him, though that wasn't unusual for the people of Core. They were the original inhabitants of the island, before the Eldani conquered it and drove them underground. They'd been called Underlings when Firal took the throne. Now they were called ruin-folk, a name they all liked better.

He knelt before her desk with his head bowed and a hand pressed to his heart. The loyalty of the ruin-folk was solid, if hard-earned. It had taken a great deal of effort and compromise to gain their love, but the dedication that came with it sometimes made her wish she still lived among them.

"Welcome, Tobias. Please, rise, so I may greet you as a friend." Firal spread her hands in invitation. Her eyes traveled to the cloaked figure behind him, who only curtsied, and stiffly at that. "Who have you brought with you?"

"She insisted on coming." Tobias offered a half smile as he rose. "She said you would find a use for her."

"And she will," the small woman said, chuckling pleasantly as she removed her dusty travel cloak. She'd been near Firal's height once, but was now stooped and gray. Her darkly tanned face was creased and leathery with age, but there was no mistaking the lively spark in her brown eyes. The woman had changed a great deal in the handful of years since Firal had seen her last. Those eyes hadn't changed at all.

Out of everyone Tobias could have brought, the man had

brought his mother. Minna, the woman who welcomed Firal into Core and fussed over her like the mother she'd never had.

Despite all her worries, Firal felt a burden lift, and she laughed. "You always know when I need to see you, don't you?"

"I tend to have a feeling, Miss Firal. Oh—Queen Firal, I ought to say. Bless me, I'll never get over that." Minna smiled. She folded her cloak over her arm and stepped forward to pat Tobias's bicep. "He's a bit more gray than the last time we visited. Distinguished, isn't he?"

Firal nodded. "Yes, he looks every bit the part of leader. Strong and capable, just the sort of man I need overseeing things in Core."

Tobias made a small sound of displeasure and brushed Minna's hand away. "Now, you two. You'll make a man's head swell." Then his face grew solemn, and he caught Firal's eye. "I've heard what happened. You have the condolences of everyone in Core, my queen. Whatever you've called me here to ask of me, know I will see it done. More, if it's in my power."

"Thank you, I will rest easier knowing it." Firal paused, unsure where to begin. She gestured to the chairs before her desk. "I have two matters to discuss with you, though I hope one of them will not require you to act. Sit, please, both of you."

Tobias helped his mother to a chair. He waited until both Minna and Firal were settled before he took a seat for himself. His posture was good, his manners excellent. How had anyone ever thought his people uncivilized?

"First is the matter of security in Core," Firal began. She rubbed her forehead, weary. "We cannot afford to close the Gate at the mine, but I will need to post several mages there to watch it. They will not interfere with your men or their duties. I expect they will leave them alone entirely, unless disturbed, in which case they will be given leave and authority to protect themselves."

"Of course," Tobias said. "But... guards, my queen?"

"I doubt she would use it, but if Envesi wants an easy way

off the island without leaving any trace of her own magic, the Gate is a perfect avenue for escape. It might also be of use to any followers she may have gained, so it will need to be watched." Firal's amber eyes flicked toward the door and she raised a hand to spin an invisible barrier around them. Neither Tobias nor Minna were Gifted; they wouldn't know what she was doing. But the door was still open a crack, and she wouldn't indulge anyone who might be outside listening. The ward would keep their voices in, but it wouldn't block anything out.

"I will need you to provide housing for the mages somewhere in Core, of course," she continued. "Will you need any additional food or supplies delivered with their arrival?"

"No, we should get along fine." He hesitated, then offered a nervous grin. "I have to say, things are much different now than when I was a child. We've lived well since integrating with the kingdom. I've never heard of anyone going hungry. It's hard to imagine anyone ever did."

Firal allowed herself to smile. It was a fine compliment, and another reminder that claiming Core as a part of her territory had been the right thing to do. Of course, even without merging the underground city into her holdings, she would have been their queen by marriage. That thought was troubling, and she lowered her eyes. "Then I'll trust you to manage things after their arrival. They will report directly to me on a daily basis, which brings me to another matter I'll need you to oversee. I realize the caverns under the ruins are vast, so I won't ask you to search them. It's unlikely you would find anything, anyway. But in the event your men notice anything out of the ordinary in the ruins or in the underground, have them report it to my mages for further investigation."

Tobias nodded. "Consider it done."

"And you ought to tell them all to be more mindful," Minna said. "No one ventures far from the mines these days, but routine makes for lazy eyes."

He chuckled. "Of course, mother."

"Thank you," Firal said. "Both for your work in tending this, and for what you've already done."

"It is my duty and honor, my queen." Tobias inclined his head and pressed his palm to his heart. "Is that all you wished to discuss today?"

Her cheer evaporated. "No. There is one other matter we need to discuss before you go."

The Overseer raised a brow, but nodded. "Of course. What else?"

This was the sticky part, full of awkward questions she didn't want to ask. Firal double-checked the ward around them before she began. "I know my leadership of the ruin-folk was only accepted because of the status granted to me by my first marriage."

Tobias frowned. Minna did, too. "Yes, Your Majesty," he said slowly. "They are content with your leadership now, though. You have more than proven yourself, even if relations between the ruin-folk and the Eldani are not perfect."

The imperfections in relations were part of what worried her. "There was a great deal of passion in your armies when I took the throne. Some initially refused to honor my lead because of what happened to your newly-raised king. Are there still loyalties to him among your people?"

Tobias opened his mouth, but his mother scoffed before he could speak. "You certainly sound the part of queen with all that dainty word-mincing, Miss Firal. There's no one here but the three of us, no reason not to speak plainly. Lord Daemon was loved." Minna sniffed and raised her chin. "But, Miss Firal, you must understand that we aren't like you mage-folk in the city. Our lives are fast and fierce, and the men in our armies now have only ever heard of him through their fathers and grandfathers."

"And even the old men who served him see that life beneath your rule is what's best for us," Tobias said. "But why do you ask?"

"Because a weakened flame can still be rekindled." Firal clasped her hands in her lap and stared down at them. "And a new war is the last thing I need."

Minna's brow furrowed, but before she could ask, the office door creaked open.

Temar stepped in and bowed, but lingered by the entry. Sensing the ward, she awaited permission to step within its bounds.

Firal beckoned her forward, concerned.

"Your Majesty," Temar said as she passed into the ward. She turned her hand to display the small, three-colored envelope she held. "An urgent message from King Vicamros II of the Triad. It just arrived."

Firal stiffened. "Did you read it?"

"Yes, Majesty." The white-haired mage bowed her head, but not before she spared a worried glance for the two ruin-folk.

"Out with it!" Firal almost snapped.

"They've found him," Temar said in a rush, keeping her head lowered. "A party has been sent for his arrest. We expect them here by mid-afternoon."

Weakened, Firal fell back in her chair. Mid-afternoon! There was no way she could have things in order by then. And if the mages had already read the note, word would escape the palace within moments. "I hope you're right about their loyalties, Tobias," she murmured.

A shadow crossed his face. "You don't mean—"

"Yes," she said, smoothing her black hair back from her face. "It seems Lord Daemon still lives, after all."

FOR THE FIRST time in what seemed an eternity, it was quiet. In reality, it had been a handful of days, but the constant flow of people and their poking and prodding made time drag. It was only made worse by the girl's crying, which Envesi found more distressing than she wanted to admit.

She didn't resent the girl's tears; they were more of a frustration than an annoyance. But Envesi didn't know how to cope with a distressed child, didn't know how to calm her or entertain her. In truth, she knew little about children at all. Despite the child she'd borne herself and another she'd created through power, she had never been a mother.

No part of her was nurturing. She had no patience, no understanding, and no idea how to offer comfort to a child who only wanted someone to love her. It was hard not to find the child endearing, with her large violet eyes and cherubic face, messy dark curls and sweet pink lips. But Envesi didn't know how to love. It was a bizarre notion she hadn't entertained since her own childhood, now centuries past, and while being around the girl was pleasant—when the child wasn't crying, that was— Envesi felt nothing more toward her than the amicable warmth one might feel for a favorite pen.

After all, Lumia—a name that made Envesi grimace when she'd learned it—was a tool, nothing more. There was no reason to feel anything else.

The girl lay sleeping on a chaise beside Envesi's desk, a cloak drawn over her to serve as a blanket. She cried herself to sleep most nights, though tonight had gone better. One of the other mages had stroked the girl's hair and murmured to her until she drifted off. It bought a few hours of peace, at least, for Envesi to study.

It wasn't necessary for the girl to be awake, just nearby. The field of energy around her was like nothing Envesi had ever felt. After days of study, the former Archmage still did not know what to make of it, and she had come no closer to determining how to use it. It was frustrating, but expected; the child's Gift was nothing like her own.

Oh, it was true they were both free mages, but Envesi's power bore a taint that was more than the strange corruption of her body. She'd learned a great deal through studying herself after she had gathered a new team of mages and unbound her power. Free of her healing affinity, she could manipulate energy from all sources and feel the flow of magic in everything around her. The white scales and the misshapen hands and feet that bore them were a small price to pay for that sort of power. But there was still a taint, a thread of wrongness in her power, like a drop of ink blossoming in a vial of water. It made her magic work in unpredictable ways, sometimes.

The girl's power, by contrast, was clean. She didn't summon magic; as far as Envesi could tell, she didn't seem to touch it at all. There was no spark of power within her, like that of bound mages. Nor did she have to wait to grow into her Gift. Like the magic that ebbed and flowed around them, it was already part of the girl. She *was* magic, in its purest form. And in that, she was more powerful than Envesi could ever hope to be.

She'd met free mages before. They could be conquered as easily as any other mages, especially when their odd customs and beliefs kept them from wielding as much power as they potentially could. They were conservative, to say the least, which had been their greatest failing. Envesi had no such restraints. Magic existed to serve mages, and mages existed to wield it. There was no reason not to explore the fullest extent of her strength.

While she could not outmatch the Alda'anan in power, she exhibited finesse in her Gift. Many of those she faced had been clumsy, almost as if they had never practiced wielding magic at all. And perhaps they hadn't. After all, the very first thing they taught their children was how to cut oneself off from the power around them, to rob their eyes of their beautiful glow. The poor fools.

But there were other things to worry about now. Learning to connect her magic to the girl's, to begin with. Envesi sighed, reclined in her chair and tapped a claw against the edge of her desk.

Everything she'd tried had failed, as if the girl's power rejected her. Whether it was because of the child's age or the taint in her own magic, Envesi didn't know. The former seemed more likely, given how oblivious Lumia was to her Gift. One couldn't simply seize another's magic for the purpose of sharing it. It had to be offered freely before one could grasp it and wield it in conjunction with their own. Trying to take hold by force ran the risk of severing the girl from power, which the former Archmage couldn't afford.

Twining her power with that of any unbound mage would have given her the extra might she desired, but anyone she unbound would face the same bodily corruption as her, and she knew from experience that not every unbinding went well. Hers had worked because she was in control. Likewise, her first two experiments had worked because there had been a team of mages present, able to tame the wild energy that surged as the bonds of affinity came free.

Her other attempts had not gone so well. Four other times she'd tried, and all four times, the mages she'd freed had burned up, consumed by the flames of raw power they couldn't contain.

Creating a new council of mages who knew how to unbind affinities and hold the new power at bay was one solution, but Envesi was unwilling to lose more to the taint. Magic flowed like a river, etching paths into the earth, digging deeper and resisting diversion. To teach others the method she knew ran the risk of pulling them into a path already colored with corruption. Finding a new method of unbinding would be difficult, but it was a necessity. Few were willing to become monsters, even for the promise of power.

The only solution was to find a new path. Studying the girl's Gift would help Envesi determine which way to go.

Behind her, someone knocked on the door frame. Simple as their headquarters was, few rooms had doors.

"Archmage," the white-robed mage murmured, glancing

toward where Lumia slept, "another report has come in. Shall I order them to track the target?"

"No," Envesi said as she pushed herself up from her desk. She paused to adjust the cloak over the sleeping child before she stalked toward the doorway. "I shall handle it myself."

The woman nodded and stepped aside to let her pass.

It was not how Envesi had planned to spend her evening, but she wouldn't miss the opportunity. She'd lost count of how many free mages she'd exterminated, but like rats in a shabby cellar, there always seemed to be one more.

Until I am able to free more of my own, she thought grimly as she made her way to the front of the tiny chapter house. Then, together, they would stamp them out, like the smoldering cinders of a forgotten flame they were.

8

EXTERMINATION

RIKKA, MASTER OF THE HOUSE OF WIND, SHIVERED AND FOLDED her arms across her chest. The breeze stirred her hair and ruffled her white robes. She had often wondered why the Archmage's tower had no glass in the windows. Most of the time, she thought it was a deliberate choice, meant to capture the island's breezes and funnel them into a building that would have been stifling otherwise. But sometimes, such as now, when cold droplets of night rain blew in to patter against the bare stone floor, it seemed more like an oversight. "There's something in the air. Do you feel it?"

Behind her, Balen, Master of Fire, raised his head. "What was that?"

"The wind," Rikka said. "There's something off about it. Something ill. Like it carries bad news."

The soft rustle of papers filled her ears. "That's exactly the sort of talk that makes the Giftless call us witches." He chuckled. "You're supposed to be grading these too, you know. Are you going to help me or not?"

She heaved a sigh and made herself retreat from the window. Dark splotches left by raindrops marred her robes. Her fingertips trailed over them without a thought, and magic stirred in answer to her call to dry them. "You think I'm being ridiculous."

"I think you're responding as many would." Balen pushed a handful of papers across the table. "I think every mage in the temple wishes they could help, but those haven't been our orders. Until Queen Firal or the Archmage herself instructs us to do something more, this is right where we need to be. Work must continue, after all, and the magelings need stability."

"I suppose so," she muttered, and didn't mean it at all.

The worst of it wasn't that work had to continue, it was that other mages had been given jobs. Anaide, Master of Water, sat in her own private quarters to comb through records and send additional information on chapter houses—both occupied and abandoned—to the queen. Shymin, Master of Healing, had been tasked with... something.

And then Rikka sat in a shared office after the magelings had gone to bed, grading papers with Balen by mage-light. Sullen, she sat down.

"Don't take it personally," Balen said softly.

She stiffened. "What?"

"That we're working. You complained about it all morning, did you think I forgot?" He flashed her a grin and for a moment, she hated that she couldn't be angry at him.

Balen's smile was like the rest of him—cheerful, charming, and projecting an unshakable sense of calm. He was a perfect example of what a Master mage ought to be. Amicable, pleasant, patient, and encouraging. His mage-blue eyes were a bolder shade than most, like the deepest blue in a summer sky, and they snapped with positivity. Rikka met his stare and tried to sulk, but his good nature soon overwhelmed her and she allowed herself a grudging smile.

"I just wish I could do more," she said with a sigh.

"You do plenty," he reassured her. "Besides, this job isn't demeaning, it's an honor. All heads of affinity are in charge of teaching, but when it comes time to leave someone in charge, we're the ones left to oversee the temple on our own. Archmage Kytenia trusts us. That should mean a lot."

"I suppose you're right." The papers in front of her were a jumble of subjects. She frowned and worked at sorting them into piles.

His smile widened, just a little.

Admittedly, there were few mages Rikka would have enjoyed sharing such a task with. Balen was easy to get along with. He was charming in many ways, too; had she been younger, she would have thought him charismatic, and certainly handsome. His features were nicely proportioned. The white hair that crowned his head was short but always ruffled, and made a pleasant contrast to his coppery complexion.

After the death of her best friend, such childish interests as handsome men had grown unimportant. Now, and always after, work came first.

The wind picked up and again, Rikka shivered. "You really don't feel that?"

"Wind is your affinity, not mine," he said, though he regarded her with thoughtful eyes. "What does it feel like?"

Deep, prickling, like a sense of discord in an otherwise orderly world. "It feels..." she said slowly, her brow furrowed. "It feels like magic."

***

ENVESI'S CLAWS, like her scales, were pearlescent white. She'd studied her own hands numerous times, but it wasn't until now that she wondered why that was. Was it because, as a mage at the pinnacle of her power, the rest of her had been scoured of color as well? The others hadn't shown rhyme or reason for the colors that emerged. Would they have been a bleached white, too, if they had crossed the boundaries that separated exceptional mages from average mortals?

The crimson droplets that welled at the tips of her claws grew larger. Beneath her crushing grip, the mousy little free mage gasped.

Ah, to bleed red. To see life escape, untainted by the corrupted magic that seeped from her body when her skin was pierced. To see such color spill from her own veins again would be one of many triumphs.

"I will give you one more chance," Envesi said as she lowered the small man so his feet could touch the floor. "Answer the question, and I may be persuaded to release you."

Her grip on his throat relaxed and the free mage gasped for air. Color returned to his lips as he panted, though his eyes retained the wild look of a frightened woodland animal. Fitting, she thought, for how small he seemed.

"What you want," he gasped, rubbing the crimson stains from his throat when she let go, "I cannot... It does not exist. I cannot help you."

Fury flared in her eyes before she caught herself. Her emotions had grown difficult to manage after the change. Even now, she struggled to contain the magic that rushed to reflect every thought and feeling. The light in her eyes faded as she regained control. "You misunderstand," she said as she flicked blood from the tips of her claws. "That was not a request."

"And you are not the first to seek it," the mage replied, his voice firm, but calm. Even now, faced with certain death, he kept such control of himself that his eyes did not glow. "The answer has not changed."

"Not the first," Envesi mused. "Who else has asked?"

"Corruption has existed since the dawn of mankind." The Alda'anan mage's brows knit together in a look that seemed half consternation, half sorrow. "And we have tread the earth since long before that time. You are not the first, nor will you be the last. Through it all, the answer will not change. You seek purification?" He barked a harsh, shallow laugh. "It is not mine to give."

Her eyes narrowed. "Very well."

She seized the flows of power in the air around her and advanced.

9

WELCOME PARTY

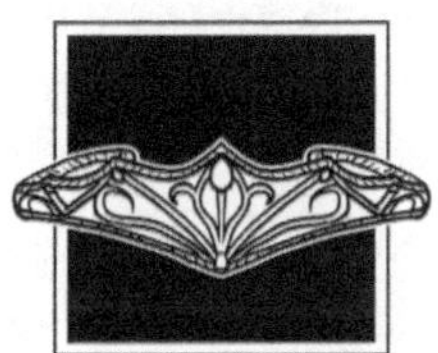

THE CITY HAD BEEN EXPECTING THEM. THE CRACKLING HISS OF THE Gate gave way to the sound of people the moment Rune stepped through the portal. Vicamros's mages had put them inside the palace walls, if barely. It sounded as if half the city had come to crowd around the gates, and the people bunched close to the iron portcullis that held them at bay. Leering faces pressed to the dingy bars and hands reached through to move in rude gestures. Amused, Rune lifted his wrists to show off the shackles that bound him. The crowds roared in response.

The rest of his escort filtered through the Gate behind him. Rune half expected Rhyllyn to try to follow them, in spite of the mages' refusal to let him into the parlor, but the Gate closed after Garam passed through with the assistance of a mage. The guards exchanged worried glances at the noise that answered their arrival.

"Awfully angry bunch," Garam said, glancing toward the palace gate and the crowd outside. "Long time to hold a grudge."

"For you," Rune said. "These people aren't human. Some of these men watched their king die."

A pair of guards moved closer, took hold of his arms and

urged him forward. He didn't resist, but held his head high as they passed the portcullis.

Garam cursed as something arced overhead.

"Shields," one of the guards called. The group moved in unison and raised their shields overhead, just as the barrage of rocks came down.

Rune glanced over his shoulder as a stone narrowly missed his head. "I'd say this is going rather well."

Garam snorted and moved closer to one of the shields. "You think people throwing rocks at your head is this going well?"

"Better than I expected." Rune shrugged.

Something hit a shield with a sick smack. A wave of brown pulp slid off the metal and splattered against the side of Rune's head as a rancid sweetness filled the air, making him gag. Rotten fruit.

"Makes me wonder what you expected," Garam muttered.

Rune chuckled softly. "A gallows."

Gallows or not, it struck him as odd that the courtyard was so empty. There should have been more guards, more mages, maybe nobles waiting at the steps to throw more rotten fruit or even spit in his face. At the very least, he expected that sort of welcome from the temple Masters. Considering the part they'd played in seeing him off, the mages would be least happy to see him of all. Their absence gave him the distinct feeling Ilmenhith and its leaders were not prepared to receive them.

The men lowered their shields as they moved beyond the reach of hurled stones. Now outside immediate danger, their pace relaxed. Though the courtyard was empty, a pair of apprehensive-looking men stood beside the tall, arched doors at the top of the palace stairs. They opened the doors in unison and stepped aside to allow the group entry.

A handful of palace guards waited inside. They fell in step with the escort without a word and ushered them toward the throne room.

The palace was no different than Rune remembered it.

Streamers in silver and blue twined around the white marble columns that lined the walkway. Live trees in massive pots stood along the walls, meticulously shaped, their trunks wound with more streamers. Banners depicting a seven-pointed star with a ring around its center—the crest of Ilmenhith—hung between them. And if the blue carpet that led to the throne room was more worn than it had been thirty years ago, he couldn't tell. He'd expected the return to Elenhiise to be difficult, but he hadn't expected the pang of homesickness that wrenched his insides.

He'd longed for this moment, an impossible dream that had lived in the recesses of his mind long after he'd given up hope he'd ever return. He had a place in the Triad—responsibilities, a beautiful estate and a comfortable house, even a handful of people who tolerated him well enough to be good company— but it wasn't home. Walking the halls of Ilmenhith's palace felt right, but his steps were more sure than his spirits. No matter how badly he wanted to return, it could never be like it was. A cold, rational voice in the back of his head reminded him of that, over and over again, refusing to give him peace.

"Her Majesty will receive you in the throne room," said one of the guards as he climbed the few steps to the peaked doors at the end of the walkway.

Rune cast Garam a look from the corner of his eye. "Did you get that, or will you need a translator?"

"Vicamros II ordered all of his councilors to learn Old Aldaanan as soon as he took the throne," Garam said. "I'll be fine. Besides, I can't imagine how it would look for a prisoner to be the one translating for his captors."

The doors to the throne room opened. Garam led the way, walking by himself. The guards filed in behind him, two by two. They kept Rune in the center of their group, though the men at his arms pressed close, as if afraid to set foot off the edges of the blue carpet. The mages came last, walking with their heads down. Instructed to keep quiet, no doubt; there were rumors that the Grand College of Lore feared being swallowed by Kirban Temple. Considering how big the temple had been in his youth, Rune thought it a reasonable fear.

He squared his shoulders as the party moved forward and inched closer to his awaiting doom. He'd mourned his decision from the moment he made it, but he would not allow himself to regret it. No matter what the people of Elenhiise thought, he was a man of his word and a man of honor, however little it may be. He would not let them see regret or fear, no matter how the feelings tried to claw their way from him.

The courtyard and great hall had been empty, but the throne room was fuller than it had been on the day he'd been sentenced to hang.

Soldiers and nobles crowded the walkway, mages in half a dozen colors sprinkled throughout their midst. The walkway of the second floor was packed with serving staff. Many leaned forward over the rail for a better look. Speculation flitted through the crowd in murmurs, but Rune stared straight ahead and pretended he didn't hear.

At the far end of the throne room, perched on a silver throne shaped like twisted vines, was the queen.

Jewels shone in her raven curls, her round face as serene as that of any mage. Her close-fitting gown accented the shape of her full figure, and the tiny gems on the navy silk reminded Rune of stars.

The guards marched forward in solemn silence. They halted at the end of the walkway, where the carpeting ended before the dais in a large circle emblazoned with the royal crest. Rune stopped in the center of the seven-pointed star and lifted his eyes.

The queen stared down at him, her face impassive.

Thirty years in exile, a looming death sentence, his execution sure to come, and all he could think of was the sweet softness of her lips.

"Daemon of the Underlings," Firal said, her voice cold and

clear, her amber eyes emotionless despite all their fire. "Thirty years ago, you escaped Ilmenhith's prison and fled execution after the murder of our king. What do you have to say?"

Rune lifted his chin. "You appear to be sitting on my throne."

The corners of her mouth twitched before she caught herself, though anger flared in her eyes. "Is that an admission of treason?"

"An accident can't be considered treason," he snapped. "If you don't believe me, then ask Kytenia. Ask Vahn. They were there, they can tell you. Or have you tried to execute them due to false claims as well?"

"But you admit you killed him," Firal said. "When you were imprisoned, the Masters of Kirban Temple accused you of attempting to usurp the throne. Considering the peremptory claim you just made, how do you plan to refute it?"

"If anyone can be accused of usurpation, it's you." Rune started forward, gritting his teeth when the guards caught his arms and held him still. "The mages wanted me out of the way. All my life, my father worked to prepare me to rule. Yet the mages refused to recognize me as the rightful heir to the throne, or even speak my name when they declared I was to hang!"

"Enough." Her voice was loud and firm, filled with confidence and determination. She rose from the throne, every inch a queen.

An odd hush fell over the crowded room. Mages and nobles alike looked at him strangely. Some peered at Firal as if seeing her for the first time.

Rune almost laughed. He turned his head to take in all the puzzled faces. All those years, and they'd never wondered what became of him? He couldn't resist a smirk when he met her eyes again. "You never told them, did you?"

"Regardless of what transpired at the end of my father's rule, I have not brought you here only to send you to the gallows." She paced to the edge of the dais and peered down her nose at him. "Instead, I offer a proposition. A chance to redeem yourself and have the charges against you waived. You will be free to live out your life in peace, on Elenhiise or off it, with your honor restored."

Words failed him and his mouth fell open. Half of him was stunned that she'd even make such an offer. The other half seethed at the suggestion he'd done something that required forgiveness. He closed his mouth as the latter half won and a scowl formed on his face. "You'll have to speak up, highness. I think there's a bit of rotten fruit in my ear from what your peasants threw at me."

She ignored him and turned instead to Garam and the mages, who waited in a half-circle at the edge of the carpet. "You have my thanks for your service. You are all welcome to enjoy my kingdom's hospitality until a decision is reached or an execution held. The prisoner shall be escorted upstairs and given private lodgings. He will be made presentable for a meeting of council, where his fate will be determined. Furthermore, he is to be kept under guard at all times, and allowed nowhere else in the palace until council has met."

"Thank you, Your Majesty. We will be glad to stay until all is resolved." Garam bowed stiffly, showing his age. Despite his study of the language, his accent was thick and his words slurred, but no one seemed to notice.

"A prisoner in my own home," Rune said. "I suppose some things never change."

Firal glowered at him. "Mind your tongue. This island has not been your home in half a Giftless man's lifetime. You'd be wise to remember it was you who abandoned it."

He started to reply, but the men around him shifted to let a pair of Firal's guards move in and take his arms.

"I will be waiting in my office," she said, giving him one last disdainful look as she turned toward the sweeping staircases behind the throne. "See that he's bathed before I have to deal with him again."

"You should have let me do the talking," Garam said.

Rune rolled his eyes. He dragged his feet as they filed down the narrow hall, and tried to pretend he didn't know where the guards were taking them. Garam wasn't the sort to lose his temper easily, but that he spoke in the northern trade tongue was a clear indicator of his mood. Most merchants and some of the mages from Elenhiise understood it, but it was unlikely the guards would. "She didn't address you. She expected me to speak."

"And you did a fine job of digging yourself a hole." Shaking his head in agitation, Garam looked ready to strangle him. "Even if you let me handle the talk during this council meeting, I don't think I can get you back out of it."

"I don't expect you to fix my problems for me. But I will admit that didn't go the way I thought it would." With the people waiting outside the palace, Rune had been sure they'd see him hang before sundown. He hadn't expected anything else, and the bitterness in Firal's first words only strengthened those expectations. Backhanded as though the offer had been, the chance to redeem himself was both startling and appealing.

His companion gave him a sidewise glare.

Rune lowered his head. "Maybe I could've been a little more polite," he muttered.

Garam scoffed. "With the look on her face, I thought the queen meant to throttle you with her own hands."

Rune couldn't help but chuckle. "It wouldn't be the first time." In some ways, seeing Firal's anger had been a relief. He'd tried to rekindle contact with her when the alliance was forged between Elenhiise and the Triad. Silence answered his efforts, making her wishes obvious. So he'd kept his distance. After so many years, he'd feared something worse than anger would greet his return. He'd feared she wouldn't feel anything at all.

And how beautiful the fire in her eyes had been. She'd

changed so little, her face a bit rounder and her figure fuller than when he'd seen her last, though that might have been for the better. She'd lost weight during her time in Core. Their time together. The memory made his throat grow thick, and he swallowed hard.

"So are we abandoning your escape plan, or do we wait until we see what her proposal is?" Garam asked.

Rune twitched and barely caught the scowl that tried to form on his face. The question was posed casually, relating suspicious information in mundane tones so the guards wouldn't think anything was amiss. He made himself study the ceiling as they walked and replied as if bored. "What makes you think I have a plan?"

"Because whether or not you expected a gallows, you wouldn't walk straight to it."

Of course Garam would expect him to be prepared. They'd been friends too long for anything else. "I have something, I just wasn't positive it would work until just now, when I spoke with Firal."

"Care to enlighten me?" Garam asked.

Rune shrugged. "It's complicated. I'll explain everything when I can, probably after this council meeting. No time now, we're to your rooms."

"Your rooms, Lord Kaith," one of the guards said as he stopped to open a door.

Garam gave Rune a suspicious look.

He smiled in response.

"Thank you," Garam said. "Send my men and my mages to me. I will need to speak to them before we meet with the queen." He peered through the doorway and arched a thick white brow. It was a good room, one of the finest guest suites. Better than what Rune suspected he would be staying in.

"Of course, Lord Kaith. Shall we call for serving staff as well?" the guard asked.

Garam nodded. "Please." He paused to frown at Rune. "And

be mindful with my prisoner. Don't forget he's my responsibility until after that meeting is held. My king would not be pleased if something were to go amiss."

Both guards bowed.

"Be safe," Rune said in the trade tongue.

"Be careful," Garam replied, then slipped into his rooms.

Despite their respect for Lord Kaith, the guards shoved Rune back into motion, their grip on his arms rougher now that Garam was out of sight. He wasn't surprised. They were men of Ilmenhith's army, both old enough that they were likely on the field when the war took place.

They backtracked a good distance before the men turned him down a smaller hallway. The rooms in this part of the palace were slightly better than the servants' quarters, meant for the low-caste attendants of visiting nobles. Better than the prison, so he wouldn't complain. He'd braced himself for the possibility of staying there again, though the memory alone made the scars on his back burn. Anything was better than that.

One of the men pushed a door open with his shoulder and shoved Rune into the small room. "You'll wait here. Guards will be up with serving girls to bathe you."

"Blonde ones, I hope," Rune said. "I'd prefer not to see any that look like the queen."

The man scowled. "Mind your tongue."

"Or what? You'll cut it out? I think Her Majesty would be displeased if we couldn't converse during that little meeting she's called."

The guard cast a glance to his companion. "Are we going to have a problem?"

"We might." The second guardsman stepped back into the hall and pulled the door closed, dulling their voices to murmurs.

Alone, Rune allowed himself a sigh.

The room they'd put him in had no windows and only one other door, which led to what he assumed was a small privy or bathing chamber. The only means for escape was the door they'd brought him through, and with the shackles on his wrists, they obviously didn't think he was a threat. The room's furnishings were sparse, but the rickety table and chair in the corner could have armed him with a club. Not that he thought escape was feasible, but until he had a solid plan, any idea was worth entertaining.

Rune sat on the edge of the narrow bed and twisted his wrists inside their shackles. So far, the only option that seemed to have merit was his first idea. Had their walk been longer, he would have explained it to Garam before they were separated. He didn't like the idea of springing surprises on his friend, but there was a chance that could work to his advantage, too. If the reactions of the spectators in the throne room were any indicator, it wouldn't be hard to stir up an outcry.

He hadn't said it outright, but he'd said enough for the clever to piece it together on their own. He'd spoken of Kifel as his father, announced his right to the throne. But there were pieces to the puzzle he didn't have yet, and how Firal had managed to hold her position as queen without explaining what happened to Ran was one of them.

Strange to think he'd need the name again, after working so hard to bury it. Even Alira no longer called him Lomithrandel; she'd adopted his new name long ago. A name Firal had given him, but one he'd grown into on his own. It was a part of him in more ways than one. From the sigil the Underling queen had etched into his hand to the rune-stone game piece that bore the same mark, which he always carried in his pocket. Not for luck or any sort of power. He wasn't superstitious. Instead it was a reminder of who he was, who he'd become, and what he'd built for himself.

Ran, he supposed, was still a part of that identity.

It wasn't long before more voices murmured outside his door, announcing the arrival of more guards. A mage, too, from the feel of it. Rune pushed himself up from the bed as a pair of serving girls and a white-robed mage he didn't recognize stepped inside. A single guard moved in behind them. A handful more waited outside.

The girls kept their heads down to avoid looking at him. They slipped through the smaller door in the back corner and the mage followed.

"Disrobe," the guard said as he closed the door behind him. "The girls will bathe you and provide fresh clothing. The queen will wish to speak to you as soon as you're clean."

The sensation of magic prickled behind him and Rune turned toward it. Magic to heat bath water was a shameful use of power, one the court mages wouldn't stand for unless it was desperately needed. For Firal to want to see him that urgently painted a grim picture of what he could expect.

"Hurry up," the guard snapped.

"Oh, excuse me. I didn't realize I'd have spectators." Rune took hold of his shirt's hem to peel it off overhead. The chains on his shackles rattled, and he paused. He couldn't undress. He turned and held out his wrists.

The guard made a low sound of frustration and opened the door just enough to request the key. A second guard stepped in with the key ring.

"We'd be fools to leave you," the first guard said, posting himself beside the exit. "A man could have any number of weapons tucked up his sleeves."

The other man sorted through the keys twice before he fit one to the irons.

"Do you trust King Vicamros's men so little?" The moment the shackles fell away, Rune shrugged out of his shirt and cast it to the floor. He wouldn't say as much, but he'd be grateful for the change of clothing. He hadn't planned on leaving home with weeks of travel still on his skin.

"Don't trust anyone much, these days," the guardsman with the keys muttered. He positioned himself beside the door with one hand resting on the hilt of his sword.

"That's probably wise." Rune raised his hands, palms out. "Especially since I don't need weapons."

The men looked uncomfortable. Rightfully so, considering he'd killed their king with his claws. Hiding his morbid amusement, Rune crept into the bath chamber.

The mage gave him one quick, appraising look before she left. If she or the two serving girls heard what had been said in the other room, they didn't show it.

Rune closed the door before the guards could join them. The chamber was small, made cramped by the claw-footed tub pulled to the middle of the room. A bucket and stool waited beside it. Finer guest baths had shelves for soaps and oils, but here, there was just a plain brown bar of soap and a shabby towel atop the stool. Impressive for peasants and low-ranking servants, he supposed, trying not to think of his private bath back home. It had been a masterpiece, a marvel of engineering ideas he'd culled from his time with the Underlings. It couldn't compare to the luxury of their communal baths, but it came close.

"I'm capable of bathing myself." He shucked off his pants and slid over the edge of the tub to sink into the water. It was a perfect temperature, just hot enough to be comfortable. One benefit of a mage-heated bath.

The girls said nothing as they moved to the edge of the tub. They were both young and pretty enough, one auburn-haired and the other a dark blonde. The auburn-haired one took the soap from the stool and the bucket from the floor, scooped water from the surface and poured it over his head. Neither responded, and they avoided his searching eyes.

"Do you want one of the guards in here with you?" Rune asked, tilting his head back as the auburn-haired girl lathered her hands and worked the soap into his hair. He would have preferred to be alone, but he wouldn't insult them by refusing to let them do their jobs, either.

The blonde girl glanced at him, then lowered her eyes. She

rolled her sleeves a little higher and reached to take one of his hands from the water. He lifted it for her, watching as she produced a stiff-bristled brush from her apron and set to work scrubbing crusted dirt from the claws on his fingers.

He frowned. "Not very talkative, are we?"

"We were told not to speak with you, milord," the fair-haired girl said.

"Why not?" he asked.

She bit her lip and gazed at him from beneath dark lashes. "They say you're dangerous."

"Bree!" the girl behind him snarled. She returned to his side, scooped water into the bucket again, and shot a glare across the tub.

Rune raised a brow, unable to hide his amusement. "Dangerous," he repeated. He pulled his hand from her grasp and twisted a curl of her hair around his finger. "And who told you that?"

Bree ducked her head. Her cheeks turned rosy. "Her Majesty's orders, milord."

"Firal?" He barked a laugh and dropped his hand back into the water. "Your queen never found me dangerous when she was in my bed, squealing like a hungry piglet at—"

The auburn-haired girl slapped him before he could finish.

Bree squeaked and recoiled.

A low growl welled in his throat and Rune turned his head slowly. The slitted centers of his eyes narrowed. He'd never learned to block out the magic. Though he couldn't seize it or wield it as he once could, it still reacted to him. The crimson glow that flooded his eyes made the girl yelp, but he caught her wrist before she could escape.

"Perhaps things have changed since I was here last, but I don't recall that being the proper way to treat guests." He held her fast as she tried to pull away, his grip firm but controlled, tight enough to trap her without letting his claws pierce her skin.

He drew her closer. "You," he said, low and clear, "will not touch me again."

"Forgive her, Lord Daemon," Bree pleaded, grasping his other arm. "Mera has a bad temper. She won't do it again."

"No," he said, loosening his grip and relaxing into the tub again. "She won't. She'll stand back and assist you today. Nothing more. After that, we won't cross paths again."

Mera shrank back, wide-eyed, and clutched her wrist.

"Now," Rune sighed and ran a hand through his soapy hair. "Where were we?"

Bree bowed her head as he offered his hand and she resumed her scrubbing, but she said no more.

It was just as well. He was in no mood for idle chatter anyway, and the girls had already served their purpose. Serving staff were useful when one wanted people to talk. In moments, they'd provided a chance to prove he was a threat, as well as a chance to stir rumors about Firal's connection to the Underlings —and him. It wasn't much, but it was a start. Dissent was a powerful tool. He could think of no better way to draw the attention he needed. If he was going to escape Elenhiise with his hide intact, he was going to need a lot of it.

CORRUPTION'S HEIGHTS

AGAINST THE BACKDROP OF THE SETTING SUN, THE VILLAGE WAS nothing more than blocky shadows. The dark shapes sat low to the ground, save one narrow building that loomed between Vahn's riders and the village proper. A guard tower, he supposed, though it reminded him more of a shepherd watching over the smaller structures beneath it.

Their stay in Wethertree had been brief, just long enough to explain their mission and order the mages back to Ilmenhith. The city's people weren't happy to see the mages go, even though he'd promised their return after their job was fulfilled. He expected the same response everywhere.

That trouble was Firal's fault. She'd been tight-fisted with the distribution of mages after she took the crown, even after Kytenia became Archmage. It was better to keep the mages close to the temple, Firal had claimed, to foster unity and prevent them from splitting into factions again. When things had settled and she finally agreed to redistribute mages across the countryside, every village had clamored to have one of their own. Not every village had been granted a mage, and the resentment between settlements was thick. On top of all that, the

Grand College's interest in acquiring temple mages had been an unpleasant additional burden.

No matter how Vahn wished they could fulfill every request, the temple couldn't spare more mages. Each year, fewer people sent their children for training, and the number of mages stationed in the temple had begun to dwindle. Every village wanted one, recognizing the value of a Gifted healer, but the temple's first Archmage still cast a long shadow.

Mages had been a driving force in the war, people said. Some even claimed they were responsible. They weren't wrong, but it was foolish to leave their children with Gifts untapped. Magic had a way of breaking free eventually, and without proper training, mages were a danger to themselves and everyone around them. Even if the temple had possessed the numbers to spare for it, one mage to a village wasn't enough to teach anyone. Much less enough to contain the threat of wild magic.

"We should be close to Eldril," Vahn said, hoping conversation would chase away his dark thoughts.

His father and the mage Kytenia assigned to the party rode at his side. For his safety, Ennil claimed, and Vahn thought he might be right. He trusted his military, but if it came to an ambush, no one could keep him safer than a mage.

Ennil made a small sound in his throat. "Near enough, but I don't think we'll make it tonight."

"We might, if we press." Vahn squinted at the guard tower. "There are several mages stationed in Eldril, aren't there, Kepha?"

The mage blinked, surprised to be addressed. "Yes, Your Majesty." Her eyes traveled farther southwest. "But I believe he's correct. I don't think we'll reach it tonight. Tomorrow, most likely. Before noon if we get an early start."

"How many mages are supposed to be there?" Ennil asked. "Enough for a Gate?"

Kepha pursed her lips. "Have you need of a Gate, Lord Tanrys?"

Vahn frowned. He'd wondered the same thing.

"Not now, no. I just wonder if we would be better served to have a group of mages ride along with us. We'd be able to Gate those we collect straight to Ilmenhith." Ennil stretched in his saddle, groaned and pressed a hand to his lower back. "Gates to move us from village to village would be better, too."

"I don't think you realize how much a Gate takes out of a mage," Vahn said, satisfied when the Master beside him nodded. "We would exhaust them within a few minutes."

"Aside from that," Kepha added, "you're assuming the mages we'd have with us would be able to reach the destinations we wanted. Any of them can get us to Ilmenhith or the temple, but unless they're familiar with a place, they can't open a Gate to it."

"So riding is the only way to reach a lot of these small outpost villages," Vahn concluded. "If there were a better way, I would have found out before we left the palace." A hint of an edge worked its way into his tone, and Ennil regarded him through narrowed eyes. Not a frown, but a look of displeasure. Vahn didn't care. He didn't say it outright, but his father understood the words not spoken: *I'm not a fool.*

"Wishful thinking," Ennil said after a time, still rubbing his back. "I'm not as young as I used to be."

Vahn snorted. "Then perhaps you should have stayed home."

Kepha bit her lower lip. No one said anything else.

They rode on for some time. The sun set before they reached the village's edge.

It was there the mage leaned forward in her saddle. Her brows drew together. "Strange," she murmured.

The single word made Vahn's skin prickle. "What?"

"I didn't think there were any mages at this outpost." Kepha paused, and her look of bemusement slowly melted into one of concern. "Have you had any reports of illness from this region?"

He straightened in his saddle, willing himself to ignore the fatigue of travel. "Why? How many are there?"

"I'm not sure," the mage said. "I can't distinguish them. More than one, but some are odd. They feel... untrained, maybe. Gifted children, perhaps."

"Can you be sure?"

She shook her head. "My assumption is temple mages. Perhaps magelings assisting Masters."

"We will exercise caution, then." Ennil pulled his mount to a stop and signaled for the rest of the group to halt behind him. "One man to investigate and ask about disease before we ride in. That way, if he's exposed to something unpleasant, there's only one person for Kepha to tend. Rather than the whole group."

Vahn nodded. "Do it."

Ennil slid from his horse and moved toward the cluster of mounted soldiers. "Ronar! Where are you?"

Kepha peered over her shoulder as Ennil disappeared among the men, then looked back to the village.

"Would they send the mages from Eldril to attend something here if it was important?" Vahn asked in a low voice.

"If it was an emergency, perhaps," she murmured.

"Should you go with the messenger, just in case?"

She hesitated, then nodded.

Ennil returned with a man close at his heels. "Ronar will head to the guard tower and see what's going on."

"I'll go with him." Kepha dismounted and offered her horse's reins to Ennil. "If people have fallen ill, they might appreciate the extra help."

Ennil nodded, took her horse and returned to his own. He waited by the stirrup and watched the pair walk ahead.

"Are you concerned?" Vahn asked casually, stretching his legs one at a time. His back and backside ached and he thought he'd walk bow-legged for the rest of the evening, but he wasn't ready to give up the advantage of horseback just yet.

His father looked surprised. "Why would I be? Even if they're beset by plague, we've a mage to heal us before infection can begin."

Vahn rubbed his chin. A plague would explain why there were multiple mages there; most people knew mages couldn't work healing on themselves. Outbreaks of disease were attended by at least a pair of mages for that exact reason. Not that they'd want to walk into a village with plague, even with a mage to support them. It was, however, a situation he hadn't considered. How many mages might have left their stations to tend needs across the countryside? Which mages should he leave at their posts in case of emergencies? How thin could they afford to be spread?

No, he thought. This was his daughter. Every mage was needed. None could be spared.

Even if it means the suffering of your people? He squeezed his eyes closed, quashing that quiet objection.

The band behind him waited, quiet. The horses puffed and stamped, the only sound aside from the singing of crickets in the grass. Vahn stared at the village, watching for movement. Aside from Kepha and Ronar, he hadn't seen a soul in the streets since they stopped. He'd have thought it strange if not for the movement of light and shadow in the windows of houses here and there. They had come at sundown, after all. People would be inside now, eating supper with their families. The thought made his stomach growl. He tried to pay it no mind.

"There," Ennil said, pacing forward a step or two.

A lone figure reemerged from the guard tower. Vahn tightened his grip on the reins as he watched Ronar make his way back to the group without hurry. Was that good or bad?

"Mages from the temple, Lord Tanrys," Ronar said as he approached. He glanced up at Vahn as if unsure it was proper to address the king, but also unsure if it was proper to give his information to someone else. "Our mage is speaking with them. There's an important Master there. I don't know her, but she's got the eye-marks."

Raising a brow, Vahn nudged his horse forward a step. The

only mages allowed to wear eye-marks were court mages and Masters who led Houses of affinity. "Why are they here?"

The soldier looked surprised. "No disease or anything, the village is safe. The Master said they were sent to investigate something. Something about magic where it oughtn't be. That was all I heard before they told me to retrieve you, Majesty."

Vahn's heart jumped in his throat. When he'd left the palace, the mages had been trying to determine where the Gate his daughter was taken through led. Had they found something?

"Mount up," he said, both to Ronar and his father. "If the temple sent them, I'll need to know what's going on."

Ronar nodded and dipped in a half bow before he hurried back to his horse.

Ennil dragged himself back into the saddle, still holding the reins of Kepha's mount. "Don't get your hopes up yet, Vahn," he said quietly. "I didn't recognize where we went, but I don't think it was here. Even the guard tower isn't big enough to hold the room I chased her into."

"That doesn't mean she wasn't here." Vahn kicked his horse to a trot. If anything, it made more sense that Envesi would have hopped from place to place in an attempt to cover her tracks. Especially if she'd landed in a location that had another mage, someone who might sense her power and send word to Firal.

He reached the guard tower a horse length or two before the rest of his group, slid to the ground and dropped the reins. Ilmenhith's horses were as well-trained as its men, and the animal would stay put unless spooked or led away. Behind him, Ennil barked orders, assigning men to tend horses and stand guard.

Vahn barely heard them as he hurried through the open door.

A half-dozen mages in Master white stood in the front room, clustered beside a table. Their conversation halted the moment one saw him. All of them were female, and most of them surprised. When the group's leader turned to face him, Vahn froze in place.

Shymin Silaron, Master of the House of Healing and Archmage Kytenia's elder sister, regarded him with a cool and neutral expression.

He'd expected an important mage, but not that important.

"I almost didn't believe it when your scout said he rode with the king." She smiled, though her expression still seemed chilly, set off by her eyes. When had they bleached? They had been a warm hazel when he'd seen her last. Now they were the same sharp, piercing pale blue of all the other high-ranking mages. All but Kytenia, anyway. "An honor to see you, Your Majesty."

"And you, Master Shymin." Vahn skimmed the faces of the other mages. His brows knit in concern. "Where is Kepha?"

"Upstairs. She asked to borrow supplies to pen a letter back to the temple, since there are so many of us here. She'll return shortly, I'm sure." Shymin moved toward him with a graceful stride, her white robes swirling around her ankles.

She was a stately woman, if not pretty like her sister. She was taller than Kytenia, almost as tall as Vahn himself, with an oval face and hair that was now more mage-white than brown. Though the blue of her eyes was jarring, she'd worn the black eye-markings of a Master of affinity for decades, the delicate pattern of swirls always the same.

Spreading her hands in greeting, Shymin watched the men file in behind their king. "How may I assist you?"

"We ride to gather mages from their outposts and send them to Ilmenhith," Vahn said. "The Archmage will need everyone she can get, and we're as fast of messengers as any others."

"Strange for the king to reduce himself to messenger duty." She raised a brow and her eyes flicked past him again. "Greetings, Lord Tanrys. You, I did expect. Though perhaps not so soon."

Vahn's eyes narrowed. Why would she expect his father?

"You have a lot of mages with you." Ennil positioned himself a step behind his son. "Should I take it to mean you've made progress with your work?"

"Not so much as we'd like." Shymin sighed and waved a hand. "Wild magic is always difficult, though I don't expect you to have any experience with it. But we are figuring things out, one step at a time."

"Temar said a number of the temple's mages were searching for where Envesi's Gate led. Have you made any progress with that?" Vahn couldn't keep a note of hope out of his voice.

Shymin blinked and arched a brow. "Of course. I know exactly where that Gate led. Why else do you think I am here?"

His heart skipped a beat. "So we're closer to finding Lulu?"

"Find her?" She laughed softly. "The mages with me are the best Masters the temple has to offer. We already know where she is."

It was better news than he could have imagined. His mouth fell open and he worked a moment before he could close it. "I have to tell Firal!"

Smiling, Shymin touched his arm and motioned toward the stairs nestled in the corner of the room. "Your mage said the same thing. Come, I'll take you to join her. We'll see about getting a message to the queen."

Vahn turned to his father, but Ennil raised a hand.

"Go ahead," Ennil said, looking pleased. "I'll see to the men."

Vahn hurried up the stairs with Shymin at his heels. They'd found her. He couldn't believe it. His heart fluttered in his chest, riding waves of blossoming hope. With enough mages, perhaps they could settle things on their own and call off the search for Ran. Things could go back to normal, and the nightmare of the past few days would be laid to rest.

Shymin slipped ahead to push open a door in the second floor hallway, then beckoned him to enter.

He rounded the corner and froze.

Kepha was on the floor, bound and gagged.

MEETINGS

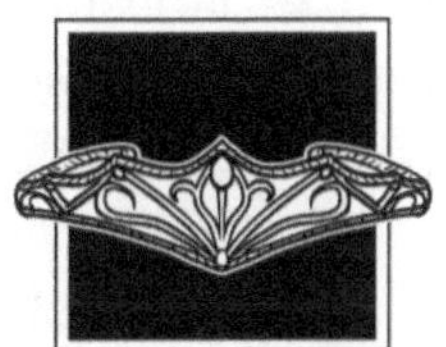

IT WASN'T UNTIL HIS EYES OPENED THAT VAHN REALIZED THE MAGES had done something to him. He didn't remember blacking out, didn't remember anything other than stepping around the corner and seeing Kepha on the floor.

Groggy, he turned his head and tried to move. Every muscle in his body ached, as if he'd just roused from bone-shatter fever. He hadn't been that ill since he was a child.

The room was dim. Wherever he was, it wasn't the guard tower in the little village outside of Eldril. He pushed himself up from the floor and sat upright, blinking at a pair of boots that stepped into his line of sight. For some reason, he'd thought he was alone.

"This isn't the way I would have handled things." Ennil towered over him, the pale moonlight marking the planes of his aging face with deep crags of shadow.

Vahn's eyes wouldn't focus. He groaned and buried his face in his hands. "Are we imprisoned?"

"We?" His father sounded amused. "Certainly not. You, on the other hand..."

His mouth was dry, his tongue sticky against the roof of his mouth. Vahn swallowed in vain and lifted his head again.

Recollection of the way Shymin greeted his father made him scowl. "You betrayed us." His voice rasped in his throat. "You never tried to save Lumia, did you?" His own father. And Kytenia's sister. Blood and earth! After all their struggles, the temple was still corrupt.

Ennil sighed and turned away. His boots crunched on the gritty stone floor as he paced toward a narrow window. Little more than an arrow slit, it let in just enough light to see. "I'm sure it's easy for you to think that. And I understand if you're angry, but believe me, what I've done has been in the best interest of our family."

Anger surged in him and Vahn tried to move. He wanted to challenge the man in front of him, strike him down and spit on his corpse. Instead he barely made it to his knees. "You kidnapped my child and handed her to a monster!"

"Your child?" his father sneered. "You're not fooling anybody, Vahn. Not even yourself. She's not yours, and anyone who's seen the girl has thought it."

Inch by inch, Vahn rose, though it took every ounce of his willpower to stand straight. He didn't know what the mages had done. He didn't feel like he'd been hurt, it felt more like he'd been... frozen, somehow. His joints creaked like hinges unused for a hundred years. "Blood isn't what makes a family. She's been mine for thirty years."

Ennil scoffed. "And for thirty years I've sat aside and watched our family legacy fade, replaced with dreams left behind by someone else."

"And you think that justifies what you've done? Giving her to an enemy of the crown?" Vahn took a step forward. His strength was returning rapidly now, his breath coming easier. The weighted feeling in his limbs began to dissipate. He walked slowly, deliberately, striding past his father and toward the narrow window. Not an arrow loop after all, as it was paned with fine glass. It was just far more narrow than a window should have been.

"I did what I had to."

"My daughter could die because of you."

"Your daughter is alive because of me!" Ennil snarled, spinning toward him. "Vilify me all you want, but don't doubt for a moment that I love her too. You say blood isn't what makes a family as if I don't know. Brant's roots, boy, look at me!"

Vahn turned his head, loath to heed a command, but desperate for answers.

"You never stopped to think it odd that the Archmage came back now? All these years after her exile, when her cause was all but forgotten? Something pulled her back here, Vahnil, and I knew what it was the moment I heard." Ennil shook his head and stared at the floor. If he didn't know better, Vahn might have thought the look on his face was shame. "You couldn't have protected her. No one could. The only reason she's safe is because I made sure she was useful."

"What are you talking about?" Vahn asked.

His father looked at him strangely. "Didn't Firal ever tell you the reason the temple was founded?"

Vahn stared at him.

Ennil's face fell. "Doesn't she know?"

"I've never heard anything about this," Vahn murmured. Despite the anger that still coursed through his veins, he felt a wash of calm. He was a king. He would not let rage get the better of him.

His father regarded him in silence for a long time. Then Ennil sighed, lifted a hand to his forehead, and rubbed his brow. "Lifetree have mercy."

Vahn looked out the window and squinted into the moonlit night. He didn't recognize anything. Even the architecture of the low city around them was unfamiliar. "It seems you know a great deal you've kept from the council, Lord Tanrys." He made himself sound as patronizing as possible.

Ennil flinched. "No," he said slowly as he made his way to the window. His voice was so low Vahn barely heard. "I know very little of what we face, and that pains me. Let me be clear. You may despise me, but through everything that's happened since before you were even born, I've done what's best for the kingdom and what's best for our family. And if you and your bride handle yourselves carefully, the kingdom may well make it through this revolution unscathed."

Vahn glared and gritted his teeth. Curse the man and the years of politics that taught him to talk in circles. "What revolution? What's happening?"

Ennil waved a hand toward the window. "Look outside, boy. You'll see the beginning."

"All I see is a city. It doesn't mean anything to me."

"And I suppose it wouldn't," his father said. "You never had a chance to visit before Relythes built that wall."

Startled, Vahn looked outside again. "We're in the Giftless lands?"

"Not anymore." Ennil shrugged as he made his way toward the door. "These are her lands now."

Vahn's head snapped back to the window. Beyond the glass, nothing had changed, but the sight now gave him chills. "The king—?" he asked haltingly.

"Alive." Ennil paused at the door. There was something in his hesitance that Vahn didn't know how to read. An uncertainty, perhaps. That he didn't know what awaited him on the other side. Or was it that he didn't want to leave? Given all that had just transpired, it was hard to believe the old man would want to stay. "Though he answers to her, now."

"So she's already taken a kingdom." A muscle in Vahn's neck pinged with discomfort. He grimaced and rocked his head to the side as he worked his fingers into the spasm. "What more does she want from us?"

"I don't think she means to rule. If she'd wanted that, she would have stayed at Kifel's side. Magic is all that matters to her. It's not what she wants from you, necessarily. It's what she wants from the mages. She founded the temple to give herself power over them. We made a mistake in wresting it from her."

"We didn't have a choice. The kingdom was falling apart around us and she was cheering on its collapse."

"I think that's generous," Ennil said. "I don't think she's capable of cheering for anything. But I'm not saying I fault the queen for that decision. I realize there was little else that could be done. Still, that doesn't keep it from being a mistake."

Vahn scoffed. "Is that how you feel about what you did? Handing over Lumia?"

A shadowy scowl drifted over his father's face. Instead of replying, he returned to the previous subject. "The problem is that kingdoms aren't enough, Vahn. You've seen yourself the effect mages have, the way people react when they hear their mages are being taken away. But no one wants to *be* a mage. They're fearsome. People are afraid of them now. Elenhiise was her plan to start over, create a culture that respected and treasured mages. That was her plan to protect them, ensure the practice of magecraft carried on. Now that's been torn away from her, and all that's left is seizing respect by force."

Ennil reached for the door. "As I said, you're free to despise me. But when the time comes and the new free mages enslave the world, I know which side I want to be on." He gave his son one last hard, meaningful look as he stepped backwards into the hall.

Vahn glowered back as he closed the door.

***

"I EXPECTED A LITTLE LESS FORMALITY." Rune adjusted the pointed cuffs of his sleeves as he took in the ten faces that stared him down. Garam was one of them, which took him by surprise, though he didn't allow it to show.

The council—plus Garam—sat in what was once his father's office, seated around tables that had been arranged into a Cshape. A single chair stood at the mouth of the open space between them. It was the only empty chair in the room.

Firal sat directly opposite that chair, her hands folded atop the table, her face serene. "Sit," she ordered quietly.

He stopped behind the chair and twisted his cuffs again. They wouldn't sit right beneath the irons the guards had put on him after he'd dressed. He'd asked for blue silk and the maids had obliged. Did the councilors think it odd that he chose the kingdom's colors? Their faces told him nothing. "Is this a trial?"

"Sit," Firal repeated, sharper.

Leveling his gaze with hers, Rune sat. He slouched in the chair and propped his elbow on the arm. "I don't see why I can't sit at the table."

"Rune," Garam prompted.

Frowning, Rune gave his friend a sidewise look.

The queen cleared her throat. "You sit before the council so that we may address your future."

He opened his mouth to speak, but closed it again when Garam glared at him. He rolled his eyes and slouched lower.

"While Ilmenhith and the rest of Elenhiise have not forgotten your crimes, the council recognizes your unique talents," she continued, "and so do I. As a result, I make an offer. Instead of execution, I present you the chance for pardon and freedom, in exchange for an act of service to the crown."

"That's what you said in the throne room," Rune said. "You don't need to repeat yourself."

Firal's mouth tightened with a look of irritation she couldn't quite suppress. She drew a breath, squared her shoulders and sat straighter. "I repeat myself for the benefit of the councilors who were not present during your arrival. Your service for your freedom. Does that appeal to you or not?"

He hesitated.

"Let it be clear," a man said, leaning forward. Rune recognized him as the wharfmaster of Ilmenhith, but he couldn't recall his name. "Your options are service or death. If the people of Ilmenhith do not see immediate value in keeping you alive, there is no reason to do so."

Firal nodded, ever so slightly.

Rune's stomach sank. The offer had caught him off guard, but he'd hoped there was more to it. That his presence was desired, that someone had finally found a way to help him come home. Yet he hadn't been arrested because he was a threat, or because of Kifel's death, or even because Firal missed him.

He'd been arrested because he was a tool.

"A choice between servitude and execution isn't much of a choice." The fire faded from his voice and he struggled to hide his disappointment. He knew it was foolish to think Firal might have wished to see him, but there had still been the tiniest sliver of hope. It should have died when he stood before her in the throne room, when she first looked at him with contempt, but it hadn't. Its slow death inside him now was more painful than he expected.

"But it is a choice being given to you," Firal said.

"Then I'm going to have to know what sort of service Her Majesty expects," he replied.

The corners of her mouth twitched. "A mage has taken something that belongs to me. I wish for you to retrieve it."

Rune snorted. "If you want someone to play fetch, get a dog."

"I did," she said. "It's sitting in front of me."

His face fell as a few councilors raised their hands to stifle snickers and hide smiles.

"Yes or no?" Firal asked.

"No."

"Then you will hang."

"I won't do something when you won't tell me plainly what it is. I thought you were capable of communicating," he snapped. "Or is your head too big for that crown of yours now? The pressure making it too hard to think?"

Her amber eyes narrowed.

"Watch it," Garam murmured in the trade tongue.

Rune ignored him. "Don't pretend you're doing me a favor by allowing me to live in a kingdom that should have been mine."

Ordin Straes, Ilmenhith's Captain of the Guard, leaned forward with a scowl. "Again you claim a right to the kingdom, reminding everyone of your crimes."

The captain had always struck him as reasonable, and Rune struggled to keep from grinding his teeth in frustration as he locked eyes with the man. "Again you fail to consider that my right to the throne existed before your king fell. Or have your eyes begun to fail you in your old age, Captain?"

Startled, Ordin drew back. Then he leaned closer, studying him. Rune lifted his chin. Good; he hadn't changed so much in thirty years that he'd be unrecognizable. As Ran, he'd worn a guise of blue eyes and tawny hair like his father's, an illusion forged by an amulet Medreal had crafted in his childhood. It had changed the color of his hair and eyes and hid his scales, but it couldn't change his face. If the captain looked hard enough, he'd realize it.

"Regardless of what you think you deserve, I am queen," Firal said. "And I'll not have you trying to rile my council while you make your decision."

Rune scoffed and straightened in his chair. "As if I have any choice. You say servitude or death, but you put forth a great deal of effort in finding me and bringing me here. No one would believe you if you said I was to die. You'd simply hold me here, imprison me, maybe torture me, until you got your way."

A look of pure offense sprang onto her face. "I do not torture my prisoners."

He burst into laughter.

The councilors shifted in discomfort, looking between themselves as he laughed.

Color rose in Firal's cheeks and she cleared her throat. "I will have an answer, Daemon of the Underlings, a people who are no more. If not now, then soon."

His laughter faded and his face grew solemn. No more? The Underlings were *gone*?

"Council is dismissed for now," she said, "as there is nothing more for us to discuss until you agree to offer your assistance. You may return to your rooms."

A pair of armored guards stepped forward to take him by the arms.

"What happened to the Underlings? Where are my people?" Genuine concern seeped into his voice. He jerked his arms away from the guards. They seized him more aggressively, pried him from the chair and dragged him toward the doorway. A handful more followed, ready to assist.

"I will go with him," Garam said, rising. "To make sure he doesn't give your men trouble."

Firal gave a curt nod. "Very well." She stood and moved around the tables with her head held high. Behind her, the councilors began to rise and straighten their clothing. She swept toward the door, but slowed just long enough to lean close to one of the guards.

"You will bring him to my private receiving parlor in half an hour," she said. Then she paused and glanced over her shoulder as Garam moved toward them. "Make sure he is alone."

Rune's brow furrowed and he turned to speak to her, but she was already gliding down the hallway, as graceful as a swan.

One by one, the councilors filed past him. Most pretended he wasn't there. Only Ordin paused to study him, his face serious and his eyes troubled. The captain's notice was a small relief, and the only one to come from this meeting. Another seed of dissent planted. With luck, it would have time to germinate before the council built a gallows in the courtyard.

"All right," Garam sighed as the last councilor disappeared. He folded his arms over his chest and adopted the more comfortable trade tongue. "At this point, I think you have some explaining to do."

Rune let his gaze fall to the floor. "Yes," he murmured. "I suppose I do."

The guards turned him toward his temporary quarters and he sent his friend an apologetic glance. "Soon, Garam. I promise."

"It's going to have to be," Garam growled. "Half an hour wouldn't be much time to explain anything, and we have to use half of that walking."

"The castle's not that big," Rune protested, though he had to admit the guards took the least efficient route through the halls possible. That was both deliberate and tactical. If a visitor didn't know the best paths to take, they'd be easier to find—and apprehend—should a visit go unfavorably. It seemed the guards had not yet noticed his familiarity with the palace.

Garam made a sound of exasperation. "How do you know? How do you know any of the things you know about this place? Your homeland? All right, I'll give you that. But you were the one who pushed for an alliance."

One of the guards looked at Rune from the corner of his eye.

"Garam," Rune prompted softly.

"You said you were passingly familiar with the island," his friend continued.

"Garam."

"Knowing which rooms are which inside the palace isn't passing familiarity!"

Sighing, Rune rolled his eyes and clamped his mouth shut. The last thing he wanted was for the guards to take an interest in what they were saying. It was easy for them to ignore it when it sounded like idle conversation, but Garam's words grew more and more heated as he went on. Sowing rumors was one thing. Stating the truth outright and in full would sooner make him look mad. Rune had tried once, sharing his story with Sera. She had laughed in his face.

Instead of responding to Garam's ongoing rant, he put his head down and pretended to be chastised. That was easy to fake, at least. After the attitude he'd presented before Firal, he deserved it. After a time, the guards lost interest.

When they reached his room, one of the guards stepped back. "Lord Kaith, if you wish me to escort you—"

"I'll stay here," Garam said before he could finish. His Old Aldaanan slurred more, betraying his agitation. "The prisoner's attitude must be addressed."

A few of the guards chuckled. They arranged themselves outside the door and let Rune and Garam pass through. Rune paced farther into the room and released a long, heavy sigh.

Garam all but slammed the door. "What is your problem?"

"Don't lecture me." Rune raised a finger, as if in warning.

"You said you had a plan, but so far that plan seems like it's just you doing everything in your power to get yourself killed. What are you doing? You walk in here, the first thing you do is challenge the queen—"

"She's my wife," Rune said, and the confession felt like acid in his throat.

Garam froze. "What?"

Squeezing his eyes closed, Rune turned away and raked his clawed fingers through his hair. He didn't know what else to say. The chain between his wrists pulled taut, an unpleasant reminder of how stuck he was.

"*What?*" Garam repeated, incredulous. He shook his head. "Oh, no. No, no, no. Don't do this to me."

"She's my wife." This time, the words were hollow, defeated. Rune bowed his head. "Or she was, before she was queen. I... I don't know what happened. The last days I spent on the island were a mess. The battle, the duels—"

"And here I wondered why you never wanted to move on," Garam muttered. "It's obvious things didn't work out, but whatever bad blood there was, you need to get over it. You're being offered an opportunity that isn't just once in a lifetime, it might be the last opportunity *of* your lifetime. You're going to die, Rune. Pushing the queen isn't going to do anything but rush you to the grave."

The door creaked. "It's time," one of the guards announced.

"Of course it is," Garam replied sarcastically. He turned to lead the way, but Rune caught his arm.

"She wants me alone."

Garam scoffed. "She wants you dead."

"Not until she gets what she wants from me." Rune withdrew his hand and stalked to the doorway to join the guards. "Wait for me. There's more you need to know. Tour the palace, ask to see the hall of portraits, something. We will speak when I'm done." He held out his wrists to let the guards guide him once more.

"Rune—"

He shook his head. "When I'm done." One of the guards grabbed the chain between his wrist irons and dragged him into the hall.

BECAUSE OF YOU

THE FRAGRANCE OF THE WARM MINT TEA WAITING IN THE PARLOR wasn't enough to soothe her. Firal poured herself a cup just the same, though her hands shook so badly that the teacup clattered against its saucer.

She hadn't known what to expect from a reunion. She'd made a point of never letting herself imagine one. Her stomach churned and her limbs felt cold, sensations she hadn't felt in the face of confrontation in decades. She thought the meeting might be awkward, but she'd never imagined it would be like that.

His anger was understandable. She suspected he might blame her for what led to his exile, and she couldn't fault him. She was responsible, whether she liked it or not. She'd had the chance to speak, to pardon or condemn him. Instead she'd chosen silence and allowed the mages to sentence him to death. It didn't matter if it was what she wanted or not; it had happened. But there was so much hate and bitterness burning in his eyes. Eyes that were cold beyond those heated feelings on the surface, that betrayed nothing. He might as well have been looking at a statue, rather than a friend or lover. Rather than his wife.

Squeezing her eyes closed, Firal made herself drink. The tea did nothing to calm her stomach or her nerves, nor did the heat of the cup in her hand grant any warmth to her limbs. She had to stay calm, no matter what she felt.

Either way, she didn't have time to compose herself. By the time she'd gotten away from the councilors and into the small private parlor adjacent to her quarters, she had precious few minutes to drink her tea and try to rein in her racing thoughts. She drank barely half her tea before someone knocked at the parlor door.

"Come in," she called without turning, taking one more sip of tea before she put down her cup on the table.

Armor rattled behind her as the guards stepped in with their captive between them.

Firal glanced over her shoulder. Rune stared at her with a cold intensity in his eyes. She avoided his gaze. "Leave him."

The men hesitated and exchanged glances with each other. "Majesty, perhaps it would be best—"

"Do not forget I am a temple-trained mage. I can protect myself. Leave him," she repeated, sharper. "And unchain him, for mercy's sake."

The guards hastened to comply, removing Rune's shackles and then retreating to the hall. They closed the door, but she heard no footsteps. They had positioned themselves outside in case of emergencies, of course.

Sighing, Firal made herself face him and let her eyes slide over his form. It was the first real look she'd allowed herself. It was remarkable how little he had changed. He still stood head and shoulders taller than her, his dark hair still jaw-length and as ragged as if cut while blindfolded. He was a little more tan, perhaps, which struck her as unusual. She couldn't imagine he saw more sun in the north. The only noteworthy difference was how far behind him boyhood now was. His shoulders were broader, his chest deeper and his frame more heavily muscled.

She gestured toward him. "You're bigger."

"So are you," he replied.

Anger blossomed in her chest and her cheeks grew red. She bit her tongue to keep it still and made herself breathe deep. She couldn't afford to rile him any more, lest it make him uncooperative. He'd always balked at being controlled, which was one of the reasons she wished Vahn had involved her in the plan to retrieve him. Leading him through a Gate in chains was probably the worst way to begin.

"Would you care for some tea?" She did her best to sound placid as she indicated the teapot and cups on the table behind her.

He did not respond.

Firal poured a cup for him anyway. "I apologize for the council meeting. There are certain protocols that must be observed, and they wish to believe they are a part of this. However, I thought it best if we discuss the details in private." She held out the cup in offering.

His eyes narrowed. "Since when does a queen pour her own tea?"

"Since I have no one to do it for me." She waited a moment longer, then carried the cup to the small table beside one of the upholstered chairs. The parlor wasn't meant for receiving more than a few guests, furnished with only two chairs and a narrow couch. Bookshelves flanked the tall table where she left the teapot. The scent of the books always reminded her of the temple's library. In the past, that scent had been soothing.

"Where is Medreal?"

"Dead." Firal sank onto the couch with her own cup of tea and adjusted her skirts before she took a sip.

Disbelief worked its way over his face.

She lowered her eyes. "A bit more than a week ago. Envesi— the former Archmage of Kirban Temple—entered the palace and killed her." Her throat grew tight, but she kept from choking on tears. Would it ever stop being hard to speak of her stewardess? The woman had been so vital to every part of Firal's life in the palace.

"That's impossible," Rune said, his voice unsteady. The emotion was surprising, though Firal supposed it shouldn't be. For all that Medreal had been a friend to her, she'd been like a mother to him.

"So I believed, at first. I couldn't imagine anyone overpowering her. But it happened, and Medreal died defending her ward." Her fingers tightened around her teacup until her knuckles turned white. "If she was powerful enough to get past Medreal, then you are the only one I know who will be strong enough to challenge her."

His eyes darkened. They were more expressive than they had been in council, giving away his thoughts, but they reflected shadows of anger now. "And you think that chaining me and threatening me with execution is going to make me want to try?"

She grimaced. How much easier this all would have been if Vahn had told her what he'd intended to do. "I'm begging you, Rune. Envesi has taken my daughter."

The corners of his mouth twitched and his expression grew cool.

Her stomach turned over. "I don't know why she was taken. She's just a baby. I expected Envesi to make demands, but none have come, which means someone must go after her. If she's grown as powerful as a natural-born free mage, you're the only hope we have."

"You remarried," he murmured.

Firal blinked at the abrupt change of subject and her brow furrowed. After all this time, had he expected she wouldn't? "You didn't?"

Rune said nothing. She almost would have preferred an outburst to the cold emptiness that returned to his eyes.

"Vahn has gone across the island with his father to find as many mages as possible to support the effort," she continued, wishing the mint in her tea would settle her insides. She took a sip anyway. "But without you, they may well be useless."

"How long did you wait?"

"I beg your pardon?"

"Before you replaced me."

She pursed her lips. "That's none of your concern."

"But finding your child is?" He snorted. "Who is he?"

"Rune—"

"Where is he, while you're expecting me to find your child?"

"I already said," she raised her voice, "Vahn has gone across the island with his father."

"*Vahn*?" he repeated, incredulous.

She lifted her chin and stared at him in challenge.

He stared back for a long time.

Dread grew in the pit of her stomach, roiling until she thought she'd be ill.

"Well," he said finally, drawing back and giving a stiff bow. He never took his eyes off her. "Good luck with your useless mages."

She almost dropped her cup in her haste to put it down. "Where are you going?"

"The dungeon, presumably, until I figure out how to get out. Again." He strode toward the door.

"You can't just leave," she cried.

He wheeled, color flaring in his eyes. "Do not tell me what I can and cannot do. You are not my queen and you never will be."

She glared back. "I'm giving you a chance to be free!"

"I am free!" he snarled. "Or I was until you dragged me back here to subject me to more punishment I don't deserve."

Firal rolled her eyes and threw up her hands. "Oh, and what do you think you deserve? A hero's accolades for conquering the kingdom? For trying to make a martyr of yourself the moment you came back?"

He raised a finger. "Brought back. You brought me back. I wanted nothing to do with this."

"As I noticed in the last thirty years without you here," she said dryly.

"Because I'm supposed to feel so welcome after your council tried to hang me."

There it was. She'd expected his accusatory tone. Firal gritted her teeth. "Do not try to blame me for this."

"No?" Rune barked a laugh and turned for the door. "Then don't pretend you have any idea what I've been through because of you."

She bristled. "Don't you walk away from me!"

He ignored her, opened the door and stormed into the hallway. The guards outside jumped and started to follow him, but Firal waved them out of the way as she picked up her skirts and hurried after him. "I'm not finished!"

"I am," he snapped.

"Come back here!" She had to run to keep up with his long-legged strides.

He turned down a long, window-lined hall and nearly collided with Lord Kaith.

The dark-skinned man spat a word she didn't recognize; a curse in the trade tongue they spoke in the north, she assumed. She understood enough to get by, but despite the burgeoning trade between the regions, she lacked real proficiency in the language.

Rune started to push past, but Lord Kaith grabbed his shoulder. "I was looking for you."

"Not now, Garam," Rune growled.

"You need to see something," the old man insisted.

"Not now!"

The councilor from the mainland held Rune in place and refused to let go.

Firal stopped a few paces behind them, puffing for breath. She'd thought it hard enough to keep up with him when they were young and traversing the ruins. She hadn't been wearing a corset then.

Lord Kaith spared only a glance for her before he frowned

and turned to lead Rune away. There was something in that look, weighted and concerned.

She frowned, too, as she let go of her skirts and followed them. When she realized where they were going, her stomach dropped.

The hall was lined with portraits of her predecessors. She'd marveled at the paintings herself, once, mused over the stern faces and the empty space where her father's portrait belonged. That had been her first visit to the palace. Kifel hadn't wanted to be displayed alongside the kings of the past, choosing instead to relish his living days. His portrait had graced the wall since the day she'd been crowned. Not long after, hers had been added beside it.

That was where the men stopped and the old councilor shared quiet words she couldn't understand. Firal closed her eyes and swallowed hard. She didn't want to see, but she couldn't make herself look away. She watched the emotions that shifted across Rune's face as Garam showed him the small family in the painting dressed with a gilt frame.

Shock, confusion, disbelief. He shook his head and took a half step back. She knew what he saw, knew from his reaction that he knew what it meant.

Seeing his eyes in her daughter's face every day had nearly killed her.

Rune turned, his expression melting from pain to anger. "You kept this from me."

She struggled to keep her face placid. "Don't pretend you have any idea what I've been through because of you."

He twitched, startled, then scowled. Looking back at the painting only once, he pushed Lord Kaith out of the way and stormed down the hall alone.

Firal stayed where she was. She heard the guards behind her and raised her voice. "He is to have free roam of the palace, as long as he doesn't disturb anything. Guard every exit, and double the patrol in the courtyards. He is not to set foot outside without an escort, and is not to leave the palace grounds at all."

"Yes, Your Majesty," one of the men said. The pair of them hurried to spread the word, leaving her and Lord Kaith alone in the hall.

The dark-skinned man turned to look at her, his face thoughtful.

"Come with me," she said quietly as she turned back toward her private parlor.

Lord Kaith followed, treading into the parlor behind her like a wary animal.

Firal settled on the couch with a sigh and looked toward the teapot. There weren't any more cups, aside from the two she'd filled with tea for herself and Rune. When Medreal lived, it seemed the right number was always on hand. She squeezed her eyes closed and fought back tears.

"He described you to me," the councilor said. He moved forward slowly and eased himself into a chair. "Many times. I suspected, when I first saw you, but I tried not to assume."

"You must think me a dreadful person," she murmured, hugging herself. A deep cold had settled in her bones, an iciness that threatened to consume her. She didn't know how to ward it off.

"I think there's a complicated story here," he said. "One he never bothered to explain."

She nodded. "You are his friend?"

"His commanding officer, for a good while. He was drafted into the Triad's army when I was young."

Firal snorted. "Then you know how difficult he can be."

Lord Kaith shrugged. "And also how loyal."

Her lip curled in distaste before she could catch herself. "So loyal that he struck down my father and then fled the country."

He raised one white brow. "So loyal that in your time of need, he's the one you call."

Except she hadn't called him. Nor had she even considered it.

She'd tried so hard to push him out of her thoughts, to the point where he was so unwelcome that he rarely crossed her mind. Firal lowered her eyes.

The councilor sighed. "Look, I'm sure this is awkward for you, but I want it to be clear I'm not here to ask questions or form opinions. I was charged by King Vicamros II to escort Rune here and see that everything was... taken care of before I returned. Nothing more."

"So you brought your friend to die?" Disgust seeped into her tone.

"He brought himself to die," Lord Kaith replied.

Firal shook her head. "I've never known him to be stupid."

"I've never known him to be happy." He spread his hands in a helpless gesture.

A small feeling of guilt crept into her and she fell quiet. The silence grew heavy. Unable to bear it, she pushed herself up and carried her cup to the table against the wall, where the teapot waited. The tea was cold, but at least pouring it gave her something to do.

"He kept that name," she said after a time, thoughtful.

"Rune?" Lord Kaith asked.

She nodded. "I thought he'd abandon it. Goodness knows he's had enough names."

"Met a mage once that called him something else. He didn't like it."

Startled, she turned. "What sort of mage?"

"A woman with white hair." A description that fit any number of mages. Which he knew, judging by his amused look.

"What did she call him?" she asked.

"Lomithrandel."

She felt sick again. Numb, she stared down at her tea and left it on the table. Even mint was no longer appetizing.

Lord Kaith studied her. "Is that a problem?"

"Maybe," she murmured. "It seems that knowledge is more widespread than I thought."

"Secrets have a way of spreading," he agreed. He gazed at her thoughtfully a while longer, then rested his elbows on his knees and laced his fingers together. "Now I have a question for you."

She looked at him over her shoulder.

The councilor met her eye. "Who is he?"

Of all the questions he could have asked, she hadn't expected that one. "He never told you?"

"He's rather tight-lipped about everything that came before our meeting. I know only what I've been able to piece together, and that's very little. That he was a noble, that he had military experience, that he was tied to your king somehow." He paused. "To your father."

"His father," she murmured.

Lord Kaith raised a brow. "Pardon?"

She grimaced. "It's complicated. But I know you heard him speak when you brought him in. In truth, he did have more right to the throne than me. But my people don't know it. When the man they knew as Lord Daemon escaped and fled from execution, no one noticed right away that Lomithrandel, the king's son, had vanished."

"A little odd, isn't it?"

"No," she said. "The nobles knew Ran was a temple mage, and mages came and went on temple business so often that it wasn't strange for him to be gone. It wasn't until months later, when he didn't resurface, that the whispers began. They accused the mages of making him disappear. Accused me. They said the temple wanted me on the throne instead of him. Had he risen to challenge me for it, I couldn't have stood against the Uncrowned Prince." Nor had she wanted to. Had he returned any time in that first year, she would have gladly surrendered the throne.

He exhaled heavily. "That explains the kingsword, then," he muttered under his breath.

She blinked. "The what?"

"Nothing," he said, waving his hand in dismissal. "So you acquired the throne through your marriage to him?"

Firal shook her head. "King Kifelethelas was my father."

Lord Kaith looked at her oddly. "I thought you just said he was Rune's father."

She flushed and faltered over her words. "Yes. I... Well, it isn't how it sounds. As I said, it's complicated. We're not related, if that's what you're thinking. My mother hid me. Rune was adopted and raised in my place. I am the one with a blood tie to the throne, but Rune was raised in the palace, with the assumption he would one day be crowned as Kifel's heir."

"You're right," Garam muttered, rubbing his forehead. "It is complicated. Seems things go that way, whenever he's around."

She stifled a laugh. "Yes, so it would seem."

"There's one thing I don't understand, though, Your Majesty." He smoothed his close-trimmed beard with one hand, thoughtful. "If what I've been told is the truth, your daughter is little more than a baby. And yet she's older than my children, who are mostly full-grown with children of their own. I know the Eldani people live longer, but..."

An unpleasant question, but one she should have expected. Even her own people thought it strange, though they were willing to forgive it as a sign of power passed through her bloodline. They weren't mistaken; they merely mistook the side the power came from. She took her cold tea and finally returned to the couch to sit. "She takes after her father."

The councilor tilted his head. "She looked normal enough in that portrait."

"She was born a free mage."

Lord Kaith cursed and thrust himself to his feet.

"Where are you going?"

He moved with a grace that belied his age, and seemed to grow taller as his movements filled with purpose. "I need to speak to the head of your court mages. And send a message to both your Archmage and mine."

Firal put her teacup aside and stood in a hurry. "What? Why?"

"Because I know why your daughter was taken." His brow furrowed with concern as he looked back at her. "And I know what the kidnapper wants."

BLOOD AND BETRAYAL

From Vahn's room, Alwhen looked like any other city. He lingered by the window, watching the rooftops as the moon crept overhead and disappeared beyond the horizon. He watched still as the sun crested the earth's rim and spilled light across the sky. Swallows darted in the early morning light, their sweeping flight only serving to remind him that he was trapped.

His room was not a cell. Its furnishings were modest but not crude, indicating he was in a noble's house, perhaps in the servant's quarters. The palace was on the other side of the city, dark and square, rising from Alwhen like the face of a cliff. If the city truly was under Envesi's control, he assumed that was where she would be. And with her, his daughter.

It was a good hiding place, he had to admit. He'd considered this half of the island and dismissed it almost without a thought. In his head, it made more sense for a mage to hide where their kind were welcome. Or where seeing one was less suspicious, at the very least.

But why bring *him* to Alwhen? The idea of being just another hostage rankled, but he couldn't imagine any other reason to capture him. They wouldn't see Ennil as a threat. His father's allegiance to the former Archmage galled him more than anything else, but Vahn could use it to his advantage. It wasn't an ideal situation, but it did provide him with a great deal of information. The question was how to get a message to Firal or the temple mages in order to relay everything he'd learned.

Or should he try to warn the temple mages? Some of them were here. The Archmage's own sister was here. The thought of Shymin made bitter bile rise in the back of his throat. They had to have trapped him on purpose. His father had set their course. Ennil must have notified Shymin, let her know where they would be. And his father had selected every last man in the band of guards they rode with. Men still loyal to him over Ordin, no doubt.

Silently, Vahn cursed his own naivety. He shouldn't have trusted his father. Medreal never had.

For what had to be the hundredth time since Ennil left, Vahn checked the door. He knew it would be locked, but checking gave him something to do, something to make him move. He'd tried to bust down the door, but it was barred on the other side, and he had nothing to slide past the door to lift the bar. Where they'd put his sword and armor, he didn't know, but they'd even taken the knife he kept hidden in his boot.

Boots. He looked at his feet, surprised he hadn't thought of it before. He still had his boots. His eyes drifted to the narrow window. The idea of breaking the glass and dropping a note was something he'd returned to over and over during the night. He hadn't, but only because smashing a piece of furniture to get a club narrow enough to use would have had mages and guards on him in a heartbeat. With a soft leather boot—if he did it right —he could break the window without making much noise.

The window was only as wide as the span of his fingers, too narrow to try to escape through. Plenty large enough to throw out something to reveal his presence, though, if he could find a way to write something.

But even if he did find something with which to write a note, what would it say? Frowning, he paced back to the window and peered at the city below. No one here knew who he was. And if the city was under Envesi's control, there was no reason for anyone to help him. Especially when none of the people milling about seemed unhappy. Everything in the city carried on as usual in the morning light. Below his prison, people ran errands and children played in the streets.

Stifling a sigh, he sank to the floor and buried his face in his hands. How was he supposed to save Lulu if he couldn't even save himself?

Eternity crawled by. Through the hours, the warm sunlight shifted its narrow outline of the window across the floor. He still sat on the floor when the bar on the other side of the door scraped out of its holdings and the door creaked open.

Bleary-eyed, Vahn lifted his head. He'd expected a servant or messenger, maybe even a guard of some sort, but a woman in the white robes of a Master mage stood there instead. She carried a tray awkwardly in both hands, and the cups sloshed tea and fruit juice over their rims as she walked.

"Good morning." Her tone was too calm to be curt, but her face was pinched, giving away her annoyance at being reduced to the role of a mere servant.

He frowned. "What's that?"

She arched a brow. "Breakfast."

Vahn squinted out at the sky. He could have sworn he'd been there forever, but the sun's position said it wasn't even yet noon.

"Will you have need of a bath before your meeting?" the mage asked.

He hesitated. She'd left the door open, but didn't seem concerned. He was no match for a single mage, especially not unarmed, but it was odd to think she wasn't worried about him trying to escape. Unless she didn't realize he was supposed to be captive. "What meeting?"

"Master Shymin will see you," she replied. "After you are ready, of course."

He tried not to grimace as he pushed himself to his feet. He'd need hours to prepare himself to face her. "I need a privy."

The mage suppressed a shudder, nodded stiffly and motioned toward the door. "Come with me. You can wash after. I will ensure your meal stays warm."

As if the temperature of his meal was of any concern. He wanted to shout at the woman, demand he be taken to the other mages, demand to see his father. Instead he tempered his response, caught his tongue with his teeth to keep it still, nodded and forced a smile. He'd do no good if he was angry, and thinking before he spoke was one place he usually excelled.

The white-robed woman led him down a shadowed stone hallway. Odd, compared to the buildings he was used to. Ilmenhith was mostly wood and plaster with a shell of pale stone. From what he could see through the narrow window, Alwhen was almost all stone. Even wooden shakes were rare. Every building he'd seen bore dark slate tiles on the shallow-pitched roofs. But they'd lived without mages for a number of decades, Vahn reminded himself. And even before the Giftless king cut himself off from the Eldani, mages had conducted little business in the eastern half of the island. In Ilmenhith, mages would snuff a fire within moments of its catching.

"Here." The mage pushed open a small door halfway down the hall, stepped back and clasped her hands together before her. She didn't seem worried about him trying to escape, but she still positioned herself in the middle of the hall.

He stepped inside and allowed himself a sigh once the door was shut. Even if he took advantage of the washbasin that stood against the wall to make himself wholly presentable, it only bought him a little time.

If Shymin intended to meet with him, she wanted something. He doubted he'd be able to bargain for much information, but sorting out what he wanted to know was important. There was no reason to think Envesi would let Lulu out of her sight, especially if what his father said was true. If the girl was useful, she'd be kept close. As precious as his daughter was, learning his father's whereabouts probably took precedence. Ennil had fooled them once already. If there was anything Vahn could do to keep his father from returning to Ilmenhith, it was likely the only good he could do.

He lingered at the washbasin after he sponged himself clean, studying his reflection in the small mirror on the wall above it. It was curious how refreshed he looked. Whatever the mages had done to him before they brought him here, it had left him well-rested. He smoothed his hair before he stepped back out into the hallway, as clean and composed as a king caught off his guard and kidnapped could possibly be.

The mage stood waiting. She hadn't moved an inch.

Vahn studied her for a time, considering whether he should speak to her or not. If she'd been sent to serve him breakfast and tend his needs, chances were she was unimportant among the mages here. It was unlikely she knew anything valuable. Without a word, he turned and made his way back to the plain room at the end of the hall.

The white-robed woman slid in after him and crossed to the table to inspect his meal. She waved a hand and thin curls of steam began to drift from the tea. Firal used magic for such conveniences from time to time, but seeing this stranger do it was oddly unsettling.

Pretending he wasn't bothered, he slipped into a chair. Despite his lodgings, the meal seemed worthy of his station, consisting of a variety of fruits and pastries served on fine porcelain. He suspected it wasn't intentional. If anything, it was just the same fare the mages allowed themselves.

"Let Shymin know I will see her after breakfast." Assuming the meal wasn't poisoned, that was. He took a pastry nonetheless. If they killed him, it would only worsen the kingdom's disposition toward them.

The mage bobbed in a graceless curtsy. "Of course." She paused before adding, "Majesty."

He lifted a brow. It was the first acknowledgment of his rank and identity she'd given. He didn't know if that was favorable or not.

She scurried from the room without saying anything else, closing the door and replacing the bar in front of it on her way. That single action told him a great deal. They didn't see him as a threat, but they still didn't want him to escape. Under supervision, they found it unlikely he would try it, but he was still a captive and wouldn't be trusted alone. Wise of them, he acknowledged; he had been considering breaking the window only a few hours before.

They gave Vahn enough time to eat his fill and drink his tea before someone returned to retrieve him. It was a different mage this time, with a serving boy at her heels.

"Master Shymin will receive you now," the mage said with a slight incline of her head. She had the same white hair and white robes as every other Master. Though he knew she wasn't the same woman, Vahn had the strange impression that she might as well have been. She moved the same way, spoke in the same timbre, looked at him with the same calculating gaze.

Vahn pushed himself from the table and strode toward her. "Thank you." He watched from the corner of his eye as the serving boy scuttled past them and busied himself with stacking dishes and cleaning the tabletop. Despite being in the presence of a mage and a king, the boy looked comfortable.

It was likely the lad didn't know who Vahn was, but that he went about his work in such an ordinary fashion indicated the mages had been in Alwhen for a while. How long, though, Vahn couldn't say. When Relythes built his wall, all communication had ceased, and the two countries had been comfortable ignoring each other. Now Vahn regretted not paying better attention to the Giftless half of the island.

As they walked the hall a second time, Vahn studied the other doors. Most were closed, but his was the only door barred. Now that he had a better look, he saw the iron brackets for the bar were a recent addition, the metal freshly forged. The chips in the stone where the brackets were anchored had not yet discolored.

The mage led him down a flight of narrow stone stairs and into another hall. This one was slightly wider than the one upstairs, but just as plain. Pale outlines on the stone showed where tapestries once hung on the walls and carpets must have decorated the floor. They passed the kitchens and a formal dining chamber, both scarcely furnished.

The thought of the mages taking the city by force had crossed his mind, but seeing every nook and cranny swept clean and every scrap of furnishing removed made him think otherwise. It was too neat, too precise. If Envesi had stormed the city and turned nobles out of their estates, there would have been chaos and a huge number of belongings left behind. This was too clean, too calculated. Whoever lived here before, they left by choice, and with plenty of time to spare.

"Master Shymin will receive you in the front parlor," the mage ahead of him said, her voice low. "Do you prefer tea or wine?"

"Tea, thank you." He lingered back a step as she opened a door and motioned him in.

Walking past her made him uncomfortable, but he reminded himself he was unlikely to find a knife in his back—if only because mages didn't need knives. Then again, magic hadn't been what killed Medreal. He drew himself up and pretended the thought didn't bother him.

Of the rooms he'd seen, the parlor was the only one that was fully furnished. Couches and chairs sat around a low table, all atop a rug in the rich vermillion that represented the Giftless kingdom. A pair of desks sat against the wall at the back of the room. Shymin sat at one, sprinkling sand over a sheet of paper to absorb the excess ink.

"Welcome, King Vahnil," she said without looking up. "I

apologize for your breakfast being late this morning. I've had trouble finding a proper cook for hire. Did you rest well?"

He stopped just inside the doorway. "I woke up on the floor after your party kidnapped me. I haven't slept since then."

Shymin turned, frowning. "Not the most restful night then, I suppose." She rose from the desk and smoothed her white robes as she crept toward him. A few feet away, she paused and dipped in a graceful bow. "I apologize for the inconvenience. This is not how I planned our meeting, but we'll have to make the best of the situation."

"I can't imagine you expected it would go better," Vahn said. "Between kidnapping my child, betraying your homeland and then kidnapping me, it seems like you set yourself up for an unpleasant meeting."

Her brows drew together and a quizzical look drifted over her face. "What makes you think I've betrayed my homeland?"

Vahn snorted. "Don't pretend you aren't aware you've committed treason. I expected better from the Archmage's sister."

Shymin's mouth twitched. "Perhaps an explanation is in order."

He resisted the urge to roll his eyes. As if an explanation would lessen her treachery.

"First," she said, "let me be clear that I do not agree with the methods used, but I am loyal to the cause. I was ordered to bring you here and speak to you, and so I have." She made her way to one of the couches, sat down and gestured for him to have a seat.

He considered standing, but a young girl in a brown dress entered the parlor with a tray of tea. The smell of it struck him as oddly appealing, and he crept forward to sit across from the mage. Being disagreeable wouldn't get him far. He was playing by their rules, now. "What cause?"

Shymin waved the girl away after the tray was on the table. She poured their tea herself. "The preservation of magic."

Vahn's brow furrowed.

"I see your confusion. I understand. The temple has always operated under a certain degree of secrecy." She pushed his cup across the table and sighed. "I'm of the opinion it hurt us in the long run. Had Envesi been more forthcoming with her plans and her knowledge, the island would be a very different place. She would still be Archmage of Kirban, for one. Instead, she sought secrecy, believing her cause would only be upheld by fellow mages."

"I don't understand," he said, taking his cup. He waited for her to drink first and only lifted his tea after he saw she swallowed and licked her lips.

"And if Envesi had been vocal about her work, perhaps you would. It may be difficult to explain now, at least succinctly. In essence, the existence of magic is threatened across the world. Only through Envesi's work in establishing the temple do we have the numbers we need to preserve our craft. Magic is fading. Failing. With each generation, it becomes weaker. In a dozen more, it will be gone, unless something is done."

Vahn hardly knew what to say. His father had hinted at such a problem, he realized belatedly, but he hadn't grasped the depth of it. Magic was deeply ingrained in Ilmenhith's culture. What would the island be like without it? How would people *survive* without it? Mages cured disease and illness, nurtured the land and even crops. The countryside had suffered with the mages spread thin. How much worse would it be with no mages at all? He shook his head in disbelief. "How can this be?"

Shymin shrugged. "Imagine a pen dipped in ink. Eventually, it runs dry. As with ink, the first marks are the strongest, boldest. The last are faint and scratchy, skipping and sputtering. Magic is the same. At the beginning of every mage's bloodline is a mage like your daughter. Powerful in ways we cannot imagine. But as the bloodline grows, the ink fades. Now we are in the last days of the stroke. The Gift skips generations. Children are weaker than their parents." She lifted her cup and smiled faintly over the rim. "And then there is your child."

A strange chill crawled down his spine. "Lulu?"

Her eyes gleamed. "Her Gift is like no other. Unrestricted, like that of the mages at the dawn of time. In her, we see hope. The chance for a renaissance of power. Envesi would never harm her, you understand. She's too precious, too vital, and a child, besides. But by studying her Gift, we have the chance of understanding how magic came to be bound, and might discover why it fades. We can restore magic to old bloodlines, ensuring the existence of mages for millennia to come."

Anger welled inside him. "Then why couldn't Kytenia study her? At home, safe, without having to steal her away?"

"Because Kytenia doesn't know," Shymin said simply. "She knows only what she was told. Her predecessor passed before he could teach her. I only learned recently, and only because Envesi reached out to me."

Something in her voice made him uncomfortable; a note of disapproval, bordering on contempt. Which Archmage it was meant for, though, he wasn't sure. He eyed her for a time, sipping his tea to hide his lack of words. It wasn't a bad drink, too weak for his preferences, but at least it wasn't bitter. Mild as it was, it still left his mouth dry.

"Why am I here?" he asked at last.

Shymin's eyes narrowed. "For Lulu, of course. Why else?"

His heart climbed into his throat. "You're going to take me to her?"

"As I said, I don't agree with some things the rest of the allied mages have done, but there's no reason to keep the girl unhappy." She paused to refill her teacup. "Considering Envesi was exiled from the island, she did not believe you would allow her near enough to study your daughter's Gift, regardless of her intentions. I did not join them until after they had already taken Lulu, so there was little I could do. Convincing them to bring one of you here took some doing, but they agreed."

Vahn found himself nodding. It made sense, though he was still disgruntled by her methods. "But why me instead of Firal?"

"They chose you. I don't think they trust Firal." Shymin offered him the teapot. He shook his head. "In any case, they thought you would be more likely to listen to reason. The plan was for me to visit the palace and give you a formal invitation, acting as ambassador between Envesi and the crown, but I arrived too late and you'd Gated out of the city no more than an hour before, on your way to recall mages."

"And it was just by chance that you ended up at the same village I was riding toward?"

She stifled a laugh. "Yes. An awkward coincidence, really. I was there to ask the allied mages stationed near there to watch for you. Your mage gave them a spook and things unraveled fast. At that point, I thought my best bet was to put you into a mage-sleep and explain fully after you woke. As I am doing now. Though I do apologize they thought the floor a better resting place than the bed."

Vahn emptied his cup and leaned forward to put it on the table. "I want to see her."

Nodding, Shymin drank half her tea in a few swallows, then rose. "Come, then. Envesi will want to see you, as well." She brushed past him and into the hallway.

He followed, but stopped halfway down the hall. "My sword and armor?"

She seemed surprised. "You won't need them. No one would disturb anyone in the company of a mage, no matter who they are."

"Where are they?" He paused before adding, "I've not seen any of my men, either. Or my mage." His father hadn't mentioned them, now that he thought about it. Not that he'd have believed a word Ennil said at this point.

"All safe, and all comfortable, I promise you." Shymin smiled. "Your men are likely sparring in the castle yard. They are being housed there until you have need of them."

"And Kepha? My mage?"

Her smile faded into a wince. "She was unhappy with us, but

she is speaking to the others. She will be given an opportunity to learn what I've told you, though more in-depth. She would be useful, since our research needs every mage available. But she won't be harmed, nor will she be held prisoner. She will be free to make a decision to join us or return to the temple."

His blue eyes narrowed. Odd. "And you don't think that would be a problem? Her taking all that knowledge back to the temple, when you just told me it was information Kytenia doesn't have?"

Shymin turned toward him, and a shadow slid through her expression. She didn't appear displeased, merely troubled. "The temple is not our enemy, Vahn. Neither are you or Firal. Kytenia will learn everything, as soon as my work here is done."

"You think she'll join your cause?" he asked.

"There's no reason to think she wouldn't." She exited the front door and beckoned him to join her. "Envesi is not a good leader, but she is knowledgeable, and her research is what will save the temple in the end."

Vahn said nothing more. She made a fair argument and he understood her reasoning, though it still troubled him. She certainly seemed earnest. If the very existence of magic was at risk, he could understand why drastic measures could be needed. But understanding warred with his heart, and whether or not their intentions were good, he couldn't forgive what they'd done.

But if she was being honest, Shymin hadn't been part of that. It sounded like she was trying to correct mistakes, more than anything, and bringing him to Alwhen was the first step. Still, something nagged inside him as he followed her across the drab stone city with its close-packed buildings. Why had Envesi sought her, and when?

It doesn't matter, he lied to himself, training his eyes on the blocky palace ahead. Soon, he'd have Lulu in his arms again. What came after that, he'd figure out later. Right now, all that mattered was his child.

The city was as drab from the streets as it was from his window. Most of the buildings had at least two floors and the structures were packed so close to one another, it scarcely seemed there was room to breathe. Narrow pathways wormed their way between the buildings, so small they hardly counted as roads. The only green he saw was a handful of weeds sprouting along the walls of houses, and they passed at least one woman with a hoe working to eliminate them. The earth was hard-packed underfoot, despite the scent of mud and the humidity that hung thick in the air.

People looked at them, but not in the way Vahn expected. They appeared curious, but aside from pausing to offer respectful nods to Shymin as she wound her way between stone buildings, they didn't appear interested for long. Mages were ordinary here, as he suspected. The city folk here were as indifferent to their presence as the people in Ilmenhith were.

The narrow pathways let out onto a wider street finished with cobblestone, where light foot traffic wove between the merchant stalls along the avenue. Shymin signaled for him to stand back as a wagon pulled by oxen lumbered past.

"I'm surprised you're able to move around the city unhindered," Vahn remarked casually, scraping the soles of his boots against the cobbles at the edge of the street to clean them. "I thought Alwhen would be less welcoming to mages after the wall went up."

Shymin let go of her robes and made for the castle at a brisk pace. People moved out of her way as she walked. "That was a long time ago. After a few decades without us, they came to understand our value. Mages were rare where I grew up, but I can only imagine how difficult life would be without any mages at all."

"That's right," he murmured. "You grew up in the southern reaches of this half of the island, didn't you?"

She nodded. "And suffered greatly for it. If I have my way,

no village anywhere on the island will have to go without a mage's presence."

"Including the settlements inside the ruins?"

She cast a shadowed glance over her shoulder. Despite the ruin-folk's allegiance to Firal, many of the temple mages still looked on them with disdain. "Anywhere."

Though the palace soared above the rest of the city, it still looked like something created with a child's blocks. Heavily fortified and thickly walled, it could have withstood any siege Vahn could imagine. The gates stood open with a pair of white-robed mages beside them, rather than guards. That struck him as odd, but no odder than the rest of his morning, and he nodded in response to their quiet greetings.

None of the mages seemed troubled by his appearance, or even surprised. Either word had moved through the city like quicksilver after his arrival, or he'd been suspended in mage-sleep for longer than he thought. He'd never heard of mage-sleep, come to think of it, but it would have been foolish to think anyone knew all the tricks mages had. Even a king.

Shymin led him up the stairs and into the palace, where both of them had to stop and blink while their eyes adjusted to the dimmer light.

Years of smoke from sooty lamps stained the walls and ceiling, dulling the illumination cast from mage-lights cradled in iron sconces. The great hall was nothing like the palace in Ilmenhith, or even like the darker, heavier furnishings his father preferred. It was low-ceilinged and square, with long, empty fire pits and longer tables running the length of the room.

Mages clad in every color of robes packed the space. They bustled about with papers in their hands, jerking the skirts of their robes away from servants carrying polished silver pitchers and trays of pewter cups. Papers, maps, and books covered the tables. Mages of every age hunched over them, lost in study.

At the head of the table, seated in a great throne of waxed oak, was not the former Archmage Vahn expected. Instead, the throne held a young man with dark hair and a worried face. A crown of twisted gold rode low on his brow.

"Who is that?" Vahn asked in a murmur.

Shymin leaned close to reply. "Mathen, the king. The grandson of King Relythes, who ruled when you were crowned."

He frowned. "My father said Envesi rules here."

"She does," she said, pushing her way into the crowd. "After a fashion."

The mages didn't notice them at first but, after they did, they moved aside with their heads bowed in deference. Most of them bowed lower as he passed. Despite where they were, it seemed they still bore him allegiance. The peculiarity of the situation clashed and tangled in his head. Once he had Lulu safe in his arms, he'd need a lot of quiet time to think.

"King Mathen," Shymin called over the din.

The young man raised his head, searching the room with a frown. His brows lifted when he saw them.

She spread her skirts and dipped in a curtsy. "Where is the Archmage?"

Vahn bristled at the title.

"Upstairs," Mathen said, half rising before she gestured for him to stay seated. He sank back into his throne. "In her parlor, I believe. I just sent some charts for her to review."

"Excellent." She smiled. "Favorable results or useful discoveries?"

"We'll see, depending on what she thinks after she reads them. Who is this?" The young man nodded toward Vahn.

Shymin stepped aside. "This is King Vahnil of Ilmenhith. He's come to see his child."

"Ah!" A grin split Mathen's features and he rose with his arms spread. "The soldier king. An honor to meet you, though I do wish it were for happier reasons."

Vahn accepted the embrace of greeting, restraining his puzzlement and mustering a smile. "I suppose I shouldn't be surprised you've heard of me, what with so many mages present. I must apologize, I didn't expect the ruler of Alwhen would be..."

"So young, I know." Mathen chuckled, rubbing his chin. He was barely out of boyhood, really, his father's crown too big on his head. "It's been two years since my father passed. I, myself, wish he'd had more time to impart knowledge before he left us. Disease is cruel that way. One of many reasons all this is so important." He waved a hand toward the dozens of mages in the room, then righted the jeweled rings on his fingers.

"Healers could have made a difference for both his father and grandfather," Shymin said. "One more reason that wall needs to come down."

"Metaphorically speaking, of course," Mathen said. "A defined border is useful for maintaining the peace, but construction of roadways linking the kingdoms is certainly a priority."

Vahn's smile became strained. "A shame Firal and I have had no opportunity to discuss the matter with you."

"All in time," the young king said, brushing away the topic as if it were meaningless. "Shall I see the two of you upstairs myself?"

"No need," Shymin said. "It looks like you have your hands full enough here. If you can convince everyone else to give us a bit of privacy, though, it would be appreciated."

Mathen nodded and returned to his throne. "Of course. I will have quarters arranged for King Vahnil, as well. I'm sure he'll want to rest after this reunion."

Shymin dipped in another bow as they took their leave. She jerked her head toward the back of the room, where wide wooden doors opened to branching halls and stairways that led both upward and down.

The pathways through the palace were simple and straightforward, the halls lined with tapestries and carpeted in the rich vermillion of Alwhen's colors. Vahn didn't think it would help him escape, what with all the mages downstairs, but he memorized the path they took anyway. They came to a halt outside a pair of doors carved with wolves, foxes, and stags, animals he recognized from books but which didn't otherwise exist on the island.

"Here we are," Shymin said breezily, knocking once before she pushed the doors open wide.

His heart leaped into his throat. Standing in the center of the room, surrounded by furnishings luxurious enough to shame his own quarters in Ilmenhith, was his daughter.

Behind her stood a monster.

NEW RUMORS

No matter how many times Kytenia stood at the window and looked across the temple's expanse from the tower, it still felt surreal.

A large portion of her life had been spent as Archmage, leading and overseeing the mages who milled in the courtyards and gardens below. Despite her knowledge and experience, she still sometimes thought it all a fluke or some horrible mistake. She had gone straight from mageling to Archmage, skipping the years as a Master she always thought she'd have. For that matter, she'd barely worn blue, having graduated to the highest mageling rank only weeks before she became leader of the entire temple.

Yet no one had contested her position. There had been a fuss among some Masters, namely those who had coveted the position for themselves, but it passed within mere days. Kytenia had proven herself knowledgeable, responsible, level-headed and determined. Even the two Masters of affinity who remained from the temple's founding had eventually acknowledged her capability, though she suspected they still envied her position.

Why, then, did she feel like an imposter every time she stood at the peak of the Archmage's tower and looked down at the people in her care?

Kytenia rested a hand against the pale stone that rimmed the glassless window. Her eyes unfocused until the colorful mageling robes below blended into the bright flowers of the gardens.

"Have we done them a disservice?" she asked quietly.

Behind her, the shuffle of papers stopped. Edagan, Master of the House of Earth, made a soft sound of displeasure. "Who?"

"Everyone." Kytenia pulled herself away from the window. Edagan was the only other mage in the office. Only a few weeks prior, that would have been unusual. Envesi and Nondar had reserved the office and parlor beside the Archmage's quarters for their personal use when they held the position, but Kytenia didn't like the idea of so much space to herself. Her upbringing had made her conscious of waste. Growing up in a crowded house, few things were so precious as space. She enjoyed sharing the office with the other Masters, but she hadn't crossed paths with them in days. She missed them—particularly her sister and Rikka, her girlhood friend.

Edagan pursed her lips and put her papers aside. "That's very broad, Archmage." She spoke the title without venom, but Kytenia always thought the Master came across as short. Edagan was old enough to be her grandmother and, while she was respectful, she had little patience to spare. Even for the Archmage.

"My entire tenure as Archmage has been spent pushing mages to the far reaches of the island. As many as Firal will allow me to send. We have mages from coast to coast now, all the way to the wall beyond the ruins. Now I wonder if that was the best decision." Kytenia paced to the edge of the wide table where the older woman worked. She laid her hand on the back of a chair, unsure if she wanted to sit. She was restless, yet weary. An unpleasant combination.

"I fail to see how it could be anything but beneficial," the Master said.

Frowning, Kytenia pulled the chair back and sat. "I am a healer. My first lessons were with Nondar, and one of the first things he told me was to learn when healing was prudent. Such a Gift is beneficial in emergencies, yes, but we've spread mages far and wide to be sure everyone has access to mage-healing. How many plagues do you think we've prevented?"

"Hundreds." Edagan waved one gnarled hand with a small laugh. "Thousands, maybe."

"And what damage has that done? How will the people we serve manage when all mages are gone? When the last epidemic is so far lost in history that none know how to treat it, or how to save the afflicted?"

The old Master grew quiet. As a rule, they did not discuss the waning existence of magic. Though his time as Archmage had been brief, Nondar insisted the decay of power was best kept out of common knowledge, and Anaide and Edagan had only taught her of the matter because of its role in the temple's founding. Nondar had passed before he could teach Kytenia everything she needed to know. As the only two Masters remaining from Kirban Temple's founding days, it fell to Edagan and Anaide to complete her training. Kytenia had never found their lessons lacking, but she often wondered how much knowledge had died with Nondar—and how much would die with her.

"Self-doubt is a luxury the Archmage cannot afford, dear girl," Edagan said at last, gentle and respectful despite the diminutive endearment. Her tone caught Kytenia off guard. The withered old mage was often brusque in manner. Had Kytenia not been looking at her as she spoke, she might not have believed the words were Edagan's at all.

"Though it is justified, isn't it?" Kytenia rested her elbows on the table. Her shoulders sagged as she exhaled.

"It always is." Edagan tidied her workspace and pretended to be distracted.

Kytenia watched her sort through her notes and papers and gathered a few pages of her own, just to have something to do while they talked. "What would you do? If you were Archmage, that is."

The old mage blinked at her. "Why should I have to do anything? Regardless of what's happening on the mainland, the temple has served the island for hundreds of years. It will continue to do so for several millennia. The best thing I could do as Archmage would be to make efforts to preserve knowledge." She paused, and a gleam came to her brilliant blue eyes. "And perhaps encourage the Master of Healing to increase studies in non-magical healing."

Restraining a smile, Kytenia bowed her head. "Yes, that does seem to be a good idea. Perhaps I could speak to Arrick and collect medical knowledge from the mainland, as well."

"Or have one of your Masters do it," Edagan said. "We are high-ranking enough to speak to Headmaster Arrick on your behalf, you know."

"I know. I'm just not sure I want everyone speaking to Headmaster Arrick."

Edagan sat back in her chair and peered at her. "Does Balen's loose tongue worry you that much?"

Kytenia snorted. Balen had been chosen to lead a House of affinity just before she became Archmage. The Master of the House of Fire couldn't keep a secret to save his life, but that was one of the reasons she trusted him. A man with no secrets was a man who could cause her little trouble. "It's not the secrets he knows that worry me, Edagan."

"But the ones he might learn." Edagan nodded.

"Precisely. And that's why it would have to be me. Or you, or Anaide, perhaps." The thought made Kytenia frown. She liked both women perfectly well, but Anaide often seemed combative. Kytenia suspected the woman had never come to terms with being passed over for rank of Archmage, even if she seemed content to follow Kytenia's lead.

The Master of Earth raised one white brow. "You've forgotten your Master of Wind."

A hint of color rose in Kytenia's cheeks. "I haven't," she said in a rush. "But you know how the mainland mages feel about my age. It's bad enough they have to deal with an Archmage as young as I am. I'm afraid they wouldn't take Rikka as seriously as they ought."

"If you want me to do it, girl, just ask."

Though the offer was tempting, Kytenia shook her head. "No, I'll tend to it myself. But if you would, keep your ears open."

"Whatever for?"

"Secrets." Kytenia's face darkened. "From mouths that shouldn't be able to speak them."

Edagan's eyes narrowed. She smoothed her hair in its bun. "You suspect temple involvement in what's going on with the girl."

"There are few of us who have worked with Lulu closely enough to know the nature of her Gift," Kytenia said. "If lips within the temple were closed, how could Envesi have learned about it?"

"She has her ways, but I do see what you mean." The old mage hesitated, then added, "I am honored that you trust me."

"You should be. There are few people I can." She tried not to think of Anaide again. Was the old woman petty enough to turn against her?

Edagan chuckled and pushed herself up from the table. "Well, we'll see if I can't add a few more to the number. Give me a handful of days, Archmage. Wherever the leak in our dam may be, it will be plugged."

Forcing a smile, Kytenia turned her attention to the charts on the table. She'd have to go through them eventually. She'd promised Firal she would review where her mages had been and who had searched their regions for the missing girl. "I certainly hope so, Edagan."

If the leak of information wasn't found, she didn't think the temple would survive.

***

GARAM WINCED as he reached the bottom of the stairs and rested a hand against the wall for support. He'd left his cane in his room. Not out of a desire to appear strong before strangers, as he might have been inclined to try in his younger days, but out of sheer forgetfulness. Age crept on him in a number of ways, stealing his peace, making his life more difficult. His knees had begun their protest when he was only halfway down the staircase, but by then it was too late to do anything except carry on. Not for the first time, he regretted the hard life he'd led in service to his king. He didn't regret the service, but most of his peers had retired young. He never saw the councilors his age suffering with arthritis.

The lower kitchens loomed ahead of him, their doors open wide to let an assortment of appealing fragrances waft out. There was another kitchen upstairs, which he'd explored first, but the scullery maid cleaning the cool hearth explained it was used only for preparation of formal meals and directed him to what she called the 'everyday' kitchens, nestled below. He'd thought it odd placement at first, set halfway below ground, but as he walked, he'd decided it made sense. The island exhibited a tropical climate. If not for the cooling shelter of the earth banked against the kitchen's walls, work in the kitchens would have been unbearable.

Ignoring the aches and pains that came from movement, Garam started forward again, this time with a bit of a limp. The kitchen was busy, though the scullery maids and serving girls clustered at the far end of it and chittered like a flock of sparrows. They cast furtive glances toward the front of the kitchen, then whispered furiously, as if their behavior didn't give them away. The rumor mill was already turning, it seemed. Garam tried not to roll his eyes. His target sat alone at the small table near the door. He carried on with a quiet grumble.

"I wish they'd just killed me." Rune didn't so much as look at him, hunched over the worn table with his forehead braced against his hand.

Garam didn't wait for an invitation before he pulled out a chair for himself. "You never were one to take the easy way out."

"But it sure would solve a lot of my problems." Rune reached for his glass and grunted in displeasure when he lifted it and found it empty. He raised his head just long enough to refill his drink with pungent amber liquid from a dark bottle. Emptying the last drop into the glass only rendered it halfway full.

Hard as the wooden chair was, it was still a relief to sit. Garam's knees ached and his legs burned, yet the days they'd marched miles together didn't seem so far behind them. He stifled a sigh and planted his elbows on the table. "But it wouldn't help that little girl."

Rune swore under his breath. He nestled his forehead into his scaly palm again and tilted his hand to shield his eyes.

A maid swept by to remove the empty bottle. Garam watched her leave, half expecting her to come back with another bottle of liquor. She didn't.

"You believe she's mine?" Rune asked in a murmur.

Garam raised one thick brow. "Do you?"

He was hesitant to reply. "I don't know."

"I suppose they could have painted her eyes any color. Though there is a bit of something in her face. The shape of her nose, I think."

Rune snorted, then sipped his drink. "You're right. They can do anything they want in a painting. My father had me painted with blue eyes. I imagine they don't have that one up in the hall anymore."

"You told me you didn't have children," Garam said. "I remember. I asked, when we were in Aldaan that first time."

"I know." Rune cradled his glass, turned it and watched its contents swirl. "Didn't think I could."

That was an odd thing to say. "I thought you weren't married long before..." Garam trailed off and cast a glance toward the scullery maids.

Rune followed his gaze and lowered his voice, even though they spoke in the trade tongue. A good precaution; one never knew who might be listening. "I wasn't." He took another drink, licked his lips and mulled his words over before he went on. "There was someone else. Before I married."

Garam nodded. "Not surprising, given your station."

"The reasons aren't important," Rune muttered. "It went on for some time, but nothing came of it. For a time I thought she kept it that way on purpose, taking something to prevent..." He trailed off and shook his head. "But it didn't make sense. For one, we were in an isolated area, with an isolated group of people. She didn't have access to those things. And for another, having my child would have put her in a position where she could claim a right of inheritance, giving her access to my father's holdings."

"But there was no child," Garam concluded.

Nodding, Rune continued. "I asked a Master who specialized in healing about it once. There was no way to test, really, but she said it was unlikely I'd ever have a normal life. I was a sickly child, I suppose because of the magic, so it seemed more likely to be me than her."

"I'm guessing you never asked her."

"No. Honestly, if the thought of having a child with me hadn't occurred to her, I didn't want to put it in her head." He sounded remorseful and more than a little sheepish as he stared into his cup.

"I can understand your doubt, then." Lacing his fingers together, Garam rested his hands against the edge of the table and wet his lips. "But the queen's not lying to you."

Rune peered at him from beneath knit brows. "What makes you think that?"

Garam frowned, his eyes drifting to the glass in his friend's clawed hand. It was almost empty again. "I spoke to Firal," he said in a hushed tone, mindful of the ears behind them. "It's not just your eyes the girl inherited, and I'd swear on my honor that's why she was taken. She has your magic, too."

Rune cursed again, louder. The maids at the back of the kitchen grew quiet.

"When you were looking for the Aldaanan, what did you find?" Garam leaned forward. "Everywhere you went, signs of magic, signs of something wrong. You know what's happening as well as I do. You suspected it, but you didn't want to say anything. The Aldaanan aren't just missing, are they?"

"I never said they were missing." Rune tossed back the last of his liquor and slammed his glass back onto the table. "I said what I was looking for didn't exist."

This time, Garam was the one who swore. "And you never thought to tell anyone they're dead?"

"What does it matter? The college mages hate them, Vicamros and his father barely tolerated them. No matter how strong Envesi is, even if she were able to rival me, she's still just one mage. The Aldaanan didn't travel alone."

"What are you saying?"

Rune scoffed and turned away. "If the Aldaanan are dead, it's because they chose not to fight. Even knowing they would die."

Garam eased back in his chair and stared at him in disbelief. "Why would they allow that?"

His companion didn't reply. In that silence, a great deal of what had transpired in the past several days made more sense.

"You never had a plan to escape, did you?" Garam asked softly. "You came here because there's no one left to unseal and cleanse your power."

Rune shrugged, his eyes lowered. "An honorable death is better than a cursed life."

"Being hung for treason is hardly an honorable death."

"It is when it's unjustified, but you allow it to happen for the sake of the place you call home." Rune shook his head. "If Vicamros had refused to turn me over, it would have crippled the Triad's economy. They've come to rely on Elenhiise too much."

"No one should die for politics," Garam said.

Rune snorted a laugh. "Pretty funny, coming from a soldier."

Garam didn't share his amusement. "Well, I'm finding that opinions change a good deal once you start getting old. The workings of the world seem different when it's your children and grandchildren in the gears instead of you."

Rune grew solemn, staring at his empty glass.

"Talk to me," Garam said.

"About what?" Rune shoved the glass away. "About how all of a sudden, everything is different? About having a purpose and a meaning? It doesn't work like that. This isn't one of Rhyllyn's ballads. I've been pulled out of everything I knew, everything I've come to love, only to be sent up against someone who's obviously powerful enough to kill free mages. All for the sake of a daughter I didn't know I had. I've never met her, never seen her face, I don't even know her name! What am I supposed to feel?"

Garam pushed himself up from his chair and pretended he didn't need the extra support from the table. "Don't know. I'm not you. But if you came here to die anyway, maybe going out as a valiant hero wouldn't be so bad."

"Where are you going?" Rune asked.

"Upstairs. I need to talk to some mages about what's going on. From the sound of those girls back there and considering the rumors you've already got going, the princess's magic won't be a secret for long." Garam took a few steps toward the stairs and paused. "The Uncrowned Prince, huh?"

Rune lifted a brow. A faint hint of amusement sparked in his snakelike eyes. "Is that what they call me now?"

"One version of you. I'm starting to think I don't know you near as well as I thought I did."

"Today's making me think I don't know myself so well, either," Rune muttered. He rose and slapped Garam's shoulder as he moved past him onto the stairs. "Do me a favor and ask one of those girls to send a drink to my room in a few minutes."

Garam nodded. "Whiskey?"

"See?" Rune smirked, though a shadow lingered in his expression. "You know me plenty well."

NEW WAYS

VAHN FELL TO HIS KNEES, GULPING BACK TEARS OF RELIEF AND elation as Lulu threw herself into his arms. He cradled the girl close and breathed her in as he pressed kisses to her temples and her ebony hair. She squealed and grinned, patting his face with her chubby hands. Only after he kissed each of her fingertips did he finally lift his head to look at the woman in the center of the room.

He had only laid eyes on the Archmage of Elenhiise a handful of times, the last being just before he descended into Ilmenhith's dungeons to free his dearest friend. Not even an hour after he'd seen her crossing the courtyard with Relythes, she'd been banished and removed from the island. He'd only gotten a glimpse then. If her face hadn't been burned into memory by the events that transpired that day, he never would have known this was the same woman.

Envesi's face was as stern and cold as ever, and her hair was the same cascade of snowy curls. Her eyes were still clear, frigid blue, but now they shone with an unnatural light. As she looked at him, her pupils thinned to vertical slits, much like those of a snake.

"Welcome, young king. She's been pleasant, though she does

ask for you often. Her mother, as well." Envesi strolled forward with a leisurely sway and, for a moment, the way she moved reminded him of Firal. With as different as the two of them were, it was difficult to remember the two of them were related.

She wore a white gown, rather than a robe, with the skirt slit to the thigh. Pearlescent white scales shimmered on her lower legs as she walked, and her three long, clawed toes splayed gracefully against the colorful carpet. Yet even stranger than her transformation was that she appeared younger than he remembered, as if her new form had revitalized her.

Vahn scooped his daughter into his arms and slowly stood. He wanted to speak, but he had no words. Instead he found himself staring at the woman's feet. It shouldn't have jarred him so badly. He'd seen the same features growing up alongside Ran, and the man had been his best friend. But this was different. It had to be. She'd done this to herself, twisted her own form for the sake of greater magic.

"Don't be so frightened, boy." The former Archmage stopped a few paces away and smirked. Despite her small stature, she made an imposing figure. "I believe Shymin was right to suggest we bring you, but I'm afraid you cannot stay long. I have important matters for you to attend."

Hugging Lulu to his chest, he took a half step back. "What do you mean?"

"Oh, I won't keep you away from her, don't worry." She waved a clawed hand. "I trust my mages have informed you what we are doing here?"

All he could manage was a nod.

"Then you know how important it is for us to win the temple over. Shymin is doing her part, and quite admirably, but we need greater leverage. We need you."

Confusion rolled through him, then bled away as anger swelled to take its place. "You kidnapped my daughter. You kidnapped me. You've taken over half the island and have a king working for you in his own palace. Why would I help you?"

Envesi chuckled. "Because you're smart, boy. Because you're angry, but you know that your father is too wise a man to be led astray. If he stands behind me, then you know you must. No matter how angry you may be."

Scowling, Vahn took another step away. "I'm not a puppet or a follower. My father helped you try to destroy my family. Why would I trust his judgment?"

Her face darkened. "Because in opening the island, you have exposed us. Doomed us. I know you believe forging ties with the north was the best thing you could do, and I forgive you for not knowing better. But I cannot forgive the mages who replaced me, who preside over my temple, who defy the very purpose of the temple's founding."

"Preservation of magic?" He couldn't keep the edge from his voice. He wanted to trust Shymin, but that meant believing what she'd said about Kirban Temple being the last bastion that could save magecraft. How could he believe that when their contact with the mainland was filtered through another school of mages, one older than the temple?

"Elenhiise was a haven, boy. A shelter for mages to thrive, so we could repopulate the world." Envesi laced her clawed fingers together behind her back and paced toward the low couches. "The old blood runs strong here. Kirban Temple has trained thousands of mages, and every one of them has provided a useful service to the island's people. In creating a culture that prized magic instead of reviling it, I ensured people would see the value in sending their children to me. Mages bore children sired by other mages for the first time in centuries. The mages on Elenhiise, the mages of Kirban, outnumber all the mages in the rest of the world combined."

Lulu patted his face, begging for attention. Vahn glanced down at her, troubled, and smoothed the girl's hair with one hand. "Why are you telling me this?"

"Because the world doesn't share our values, and our way of life must be preserved. They seek to eradicate magic. They will not allow our sheltered population of mages to exist in peace. A war is coming and we are in need of allies." She sat on the edge of a couch and drew one knee over the other, exposing an indecent amount of thigh.

Vahn tore his eyes away, uncomfortable. How could this be the same woman? He was sure she'd had wrinkles around her eyes and age spots on her hands when she was exiled. A far cry from the womanly figure before him, who seemed no older than Firal.

"Of course," Envesi continued, resting a claw against her cheek, "I mean no harm to your little kingdom, or the temple. Both will be allowed to operate as they please, as long as my needs are met. I can also promise that your cooperation will make life more pleasant for everyone. A gift, perhaps, or an act of service to aid you. Tidings of my goodwill." Her snakelike blue eyes drifted to the girl in his arms. "Perhaps an addition to your family would be well received."

His mouth fell open. "How did you—"

"Your Master of Healing is assisting me. One of the first questions she asked was how to treat secondary infertility. I am aware of your struggles, young king, and while I am sure they've told you the issue is not uncommon, I am equally sure they don't know how to address it." She smiled mirthlessly. "Do not forget that I am an unparalleled healer. More talented than any I've ever encountered, and capable of correcting sickness of both body and mind."

A child of his own. He hugged Lulu close, savoring her presence. He loved the girl more than words could express, loved her as well as if she'd been his own child, but the jealousy that he would never share a blood connection with his wife had always simmered beneath the surface. Not against the girl, but against her father, absent after the storm he'd created. Ran had a year worth of chances, opportunities to return and claim responsibility for everything he'd done. How could Vahn feel anything but jealousy and resentment when the man had tried to resurface a single day after Firal had chosen a new path?

But to think of a growing family. A brother or sister for Lulu. A blood bond to finally cement all of them together, creating a link between him and Firal and the girl he'd raised as his own.

Vahn had given up on the idea of more children long ago, after every mage on Elenhiise with a healing affinity had inspected Firal and concluded there was nothing they could do to help. More than one mage had told him Nondar would have had the skill needed to treat her, but Nondar had passed long before they'd had any clue it was an issue.

A tempting offer, one that tugged at his heart. Had it been any other mage in front of him, he would have leaped at the opportunity.

Yet did he have a choice? Vahn had no Gift, no way to stand against this woman, and he suspected she wouldn't take no for an answer. That she knew his deepest desires at least gave him a way forward.

Vahn kissed his daughter's temple and crept forward to sit across from the white-haired mage. "Tell me about what you're trying to achieve, and what you need to make it happen."

She quirked a brow and smirked. "Caught your attention, did I?"

"I won't make any promises," he said, raising a finger in warning. "But it's always possible that an agreement might be arranged."

"Very well, child." She stretched, draped an arm across the back of the couch, and sighed. "Where to begin..."

No one stopped Rune from emptying his assigned quarters and making off on his own. There were few things in his temporary room, but he wasn't about to leave anything behind. He heard guards following him, though they gave him a wide berth. They peered around corners to see where he was headed, but let him carry on. Rune found it amusing. He didn't intend to leave the palace. Perhaps that he headed deeper into the maze of hallways made them feel more at ease.

They seemed somewhat confused when he stopped by Garam's quarters, likely because the man wasn't there. But Rune didn't need to speak to him to recover the rest of his belongings. He didn't have to search long before he found his sword and added it to the collection of things he carried beneath his arm. He kept it wrapped for now; he didn't need any fuss over whose it was, but he wasn't about to let the blade slip out of his possession again. The thought conjured memories of his first meeting with Garam and he fought a smirk. The captain had mistaken the sword for stolen, setting off the whirlwind of events that thoroughly tangled Rune in northern politics.

At first, he'd doubted whether it was wise to bring it. Wrapping the blade and stashing it with Garam's things had been the best solution. It was there if he needed it, but hidden from sight until the time came. Were things to go sour, it would be easy for Garam to take the kingsword and return to the Triad with it. Arrick and Redoram could study the blade, then pass it on to Rhyllyn as part of the grand estate left behind. A dismal thought, but necessary in times like these.

Rune climbed another flight of stairs at a leisurely pace, taking in the small changes around the palace as he walked. The guards eventually lost interest in his meandering, and his entourage dwindled to a single follower for a time. Then he gave up as well, leaving Rune in peace.

Even alone, he didn't rush. There were new paintings, sculptures, tapestries and vases to admire, all riches brought by the increased trade with the mainland. Some rooms had been plastered and painted and were no longer the cold stone he remembered, but otherwise, little had changed.

"Ran," a voice behind him called.

Rune stopped and turned back.

Ordin Straes strode up the hallway toward him. The man slowed as he neared, regarding Rune with apprehension.

Rune raised a brow and looked at him expectantly.

"Lifetree's mercy," the Captain of the Guard breathed after a moment, and wiped his face with one hand. "It is you."

"Good to see you too, Captain." Rune shifted the bundle under his arm and offered his hand.

Ordin studied his claws for a long time before he shook his head and drew back, his face pinched with distress. "What happened to you?"

"That's a complicated story." Tipping his head toward the end of the hallway, Rune started off again. "Walk with me."

The captain fell in step beside him, staring straight ahead. "They said you were dead, you know."

"I imagine that would be a common belief, given how long I've been gone." Rune couldn't help a smirk of amusement. Was the man here because of the rumors already crawling through the palace, or because he'd figured things out on his own? The latter seemed more likely, but Rune wasn't about to ask. Rumors were most useful if no one knew where they started. Especially since that meant the creator could hide behind anonymity if something went wrong.

Ordin's jaw tightened. "I owe you an apology."

Rune blinked at him. "For what?"

"I ordered your capture, the night that..." Ordin trailed off. "I've cursed myself for that breach of conduct many times over the years. None so violently as this morning, when I realized it was you I wronged."

Rune snorted. "How does that make it any different?"

The captain shrugged and clasped his hands together behind his back. "Because I helped train you when you were young. Before I replaced Ennil Tanrys as Captain of the Guard. Because I always told your father you were too soft on your opponents in combat. I don't believe the young man I knew was capable of killing in cold blood."

"Would that I were still the same young man," Rune murmured. "Time changes all of us, Ordin. Hardens us."

"But you never intended to usurp your father's throne."

"No," Rune said, shaking his head. "My father's death was a tragedy, but there's little to be done about it now, and... that's something I'd rather not discuss. Tell me, did the queen inform her council what she has asked of me?"

"Not all of them," Ordin admitted. "She spoke to me, but only because I insisted."

"And what do you think of the princess's disappearance?" The title felt odd as it rolled off Rune's tongue. He wouldn't incriminate himself as the girl's father just yet. He still wasn't sure he believed it. Garam seemed certain, but Garam's life wasn't at risk of being upended over such a discovery. Selfish as Rune had become, he acknowledged that the secret protected Firal, too.

The captain's mouth twitched with a suppressed frown. "I think I wish it were a simple kidnapping. A scoundrel after a ransom. Something like that, I could understand. But this..." He trailed off and shook his head.

"There are always motives," Rune said.

"I didn't say there weren't. The problem is that whatever this one is, I have a feeling it's greater than I—or any of my men—are ready to deal with."

The man's candor was a surprise, and strange. Rune never expected he'd be able to slide back into any of the positions he'd held before, but Ordin spoke as calmly as if he'd never left. They'd never been friends, the captain plenty of years his senior, but they had worked together a number of times. As the captain said, he had been responsible for overseeing some of Rune's sword training, on top of instructing him in military strategy. Such things were expected of a potential heir. Ordin sounded no different than he had in those days, speaking as if he were sharing battle strategy with a student, though the weight of his words was greater.

"I think you're right." Rune didn't like to think about it at all, but if Firal had told Garam the truth, it made more sense than he wanted to admit. "I do think it's the beginning of something. But I don't believe we're in real danger just yet."

"What do you know?" Ordin asked in a murmur.

"I trained with mages of similar strength during my time on the mainland. But they—the Alda'anan—were pacifists, and after what I'd learned in the temple, our skills were incompatible."

Ordin nodded. The man remembered Rune's short-lived position as a court mage, then. Good.

"Over the years, the Alda'anan disappeared." Rune bit the inner corner of his lip and worried it in thought. "I think the princess's kidnapping has something to do with that."

"With disappearing mages?" The captain sounded skeptical. "She's just a girl."

"Yes," Rune said, "but her nursemaid was Alda'anan, using the island as refuge. Medreal was killed before the girl was taken. From that, it's probably safer to assume that Medreal was the real target."

"And the girl was just an additional complication," Ordin concluded.

Rune nodded. "That's a guess, at least. I won't know anything for certain until I can speak with the temple mages. I believe they'll be able to answer some of my questions."

"It's difficult to catch them for a meeting these days," the captain said, rubbing his chin in thought. "But I might be able to help. Let me go speak to Temar."

The name surprised him. "Temar is still alive?" Somehow, when he'd heard Medreal had been killed, he'd assumed other palace mages would have suffered the same fate.

"And as lovely as ever." Ordin chuckled and smoothed back his dark hair. He'd always fancied the mage, but for reasons Rune had never determined—or cared to find out, truthfully—he had never acted on his interest.

"That's a start, then. I'll need to speak to one of the high-ranking Masters. Nondar, maybe—"

"Archmage Nondar has been deceased for nearly thirty years," Ordin interjected.

Rune paused. They'd named Nondar Archmage in Envesi's absence? Likely the best choice they could have made, but he'd never expected the old man would have passed away. He'd never gotten along well with Nondar himself, but he recalled the mage's fondness for Firal, an element that would have been useful in gaining the temple's favor. As much as Rune resented the mages—for their treatment of him, for his exile, for his very existence—he couldn't deny that he would need their cooperation if he was going to do anything. Of course, whether he was going to do anything or not, he hadn't yet decided.

"I apologize," the captain added. "You've been gone a long time."

"Who leads the temple?" Rune asked.

"Archmage Kytenia was raised immediately following Archmage Nondar's death."

Rune froze in the middle of the hallway. "*Kytenia* is Archmage?"

Ordin stopped a few paces ahead and turned with a frown. "Is there something wrong?"

Rune could have laughed. For the first time since his arrival, something worked in his favor. "No, no," he said hastily. "It's just I've been gone a long time, as you said. I studied alongside her in my days as a mageling. She's come a long way. Is there any chance I may have an audience with her?"

"The Archmage is very busy," the captain said. "But... well, Temar may be able to do something. I will send word." He shifted on his feet, hesitant to leave. "Where are you going now?"

"My quarters," Rune said, shifting the bundle under his arm. "I trust Firal hasn't given them to anyone else."

"Not that I am aware of, your—" Ordin stopped short,

suddenly flustered. He'd barely caught the title before it rolled off his tongue.

"No titles. Not anymore." Rune offered a sympathetic smile and clapped the man on the shoulder.

Ordin rubbed his forehead, troubled. "What am I supposed to call you, then?"

"You could try Rune," he suggested, lifting his scarred left hand. "It's what most people call me now."

"Odd," the captain said. "Though I suppose times are odd as well, aren't they. Very well. Make yourself comfortable in the palace. I'll send word as soon as I know something."

"Thank you, Ordin," Rune said earnestly.

The man only nodded, then trudged back the way they'd come.

The last branch of the hallway turned into a wide walkway lined by graceful doors. Firal's private quarters would be halfway down the corridor, if she'd moved into the ruler's suite. Rune tried not to think of her sleeping arrangements as he strode past the double doors without allowing himself to look at them. His quarters had been farther down, near the end of the hallway where the serving staff had their narrow access staircase hidden behind a tapestry. He'd made use of the passage often, slipping through the back ways to escape his father's watchful eye.

He lingered outside the door for a time before he tried it. He didn't expect his old rooms to be locked, though he did expect they'd be in use. When the door groaned inward on stiff hinges, the darkness and dust on the other side came as a surprise.

Furniture loomed as ghostly shapes, draped in pale muslin and barely illuminated by the narrow shafts of sunlight that peeked in through the curtained windows. Dust motes swirled in the air as he stole inside and pushed back a curtain. He blinked away the sudden blindness and left his belongings on the floor. Then he pulled a covering off a tall shelf, coughing as stale dust filled his throat and nostrils.

Nothing had changed, so far as he could tell. Books and

trinkets still lined his shelves, and a peek inside the wardrobe showed all his clothing was still there, too. He coughed into the crook of his elbow as he waved away dust clouds and pulled the wardrobe doors wide. Once his throat cleared, he dug for the small box he kept in the bottom.

It wasn't locked—he rarely locked it—but that the box proved empty was still a slight frustration. The amulet he'd worn in his youth would have been useful, with its strange illusory magics that hid his true form, but he couldn't recall what he'd done with it. He vaguely remembered putting it away, though that could have meant here or in Core.

"Shouldn't expect an easy way out," he muttered to himself, clapping the box shut and putting it back.

"Looking for something?" a man asked from the doorway, an edge in his voice.

Rune glanced to the guard and frowned. "Yes, actually." He stood and closed the wardrobe. "Catch a maid in the hall and have a handful of them sent up to clean. I've not looked at the private bath yet, but I expect it's no better. And have one fetch a seamstress. If I'm to be held here for any length of time, I'm going to need new clothing."

The guard opened his mouth, but Rune went on before he could voice his anger.

"Oh, and I'll need a handmaiden for the afternoon, to manage errands for me since I'm evidently not supposed to leave the palace. Have Bree sent to tend me." He smirked and brushed dust from his sleeve. "I liked that one."

Flustered and scowling, the man stormed off.

Rune doubted he'd do as he'd been asked, but it got the man out of his way. He pulled the wardrobe open again as an afterthought, took a coat from inside and drew it on. As he expected, it was too snug through the shoulders and chest, the sleeves were much too short, and the standing collar didn't quite make it around his neck. He removed it with a rueful chuckle. Strange to recall he'd thought himself a man when last that fit.

He tossed the garment onto a covered bureau as he made his way to the bed.

The cloth canopy had been removed, likely at the same time the furniture was covered. The fine down mattress and bedding were still there and draped with more muslin, which he folded back so he could inspect the blankets underneath. Discolored with age and as stale as the dust floating in the air, they'd have to be replaced. That was work for the maids, then. He left it alone and turned to pull the covering off the low table beside the bed instead.

A book still lay there, pages open and facing down to keep his place, just as he must have left it thirty years before. He barely glanced at the title on the spine—some history of some sort that he didn't recall—as he opened the table's drawer and fished inside. There were a few things he had to push aside to open the false panel in the back but, when he did, his claws found the fat coin purse just as he'd left it. A small relief; he doubted he'd be allowed such easy access to the royal vault as he'd been blessed with in his youth.

"Your lordship requested me?" a small voice squeaked from the doorway.

Rune turned, surprised. He hadn't expected anyone so soon, especially not the maid he'd asked for. Bree stood just beyond his quarters, fidgeting with the edge of her apron, her face a mix of eagerness and apprehension.

"Yes," he said after a moment, bouncing the purse in his palm to make the coins jingle. "I did. Are there more maids coming?"

"They've been called for, m'lord. They'll be off fetching cleaning supplies, I expect." Bree dipped in a curtsy before she shuffled forward. She was small enough to be childlike, shorter even than Firal. "Do you wish me to wash your hair again?"

"No. I need you to manage some business in the city for me. I've already requested a seamstress, but I need you to take care of a special job." He opened the purse and sorted through coins as he spoke. She'd do what he asked, even without payment. That was her job, for as long as he was a guest in the palace. Coins simply had a way of making the world work smoother. He drew a slim silver coin from the pouch and rolled it between his claws. "I need you to find a silversmith. One who can complete something for me as soon as possible. I'll need the smith to come here, of course. I trust you can see to it before the day is out?"

She eyed the coin, nodded and inched close enough for him to lay it in her palm. "I'll have one to meet you within an hour, m'lord."

"Perfect," he murmured as he drew the strings on the purse tight. "I knew I was right to pick you."

Bree blushed, but curtsied again before she scurried back into the hall.

Rune watched her go, weighing the money in his hand. He thought about putting it back, but slid it into his pocket instead. He crossed to his long-abandoned desk and chair to wait. The cleaning staff would be there before the seamstress. Who knew how long it would take Bree to find a smith who could fit in a rush service, much less for a price that wouldn't empty his hidden savings in a single swoop. He'd have to remember to pay the seamstress first. But it would be worth it.

Looking back, he realized he should have commissioned such a piece long ago.

16

UNHAPPY REUNIONS

GRIPPING HER SKIRTS UNTIL HER KNUCKLES GREW PALE, KYTENIA hurried past the mages in blue-trimmed white that clustered in the Gating parlor. Temar would be close on her heels. The court mage could deal with the lollygaggers on her own.

Kytenia had been surprised when Temar and a handful of other mages in Ilmenhith's colors appeared at the temple. Court Masters were not messengers, yet Temar carried an urgent message for the Archmage. After Kytenia heard it, she understood why the woman had chosen to deliver it herself. There was no doubt that Temar's visit to the temple would set tongues wagging in the palace, though, and Kytenia didn't envy the task of putting a stop to whatever new rumors emerged.

Despite Vahn's insistence their trip to the Grand College would prove fruitful, Kytenia had doubts about whether or not their request would yield any results. She had suspected who he might have called, but it had been too long, too quiet, to think such a call would be answered. Especially so soon after it was delivered. Had it even been a week since their meeting with Arrick?

Ordin Straes waited in the hall, just as Temar said he would. The man bowed with his fist pressed to his chest. "Archmage."

169

"Captain." Kytenia offered a stiff nod in response, her fists curled tight in her skirts. She should have changed into proper robes before coming. She'd been in her quarters copying notes, and her old yellow work dress was stained with ink in half a dozen colors. Hardly fit for the Archmage of Kirban Temple.

The Captain of the Guard was as tight-lipped as Temar had been. He turned to lead the way without another word. She didn't blame him. Word that the Archmage had jumped to visit a prisoner in the palace would spread soon enough on its own. They didn't need the rumor to spark before she even made it upstairs.

Guards and serving staff looked at them oddly as they passed and, belatedly, Kytenia realized her shabby dress might have been more of a blessing than a burden. Not everyone in the palace knew the Archmage well enough to identify her at a glance. Without the white robes and ink eye-markings of a high-ranking Master, she didn't stand out. All they saw was a woman with white at her temples creating snowy rivers that disappeared into the curls of her auburn hair. For once, she was relieved her eyes hadn't yet changed to mage blue.

Though she silently wished the captain would move faster, they reached their destination soon enough. Instead of knocking, Captain Straes walked straight to the door and thrust it open, to the surprise of the people inside.

A handful of maids paused their work to peer at her with expressions of befuddlement. Farther from the door stood her girlhood crush, his arms spread, the seamstress beside him frozen mid-measurement.

"Kytenia." Ran—or should she think of him as Daemon?— smiled as he spoke her name. He lowered his arms and waved the seamstress back. The woman looked annoyed, but she held her tongue and turned her attention to her pad of notes.

Kytenia lingered by the door and cleared her throat. "So you are here. Shall we speak in private?"

Catching the hint, the serving staff gathered their supplies and slipped past her to wait in the hall. The seamstress started to leave, but Ran put up a hand to stop her.

"Just a moment. Let her finish." He spread his arms again and the woman lifted her measuring tape to take the last handful of measurements.

"Did you have colors in mind?" the woman asked as she went over her notes one more time.

"Blue." He shifted on his feet as she finished, twisting his wrist to indicate the cuff of his sleeve. "And silver embroidery, with scrollwork at the cuffs and collar, as well as across the shoulders."

Kytenia raised a brow at the choice.

The seamstress nodded. "Is that all, my lord?" She gave Kytenia a sidewise glance. She didn't seem to recognize her, as Kytenia feared the serving staff might, but the way she looked at her seemed troubled.

"For now. Thank you." He passed the woman a small velvet purse and waved her away before he turned to Kytenia again.

The Archmage straightened where she stood, but didn't move until the seamstress stepped into the hallway and closed the door behind her. Then Kytenia paced forward, more calmly than she felt, and wrapped him in a hug.

He seemed surprised, but closed his arms around her and chuckled. It was the first time she'd ever embraced him. The solid feeling of his muscled form against her only served to make it more surreal. His arms tightened around her slender frame, just slightly, and for a moment she suspected he was just as grateful for the contact as she was.

"I didn't believe it when Temar told me," she laughed, despite herself. "All these years, not knowing if you were even alive—"

Frowning, he pushed her back. "Firal never told you?"

Kytenia wiped her eyes and regarded him curiously. That was an odd thing to say. "We never knew. We didn't even know if you'd made it off the island. Vahn seemed to think you'd be on the mainland, but..." She trailed off, swallowed hard and leaned in to hug him again. "It's just such a relief to see you in one piece, after all these years." She didn't want to admit she'd given up the thought she ever would. Firal had avoided speaking of him after his disappearance, the hurt too deep. Out of respect, Kytenia never asked.

"It's good to see you, too. I hear you're Archmage now."

She nodded. "It's hard to believe. Even for me, sometimes. Shymin is Master of Healing, and Rikka is Master of Wind, too."

He snorted in amusement. "How far we've all come."

"And now you've come home." She smiled, though her cheer was quick to fade. "If only it were under better circumstances."

"Circumstances," he murmured. His expression darkened and he drew away. "I feel like I've heard that word a lot lately. But that's part of why I asked for you. Ordin wasn't sure he could convince you to come, but I'm glad he did."

"Well, it's hard to refuse the Uncrowned Prince," she teased.

He looked troubled.

"What?" Kytenia arched a brow.

"That's not a title or name I want anymore."

She couldn't argue with that. With a troubling history behind him on Elenhiise, it should have been obvious that he'd forged a new life for himself elsewhere. She crossed her arms and made herself smile at him again. "Who are you, then?"

He snorted. "On the northern or southern continent?"

Kytenia blinked in surprise. "You've traveled that far?"

"Rune Kaim-Ennen in the north," he said, ignoring the latter question in favor of the first. "Champion of the Royal City Arena and vassal to King Vicamros II."

"And in the south?"

"Ruali Dreamhunter."

"Peculiar names," she chuckled.

He shrugged.

"Well, since your liege is in the north, I suppose Rune will do." She kept her arms crossed as she paced around the room.

His quarters were only half clean. She couldn't imagine why he'd been put there, with all the space available in the palace. "So you wanted to speak with me. I'd say I'm flattered, but I'm guessing it has more to do with me being Archmage than with me helping rescue you, all those years ago."

"Don't think I don't appreciate it." Rune followed her with his eyes. "Right now, the most important thing is why I'm here."

The lack of urgency in his words startled her. He spoke as if it were business, nothing more. Not the life of his child hanging in the balance.

"I've already done everything I can to help," she said. "I'm not sure what else you expect of me."

"I didn't ask you here to tell you what to do. I asked you here to warn you about what we're facing." Stormy shadows filled his violet eyes.

"Free magic," she finished for him.

Now he looked surprised.

She drew herself up and looked him square in the eye. "I am Archmage now, Ran. Rune." The name still felt awkward on her tongue, but it was no worse than seeing him as he was. For most of her life—for the span of their delicate friendship—he'd masqueraded beneath illusory magic that changed his hair to tawny and hid the scales on his arms and legs. Even now when she thought of him, that was the image conjured in her mind, though she'd known his true appearance for years. It would take some time to adjust.

"I am aware of the practices of those before me," she continued. "As I am aware of your origins, and what the former Archmage sought to do with your power."

He grew solemn. "Then you know what we have to do."

That gave her pause. There was a gravity to his words that unsettled her, a heat buried in them that threatened to burn its way to the surface. She hesitated to reply.

What *did* they have to do? She knew the former Archmage couldn't be allowed to go unpunished after what she'd done.

And if exile worked, the woman wouldn't have come back to the island to begin with.

And neither would he.

True, his exile had been more self-imposed, but what other choice did he have? If he'd stayed—even if he'd hidden in the underground—he would have been found and taken to the gallows eventually. Especially once the Underlings had submitted to Firal's rule. But neither Rune nor Envesi were welcome on Elenhiise, and the reasons why mattered little.

"We cannot kill another mage," she said at last, though stifling doubts rose within her as she spoke. Did mages on the mainland adhere to the same rules of conduct as the island mages? He'd been raised under the same tutelage as she had, even if his Gift was different. Had his time away from the island changed his understanding of their laws?

"I'm not talking about killing her." Rune sounded irritated at the suggestion. The scowl on his face came as a relief. "With the kind of power she has now, I don't think that's possible. The best we can do is sever her. Hopefully before she learns how to share power with the girl."

Her relief drained away and a knot of dread formed in her stomach instead. "What?"

"I couldn't link my magic with that of the Alda'anan, but there has to be a way. That's why she took the girl. It must be. If she really is a free mage, then—"

"No," Kytenia interrupted, waving her hands. "The other thing you said. Sever her?"

Rune's brow furrowed. "What else are we supposed to do?"

That wasn't what she meant, either. She opened her mouth to explain, then grimaced. It served her right, after lording her knowledge over him only a moment before. "When you say severing—is that a practice among mainland mages?"

He stared at her for a moment before understanding lit in his eyes. "You don't know what I'm talking about, do you?"

"I have an idea," she said, defensive. It would have been

difficult not to gather an idea of what it meant, just from the word alone. "I'm just unfamiliar with how it is done. Certain practices are outlawed here, you'll recall." That let her save face, at least.

Rune considered that for a moment and then shook his head. "Now that I think of it, I shouldn't be surprised. I'm not even sure you can do it. It might be something only a free mage can do. You have to be able to catch the flows and manipulate them directly. All of them, all at the same time."

Even at a level of strength befitting an Archmage, that was beyond her ability. She could influence the flows, if she spent her own energy to do so, but she could not tap elements outside her affinity any more than she could open a Gate on her own. "That shouldn't be a problem, since you're here."

The corners of his mouth twitched, and a deeply troubled expression flitted across his face before he caught himself and replaced it with a mask of cool neutrality.

Why would that bother him? Kytenia's eyes narrowed and she started to speak, but a knock at the door cut her off.

Captain Straes didn't wait for a response before he opened the door. "Archmage," he said, taking a half step in before he realized she was only a few feet away. He froze.

She lifted a brow. "Yes, Captain?"

He glanced between them, his face pinched with worry. "A message from the temple. They need you. Now."

***

EDAGAN WAS NOT what most people considered friendly. She did not even label herself as agreeable. But she was Master of the House of Earth, and she was good at her job. And so she found herself—yet again—surrounded by hapless and hopeless magelings who couldn't tell a pebble of sedimentary stone from a wart on their own backsides.

Sighing and rubbing her eyes, Edagan strained not to snap at them again. They were trying their best, she reminded herself. They wouldn't have been sent to her if they didn't have potential. It wasn't their fault she didn't enjoy their company. She didn't enjoy anyone's company, though she tolerated some better than others.

"I think that's enough for today's class." Edagan closed her notebook and tried not to look at the disappointed faces. Field study was never pleasant for her, but the magelings adored it. It was the only time they were allowed to set foot inside the ruins, even if it was just the outermost rings. In days past, even that was forbidden. One of many things that had changed under Firal's rule, Edagan supposed.

The magelings in their colored robes shuffled into a line, preparing to file out. One lonely figure in white—the only other Master who had come today—moved to the back of the line to herd them along, indicating Edagan would be stuck leading the entourage out of the ruins. A shame, really; she had hoped to send them off ahead of her and take a moment to herself to investigate what looked like the opening to a cavern.

Resisting the urge to sigh again, Edagan turned to address the class. "We will resume today's lesson after—" She stopped short. The small hairs on the back of her neck prickled. She shivered and the hairs on her arms rose, too. A ripple of energy in the air. Something wild, like the crackling flows of a Gate, but worse.

Neve, the Master at the other end of the line, held out a hand as if to keep everyone still. "What is that?"

Edagan frowned and started to reply.

A whistling shriek drowned out her words. The explosion that followed sent her to her knees.

"Down the hall!" Edagan barked over the cries of the magelings. "Farther into the ruins!"

The magelings scurried down the corridor, some on their hands and knees. Edagan spun toward the temple, though she couldn't see over the labyrinth's walls. Only a plume of smoke drifting into the clear blue sky indicated anything was wrong. Any other time, she might have thought it a training accident, nothing to be concerned about. But she recognized that foul feeling in the air, a rotten, tainted sort of magic she had not felt in decades.

Archmage Kytenia had only just mentioned its source the other day. The thought gave Edagan a chill, and she hurried to follow her class into the depths of the ruins.

The opening at the end of a hall that caught her attention earlier in the day wasn't far. The magelings poured into it with little direction. It proved to be a collapsed entrance, but the cavernous front provided refuge for now. Besides, if necessary, they were all mages proficient with earth. Digging a way down to the tunnels of Core wouldn't be difficult.

Edagan lingered by the opening. Neve moved close, the young woman's face troubled. Younger, Edagan corrected herself; Neve had worn Master white since the early days of the temple. Even with the slowed aging experienced by skilled mages, the corners of Neve's eyes and mouth were crinkled from the passage of time.

"What should we do?" Neve asked in a murmur.

For the dozenth time since their excursion began, Edagan struggled not to frown. "Well, one of us will have to go inspect whatever is going on. Rest assured it's nothing good."

The magelings clustered behind them, most huddling beside the collapsed stone at the back of the cavern. Neve regarded them thoughtfully. Edagan tried not to. They were a pitiful lot, a mix of magelings in every color robe, a muddled mess of gray, lavender, yellow, green, and blue. None useful against trouble, and none of them yet strong enough to aid in the opening of a Gate.

"I'll go see what I can learn," Edagan said as she adjusted the standing collar of her white robe and ignored the few stray strands of white hair that had fallen from her stern bun.

"Are you sure?" Neve asked.

"You're better with the children than I am." Edagan didn't care if some of the magelings were old enough to have children of their own; they were all children compared to her. "Look after my class and I'll be back shortly."

Without waiting for a response, she trudged back out into the ruined corridor and oriented herself to the position of the plume of smoke that rose from temple grounds.

What she was going to do when she reached the temple, she didn't know. For now, she was just relieved to be away from the magelings long enough to think. They were a noisy lot, and their presence was distracting. But they were her magelings. Whether or not she liked being around them, they were her responsibility. She straightened her posture as she walked and pushed them from her mind. As long as they were hidden away with Neve to stand guard, they'd be safe.

The mages in the temple were another story.

Edagan rounded a corner into the last ring of the ruins and froze. The temple walls were only a short distance away, across an open field. The temple itself was quiet and nothing seemed out of order, save the churning cloud of smoke. It rolled steadily from somewhere in the temple grounds, the mark of a constant flame, and the air sizzled with enough power to make her stomach turn.

In spite of the smoke, the temple grounds were quiet and still.

She started forward and took only a handful of steps before a lone figure in white emerged from the shrubbery that filled a gap in the temple wall. The gardens had once been sufficient for privacy; the mage-barrier kept out intruders more effectively than walls ever would.

Whoever it was, the Master saw her and signaled for her to stay put. Edagan retreated to crouch behind the crumbling outer wall of the ruins. Her knees protested, but she remained still.

The Master mage across the field lingered beside the bushes for a long time, then bolted across the field as if afraid to be seen. He'd come halfway before she caught a sense of his Gift, letting her identify him before her aging eyesight could make out his face. Balen was the Master of the House of Fire. What reason did he have to be sneaking about, unless something had gone terribly wrong?

"What in the world is going on?" Edagan snarled in a whisper the moment he was close enough to hear.

"Walk," Balen replied, taking her by the elbow and guiding her farther from the temple.

Free magic still burned in her senses, though it faded as they moved. She growled beneath her breath. "Speak, boy."

"Anaide and Shymin are in the Archmage's tower," Balen murmured. He was unflappable as always, calmer than she thought a Master of Fire should be, but that was one of the reasons they'd chosen him as Alira's successor. The Master of a House needed to be calm, patient, and good with magelings. Or calm and patient at least, Edagan thought ruefully.

"I was the only one outside when the Gate opened." Balen paused, looking back and forth. Edagan turned him in the right direction and continued toward the refuge where her class awaited while he went on. "The king came through with his daughter in his arms."

Edagan stopped mid-stride. "That's the best news you could have brought!"

"No," Balen said, hurrying her onward. Worry puckered his brow. That sort of expression on him was reason enough to be concerned. "He's a prisoner, I believe. He's in the company of... of the previous Archmage, I think."

"You think?" She tried not to scoff. "She raised you as Master!"

"If it is her, she's... changed, Master Edagan." His tone was stiff, uncomfortably formal.

It made her stomach lurch. "Lifetree's mercy," she breathed, stopping to rest a hand on the wall beside her for support. The free magic burning in the air suddenly made sense. It wasn't Ran. It was worse. "She's done it to herself, hasn't she?"

Balen paused a few steps ahead. "Done what?"

She dared not try to explain. "We'll go down," Edagan said, steeling herself and moving on. "Chisel our way to Core. We'll have to get word to the capital somehow." How they would manage that, she didn't know. Even with three Masters and a whole gaggle of magelings with an earth affinity, it would take hours to dig their way through the collapsed stone and find a way to Core. Even if they managed it sooner, who knew how long it would take to find their way out of the tunnels? Her strength in her element gave them an advantage, but even that would only get them so far.

Belatedly, she realized she hadn't asked about the fire. "The smoke, what is that?"

"A disagreement between Envesi and Anaide."

She moaned. "And when she comes face to face with the Archmage, I expect it will only be worse."

"The Archmage is in Ilmenhith," Balen said.

"Ilmenhith? Why?" Edagan shook her head. "No, don't answer that. Whatever the reason, it's a blessing right now. We must figure out how to get a message to her."

"I asked a group of Masters to send word to Wethertree before I came to find you. With fortune, they've managed to do it. The mages in Wethertree were meant to send mages from the countryside to Ilmenhith. If they're still in Wethertree, they will know how to reach the queen."

"You've done well, Balen."

He blinked in surprise. And with good reason; she didn't offer praise lightly or often.

She didn't give him time to bask in it. "Now roll up your sleeves," she said, doing just that as she descended into the collapsed cavern where Neve and the magelings waited. "We have rocks to move."

They may as well have been a mountain.

RESTLESS DISCONTENT

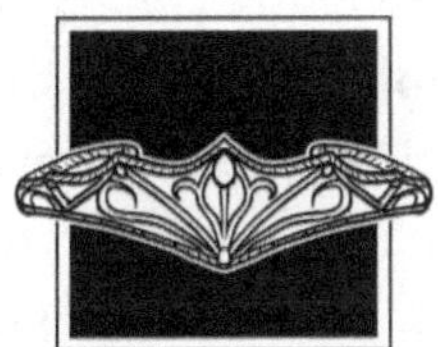

Unseasonably cold rain pattered against the glass in the parlor's front windows. Rhyllyn hovered beside them, his fingers twitching with the desire to wipe the droplets away. He could, from inside; all he had to do was use his magic. The power came so easily now, but he knew wiping the window clean would change nothing. He'd see no better in the water's absence, and the path on the other side of the glass would still be empty.

Behind him, the soft rustle of fabric announced the fact he was no longer alone. He was always aware of Alira's presence, to an extent, but it felt different when she was nearby. Her Gift whined in his senses, like a mosquito hovering beside his ear. Unsettled by the comparison his own thoughts provided, he brushed a hand over the side of his head, as if to ward away the buzz.

"He's not coming back, dear heart." Alira's voice was soft and tried to be soothing, but it only served to make him more miserable.

"You don't know that," Rhyllyn murmured, and he surprised himself with how much he meant it.

Alira had no more than returned from Roberian's capital city. She'd seen the uproar herself. Surely the Triad wouldn't have churned itself into a fury over the mere possibility of a hero being slain.

She sighed. "You only hurt yourself by coming to the window like this. I know you must grieve, Rhyllyn, but please, let someone be there for you. If not me, then one of your friends."

He'd tried to stop returning to look out the window, but he didn't tell her that. As the hours slid by, it grew to be something like a sore he couldn't stop picking. He should have been baking, studying, practicing with his instruments—anything other than standing in the small parlor in the front corner of the house, staring out through the glass as if he might see something on the other side.

His brother had never even gotten a chance to unpack his bags.

"He's faced plenty of horrible things and come back in one piece," he said after a time. "He's traveled all over. Faced monsters and thieves. He's been to war so many times. How could he survive all of those and not this?"

Alira couldn't quite restrain her snort. "Half the stories he's told you are gross exaggerations."

"You don't know that," he found himself repeating. "And just imagine the stories he hasn't told me."

This time, her sigh was heavy, defeated. "Very well. I'll let you brood. I'll be in the kitchen if you need me. We still need to eat."

"Yes, ma'am," Rhyllyn agreed absentmindedly as she retreated from the doorway. He let himself stare at the empty, muddy path outside for a moment longer, then finally pulled himself away.

No matter the situation, he didn't want to be labeled as *brooding*. He wasn't that sort of person, but his brother was, and the last thing Rhyllyn needed was for that comparison to be drawn.

He'd been alone in the house plenty of times, but he didn't

know how to explain things to Alira. The whole house felt tense, tight, like the spring-wound butterflies Rune had made to entertain him when he'd been small. It felt no different than any of the other times his brother had left on an expedition. The manor waited, and Rhyllyn waited with it.

Instead of lingering in the dim, gloomy parlor, he made his feet move. His claws clicked against the fine parquet flooring in the foyer as he padded across it. He probably should have turned down the hall, gone to see if Alira needed help in the kitchen, but he couldn't make himself seek her out so soon. Instead, he crossed into the study on the other side of the house.

If the parlor was dim, the study was downright shadowy. It was best for the books, Rune always said, though Rhyllyn suspected the thick curtains had more to do with his desire to shut out the world when he was studying than any urge to protect the countless volumes that lined the shelves. Most of the books were not uncommon or even particularly valuable, as far as Rhyllyn knew, and there had been times he passed the study door and saw a glint of sunlight beneath its edge.

He wished it were sunny enough to let some light in now. Instead, he waved a hand over one of the fine oil lamps that sat nestled among books and papers on his brother's wide desk. A flame sprang to life inside and he blinked against the glare.

A handful of Rhyllyn's instruments sat in the study; it was his favorite place to practice, and when Rune was home, he seemed to enjoy the music. Rhyllyn brushed his clawed fingers over the neck of his favorite lute and was rewarded with a few soft notes, but his eyes traveled to the large map pinned to the wall above the desk instead.

Dozens—if not hundreds—of marks colored its surface. The chalks were somewhere in the desk's top drawer, if Rhyllyn remembered right. He pulled it open and rooted around for the box.

Some of the marks represented places he'd been. He'd chosen a cheerful orange as his color, while Rune's marks were a combination of blue, red, and green that apparently meant something, though Rhyllyn couldn't fathom what. Some areas were shaded in, others circled, but for all that the known world was wide, there was little left untouched by chalk.

He found a piece of red, instead of his orange, and turned it between his claws.

Most of his brother's time had been dominated by his exploration, a search for the Alda'anan mages Rhyllyn had never so much as met, but whose existence had still shaped his life. Despite the time he spent traveling, Rune had always found time to be present for him—and when it came down to it, that was what Rhyllyn believed he missed the most.

A return from travel was supposed to be a joyous time. A time for new stories, new songs, new trinkets brought back as gifts for loved ones and friends. Instead, it had heralded quiet, discontent, and yes, grief.

Rhyllyn swallowed thickly and raised his chalk.

"I've warmed some bread and fruit preserves from the cellar," Alira announced from somewhere beyond the open door. "I thought you might—" She stopped short as she reached the doorway and saw him before the desk. "What are you doing?"

"I asked him why he didn't look here, once," Rhyllyn said, his hand hovering over the map. "He grew quiet when I did. That was how I knew what it was." A home he'd always known existed, that his brother refused to speak of.

Alira tilted her head and watched as he pressed the chalk to a tiny point near the center of the ocean, halfway between the north and south.

"He said, 'Ithilear's a big world. In a place as small as that, people don't even know the world has a name.' But he never told me anything else." Slowly, Rhyllyn twisted the chalk, leaving a bold red mark atop the island's delicate outline. "It's so small, the country's name isn't even printed on the map. But I guess now he'll know if the Alda'anan ever reached it, won't he?"

As he lifted the chalk from the map, the colors blurred. It took him a moment to realize there were tears in his eyes.

Wordlessly, Alira swept into the study and gathered him into her arms.

Though he felt no shame for his display of emotion, he worked to hold back his tears. Letting them loose was tantamount to admitting defeat, and until he received word or Garam returned alone, he chose to cling to hope.

They were closely matched in height, and Alira cradled the back of his head to settle his brow against her shoulder. He relented and allowed that much, though he bit his tongue and inhaled deep to keep hold of his emotions. After a time, he wrapped his arms around her ribs and let himself be comforted. If Rune had become his brother, Alira was the closest thing to a mother he'd ever known, and he was not too old to admit he still needed to be mothered sometimes.

"It just isn't fair," he murmured into her white robes.

"It isn't," she agreed. "But if things were fair, he never would have left that island, and we wouldn't have met, dear heart."

Rhyllyn rolled his eyes and held back a huff as he removed himself from her embrace. "That doesn't make it better." Nor had it made things better when his brother said the same thing.

"No, but it may bring you peace, in time. Come. Eat." She beckoned him toward the hallway.

Reluctantly, he followed.

The kitchen was no cheerier than the rest of the house, but with the fire in the oven stoked, it was warm enough to chase away the chill of the rain. Alira led the way to the worn wooden table where they took most of their meals, and Rhyllyn sat with a frown.

She crossed to the counter once he was settled. "Let me make you some tea. There are things we should probably discuss."

"I don't want to talk."

"Then you can listen." Alira waved her fingers over the kettle and it began to steam. Her sway over fire was always impressive, but given what he knew of her history, it was no surprise.

Rhyllyn slouched, but didn't argue. A moment later, she sat a plate of warm bread and berry jam before him, followed by a cup of hot tea.

She sat across the table from him with her own cup in her hands. "Tomorrow morning, we will need to visit the capital."

"Roberian?" He curled his fingers around his tea and found himself grateful for the warmth that seeped into his scales.

"The Royal City. I had hoped to go alone, but I think it will be best if I take you with me." Her grip on her cup tightened. "I already told you the news was not well received. Your brother always was an influential man, and between the king's mages and the Iron Children, it seems there are spaces that will need to be filled."

The suggestion was so blunt, it made his skin crawl. "It's too early to discuss who's going to replace him."

"Rhyllyn. The entirety of his estate falls to you, which means there will be social obligations, too."

"He's not dead," Rhyllyn snapped.

"I did not say he was," Alira replied, with more patience than he probably deserved. "But you cannot deny that he left you in charge of things here, and that means you will need to be in charge of his affairs in the Royal City, as well."

He squeezed his eyes closed. "I'm not ready."

"I know. But many things you weren't ready for have befallen you, and you've risen to the challenge every time. I don't ask this of you lightly, dear heart, but if there's any example he's set for you that I hope you're willing to follow, I hope you've learned his courage." A soft note of admiration colored her voice, and Rhyllyn cracked an eye to squint at her.

"I thought you said his stories were exaggerations," he said.

A hint of a smile crossed her lips. "And they are. Surely you don't believe there are things like giant well-worms, or ancient underground trees?"

Rhyllyn picked at the crust of his bread and slouched deeper in his chair. "There might be."

"And I will concede that, but I've certainly seen no evidence." She lifted her cup to her lips and took a long sip of tea. When she lowered it, she sobered, her eyes pinched with concern. "What I have seen evidence of is trouble. If we address nothing else in the Royal City tomorrow, we must visit with Vicamros. I suspect he's in need of a friendly face."

"Fine," he said, and he meant it. Still slumped in his seat, he lifted his bread from his plate and took a large bite. Alira wouldn't ask any questions if his mouth was full, and from the way her eyes narrowed at him, she knew he was avoiding conversation.

Still, it seemed enough to dissuade her from unpleasant topics for now. She sipped her tea again and the kitchen grew quiet, save the soft, distant rumble of thunder outside.

At Alira's insistence, they Gated directly into the palace. The mages present in the Gating parlor frowned at them in disapproval, but Rhyllyn hardly cared. Rune had always come and gone from the palace as freely as he pleased, with or without permission to use the parlor, and Rhyllyn had no reason to think the king would begrudge them an unannounced visit. Especially not when Alira had pushed so hard to get him out of the house.

Though he hated to admit it, the brooding she had accused him of seemed far more appealing than the Royal City. Their direct transport into the palace might spare him from hearing the discontent he was certain had taken the city, but the people in the palace knew him. The moment they stepped from the parlor and passed a handful of guards outside its door, he received his first sympathetic glance.

He's not dead. He fixed the thought firmly in his mind and kept his face from showing feeling as they traversed the palace with Alira in the lead.

Halfway up the winding hall, she flagged down a councilor. "Is King Vicamros in his council, or is he in the throne room downstairs?"

"His private offices," the man answered in a murmur. His eyes flicked Rhyllyn's way, but there was no apology in his glance. Instead, his gaze darted away again, quick as a dragonfly.

Rhyllyn lifted his chin. How many of the wretched councilors had pushed to have his brother sent to hang? The only council members he could be sure were friends were Redoram and Garam, and Garam had not yet returned. *Which means he's still alive,* Rhyllyn reminded himself. *Until Garam comes back, he has to be.*

Alira offered a brusque thank-you and returned to Rhyllyn's side. "Come," she said as she took his arm. "He'll be happy to see you, I'm sure."

"I'm sure," Rhyllyn repeated in a grumble.

She escorted him to the king's office, offering a polite nod to each and every guard stationed along the way—and there were many. More than Rhyllyn was accustomed to seeing, with a half-dozen of the king's personal guards stationed just outside the office door.

He tried to hold to his sour mood as she knocked, but the moment the door opened and it was the king himself who stood on the other side, all his frustration slipped away.

Vicamros straightened and wiped a hand over his face, though it did nothing to hide his weariness. Deep shadows smudged the space beneath his eyes, and his expression could be described as nothing other than bleak.

"Alira," the king said, his voice far more rough than usual. "I didn't expect you. Or you." His eyes drifted to Rhyllyn, and a new line of worry threaded itself between his brows.

"Majesty." Alira spread her white skirts and dipped in a

curtsy, then nudged Rhyllyn's side as if to remind him to show the same respect.

Instead, Rhyllyn stepped forward and wrapped his arms around the king's ribs.

A pair of guards surged toward him, but Vicamros raised a hand as he stumbled back a step and then regained his balance. His arms closed around Rhyllyn's shoulders, and from the way they tightened until it grew difficult to breathe, Rhyllyn knew the king needed it even more than he did.

"Come inside," Vicamros said at last, motioning for Alira to join them. The half-dozen men outside the door moved to follow her, but the king raised two fingers, and only two slipped inside. Once they closed the door, he returned to his desk and sat with a heavy sigh.

"Are you well, Majesty?" Alira asked.

Vicamros's mouth twisted with something that was halfway between a grimace and a rueful smile. "No. I've not slept."

"I can tell," Rhyllyn said.

The king seemed to deflate. "I fear I've made a grave mistake."

"I think you're right," Rhyllyn agreed.

Alira shot him a warning look.

He ducked his head and pushed his clawed toes at the plush carpet underfoot. "He said it."

"I did say it." Vicamros leaned his elbows against his desk and rubbed his forehead. "And I mean it. I've gone over the council meetings in my head so many times, and I can't see any other way to handle things, yet..." The sigh that escaped him said enough without him needing to finish.

Rhyllyn crept forward. There were no empty chairs in the king's office, so he stood before the desk instead. "He went by choice, Cam. He knows what he's doing."

"And I wish I knew what that meant." Vicamros lifted his eyes to Alira, hopeful.

She merely shrugged in response.

His shoulders sagged and he reached for a paper. "In any case, I'm glad the two of you are here. The council is satisfied with the decision made, but there are a number of groups who are less forgiving. Councilor Parthanus holds a great deal of sway over the scholars these days, and they seem to feel they've been robbed of an asset."

"They aren't without a free mage," Alira said. "It will take time, but Rhyllyn will be able to continue any projects they began and were unable to complete."

Rhyllyn tried to smile, but found he couldn't. One of those projects was determining the source of the corruption in his brother's magic, in hopes it could be cleansed without the Alda'anan. Without Rune, was there any reason to continue? Rhyllyn had scales of his own, but they didn't bother him like they'd bothered his brother.

He caught himself too late and his brow furrowed. How easy it was to slip into thinking of someone as gone.

"Do you disagree?" Vicamros asked.

"No," Rhyllyn said hastily, mindful to return his face to neutrality. "Just thinking. It's... it's a big role to step into."

"And not one you're eager to take, I'm sure."

"No," he repeated, softer. "It's too soon."

The king nodded as if the statement had lifted a burden from him. "Then we will wait. For now, I will instruct the scholars to give you time. That will likely appease them, but I'm not convinced the Children will be so easy to please."

"They never are," Alira sighed.

Rhyllyn was more eager to work with the scholars than the Iron Children. That was one role he doubted he could fill with ease. Everything they did revolved around machinery and its development, and Rhyllyn was no engineer. Nor did he share their disdain for magic, which was what drew their council together in the first place—and drew his brother into their midst. There were some practices Rhyllyn agreed with, and he enjoyed seeing the creations their society produced, but he held no desire to be part of their work.

"Maybe you can just tell them to wait, too," he suggested halfheartedly.

That drew a chuckle from the king. "Somehow, I don't think that'll work."

"Why not?" Rhyllyn fidgeted where he stood, feeling more a child than he ought in the company of a friend.

"Their motto," Vicamros said, and the distant look in his eyes gave him the appearance of a man haunted by the events he'd tried to halt. "Progress never waits."

18

DISTRACTION

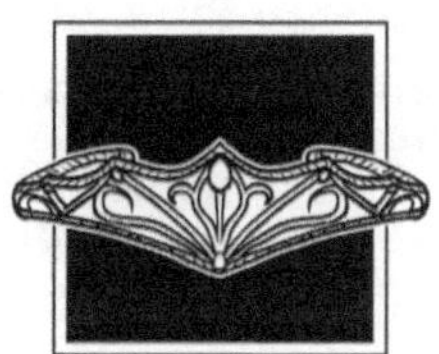

RIKKA WATCHED UNTIL THE WHITE OF BALEN'S ROBE VANISHED INTO the ruins. Only then did she allow herself a sigh of relief. Somehow, she feared more for the safety of the mages outside the temple than that of those within it. Perhaps because as long as they were in the temple, they could be conquered along with it. Those who ran put themselves at risk.

She spun from the gardens and hurried back to the tower. Part of her wanted to flee alongside him, but with Anaide and Shymin trapped in the tower and Edagan already in the ruins, there was no one else left with the authority to carry warning to Kytenia and the queen.

Yet she still wanted to run. Running was easier than facing the anger that swelled within her and threatened to burn her up from the inside out. The woman in the tower with the other Masters was worse than an enemy to the temple or the kingdom. Envesi's actions had left Ilmenhith crippled when it needed mages the most. The lack of power had driven magelings onto the battlefield to quell a fight that wasn't theirs. In that battle, Rikka had lost her dearest friend.

Pushing away thoughts of Marreli's death was a struggle. They fought Rikka's efforts to focus, even as she gathered every white-robed mage on the first two floors of the Archmage's tower and waited in tense fear for them to combine forces and open a Gate. She didn't have time to dwell on old anger, even if the loss still ached every time it crossed her mind. Right now, the queen needed her.

The thought tumbled free before she caught it and Rikka gave her head a twitch as if to discourage any others. It had grown hard, over the years, to think of Firal as her friend. Firal was the queen first and a mage second; friendship came somewhere after that. Friendship with all her former comrades seemed to come somewhere after that. Rikka's duties as a Master mage consumed her.

Or maybe she'd surrendered herself to them after her friend's death, as a means of protection for her own tender heart. There had been a time where Shymin, trapped farther up the tower in the presence of the treacherous former Archmage, had been something like a sister to her as well. Yet the fear and anger that clawed at Rikka's belly didn't touch her guarded heart. These days, it seemed nothing did.

Except Balen, she thought as the portal stabilized and she pushed through to the other side.

After so many years, perhaps another friend had begun to worm his way in.

The courtyard was not as lively as Rune remembered. In his youth, he'd stood and watched for hours while the guards trained below. There had been numerous rows of them then. Now, only a handful of men in off-white gambesons worked their blades in the yard outside the castle's barracks. The curve of their blades marked them as cavalrymen. As few as the island's horses were, Rune had always found it curious that so many soldiers trained as part of the cavalry.

"Did you bring your sword?"

Rune started and twisted away from the window.

Ordin didn't smile, but a hint of interest lit his eyes.

It was unlikely the captain would bat an eye at the unusual blade being in his ownership, but Rune was unwilling to risk an oppositional reaction. It had graced his father's side for too many years to go unnoticed here. "Why do you ask?"

"Because you look like you want to join them." The captain nodded toward the windows. "A good number of the horsemen have gone with the mage recovery party. Those who remain would probably benefit from a little excitement."

Rune snorted. "The last thing I want to do is rile up a bunch of guards who don't recognize me. Besides, I'm not allowed out of the palace."

"It's a big palace," Ordin said. "There are other places to practice."

Half a dozen came to mind before Rune dismissed the idea with a frown.

"Unless you don't participate in swordplay anymore?" The captain raised a brow.

"On the contrary," Rune muttered, "I participate more often than I'd like."

Ordin spread his hands in invitation. "Indulge me, then."

"The Captain of the Royal Guard sparring with a prisoner who's skirting execution probably isn't the best look."

"There's no reason they have to see." The captain glanced out the window. "I have my own reasons for curiosity."

Rune drew back from the sunlight. "So you can know what to expect if I turn on you?"

"So I can see how far my student has come." Ordin's eyes glazed as he watched the men below. "I've trained a lot of men. Most of them, I know what they're capable of. I've seen them continue to develop their skill, or else seen them give up and pursue other things."

"And I'm a mystery," Rune finished for him. "What if I like it that way?"

The captain cracked a sly grin. "I always assumed you did."

A hint of guilt tugged at Rune's heart. Looking back, it had become harder to rationalize the need to hide his nature. His father had feared his exclusion or mistreatment. Yet the people of the Triad had accepted him, as had the ruin-folk. Some feared him, and Rune supposed that was their right, but he'd earned respect and made a name for himself among both groups. Why had it been necessary to hide from his own people?

"My father should have told you," Rune said at last.

Ordin inclined his head in the slightest nod of agreement. "Perhaps we wouldn't be here now."

"I'd settle for escaping the noose." Slowly, Rune turned to retreat down the wide hall. "I'd imagine the ballroom is empty?"

The captain turned after him with a new spring in his step. "I can't see why it wouldn't be."

"And you don't have anything better to do?"

"The mages will need me before long, but I can spare a few minutes. In full honesty, I'd appreciate a bit of a distraction." The captain fell in to walk at his side.

Rune nodded. "Then bring me a sword."

"What's your preference?"

"Hand and a half."

"Like your father," Ordin noted.

Again, Rune nodded. "I used his blades a lot. Always wanted to be just like him. I suppose I always fell short."

"I think he would disagree," the captain murmured.

Rune shrugged. "It doesn't matter. He's dead."

They parted ways at the foot of the stairs. The captain disappeared around the corner while Rune carved a path through the heart of the palace, toward the ballroom he'd come to resent. In his youth, the room had filled him with anxieties. Fear he'd be discovered as the monster he was had dominated so much of his life.

Serving staff watched him pass, their expressions ranging

from curiosity to fright. Good. Let them be afraid. After all the years he'd struggled with fear, it was someone else's turn.

When he reached the ballroom, it was not dark, but the pillars that stretched to the ceiling cast strange shadows in what daylight filtered through the glass skylights. At the far end of the room, the balcony that overlooked it all seemed shrouded in shadow, the space at the balustrade where his father had watched every event heartachingly empty.

Rune stood staring at that empty place when the Captain of the Guard rejoined him with a second sheathed blade held at his side.

"Hand and a half," Ordin said as he passed it over.

Rune curled a clawed hand around the sheath and raised a brow at the weight. His father had always reserved the best blades for his use and that of his personal entourage. Curious, he pushed the hilt with his thumb and slid the sword free. It rasped softly against the edge of the scabbard and gleamed in the weak light. "Whose is this?"

"Mine." The captain stepped back and drew the sword belted at his hip.

"I thought you favored longswords?" Rune laid the scabbard on the marble floor and paced forward to join Ordin in the open center of the ballroom.

"I did, when I was younger." The captain moved through a few forms etched into Rune's memory from drills. "I suffered an injury in my left shoulder that made it harder to rely on."

On the third form, Rune joined him, their movements fluid and synchronized. "Dangerous information to give an enemy."

"Are you?" Ordin asked, the question so mild it seemed he didn't care to hear the answer.

Rune considered for a moment before he answered. "Perhaps. Your queen seems determined to make it so."

The captain made a soft sound of disappointment in his throat as he led the transition into a new stance. "There are rumors in the palace."

"There always are." The sword in Rune's hand bore a pleasant balance, though it was a shade heavier than the kingsword he'd grown accustomed to. He adjusted his grip with the weapon at arm's length.

"What you're doing is dangerous, Ran."

Rune twitched at the name and lowered his blade.

"Not just for you," Ordin continued. "You're putting Firal in danger, too."

Adjusting his grip on his sword again, Rune eased into a combat stance and turned to face his former mentor. "She put herself in danger when she dragged me back here."

"So you do consider yourself a threat?" The captain met his eyes and then moved into an experimental swing. Their blades met in a feather touch and the sharp edges whispered as they slid together.

Rune pulled back. "We should be using wasters. These are good swords."

"We use what I say we use." On the second swing, Ordin did not hold back. The captain lunged in and this time, when Rune raised his blade to block, the metal rang a single sharp, clear note across the empty ballroom.

Not a match to see his skills, then. Nothing for old times' sake. The captain had brought him a real sword for a reason. Although given to his passions, Ordin was a good man and a good judge of character. Right now, at the end of his sword, he was judging Rune.

Dauntless, Rune shifted his balance and abandoned his reserve. The captain wanted a fight. He'd get it. Years of practice gave him remarkable grace with a blade, though if the captain was surprised by the sudden shift from performance to purpose, it did not show.

They were unarmored. The skirmish wouldn't last long. Fast and furious, the blows exchanged either slipped wide or bounded off a deflecting blade. Step by step, Rune pushed the captain back. Anger and frustration fueled every strike, a heated outpouring of feeling he couldn't express any other way.

On the third step, Ordin shifted to defense and a light of uncertainty shaded his eyes. He blocked a blow destined for his head and the force knocked him off balance. The captain staggered back and braced to be struck down.

Rune's sword swept down in a two-handed, overhead strike that stopped a hair's breadth from his one-time teacher's blade.

Slowly, Ordin opened his eyes. Rune hadn't noticed the man had screwed them shut.

Letting his weapon sink to his side, Rune stepped back, breathing hard to catch up with the racing of his heart. "My fight is not with you."

The fight was over, abandoned prematurely, sparing the captain his pride. Ordin grew solemn. "You're an honorable man."

"Worse things have been said about me." Rune twisted his hand to offer the sword, hilt first, back to its owner.

The captain took it, his face grim.

Rune took another step back. "The mages will need you."

"Yes," Ordin said, regarding him with a thoughtful frown. "Or maybe you are what's needed."

Resisting the urge to curse took a great deal of strength. "Go."

Nodding, the captain turned toward the great double doors through which he'd entered. "We'll fight again." The statement was simple, matter-of-fact. Somehow, Rune didn't think he was wrong.

"With luck," he called toward the captain's back, "it'll be on the same side."

19

GHOSTS OF THE PAST

His blood still burned. Rune wiped the back of one hand across his forehead as he leaned against the rail and gazed down into the grand ballroom. He'd already straightened his clothing and smoothed his hair, but the flush of anger that churned to life in that brief match did not want to abate.

Staying his hand hadn't been hard; he'd never intended to harm Ordin. But he hadn't intended to display his full ability, and the fury that had sprung forth in their brief match proved difficult to contain. Halting the fight had offered no relief. Had they been using wasters instead of steel, he would have pushed harder. As it was, instead of the match cooling his head, it left him more like an animal in a rattled cage.

Maybe holding their sparring match in the ballroom had been a bad idea.

The room was spacious and offered the privacy they'd both wanted, but it harbored too many memories. The last time Rune set foot in the ballroom, his father had stood in the exact place he leaned now. He'd approached him then, offered information he'd hoped would quell the storm he knew was coming. Now, looking back, he didn't know how he'd ever believed such a thing possible. He laced his clawed fingers together and closed his eyes.

It had been easy to hide from the gravity of everything he'd done. No one on the mainland knew the atrocities he'd committed, nor did they care. Even now, Garam followed him to what might as well have been the far reaches of the world, more of a companion for moral support than a politician there to carry out business.

Not for the first time, Rune regretted that he'd never been more open with his friends. If they'd known about his father's death, about the blood on his hands and the nightmares it still sometimes gave him, perhaps things would be different. Maybe Vicamros would have fought harder to see him spared.

Or maybe he would have killed him, himself.

"Wouldn't that have been easy for you?" he murmured. Disgusted, Rune pushed himself off the rail.

The last thing he should be doing was wallowing. Every minute he spent in the palace was one minute closer to an execution he couldn't stave off forever. He could almost feel the rope around his neck. Sooner or later, they'd grow tired of giving him slack.

The click of his claws against the cool stone floor seemed loud in the empty ballroom, each tap echoing back to torment him further.

Had they held balls in his absence? Had the traditional masquerade been carried out in the years that followed his father's death? He'd grown so used to the way life moved on the mainland, where he was surrounded by Giftless men and women. The speed at which they lived made it easier to move on. Here, it felt as if no time had lapsed at all.

At least, not in Ilmenhith. Here, the people still knew him, even if they resented him. But he hadn't yet figured out how to reach Core and learn what had become of the ruin-folk he'd once called his people. In the wake of the misunderstandings that surrounded Kifel's demise—misunderstandings he'd originally hoped to eliminate, and in the end only managed to make worse —it was all too easy to assume the punishment he'd received in the palace dungeons had been extended to the ruin-folk, as well.

Rune raked one hand through his hair as he stepped from the ballroom and closed the door behind him. He should have thought to ask Ordin what happened before the man slipped away. No one else in the blighted palace would answer his questions, except maybe Kytenia. Maybe what precious little luck he had would grace him with another opportunity to speak with her.

No more had he fixed that thought in mind than he rounded a corner and found himself blessed with something else.

A pair of men in the hallway turned toward him, one so unexpected that Rune blinked twice and squinted at his face. "Davan?"

The man murmured something to his companion, who nodded and hurried on alone. Then he turned, a hint of uncertainty on his face as he pressed a fist over his heart and offered a slight bow. "Tobias, sir."

"Tobias." Rune's brows rose. Of course it was. It had been years since he'd set foot on the island, and Davan had already been in his prime. "I'm sorry. You just…"

A nervous smile curved Tobias's lips. "No apologies necessary, Lord Daemon. It's an honor to be mistaken for my father."

The title startled him, and Rune's brow crinkled. "I'm surprised you remember me. You were just a child, the last time I saw you."

"You make a strong impression, my lord. Though I must admit it's strange to see you…" Tobias trailed off, though his smile returned with more strength and sincerity. "Time doesn't favor all of us so well." The wings of silver in the younger man's hair spoke of that. His face was worn, pinched, as his father's always had been. The life of the ruin-folk had never been easy, but Rune had hoped to make it easier.

Rune shook his head. "What are you doing here? When I arrived, Firal said the Underlings were no more. I thought—"

Tobias cocked his head. "She said what, now? That makes no sense. The ruin-folk are more plentiful than we've ever been."

A wave of relief hit him so hard that Rune thought he might fall to his knees. "You survived."

"Aye, my lord. Better than, really. After you were..." His mouth twisted and a muscle in his jaw worked a moment before he found diplomatic words. "After your departure, the queen sent a summons for us. My father brought all of Core to Ilmenhith to answer her call."

"Your father is the only man I've known who could have made that happen," Rune murmured. "Is he...?"

"Gone," Tobias said, with wistful fondness in his eyes.

As easily as relief had come, it was washed away by that single word. A deep ache lodged itself in Rune's chest. He swallowed hard and nodded. Medreal. Nondar. Davan. How many of the steadfast figures in his life had been swept away in his absence? "I was honored to have known him. Your father taught me a great deal. He was a good man."

"He often said the same about you."

Rune held back a frown. "I expect that wasn't a popular sentiment, after what happened."

"Why wouldn't it be?" Tobias tilted his head again. The sincerity in the habit was reassuring. "There were plenty of men who saw you on the battlefield. Core knows exactly what you did, and they've always respected you for it."

"What I did?" Rune asked, though haltingly. That word of his duel might have returned to Core with the soldiers had never crossed his mind.

Tobias gave a single nod. "You challenged the king to a duel, sparing the rest of the army. You won, but tried to spare the king's life. You carried yourself with honor until the end. When you were taken, no one blamed you. We had hoped you would be released, but no one seemed to know what came after that."

Honor. There was a word he heard too rarely. Rune gave a soft snort. "I wish my recollection of the night was as favorable."

"I don't imagine it ended as well for you as it did for Core's army." The look Tobias gave him was weighted with knowledge and sympathy. Had he heard, somehow, what imprisonment had entailed? Or was it an assumption, based on the cruelties the Underling queen had once inflicted on those who crossed her?

Rune chose not to ask and instead returned to his previous question. "Did all of you stay in Ilmenhith?"

Tobias shook his head. "Some did. Most of us returned to Core at the queen's behest. It's a good home, and it has everything we need. The majority of the ruin-folk were happy to return, but the ruins are considered part of Queen Firal's lands, now. We're hers, and so is the mine."

The mine. The reason Rune had swayed Vicamros to ally with Elenhiise. Of course she would have sent people back to manage it. He didn't know whether to be thankful, or curse himself for making the island so useful.

"My father served as the mine's overseer and a part of Ilmenhith's council," Tobias continued. "I took over once he passed on. I'm not in Ilmenhith often, but when my queen calls, I answer."

"As if you have a choice," Rune muttered, rubbing the back of his neck. But why had she called Tobias, of all people? To issue orders, or to taunt Rune with her control over his people?

A hint of nervousness returned to the man's face. "I was not present when you were brought before the throne, but I heard what happened. I won't pretend to understand what's taken place between the two of you, and I'd prefer not to know. She's asked me to guard the Gate in the mine, and I will, but I won't be involved beyond that. Once the mages she's sending are ready, I'll be going back to Core."

"What will you do until then?" Part of him hoped it would take a while for Tobias to depart. Rune had often hoped word of the ruin-folk and how they fared would make its way through the trade Gates, but it never had. The opportunity to ask questions was precious, but there was a stiffness in the way Tobias stood that said he wasn't sure how to behave around their one-time leader. Pressing would do no good, but if the man was bored, perhaps he'd be willing to seek deeper conversation.

Tobias shrugged. "I was on my way to the library."

Not the answer Rune expected. "Is literacy more common among your people, now?"

"Yes, but I'd actually hoped to speak to the scholars. We've been stuck on how to repair one of the lifts for some time. I was hoping to see if they'd made progress in solving the problem."

Rune straightened. "Are the schematics here?"

"Yes, there are copies in the library here, in the temple, and in Core, of course." Tobias hesitated a moment, then offered a smile Rune dared say was almost timid. "Would you care to see them?"

"I would love nothing more," Rune said, and the eager honesty that seeped into his voice seemed to put the man at ease. He'd frequented the library in his youth. There was a chance the scholars would recognize him, too, and the more people who realized who he was without him having to say it, the more likely he was to escape whatever fate Firal had planned. Already, the invisible noose around his neck seemed a little looser.

He motioned for Tobias to lead the way, and he did.

"I understand we have you to thank for a good portion of the repairs," Tobias said as they walked.

"How do you figure? I wasn't here. The lifts weren't operational when I went into exile."

The man shrugged. "My father said your research and notes were what got them started. A good portion of the work had to be completed by mages, which was easier, after we settled under Queen Firal's rule and the temple mages became our allies, but he assumed you'd intended to manage most of the repairs yourself."

"I had," Rune admitted. "I simply never had time."

"A problem many of us face," Tobias said.

They scaled to the second floor and Rune shared several shortcuts through the halls. Eventually, they arrived at the library's doors, and he motioned for Tobias to precede him. The younger man nodded his thanks, and Rune found himself wondering briefly at how easy it was to think of him as young. Tobias was more than a hundred years his junior, yet he'd aged like any other Giftless man. His life would be fast and fleeting, and he'd lay on his deathbed before lines of age found their way to Rune's face—if that happened at all.

He'd once assumed he would age like the Eldani and walk the world for several hundred years. That was before he'd understood the near-immortality of free mages. With his power sealed, would he pass before Firal, or after?

Before, idiot, he reminded himself with a quiet snort. *You're still slated for execution if you don't cooperate.*

"Here we are," Tobias announced. He pulled a thick roll of paper from a rack and double-checked the label on its end before he used the roll to point at a table. "Move those books there, will you?"

All too happy to abandon that dismal train of thought, Rune gathered the books and moved them to a nearby desk while Tobias spread the schematics out on the table and found weights to hold the corners.

Across the room, one of the librarians peered at them from behind a large table, but made no move to stop them, or even investigate what they were after. Rune opened his mouth to ask which of the scholars were involved in the study of the ancient lifts, but halted when he felt the weight of the librarian's eyes. He stared back, silently willing the man to recognize him.

Tobias didn't seem to notice the exchange. He traced outlines on the map and motioned for Rune to join him.

The battle of wills ended, and Rune tore his eyes away to return to the table. The map of the underground was incomplete, but it didn't matter. The important parts were there.

"We've gotten most of them running," Tobias said as he fished a box from the broad map table's drawer. He took a handful of colored glass stones from the box and laid them on a number of circles Rune recognized as lift locations. "Some better than others, but that's likely the best we can hope for. They're as old as Core, and who knows how old that is."

"Might as well be as old as the world itself." Rune touched a claw to one of the circles left unmarked. "This one?"

Tobias blinked at him. "How did you know?"

"Because it always gave me trouble." There was a box of chalk in the drawer, too, if Rune remembered right. He searched for it with one hand while he studied the others. "It looks like almost all of the rest are operational. How long has this taken?"

"Her Majesty put a lot of effort into getting the ones related to mine function working in the first year of her rule." The glass stones came in multiple colors, and Tobias rearranged them to color-code the lifts that had been working longest. The green stones gleamed in the soft light.

Rune studied their layout for a time, then nodded. "Makes sense. The more lifts working, the better the mine's production. Faster getting things in and out, at least."

"Aye. Fast as we can, anyway. It would be better if we had an alternative to the hand carts. The deeper the mine shafts get, the harder it is to transport waste rock and ore."

Two or three of the lifts that remained without stones were ones Rune knew he had examined. Studying the mechanics left by the Alda'anan—a people he hadn't known existed then—had been one of his favorite pastimes in his youth. Strange to think how they had influenced him, even then. "I have suggestions for that. Get me a paper?"

Before Tobias could take a step, the librarian appeared at his side with a sheaf of paper in hand. He laid it atop the map without a word and returned to the rolled maps to retrieve another.

Rune took the top sheet and gripped a piece of chalk

between the first knuckles on his first two fingers. "I'm sure I don't need to explain the idea of a rail cart?" He sketched lightly at first, tracing hallways he recognized as mine shafts onto the new paper. Then he drew in rail paths and junctions, and sketched examples of what the rails at each junction might look like.

"I can guess what it means," Tobias said. He craned his neck to study the illustration. "These levers would move the rail?"

"So the cart never has to be removed from them, yes. They'd allow you to switch the path the cart takes." A drawing of the lever mechanism went down on the paper, followed by an example of what the cart itself might look like.

"They have these on the mainland?"

Rune rocked his free hand. "They're in development. Some of the mines in the northern parts of Roberian have begun to implement them, but mostly, Vicamros wants to use rail systems for transport of people and goods. We've been working on it for years, but there's been some opposition, so progress is slow."

"We?" Tobias asked.

"A group of scholars in the Royal City," Rune said. "I enjoy working with them, when I can. They like building things and I'm good at breaking things, so we make a good team."

Tobias snorted a laugh.

"Here are the diagrams showing how the known lifts operate," the librarian put in as he laid a handful of rolls at the edge of the table. "Will anything else be needed, Your Highness?"

The chalk snapped between Rune's fingers. His eyes flashed to the librarian's face.

The grim older man merely raised a brow.

"No," Rune managed after a moment. "That will do for now. Thank you."

Tobias observed the two of them with a curious tilt to his head.

The librarian returned to his desk without further comment.

He'd recognized him. That much, Rune had hoped for, but the title had been completely unexpected.

He gazed after the old man, his brow furrowed.

"You're remembered most places," Tobias said softly, as if reading his thoughts. Perhaps they were easy to guess. "In Core, you're remembered as a hero."

"But you answer to Firal now," Rune murmured.

Tobias inclined his head. "Aye. And that won't change. She's been good to us. Worked hard to make the Eldani accept us, see that we had value to offer. But if you ever decide to come back, well... there would be a place for you with the ruin-folk, I'm sure."

How many times had he wished for exactly that? A chance to step back into his old life, to pick up where he'd left off? "I wish that were my choice to make." Rune took a new piece of chalk from the box and resumed his drawing. "You'll need to make one of these. It's a hand-car. With a man on either side to work this arm, it'll roll much faster than a man on foot can push it. It's harder to move with a heavy load, but it'll still be faster than dragging handcarts up and down the tunnels."

Tobias took the drawing when it was finished. "You design these with your mainland scholars?"

"Mostly, I damage them after they're built. But you learn how things work when you have them in pieces." There was still the non-functioning lift to think of. Rune turned his attention to the rolled schematics the librarian had brought. He unrolled one and paused. "Where did you get these drawings?"

"Those? They were copied from a book the queen gave us. Why?"

Rune's brows knit. "I kept a journal of diagrams. I drew everything I found. These look like..."

"One of your drawings," the librarian put in from across the room. "I was in charge of copying them from the original volume. The book is in the queen's possession, but if you wish to compare my work to the original, I am sure she would be willing to lend it to me for a time."

"No, thank you." Rune spread the paper atop the map that was already out. "I remember them. Here, Tobias. Did you replace this guide chain?"

The younger man nodded. "Aye. The broken one was a beast to remove, but one of the mages was able to thread it through the channel. She replaced it, too. One of the high-ranking Masters. But the new one doesn't seem to do anything."

"Because there's a wheel inside this wall." Rune tapped a claw against the diagram, right below the chain. "I think the teeth on it are broken, but I never did figure out how to get in there to replace it. A mage with an earth affinity might be able to find a way in."

"Or maybe you could pay Core a visit, yourself," Tobias said.

Rune lifted his head. There was something new in the other man's eyes, a soft, wistful sort of hope that made his stomach lurch. "No," he said after a moment. "I don't... I don't think I can."

The light in Tobias's eyes faded, but he was no more solemn than he had been through their whole conversation. "I understand, Lord Daemon. If you ever change your mind, though..."

"Of course," Rune said, and left it at that. He moved the schematics and stared down at the map as Tobias placed a few more stones and explained where they might find more damaged mechanisms, but the words filtered through his head without understanding.

All his life, he'd sought to make a difference, to aid these people and help make his country whole. Now, he couldn't even aid them in the repair of a simple mechanical lift. Just like he could do nothing to meet Firal's demands.

He closed his eyes and pretended to be lost in thought as the mine's overseer droned on.

How long would the seal on his magic haunt him?

CONFLICTING MESSAGES

SMOKE BILLOWED FROM THE HOLE IN THE WALL. THE STONE ITSELF sizzled, trailing to the floor in glowing rivulets to form molten puddles. The carpeting and furniture scorched around it, even as the glow faded and left rippled slabs of cooling stone in the middle of flickering flames.

Anaide stared in disbelief. The Master of Water had seen many things in her lifetime, but even Lomithrandel—abomination as he was—had never done anything like that.

"Now," Envesi sighed as she eased back into her chair, "let's try to be more civil, shall we?"

Anaide paled, sank into her seat and gripped its arms to keep her hands from shaking. Her knuckles turned white with effort.

The shockwave of energy had missed her head by inches. Now that she'd seen its effect, she didn't think the monster across the parlor had been aiming for her. Envesi had too much control over her power for that. Even now, with all the force of the world at her fingertips, the woman managed to keep her too-blue eyes from glowing. Despite all his training, that was a trick Lomithrandel had never learned.

"As I was saying," Envesi continued, inspecting her claws. She seemed fascinated by her new appearance, which made

Anaide wonder how long it had been since she'd changed. If it was a recent development, then her control over her new and greater gift was even more frightening. It would only get better with time. "The king expects cooperation. If your new Archmage takes issue with that, she may speak of it with him." She sneered as the title she used to hold rolled off her tongue. "It isn't my intention to incapacitate any mages. Every single one of you will be needed. Your value has not diminished, in spite of your wrongdoing against me."

They had done no wrong. Everything said at the meeting that led to Envesi's exile had been true. Anger nettled at her, but Anaide only nodded. She didn't dare snap at the woman again.

"Where is the girl? Your acting Archmage?" Envesi asked.

Anaide hesitated and glanced around the parlor. Edagan was in charge of student exercises today, but the rest of the temple's council had been present. Only Shymin remained, her face a cautious mask of serenity. Where had Balen and Rikka gone? No; she couldn't let herself be distracted. Perhaps one of them had already managed to notify the queen. Or else they'd been captured by the league of rebel mages that came through the portal with Envesi.

The Master of Water wet her lips with her tongue. "Looking for the princess."

Envesi raised a brow. "Is that so? Well, in that case we'd best let everyone know she's with her father. You, there." She turned her head and beckoned Shymin closer.

The Master of Healing remained calm as she came closer, her thin hands clasped in front of her waist. She didn't have the same death grip Anaide had on her chair. The young woman's composure was admirable.

"Carry a message to your queen, letting her know her husband and child are in the temple. With me." The corners of Envesi's mouth curled with a smile that was both amused and savage.

Shymin bowed her head in acknowledgment and turned to

leave without a word. Silently, Anaide prayed the girl would squeeze as much information into the message as possible.

"Naturally, I will assume immediate control of the temple mages. We can't afford to waste time." Envesi rubbed her claws together, smirking. "The king agrees that with magic's existence at stake, I will need every resource at my fingertips. Call your council together so we may decide our next course of action."

"Of course." Anaide faltered over the words, wishing she could remain as collected as the Archmage's sister. Bless the girl; they'd made the right choice in raising her to Master of a House for certain.

Envesi nodded and waved her away. "Go on, then. Not a moment to spare. I'll be in my office."

Anaide bowed her head, pushed herself up and hurried toward the door.

"Oh, and Anaide?"

She paused, turning back to the reptilian monster that lounged with her legs crossed.

Envesi's snake-slitted eyes narrowed. "I will be referred to by my title."

Anaide swallowed against the thick dryness in her mouth and nodded. "Of course," she said, though the words made her stomach turn. "Archmage."

***

The air outside the Gating parlor still hummed with enough energy to make Kytenia's hair stand on end. She rounded the corner into the hallway and skidded to a stop with a yelp.

Rikka clapped a hand to her chest, her blue eyes wide and her cheeks flushed. "There you are!"

"What's happened?" Kytenia asked in a rush, then winced at her own lack of manners. "Are you all right?"

"Fine." Rikka stepped back and smoothed her white robes.

She didn't look fine; she looked shaken to the core. "It's the king. And Firal's daughter. And the Archmage."

Kytenia blinked. "Me?"

"No," Rikka said, grimacing. "The other one."

Her brow furrowed. "Arrick?"

"Envesi," Rikka replied.

Kytenia should have been angry that Rikka used her title for the exiled woman, but she couldn't fault her. There was still a sense of awe that came with Envesi's presence, even without the free magic Rune warned her about. Envesi had been the first Archmage of Elenhiise and had held the title when Kytenia and Rikka were children. The woman had never been anything other than terrifying.

Kytenia hoped she didn't look as wan as she felt. "What has she done?" And what did it have to do with Vahn? The image of him at Envesi's mercy flashed through her head and turned her stomach. After so many years, she still felt something for him, though it had cooled to the sort of warm affection she felt for her siblings.

"They're at the temple," Rikka said, lowering her voice. "She asked to speak to you, but we were holding council. Anaide decided we should meet with her in your absence. I came to you as soon as I could get out the door."

"They? Vahn is there?" Now Kytenia felt ill. He should have been at the other end of the island, rounding up stray mages and sending them to Ilmenhith.

Rikka nodded. "With Lulu. He didn't see me, but I saw him. I think she's taken him prisoner too."

"Then we have to tell Firal." Kytenia picked up her skirts and turned to lead the way. She only made it a handful of steps before she realized she didn't know where Firal was.

Fortune intervened the moment she rounded the corner and found Captain Straes waiting politely out of earshot.

"Captain," Kytenia said, "I need to speak to the queen right away."

He jerked as if surprised. "Shall I find her and send her to meet you, or do you need to accompany me?"

"Archmage," Temar called from behind her.

Kytenia groaned, looking over her shoulder. "Rikka, could you?"

"I'll go with him and tell Firal." Rikka smiled and touched her shoulder in reassurance. "We'll be in the private parlor by her quarters when you're finished. I'm sure it's best we keep this quiet for now."

Forcing a smile of her own, Kytenia nodded. That her sister and one of her dear friends were Masters at the top of the temple was a blessing she was thankful for every day. "I'll be along soon. Don't worry."

Temar waved her back into the Gating parlor and Kytenia hurried to join her, stifling her irritation. What could possibly be more important than telling the queen that her husband had been captured? She tried not to think about the implications of the former Archmage being in the temple. The woman had been stripped of her rank and exiled. There was no doubt it would be an unfriendly meeting.

Kytenia rounded the corner into the parlor with harsh words ready on the tip of her tongue. The moment she saw her sister come through the Gate, they slipped away. Dread turned her heart to ice.

"Oh, you're here!" Shymin smiled, her mage-blue eyes sparkling. "I expected you'd be with Firal. No matter, I can carry a message to her if you wish to return to the temple right away."

Wary, Kytenia lingered beside the door. Shymin's attitude was the complete opposite of Rikka's. Why would her sister be happy when their friend was frightened? "What sort of message?"

"King Vahnil has been reunited with his daughter. They await the queen in the comfort of the temple." Shymin practically beamed as she recounted the news.

"Why didn't they come with you?" Kytenia glanced at the

archway against the wall. She couldn't see the Gate, not from this side, but she felt the last of its crackling power fading as the portal closed. "Surely Vahn's as eager to bring Lulu home as anyone else."

For a moment, her sister's cheery demeanor faltered. "They are in the company of mages who wish to speak to you. Allies who have information they feel is urgent to discuss. Vahn has joined them and agreed that temple business is best kept within the temple."

Allies? Kytenia's skin crawled. Didn't Shymin know Envesi was there? Didn't she know Vahn was a captive? Kytenia inched forward, casting a sidewise glance to Temar. The Master of Ilmenhith watched them both with a frosty look in her eyes. Yes, there was something amiss. Temar saw it, too.

"A messenger came through just a moment ago saying the temple had been invaded by a hostile force," Kytenia said.

Startled, Shymin stiffened. "Who told you that? That's ridiculous."

"A mage sent by Anaide. She said the former Archmage was among them."

Temar straightened, ready to seize the flows of power that drifted on the air.

Shymin hesitated, then nodded with a quiet sigh. "She is. But she means no harm, Kyt. You need to speak with her. You'll understand once you hear what she has to say."

"Understand?" Kytenia almost laughed. "She kidnapped Firal's daughter and murdered the girl's nursemaid!"

"I know," Shymin said, exasperated. "But you have to listen. She knows things, Kyt, things none of us have access to. Knowledge that went with Nondar to the grave. She can fix it! She can stop the decay of magic!"

The determination in her sister's tone sent a chill down her spine. The decay of magic. If Envesi had announced the decay upon her arrival, Shymin should have been surprised, concerned, maybe overcome with disbelief. Instead she spoke with confidence that came from long-held knowledge, while discussing a secret only Anaide and Edagan should have known.

"I don't know what you're talking about," Kytenia lied.

Shymin's face fell. "I know. That's why you must speak with her."

Power lashed out beside them and Shymin shrieked as the air itself wrapped around her like invisible cords.

"Traitor!" Temar snarled as her face crumpled into a vicious scowl. "How could you? The Archmage is your own sister!"

"Temar!" Kytenia barked. She shot a panicked look in her sister's direction, but the order to release her died before it could escape. How could she defend her? She'd been moments away from snaring Shymin on her own.

"The state of magic was a secret sworn to the head of the temple," Temar said. "Her knowledge betrays her."

"As it betrays you," Shymin snapped.

Kytenia raised a finger to order a halt to the argument and glared at the court Master. "Temar, what are you on about?"

The Master of Ilmenhith hesitated, but her grip on the flows of air around them never loosened. "You truly don't know?"

Drawing herself up to look as imposing as she could in a dirty dress, Kytenia peered down her nose at the older woman. "Tell me what you've heard."

"Archmage, I don't think now is the time—"

"Now!"

Temar winced. "I have had many duties in the palace, Archmage. One was to watch over the Uncrowned Prince." She spared a glance for Shymin. "I was told of his purpose, so I could understand the importance of my task."

"And now you." Kytenia turned her glare onto her sister. "How did you learn this?"

"I..." Shymin faltered, her mouth working without producing sound.

"With all due respect, Archmage," Temar said, "I think it best if we speak further in private."

Kytenia's jaw tightened and she gave a stiff nod. "Yes, of course. We shall see what the queen has to say of the matter. Perhaps Her Majesty has heard of this decay of magic, as well."

Shymin flinched at the acid in her tone, but said nothing more. Her stiff posture eased as Temar let her go, but the Master mage stayed close, ready to seize her again. Kytenia was grateful for the intervention, but the knot in her stomach only tightened. She fought the rising illness and stayed composed.

When she'd spoken to Edagan about watching for leaks within the temple, she'd never imagined her own sister might be one of them. Worry, anger, and disgust mingled inside her, creating the most nauseating fury she'd ever experienced.

"Kytenia," Shymin said softly, walking close behind her. "Envesi is trying to help. I know it's difficult to hear after everything that's happened, but I really think you need to speak to her. As Archmage, you owe the temple that much."

Temar made an angry sound deep in her throat.

"The temple still looks to the royal family," Kytenia said, keeping her voice calm through some power she hadn't known she had. "We speak to the queen first. Until then, we will discuss it no more."

Shymin bowed her head and fell silent.

Temar strode beside her until they reached the queen's parlor, where she slipped in ahead of the two of them to be sure Firal was ready to receive them. Kytenia eyed her sister, nervous. If Shymin lashed out at her, would she be able to do what she needed to protect herself? The thought was troubling, but she didn't have long to think before Temar waved them in.

Though Kytenia expected to find Rikka there, the Master of Wind was not in the parlor when Firal beckoned them inside. Likely for the best. Rikka had no love for the previous Archmage. Hearing Shymin take the woman's side might have sent her into a rage. Few people liked Envesi, but they had lost Marreli—Rikka's best friend—in the the war the woman engineered. They all had mourned the mageling's death, but none so deeply as Rikka. They had been the closest thing to sisters. Looking at her own sister now, Kytenia only just began to understand that loss.

Firal stood to greet them, though there was no friendliness in her amber eyes. "What is the meaning of this?"

Kytenia wished she knew. "Shymin comes bearing news from the temple as well. Her version is... different from what you may have already heard."

Lifting her chin, Shymin stepped forward and spread her skirts in a curtsy. "I have spoken to King Vahnil," she announced, making both Temar and Kytenia look at her in surprise.

Firal raised one dark brow. "Before or after he was taken prisoner alongside my daughter?"

"He is nobody's prisoner, Majesty. He is in the temple of his own free will. He is helping Envesi plan actions to instill safeguards that will preserve the existence of magic."

"Don't pretend this is some urgent matter," Firal snapped. "Magic will be here for centuries, no matter how diluted the old blood is. It isn't some limited resource that's at risk of disappearing overnight."

Kytenia stared, dumbfounded. Did *everyone* know? Magic's failing was supposed to be a secret!

"Yes, I know what Envesi thinks she's doing. And I know you all foolishly think the shape of your ears means you're something special." The queen's eyes flashed fire, her cheeks flushed with anger as her gaze fell on Shymin. "It's a lie, fabricated by the very woman you're defending. You've spent your whole life lamenting that you're half human, certain it affects your station in life. It's nonsense. The rest of the world knows better. The Eldani are nothing. Mongrels. There was only one true mage living on this entire blighted island, and Envesi killed her!" Curling her hands to fists at her sides, Firal stormed past them with tears brimming in her eyes.

Kytenia turned after her. "Wait! Firal, where are you going?"

"I've had enough of this," Firal said, heaving the door open and glowering at all three of them. "Throw your sister in prison. Leave her to rot. I won't have corruption breeding in my kingdom. I will have my family back, one way or another, and don't you dare think you have any right to stop me."

The door slammed closed, making all of them wince.

A hush fell over the parlor and lingered until Temar cleared her throat. "Well then," she murmured. "Who are we to disobey the queen?"

Kytenia said nothing and turned to face her sister. All that could happen now would be unpleasant, but the Master of Ilmenhith beside her was right. Who were they to disobey?

"BRING me the reports on the mages returning to Ilmenhith. How many have been found, and how many have arrived." Firal didn't so much as look at the guards as she swept past them on her way out of her private parlor. Only one fell in step behind her. The others ran to fulfill her orders as she made for her office. As if by magic, two more guards appeared in the hallway to station themselves at her office door the moment she arrived. One of the guards slid into her office ahead of her to ensure it was empty. She tried not to roll her eyes. Few people posed any danger to her. With as angry as she was at the moment, the Giftless were not high on the list, and she would have sensed a mage's presence already.

Still, she waited for the guard to emerge and give her the all clear. As she waited, Ordin Straes appeared at her heels.

"Is Rikka well, Captain?" she asked without turning to face him. The guard returned to the doorway and nodded, and Firal stepped inside.

"She'll be all right. She's settled in one of the guest suites. I expect she'll feel better after she has a bite to eat." The captain hesitated at the doorway, sensing her temper. Unwilling to rile her further, he awaited her command.

"Come with me." Firal's tone was curt, but she felt no remorse. "I need to speak to you. And Temar, as soon as she's finished in the dungeons."

Ordin repeated that to one of the men by the door and the guard hurried away to retrieve the court Master. Then the captain cleared his throat and followed Firal to her desk. "May I ask why Temar is in the dungeons?"

"Not now." She'd barely taken her seat before the door swung open and a white-robed mage hurried in with an armful of papers. Not Temar, but the answer to Firal's first order.

The Master plopped her collection of papers onto the desk, bowed to the queen and then to the captain, and waited for the flick of Firal's fingers before she took her leave.

Firal bit her tongue to hold back a sigh after the woman departed. The papers delivered were a jumble of rolled maps and missives, along with a few pages that were unrelated, save a few hasty notes scribbled in their margins. She shouldn't have expected proper reports and records so soon after Vahn's departure, but a handful of days should have been enough to at least begin organization.

Ordin's brow creased and he ran his fingers over the curled edge of a map. "Mage outposts?"

Sparing a glance for the open door, Firal spun a hasty ward around them. "If the temple is under siege, I need to know the location of every last mage on the island." Every mage trapped inside the temple was one more shred of hope Envesi could tear away from them. Were the temple mages prisoners, too? Or were they there with the former Archmage by choice? Firal thought of Vahn and their daughter and her throat constricted.

As skilled a fighter as he was, Vahn was not Gifted. He couldn't hope to defend himself against mages of any persuasion. If any of the traitors raised a hand against him, would anyone come to his aid?

Ordin tapped a finger against the hilt of his sword and frowned in thought. "Should I summon Master Rikka? She may be able to give you an estimated number of mages currently in the temple."

"No, not yet. Rikka will need her rest. Kytenia will be able to answer that question. Summon her along with Temar, but send another mage down to replace them. We will need a Master posted in the dungeons at all times." Firal had never imagined she might have to give such an order. To her knowledge, the only other time a mage had been imprisoned in Ilmenhith was when... She caught her lower lip in her teeth.

Had there been mages posted there to keep him from reaching the flows of power that hovered all around them? She didn't recall it being necessary. How had they kept him from using his Gift? Or had they? He'd escaped while she cast Envesi through a Gate to the mainland, exiling the woman to the Grand College in Lore. Perhaps he'd merely waited until everyone was too distracted to notice him wielding the power he needed to break free of his chains.

Firal blinked to clear tears from her eyes and gave her head a small shake. Thoughts of Rune made anger bubble inside her. She couldn't afford that distraction now.

"If you would, Ordin, also summon a maid with a tray for tea. Mint, if you please." She didn't exactly feel ill, but there was an uneasy knot in her stomach that made her think any additional stress would make her vomit.

"As you wish, Majesty." The captain bowed from the waist with a hand to his heart, then retreated beyond the ward to relate further instructions to his men.

Letting the ward fall, Firal unfurled a map across her desk, dropped weights on its corners, and traced chalk notations with her fingertips.

Most of the mages from Wethertree had returned, leaving only enough Masters behind to open Gates for the transportation of those the king's men were supposed to send back to the temple or Ilmenhith's chapter house. So far, only a handful more mages had appeared, though messages had come from a half-dozen others to verify their impending return to the capital.

She followed the names of mages and outposts from those messages, drawing a curving line down from Wethertree toward Eldril. That was the region Vahn must have been taken from. If she sent a team of mages back to investigate, perhaps she could gather a list of names and identify some of the traitors.

Could she spare any mages for such a task? It seemed minuscule in comparison to the problems looming before her. Though punishing those who turned against her would have given her great pleasure, she couldn't leap to anything that would hinder the rescue of her husband and child.

Still, there was something to be gleaned from knowing where he was found. The region was isolated and Vahn's group had traveled in secret, not telling anyone where they were headed next. If a group of mages had been ready to intercept them, it meant a turncoat in his company. The mage assigned to the party had been selected by Kytenia, which left her with one other likely suspect.

Her fingers crumpled a missive and her jaw tightened until she felt it twitch. Would he have betrayed his own son?

"I'll take it, thank you." Ordin's voice jolted her from thought. She'd almost forgotten the captain was with her. He drew a tea tray from a maid's hands and pushed the door closed with his elbow.

He cleared his throat as he placed the tray on the edge of her desk. "Temar is on her way. Archmage Kytenia will be up shortly after. She wished to speak to the prisoner in private first."

Firal nodded. There were few people left she felt she could trust, but Kytenia was one of them. After everything Kytenia had done for her, anything less than unwavering trust would have been an insult. If the Archmage desired a moment alone with her sister, it was the least Firal could offer. She poured herself a cup of tea and willed herself to relax. Aside from organizing her thoughts, there was little she could do until they arrived.

The tingle of Temar's presence entered her senses long before the door opened.

"Is all well, my queen?" The court mage was short of breath, but she smoothed her hair and righted her robes in an effort to look presentable.

"What do you think?" Firal snapped before she caught herself.

The woman flinched, but said nothing.

Firal closed her eyes and drew a deep breath. "I'm sorry. I don't mean to take it out on you. Temar, how many stations still hold multiple mages?"

"Not many." The Master crossed to the desk and leaned over the map. "These two, for certain, but the largest outpost was the chapter house in Wethertree."

Firal marked each station indicated with colored chalk. "Are you able to retrieve these clusters of mages by Gate?"

Temar pursed her lips. "I thought we'd decided not to try."

"Well, I need as many loyal mages as possible now, or I'll have no hope of pushing back."

"Pushing back against what?" Kytenia slipped in from the hallway, as graceful and beautiful as ever, despite her stained yellow dress.

Firal opened her mouth to answer, but her jaw hung open in surprise when someone followed Kytenia through the door. With the news of Vahn's capture, Rune was the last person she wanted to see. Yet there he was, like a thorn in a tender part of her she couldn't reach. "What is he doing here?"

Kytenia blinked at him over her shoulder. "Given everything that's going on right now, I thought he should be involved."

All the anger Firal had tried to suppress came roaring back, heating her blood until she thought she'd explode. "If I wanted him present, I would have summoned him."

Rune scoffed. "Then why am I here? I could be comfortable at home in Roberian, but instead—"

"Firal, Vahn thought he could help." The Archmage drew herself up to an imposing air, stained dress and all. "He called him for a reason."

"Wait." Rune raised a clawed finger and stepped between them. Firal drew a breath to deflect questions, but he turned his back to her, his attention on Kytenia. "Vahn was the one who summoned me?"

Exasperated, Firal turned back to her maps. "I don't have time for this. We need to act now, and unless he's going to lift a finger to help—"

"Lift a finger, or fall at your feet while you order the stars to align to your pleasing?" Rune sneered. "You've yet to present even a halfway thought-out plan, but still expect me to make miracles happen."

She gaped. Ordin and Temar shifted uncomfortably beside the desk, avoiding looking at either one of them.

Ruddy light flashed in Rune's violet eyes. "Speechless? That's unlike you."

Heat crept up her neck, alongside her rising temper. Her heart thumped against her ribs as if it meant to beat him itself. "I am a queen. You will not speak to me that way."

He almost laughed. "Or what? You'll hang me? That's what you wanted me here for in the first place."

Flustered, Firal crumpled another paper in her hands. "I didn't want you here at all!"

"Why not?"

"Because I hate you!" The words tore free by their own power and left her throat raw. They bit hard and cut deep, cooling his expression to neutrality.

Rune lifted his chin and the light faded from his eyes. At first she thought him wounded. Then his lips curved with a hint of amusement. "Took you long enough."

He turned to offer a stiff bow to Kytenia, ignoring the others present. "Excuse me, Archmage."

"You are dismissed," Firal added weakly.

"I wasn't waiting for permission," he replied flatly as he let himself out the door.

Brooding silence weighed on her until she collapsed into her chair and covered her eyes to hide the burning tears.

Ordin cleared his throat. "With all due respect, Your Majesty," he murmured, "I think we may be rushing. If we are to act, we will need the support of the council."

Temar nodded. "Captain Straes is correct. If we are forced to act against a group of mages invading the temple, it's best to discuss the matter thoroughly before action is taken."

"We can summon the council members and speak at dawn," Kytenia added. "It would be best if you had some idea of what you wish to say before then."

Her throat constricted and Firal swallowed hard, willing herself not to cry. "We can't wait that long, can we?"

"We must." Temar spoke gently but firmly, compassion in her eyes.

"I don't mean to take sides, my queen, but he was correct in that we need a clear plan." Ordin leaned over her desk and removed a weight from the corner of the map. He turned it over in his hand before he planted it atop the symbol that marked the temple's location.

"I will see what mages I can gather, but their number will be small." The court Master gave a gentle curtsy. "By your leave, Majesty."

Firal stared at the weight on the map and blinked to dissipate her tears. She hadn't chosen the heavy figurines for any particular reason, they'd simply been what was at the top of the box. The tiny obelisk that stood atop the temple marker seemed to loom over the rest of the map. "You are all excused."

Ordin bowed and followed Temar to the door.

Kytenia lingered, her eyes on Firal like a leaden weight. "If you mean to involve him, he will need to be in council tomorrow morning. Regardless of how you feel, it's clear Vahn wanted him included and thought he would make a difference. Otherwise, he wouldn't have gone through the trouble of finding him."

Unable to look at her friend, Firal closed her eyes instead. "He refuses to help."

"To be fair, you've not been the kindest in your method of asking." Kytenia smiled sadly, picked up her skirts and made her way to the door. She paused halfway and looked back. "Perhaps you could soften your tone, just to see what happens."

The silence after Kytenia departed bred bitter discontent, her words hanging heavy in the air.

Firal clenched her teeth and buried her face in her hands. Rune had always been difficult and often frustrating. But he had, it seemed, gone to great lengths to irritate her as deeply as possible since his arrival. Yet she couldn't blame her reaction solely on him, and the knowledge twisted up her insides until even mint tea could offer no relief.

How could she soften her tone with all the resentment she still harbored?

DEEPER

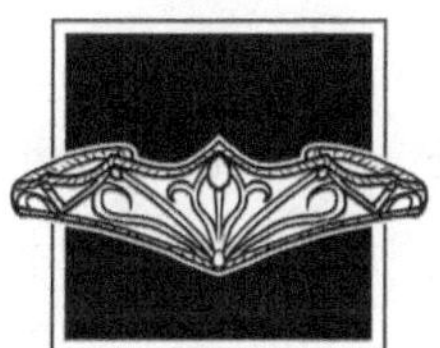

Sweat rolled down Edagan's temples and between her shoulder blades, making her squirm. She paused to wipe her brow on a sleeve that would never be white again. Her robes clung in uncomfortable places and her gray-white hair stuck to her face and her neck. For a fleeting moment, she regretted the sliver of vanity that demanded she keep her hair long. Her stern bun had come undone some time ago, but frustration kept her from tying it up again.

Magelings milled behind her, restless and nervous, whispering among themselves but reluctant to speak to her. She'd snapped at them more times than they deserved, but she was unwilling to apologize yet. The less they bothered her, the sooner they'd reach their destination.

Digging out the collapsed tunnel they'd taken shelter in had been easy. It was what came after that gave them struggle. The winding corridors beneath the ruins doubled back on themselves like twisted snakes, impossible to navigate. Not long after they began, Edagan and the other Masters decided it best if they forget trying to remember which turns they'd taken. Instead they had decided to push down through the earth, split rock and break through the walls that separated the tunnels. Steep drops opened before them more often than Edagan liked, forcing them to pause and lower magelings into each new passage a few at a time.

Even worse, the air was damp and stale. The smell of mold made her nose itch and her eyes water. Her mouth was dry despite the water Balen pulled from the air for them to drink—the man was all but useless when it came to shifting earth—and the sweat on her skin grew icy and clammy in the cold underground air.

Edagan struck the wall of the tunnel with the flat of her palm and grimaced as stone split, but failed to fall away. She was growing tired, and the magelings were already too exhausted to help.

"Perhaps we should reevaluate the situation," Balen murmured, giving voice to thoughts she didn't want to admit.

She gritted her teeth and closed her eyes as she leaned against the wall for support. The earth hummed to her senses, teasing her with visions of the world both above and below. It was disorienting, but helpful, and was also a trick none of the magelings had conquered. Neve was some help, but most of her energy was devoted to keeping the magelings organized.

Edagan swore they had to be close to a passage that would lead them to the underground city, but the looping tunnels muddied her perception of the earth. For all she knew, they'd been going in a slow spiral instead of the angled downward descent she'd intended for them to take.

Balen rested a hand on her shoulder and leaned close to offer more water. It was pure and tasteless, and the only part of their trip that had worked as planned.

Truthfully, she'd been surprised the man was adept with water, given his opposing elemental affinity. It made little sense, but she was grateful. She accepted the sphere of liquid and watched its surface as she took over the energy needed to hold its shape. It wobbled but held, the ripples serving as testament to how weary she really was.

Swallowing back a sigh, Edagan drank from the sphere's surface until it dwindled to nothing. Then she licked her lips to speak. Before any words escaped, Balen spun a small ward around the two of them. Bless the man; at least he'd kept his composure.

"I believe we may be in trouble," Edagan said. "We can't possibly continue on like this, and we have no supplies." She didn't sound as defeated as she felt. Though she would have liked to claim composure, more of it was pride. Balen was young. She had been Master of Earth for longer than he'd been alive. Showing cracks in her facade simply wouldn't do.

"I've been watching for foraging options," Balen said, "but we're too deep for roots and I haven't seen any fungi."

"I don't know how much farther we can go. I will rest, but there are more tunnels here than I realized." She glanced toward the cracks in the stone wall and frowned. They had worked their way through more walls than she'd been able to count. All the temple's books on the ruins said the catacombs underneath were vast, but she'd never anticipated what that really meant. The combination of natural and manmade corridors created more passages than there were tunnels in an anthill. Looking back the way they'd come, the multitude of openings reminded her of holes in a sponge.

He followed her gaze and dropped the ward. There was little else to discuss. Going back to the temple wasn't an option, especially not after they'd fled.

"It's incredible, isn't it?" Balen said as he studied the open tunnels above. "No wonder the ruin-folk were able to hide here so long."

"And no wonder they developed such wealth. A number of these passages held running water at some point. Anyone with time to dig in the gravel would find corundum and gold by the handful." Edagan smoothed back her hair, ignoring the streaks of dirt her hands left at her sweat-dampened temples. "With fortune, we'll reach the city soon. I think I'll sit and trace the tunnels to see if I can find any shortcuts."

Balen chuckled and lowered himself to the floor. "How fortunate we are. Of all people to be with in the underground, we're led by Edagan, the legendary Master of the House of Earth."

The false bravado made her sniff, but she didn't miss the way the magelings behind them seemed to relax. He really was good with the children. She couldn't think of a Master she'd rather have trapped with her for this disaster.

"Yes," she said, elevating her voice so the magelings would hear. "We're very fortunate, indeed."

She sank to the floor with a long exhale and tried to ignore the tingle of mold in her nostrils when she drew breath again. Her palms flattened against the cool stone beneath her. Closing her eyes made it easier to concentrate. Had she not been so tired, she would have warded out the sound of the murmuring magelings as well.

The earth beneath her palms sang to her, a low, soothing thrum punctuated by the percussion of shifting stone. She didn't often connect to the earth that way. It could be overwhelming, and its power tried to seep into her when her guard was down. This deep underground, that sort of power could consume her. It would petrify her body, if it didn't burn her up first.

"Tell me, friend," she whispered, pressing her hands down until stone and soil filled every fingerprint. "Where must I go?"

No matter her connection to it, the stone against her skin would never communicate with her in the way her words implied. But speaking to it made the connection easier, helped her relax, helped her spread her awareness through the cracks and crevices in the stone.

The vibrations of energy were always present, shifting as the world's plates moved, and each moment she spent connected to that power gave her a clearer visual of what waited below.

Thousands of tunnels created a tangled web of emptiness,

places where no energy existed to answer her call. They reached deeper than she ever imagined, sprawling in every direction, muddling her senses until she thought looking farther was hopeless.

Then, what seemed miles away, she felt it: the void of a cavern so vast it could only be what they searched for. Latching onto the edges of that emptiness, Edagan sent one final push of energy, seeking the tunnels connected to it. Light filled her mind and vision and for one glorious moment, she swore she saw everything.

Power hummed in her senses and filled her form until it seemed her heart pulsed in time with its ebb and flow. Land shifted, moved, breathed like a living thing. The outline of the island and the oceans beyond it hung black in her vision and, all at once, a single twisting path burned so brilliantly before her eyes that she feared she'd never see again.

Heat rose inside her head, planted a low whine in her ears. Her hands left the floor and the world departed from her senses as if torn away. Edagan gasped and her body went rigid as her own energy snapped back like a whiplash. Her sun-withered skin rose in gooseflesh as the power surged through her and settled, leaving her dizzy and disoriented. Blinking to clear her vision, she found Balen hovering above her and realized she was cradled in the young man's arms.

His expression softened into a worried but understanding smile. "I thought you'd gone too deep, my friend."

Despite the drink she'd had only moments ago, her mouth was almost too dry to let her speak. "Almost," she croaked, sitting upright but not deterring him when he supported her shoulders. "But not today."

"What did you learn?" The corners of his eyes grew pinched as he spoke, as close to a wince as she'd ever seen him come.

She patted his hand and pushed herself up. As she found her strength, she closed her eyes and breathed in deep. Her head spun, but she ignored it, and the dizziness went away. "Enough. Come along, children," she called.

The magelings perked up and climbed to their feet. They looked a bit refreshed. Good; they'd need their strength.

"I'm not sure we're ready for more digging, Master," a girl in blue robes ventured.

Edagan sniffed. "No need, child. We're walking."

RUNE LIFTED his head from the cushion of his folded arms and growled beneath his breath. Frustrated and exhausted, company was the last thing he wanted. Yet the knock at his door had been firm and insistent. Would these people never give him a moment of peace?

The knock came a second time, harder, and he gritted his teeth as he pushed himself up from the table. The table rocked and the floor felt uneven beneath his clawed feet. Perhaps that last drink had been one too many.

His rooms were clean now; new linens made the bed and the furniture had been polished until it shone. The curtains were still open. Familiar stars glittered in the night. It had been ages since he'd seen them from the island, but he wasn't in the mood to stargaze. He wasn't even certain what time it was. After all their cleaning, the maids had forgotten to wind the tall clock beside his desk. It stood silent, its hands askew. His father had once told him that a timepiece was the most valuable thing a man could own. Clockworks were rare and exceptionally expensive, but their value came from the reminders they offered, rather than the price they could fetch. There were only two in the palace. One in his quarters, and one in his father's office. Firal's office now, he supposed.

Again someone knocked, and this time tried the door. Rune hadn't locked it and it swung open on freshly oiled hinges.

He scoffed and stopped where he was, halfway across the room. "Of course, come in. How fortunate that I'm decent."

"An interesting word to describe yourself," Firal murmured as she slipped inside and shut the door behind her. She was alone.

Of all the people who might have come to see him, he hadn't expected her. He shifted on his feet and watched, wary, as she moved closer. She walked with her head bowed, defeated and resigned. A far cry from the defiant queen who'd threatened to hang him just the day before.

Only hours ago, she'd said she hated him. The words tore to shreds what tender pieces remained of his heart. The whiskey clouded his senses, but hadn't soothed the hurt. His jaw tightened. "Why are you here?"

"Because I need your help." She looked at him from beneath dark lashes, her eyes glassy and troubled. "Envesi has moved into the temple. Our daughter is there and so is Vahn. If you're going to retrieve our child, this is the easiest opportunity you'll have. All you have to do is Gate in and out, and bring them back with you."

He hadn't expected an apology, but that she crept in with more demands so soon left him incensed. She made it sound as if opening a Gate was so simple. To be fair, he supposed it once had been. He crossed his arms. "Why don't you have your league of mages do it, then?"

"Because I don't know if I still have mages on the other side, and I can't risk sending a dozen through to do it. They'd be noticed. If it's just you, then there's a chance."

Reasonable, he had to admit. Half of him had hoped for some rash, half-brained notion of what he was supposed to do. But her reasoning was sound, and harder to reject.

Still, on top of assuming he would help after the way she'd spoken to him, she assumed he was still capable of facing the former Archmage on his own. Such an expectation would have been laughable even if he'd been at full strength.

"Wait," Rune said, raising a claw. "Why is Vahn there?" The mention of his one-time friend's name had almost escaped his notice. The alcohol must have dulled his wits instead of his heartache. "I thought you said he was riding across the island."

Firal shook her head. "I don't know what's happened or what took him there, but both Rikka and Shymin said they saw him there. Rikka said he was a captive."

He frowned, the only outward hint of the emotions that warred within him. For years, Vahn had been his friend—his dearest and only true friend, at that. More than once, Vahn had laid his life on the line for him. Rune's heart leaped at the opportunity to repay the favor, but the bitter, selfish part of him reined it in. In his absence, Vahn had taken his wife, his child, even his crown and his place in the palace. How genuine of a friend could he be?

"I can't seem to convince you any other way, so I've come to ask your help," she said, pacing closer. "Not order it. I will hold council at dawn to decide what we will do. I can grant you clemency and power, give you a title and holdings. Wealth, land. Whatever you ask, I will give you as reward." She stopped only a step away.

He searched her face, his eyes narrowing. "Anything?"

Firal swallowed and dropped her gaze to the floor. Her hand traveled up the front of her bodice and lingered at the base of her throat, saying more than words could. "Anything."

Again emotion warred within him. How could she spit such venom in her office, then offer herself to him like that? Anger roiled against the heartache that swelled in his chest. He wanted to touch her, hold her, kiss her until she couldn't breathe. He wanted to throw her words back at her, tell her he hated her and see if it tore at her heart. And he hated that she stood so close.

It would have been so easy to take what she offered. Already he imagined the salty flavor of her skin and the way he'd fit between her supple thighs. It had been years—a lifetime, for some Giftless men. Weren't feelings like this supposed to fade?

Despite all the hurt and anger that scorched him from the inside, he wanted nothing more than to drown in her amber eyes and lose himself inside her. It was primal, base, but he knew it was the only way he could convey the depths of his feelings. He'd always thought himself good with words. Nobility had to be. With the storm of emotions she caused, words could never be enough.

Yet all the longing that surged within him couldn't drown the resentment that welled up alongside the tide of desperation. She'd made her wishes clear when he'd written a letter to ask forgiveness and beg an audience. The silence that answered had been enough. She'd moved on and remarried. How little must she think of him, to believe he would lay with another man's wife? How little did she know him, after all the times he'd laid his heart bare?

"I can't help you." Rune stalked back to the table he'd had brought to his room and drew back his chair.

Firal's mouth fell open and tears welled in her eyes. They clawed at his bleeding heart, so he didn't look at her again. Instead, he focused on refilling his empty glass.

"I'm speaking of your daughter!" she cried, clutching her skirts in her fists and storming to the edge of his table.

"And you didn't think to speak of her any time before now," he snapped. "Before a moment where everything you think I can do offers you a convenience. In all these years, you never thought I might want to know I had a child?"

"I was protecting her!"

"A fine job of it you've done," Rune murmured over the rim of his glass as he sat down and took a sip. It was crude whiskey, nothing like what he could get on the mainland. But it was strong, and it would do. The floor would roll like the seas beneath his feet before he was ready to stand again.

Her cheeks flushed with anger, but she kept control of her tongue better than he expected. The woman he'd known would have flayed him with words. Instead, she remained cool and collected as she drew herself up with a sharp inhale. "You were supposed to save us."

He swirled the liquor in his glass and shrugged. "I'd say I'm sorry to disappoint you, but I don't really care."

Firal's mouth tightened and the fire in her eyes turned to frost. "So," she said, smoothing her skirts. "You've become just as much a monster on the inside as you are on the outside."

The words cut deep, stabbed and twisted until everything in him came apart. Grief swelled and turned his stomach as the last tiny flame of hope he'd harbored extinguished, but the facade he'd carried since childhood never faltered. Ignoring the soul-deep agony that chilled his heart, he offered a smug smile and raised his glass as if in toast.

Her face crumpled as she spun on her heel and stormed from his room. She slammed the door behind her so hard, it rattled on its hinges.

His smile twisted to a snarl as the room fell silent, leaving only the sound of his drumming pulse to hum in his ears. Too quick, too loud. Stifling a roar as he came out of his chair, he flung his glass after her.

It fell short and shattered on the floor, followed by the near-empty whiskey bottle.

A monster, inside and out. Those words bit to the core, echoing and amplifying everything he'd ever hated about himself. Everything he'd always feared. The table tilted under his hands as he shoved himself back. The chair got in his way. He kicked it aside and it toppled with a crash.

Rage burned in his chest and was mirrored in his glowing eyes. Gleaming, ruddy light danced around him, glinting off polished candlesticks and windows, mocking him from every angle.

She'd been the only person who ever mattered, the only one he'd wanted to impress, the only one who ever made him think he could be something more than a beast. Yet to her, that was all he was.

The standing mirror shattered before he realized he'd thrown something at it. The glass cackled as it hit the floor, taunting him as claws burrowed into his arms. The scent of acrid iron filled his nostrils and made him sick.

Howling in anger and defeat, he fell to his knees and gritted his teeth against the pain as he rent rows of scales from his arms. Blood flowed down his fingers, sticky and hot, plastering the tatters of his sleeves against his torn flesh.

Worse than anything, the pain or blood or the roar of his heartbeat in his head, was the aching knowledge she was right.

DECISIONS

THOUGH RUNE HEARD SOMEONE KNOCK, THE SOUND WAS LOST IN the haze of memory between wakefulness and sleep. The clack of the door's latch roused him.

"Oh," a girl's voice squeaked from the doorway, and the door closed again.

Rune closed his eyes. He didn't recall falling asleep, but the throbbing in his head made it hard to think. Stars still speckled the sky outside the windows, though he'd been on the stone floor so long, it no longer felt cold. His body ached from laying there, but the pain in his arms made it easy to ignore. Still, he didn't move, silently wishing for the empty embrace of sleep to take him again.

It wasn't allowed the chance. Again the door opened, this time with the rustle of skirts and the quiet padding of slippered feet.

"Fetch a mage, and bring warm water and a rag," said a soft, motherly voice above him. Gentle hands touched his shoulder and stroked soothingly instead of shaking. "Come along now, my Lord Daemon. Her Majesty calls for you."

She touched his bicep and coaxed him upright with gnarled

fingers. He didn't resist, moving mindlessly as she guided him to his feet and steered him toward the table. His legs were unsteady, but she was an unwavering support beneath his arm.

"Here we are," the old woman murmured. She caught the overturned chair with her foot and pulled it close enough to stand it upright. Then she guided him down onto it, her touch strong and confident.

His shoulders sagged as he sat, his head bowed. He stared at his hands in his lap without seeing them. He didn't want to see. What wasn't crusted with black blood was still green, glittering in the feeble light of the candle a maid placed before him.

The bowl of water clacked against the table as the girl put it down in front of him. He smelled the steam from where he sat.

"What is it?" another familiar voice asked from the doorway. A flurry of footsteps echoed in the room as the maid hurried out and someone else hurried in. Hushed whispers in the hallway were muted when the door swung shut.

He closed his eyes again.

"He needs healing, miss mage." The old woman took hold of one of his arms and moved it aside. Leaning close, she pulled a knife from her belt and cut open the front of his shirt. Carefully, she peeled it back.

"What happened?" the mage asked as she hastened to his side.

"It doesn't matter," the old woman replied gruffly. "It's over now." She drew off his shirt and behind them, the mage made a quiet sound of surprise. The air that kissed his scarred back was cold, sharp.

The old woman dunked the rag into the water and wrung out the excess before she laid the cloth against his wounded arm. He winced, but didn't pull away.

"I'll be brief," the mage murmured. She pressed cool hands to his shoulders, her thumbs against his neck. The chill made his skin rise in gooseflesh, the reaction only magnified by the eerie feeling of her energies pouring into him.

A wash of warmth followed and the pain in his head and his arms subsided as his torn flesh knit itself back together, as seamlessly as if it had never happened at all.

"You've been through a great deal, my lord," the old woman said, refreshing the rag and sponging his arm until his scales began to come clean. "But the queen needs you."

"No one needs me," Rune croaked. "They need something I can't give."

She huffed and reached for his other arm. "Oh, hush now. There's no time to be feeling sorry for yourself. We need the leader you were, my lord. Even my boy says it."

He tilted his head just enough to look at her. The dark eyes in her bronzed face looked so stern and piercing, he would have recognized her even in the dark. She'd been good to them; a friend to him and like a mother to Firal. Minna's presence should have been a relief, allayed his fears that the people he'd been forced to abandon had struggled without him. Instead, it served as one more harsh reminder of his failures.

He lowered his gaze again, afraid she'd see through him now that his facade was cracked. "I'm not that person anymore. I can't help anyone."

"Don't be silly." The mage knelt beside his chair. Rikka had worn yellow robes when he'd seen her last, though she—like everyone else—had changed. Her transformation was minor, less noticeable than the white wings in Kytenia's hair.

Rikka's eyes had always been blue; now they were just bluer. Her hair was a different shade of red, now sporting the orange tint of henna. It was difficult to think of her as a Master. A Master of a House of affinity at that, with delicate black markings painted at the corners of her eyes. It hurt to think how many of them must be stronger than him now.

Rikka touched his bare shoulder, her fingertips gentle and reassuring. "You're the only person they knew to call for help. Your daughter is counting on you, Ran."

Startled, he glanced at Minna. The old woman nodded and continued her work without a word.

"How did you—" he started.

"I was there when Firal found out," Rikka said. "A few days after you escaped, right before her formal coronation. She was ill and Kytenia offered to heal her. But it wasn't the sort of illness that could be healed." She smiled sheepishly, though the expression was quick to fade. "That was when we found out you'd been married. Firal was so frightened. Worried about her safety and the safety of the baby. So Kytenia told Vahn to marry her."

The words took a weight from him. Rune lifted his head, just a little, but found the movement easier. "Kytenia told them to?"

Rikka nodded. "It was the only thing she knew to do that would ensure they'd be safe. Nobody was happy, but everyone thought it best. I think it was hardest on them. Vahn and Kyt, I mean, since they had planned to wed."

So Vahn hadn't stolen his wife. With all the bitterness that came from learning of their union, this new information was a relief and a blessing. Rune had asked Vahn to protect her. He never would have imagined that was what it would take.

"There." Minna gave his arm one last swipe with the rag and dropped the cloth into the murky bowl. "Just like it never happened."

"Thank you," he murmured.

Minna offered a sad smile and patted his hand. "Now to get you ready. The two of you will have to chatter later, miss mage. Council will be meeting soon. That's why someone was sent to fetch him in the first place."

"Of course." Rikka blushed and pushed herself up. "I'll see you at the meeting, Ran."

Minna hurried her along, then paused at the doorway to take bundles of things from the maids waiting outside. None of the girls dared do more than peek inside, though they whispered furiously amongst themselves until Minna shut the door in their faces.

"Rotten little gossips," Minna grumbled as she carried the bundles to the bed. "That sort of behavior would never be tolerated in Core."

She unfolded the cloth wrappings and held up a coat to inspect the embroidery. "I hope one of these fits. I know you asked for something to be made, my lord, but you'll need to be properly dressed before it arrives. Can't have you tending a formal meeting in..." She trailed off, her mouth twitching. The tatters of his bloodied shirt lay on the table before him. "Well, I'm sure one of them will do."

Rune tried not to sigh. "What good am I going to do in a meeting of council? I don't have the power to do what they ask."

"You'll do as much as anyone, I suspect." She lifted another coat, shook her head and cast it aside without a second thought. "The best you can, given the circumstances. Ah, this one should do. Let's see if it fits."

Easy for her to say. They hadn't threatened to kill her over a lack of cooperation. And no matter how he tried to put on a brave face and pretend it didn't bother him, there was still a part of him that went cold with fear whenever the thought of execution crossed his mind. The same cowardly part made him wish he could run and escape all the problems that had erupted since his arrival.

Minna returned to his side with a thin shirt of white linen in her hands. A coat in the near-unchanging high-collared style of Ilmenhith hung over her arm. The color she'd chosen surprised him, for all it had seemed like a good idea the day before.

"I don't know—" he started.

She didn't let him finish, pushing the clothing into his arms. "Come on, now, get dressed. I didn't think to send for trousers, yours will just have to do. Fortunate they're dark. They won't show much dirt."

He frowned as she scuttled back to the bed and busied herself with folding the discarded clothing, but he didn't have many choices. If he didn't attend Firal's meeting willingly, he had no doubt she'd have her guards strong-arm him. He pulled on the clean shirt and rose to shrug into the blue coat. He trailed his claws over the silver embroidery on the sleeves and paused. He'd seen this coat before.

It was his father's.

"Minna—"

"You'd best hurry," she interrupted, returning to straighten his cuffs and collar. Then she stood on tip-toe to place something on his head. He twitched as the cold metal settled against his brow.

"There." Minna cupped his face in both hands and smiled warmly, though tears filled her eyes. "What a king you would have been, if only you'd had the chance to lead us."

Rune touched the back of her gnarled hand with his claws, his brow furrowed. "I'm not fit to lead anyone."

"I think you might be surprised, my lord." She patted his cheek, stepped back, and wiped her eyes. "Go on, now. You've a little girl who needs you."

"I can't help her." His voice cracked.

"And who says you can't?" The old woman stared up at him with her lower lip in a defiant pout.

"They want me to do things I'm not capable of anymore. They want me to be a hero, but I'm..." he trailed off, flexing his clawed fingers until he curled them into the palms of his hands.

Minna huffed. "Who's to say you can't be a hero? No one gets to decide that but you. Heroism is a choice, Lord Daemon. Lifetree knows you've already been one to us."

Rune's brow furrowed and he squeezed his eyes closed.

Gently, her hand touched his jaw. "Chin up, Lord Daemon. Never forget you were our king by right."

He opened his mouth to protest, but thought better of it and bowed his head. He'd have time to argue with Minna later, when there wasn't a risk of guardsmen apprehending him for truancy. Instead, he ran his fingers over the embroidered cuff of his coat and turned toward the door. "Thank you, Minna."

She didn't look at him again, simply sniffed and waved him away as she returned to folding and sorting the unneeded clothing on the bed.

Squaring his shoulders and lifting his head, Rune strode into the hallway and pretended he didn't see the serving staff milling about in their pre-dawn work. His fingers twitched and he forced them to be still, lest he find himself touching the embroidery again.

Part of him wanted to remove the crown and inspect it, fearing it might be one of his father's as well. The one he'd commissioned for himself wouldn't be done until that evening and, while he'd requested one similar to what Kifel had worn, he wasn't so bold as to wear one styled after the king's.

Workers stopped to look at him, some pale, others spooked. Did he look so frightful, dressed as he should have been? He had to admit Minna was right. The kingdom's colors were his by right, if not by birth. And though he knew the finery he wore belonged to his father, he doubted anyone else would recognize it. He knew because of the way he'd hung on his father's sleeve as a child, the way he'd studied the man's posture and tried to mimic it, the way he'd tried to engrave every word of approval into his memory. His throat tightened and he banished the thoughts as he made his way toward the council chamber.

The council met in a room adjacent to the office Firal now called her own. He'd been there a thousand times, but only as a spectator, a child with hopes of someday earning the right to his father's place. The door was closed. He didn't knock.

Conversation inside halted as the door creaked open and he stepped through. Firal sat at the head of the table, staring at him in a mix of irritation and surprise.

Rune half expected some sort of outburst. He knew the risk

of appearing in the kingdom's colors with a crown that wasn't his. Instead, everyone present just gaped.

Ordin was the first to compose himself. The captain rose to his feet with awe in his eyes.

With her lips still parted in surprise, Kytenia followed. Then Rikka, Temar, Garam, and Tobias. One after another stood until only a few council members and Firal herself were left seated, the queen's mouth tightly pursed. If Rune hadn't known her, he might have thought it disapproval on her face. But he recognized something deeper in her eyes, something complicated and thoughtful.

"Majesty," Rune said, pressing a hand to his heart as he bowed. It was the first sign of respect he'd shown her. It caught her off guard, as he suspected it might.

"As I was saying," Firal said, tearing her eyes away as if he were no more of an interruption than a servant with poor timing. "There's no reason to believe they'll be released without action, either way."

Despite Firal's indifference, those standing remained on their feet until Rune rounded the table and took his place in the only open chair. Placing him between Ordin and Garam made sense, given their positions. Ordin was chief of Firal's security and Garam had his self-proclaimed responsibility to see affairs carried out on the island before returning home. Yet Rune couldn't help but wonder if it was chance or oversight that he was placed between the two people he figured were his closest allies.

Everyone sank back into their seats after he settled, earning him a dark look from Firal. He returned it levelly, his face unchanging.

"It's obvious she's trying to prod you into action, Majesty." Ordin rubbed his chin, though he looked like he'd rather rub his eyes. Everyone but Firal looked half asleep.

"As I said, now is the easiest time to act. I could have my child in my arms before noon." Firal was curt, impatient.

"A Gate in, a Gate out. I requested it before. Now I demand it."

"I have no way of organizing mages in the temple to open a Gate back to the palace," Kytenia said. Her voice was gentle but firm, and Rune mused over how it matched her appearance. She'd traded her charming yellow work dress for the stern white robes that suited an Archmage, but her face still bore a pretty sort of kindness, as it had for as long as he'd known her.

Firal snorted. "We shouldn't need them."

"Why wouldn't you?" Rune traced shapes on the tabletop with one claw. Its surface was worn from years of use, dented and etched with countless words where pens had pressed too hard against paper. His thoughts drifted to how many decisions penned there should have been his to make.

"I already told you—"

"And as I told you, as I've said since the moment you first laid this task at my feet, I cannot help you." Rune met her glare and raised a claw before she could speak. The desire to answer in belligerence floated to the surface, but he disregarded it. Anger had gotten him nowhere. It didn't matter how hot his hurt still burned. He was tired, and nothing was going to change Firal's mind. "Which you have continually misunderstood, choosing to take my words as refusal instead of what they are. I am not capable of doing what you ask."

Her eyes narrowed.

"You're demanding something far beyond my reach," he continued, reclining in his chair. "Even if it were a good plan, I don't have the strength needed to transport us to safety, much less face a mage like Envesi."

Firal shook her head as if to free herself from the weight of his words. "What are you talking about?"

"Magic." Garam looked between the two of them and frowned deeply.

Rune nodded. "Even if I still possessed the strength I used to have, you're expecting me to stand alone against someone who was able to kill one of the most powerful mages the world has ever known." His throat tightened as he spoke of Medreal. He swallowed hard to clear it.

"What do you mean, the strength you used to have?" Firal demanded.

"Tie magic with me."

She made a sound of disgust. "I'm not an idiot."

He shrugged.

On the other side of the table, Kytenia pushed herself up. "I'll do it."

"Don't be foolish," Temar hissed.

Ignoring her, Kytenia made her way around the table as Rune rose. She bit her lower lip and extended her hand.

He laced his fingers with hers, offering a gentle squeeze for reassurance. Slowly, energy trickled forth to weave their power together. She prodded the air around them and he led her in reaching for the power she couldn't tap on her own. It slipped away like grains of sand through their fingers, while the seal on his magic lit within him.

"Oh my word," Kytenia breathed. Her voice sounded pained.

"What?" Alarmed, Firal planted her hands on the table and half rose from her chair. "Kytenia?"

The Archmage opened her eyes slowly and looked at Rune in pure pity.

"Kytenia?" Firal prompted.

The Archmage shook her head. "I... I don't know. It's there, the power, but there's something..." She probed his energy, this time exploring him instead of his connection to the energy around them. She found what she was looking for with relative ease, some inexplicable force that pushed back when she tested it.

He flinched as the first warning pangs sparked in his chest. He'd never quite determined how the seal was connected to him, or to his power, but he always felt it there first.

"I don't understand," she murmured. "I've never seen anything like it."

"A seal," Garam said. "Something barring him from reaching any real power, put in place by mages much stronger than you."

Kytenia's eyes filled with sadness. "Can you even do anything?"

"Enough to survive," Rune replied. "Not enough to face someone like Envesi."

"Then what are we supposed to do?" a small man near Firal asked. He looked familiar, but Rune couldn't place him. The council had changed since his father's rule; he didn't recognize any of the people who hadn't stood when he entered.

"Come up with a better plan." Ordin drummed his fingertips against the table. "Archmage, it's your temple. How do you want to handle the invasion?"

Kytenia hesitated.

Rune squeezed her fingers again and she started. Had she already forgotten she held his hand? She watched his face, thoughtful. Slowly, her fingers shifted between his, tightening their grip. It was a gentle display of solidarity, and perhaps something more. The contact gave him comfort. He suspected it did the same for her.

"I suppose the first thing we should do is determine if it really is an invasion," Rikka suggested. "There were a lot of mages with Envesi, but I can't say if they were loyal to her. I saw several faces I recognized, including Kepha."

"Kepha?" Temar gasped. "But that would mean they captured King Vahnil's entire party! Was she a prisoner?"

Rikka shook her head. "She looked well and walked freely among them."

Garam cleared his throat. "Excuse me, but how many mages are we talking about, here?"

"More than Aldaan," Rune said, pulling away from Kytenia and sinking back into his chair. The moment he broke contact, the tie between their magic dissipated. "More than the Grand College probably counts in its ranks."

Garam let out a low whistle and rubbed his white beard.

"But we don't know that they're all against us," Rikka insisted.

"And how are we supposed to find out?" Ordin asked.

"Simple," Firal said, drawing startled glances from everyone at the table. "We ask Envesi. We already know she wants to meet with me. We'll just have to work that to our advantage."

Kytenia bowed her head and lingered behind Rune's chair. "I don't think we'll need to consult Envesi directly. Not for that information, anyway."

Rikka and Temar looked troubled.

Rune lifted a brow.

"What do you suggest?" Ordin asked.

"Yesterday, when Rikka brought word of Envesi's arrival at the temple, she was followed by my sister." Kytenia paced back to her chair and stood behind it with her eyes downcast. "Shymin told a different story, implying Envesi came peacefully."

"Even though we already know she's holding my family captive." Firal shook her head and rubbed the space between her brows as if to keep it from crumpling with anger. "You're right. She knows more than I've given her credit for. More than I suspected or hoped, as well. So we speak to Shymin. Then what?"

"Precisely my question." Ordin leaned forward to rest his elbows on the table. "We ought to have a solid idea what we're doing before anything else."

"Preferably something better thought out than opening Gates directly into the viper's nest and shoving people through," Rune said dryly, earning himself several glares. "I'm sure Captain Straes will agree that was a terrible idea to begin with. What's supposed to come from snatching prisoners out of Envesi's grasp? No one could honestly think that would be the end of it."

Color bloomed in Firal's cheeks, though whether it was from anger or embarrassment, Rune didn't know.

"He's right." It was the first Tobias had spoken. That he spoke at all surprised the others at the table. He sat with his arms folded over his chest, frowning and staring at the table without seeming to see it in front of him. "Snatching them out of her grasp without hearing what she wants would only make things worse."

Firal threw her hands up, exasperated. "Then what do you propose we do?"

"With all due respect, Your Majesty," Tobias said, "I think we should ask the only person here who has experience fighting mages."

Rune twitched as all eyes turned to him.

"Make a habit out of it, do we?" Garam intoned.

Shrugging, Rune sank lower in his chair. "Not intentionally."

"Tobias has a point," Ordin said. "Out of all of us who fought in the war, you're the only mage who was on the other side."

"Not that I did much fighting then, but I did learn a few things serving under Garam." Like the captain beside him, Rune leaned against the table and laced his fingers together.

"And you worked with the Aldaanan," Garam added. "Between their abilities and yours, you know what we're up against."

Firal nibbled her lower lip for a time. Eventually, she sighed and leaned back in her chair. "Then speak. What would you have us do?"

"We'll need mages," Rune said. "Lots of them. If her power is anything like what I've seen from free mages in the past, she's strong, but not infallible. One on one, any mage against her is useless. But if we have a big enough group..."

"Swarm and overwhelm," Garam said thoughtfully, stroking his jaw with his thumb.

Rune nodded. "Just like the college mages tried to do to us in

Aldaan. It was all I could do to hold them off then. With the team of mages on my side, we might have an edge."

"And if the temple mages have turned against us?" Temar asked.

"There are more mages in the world than just those in Kirban. We'll collect the loyalists in one place and add to them. The Grand College will support us. They won't have a choice. Elenhiise is too valuable to Vicamros for the college to turn a blind eye." Or for Vicamros to save the champion of his arena, Rune thought ruefully. He didn't blame the king for what he'd done; politics always took precedence over personal matters, even when you weren't in charge of what might as well have been an empire. But he wouldn't deny it stung.

"There are schools in the south as well," Garam said. "I know someone influential down there. We can contact them, too."

Kytenia shook her head. "Mages against mages. Who ever thought it would come to this?"

Garam chuckled. "It's more common than you might think."

The mages on the other side of the table looked at him strangely.

"So we talk to Master Shymin to determine the state of things, gather what mages we can, and put out a call for others," Tobias said, ticking off his fingers and neatly brushing away any discussion on that topic. "Shouldn't we figure out what we're going to do to rescue the captives? That is what started all this, isn't it?"

"No." Rune kept his tone calm and level despite his rising irritation. "Don't misunderstand. They are important, but there's nothing to be done about the captives until Envesi is dealt with. Anything we do to try to remove them from her grasp now will only make things worse. Opposing her means we must do one of two things, or this will never end."

Kytenia raised a hand to her mouth, aghast. "You're suggesting we kill her?"

He'd almost forgotten the mages of Kirban adhered to

different rules. According to the temple, killing another mage was forbidden. Convenient for Envesi, but not surprising, considering she'd written most of the rules and shaped them to meet her own agendas.

"Kill," Rune agreed, "or sever her."

All around the table, faces shifted between surprise and confusion.

"Sever?" Firal repeated at last, though she shivered as the word left her tongue. She already had an idea of what it meant, then; her tone conveyed disbelief rather than failure to understand.

"Is such a thing possible?" Rikka murmured, rubbing her arms to ward off a chill of her own.

"The Alda'anan teach against it," Rune said. "But they aren't here, are they?"

Tobias cleared his throat. "Forgive me, but there are no mages among my people. Save the youngest generation of children, that is, some them being born of unions with surface folk. I'm not familiar with this term, but it relates to magic?"

Garam nodded. "Cutting a mage's ties to magic, in essence. Removing their ability to bend energy to their will."

Tobias's face crumpled in disgust. Even they had grown used to the comfort and convenience of mages in their midst.

"And you know how to do this? Sever someone from power?" Firal asked, giving Rune a hard look.

He nodded.

"You've done it?" Her voice took an edge.

He met her gaze, unwavering. "When necessary."

She shuddered and turned away. Echoes of her words the night before haunted him and left him to wonder how firmly this helped cement it in her mind.

"I'm reluctant to agree to something like this, but I understand where you're coming from." There was a pinched look around Kytenia's eyes, but otherwise, her face was smooth. She'd grown used to difficult decisions, it seemed. This was just one more for her to handle. "Of the options, I think cutting her off from power is better. Not because it spares her life, but because I can think of no better punishment for misusing her Gift than forcing her to spend the rest of her days without it."

Rune's brows lifted and the crown shifted against his skin in an odd reminder of its presence. He hadn't considered that, and hearing it from Kytenia's mouth came as a surprise. In a single sentence, she'd changed a great deal in his eyes. Severance was a cruel punishment for a mage, but well deserved. He nodded in agreement.

"However," the Archmage continued, her expression growing stern. "If that's the route we take, the knowledge of severance—and how to perform it—will need to be a closely guarded secret. That's not the sort of thing we can risk other mages learning how to perform."

Ordin frowned. "This isn't common knowledge? I'd have thought you'd at least be familiar with the idea, Archmage Kytenia."

"I don't think this knowledge is something you need worry about, Archmage," Rune said. "Even if other mages saw it done, most wouldn't have the capability to perform a severance. I'm not sure any could. As far as I know, severing can only be done by a free mage."

"Which means you?" Firal tilted her head. "After we just discussed your lack of strength?"

He hesitated.

"We have options." Garam leveled a hard look with her, an action that bordered on inappropriate. He was an esteemed visitor, well respected and entrusted with the responsibility of managing Vicamros's business in the man's absence, but he was addressing a queen. Others at the table shifted in visible discomfort, and he softened his tone. "If he thinks he can do it, then we'd all best believe he knows a way to see it done."

"Yes," Kytenia murmured with a wry smile. "His reputation for determination persists beyond anything else."

"Has the island forgotten me already?" Rune couldn't resist smirking at her. The look put a hint of a twinkle in her eye.

Ordin snorted a laugh. "I'm sure you wish you could get off so easily. I don't think the island's people have forgotten either one of you."

Firal's face darkened. That smothered the brief spark of mirth, and both men's smiles faded.

"Watch yourself, Captain," Rune said, shifting back in his seat. "Seems we aren't supposed to talk about that just yet."

Ordin cleared his throat and grew sober.

Rune straightened the sleeve of his coat and pretended not to notice the familiar embroidery. "As Garam said, it's still possible. I can use magic, I just can't reach it. But because my own power is bridled, I'm able to tie it with that of other mages. Something I couldn't do safely before."

Firal bowed her head to hide a knowing look.

He pretended not to notice that, either. "I can draw power through others, but I'd need a lot of mages to work with." He'd learned the hard way to control what he drew. Used to limitless power as he was, the might he drew through others was enough to risk burning them to cinders. He'd never figured out what made his abilities different, aside from that bound mages had restrictions woven into their very beings. Near as he could figure, tearing those restrictions down by pulling too much energy simply made people come apart at the seams. He'd never gone that far—not yet—but he'd come close. Those memories still haunted him. The people who shared their power with him were allies, friends. The only way he could be sure they'd be unharmed in a fight against a mage like Envesi was to be certain there were enough of them present and connected.

"How many mages?" Temar asked.

"As many as possible. Ten Masters from each major affinity, at the very least. If I had it my way, the entire temple."

Firal gaped. "I don't think you realize what you're asking for."

"And I don't think you have any idea what she can do," Rune almost snapped. "If you'd seen half the things I've seen free magic do, half the things I could do once I had a teacher who understood my power, you'd know I'll need access to every mage we can find."

She hesitated, considering. She'd seen him open Gates alone, without even exerting himself, when it took at least half a dozen Master mages to do the same. Shouldn't that have been enough?

"You'll have however many mages we can spare." Kytenia sounded resolute, though her eyes betrayed her uncertainty.

Rune didn't blame her. He knew he was asking for a lot. That Kytenia was willing to at least try to accommodate him was a comfort. No matter how friendly their meeting had been the day before, he hadn't been sure he could rely on her. Still, there was a look about her that made him decide to speak with her privately later. No matter how dangerous Envesi was, he had to remind himself that he was only a step less so. If that, he reminded himself; if he had enough mages to supply the power he couldn't reach on his own, he suspected they would be on equal footing. Regardless of who was stronger, he had the advantage of formal training in the use of free magic. Envesi didn't.

"So we speak to Shymin, collect loyal mages from the temple and allies from the Grand College, send Lord Kaith to speak to the southern mages," Rikka said, ticking off her fingers. "Then what? We hunt the woman down and try to peel away her power?"

Rune started to speak, but a strange prickling on the edge of his senses silenced him. He turned his head, his brow furrowed.

Uncharacteristically, Kytenia cursed.

"Is that Anaide?" Rikka pushed herself back from the table and started to rise.

"Coming this direction. Someone must be bringing her." Kytenia turned toward the door and squared her shoulders.

The faint energy signature—something unique to each mage —grew clearer, verifying Kytenia's assessment.

Firal gripped the edge of the table, but relaxed after a moment. "She's alone." Or at least, there were no other mages with her.

"Don't relax just yet. She's coming from the temple. I can't imagine she has good news." Kytenia turned to Rune and grimaced. "And no matter what news she brings, we can't let her know you're here. Not yet."

He nodded. He didn't like the idea of hiding, but she was right. If Anaide came from the temple, she came bearing a message, and she'd be expected to return. For once he was grateful for the seal on his power. It muddied what others could sense. If he couldn't touch magic by himself, there was little for other mages to feel. He blended into the background unless he actively tried to reach for power, or tried to work his own energy into something useful. This time, it would let him slip away unnoticed.

"We'll call you back as soon as we know what's going on," Kytenia said. "You'd better hurry, so you don't run into her in the hall."

"I'll escort him back to his room." Garam stood, masking a grimace as he straightened.

"We will call for you," Kytenia repeated.

Rune frowned, but said nothing. Silent, he slid into the hallway and turned east.

"I don't mean to complain," Garam said behind him, "but I'm not as young as I used to be. You might want to slow down just a little."

Stopping just long enough for his friend to catch up, Rune gestured to a narrow side passage that led to stairs. "We're going that way."

Garam's dark eyes narrowed. "I thought we were going to your room?"

"If that really is Anaide, I don't want to be anywhere she might think to look for me if someone in there slips. Besides, I need to speak to someone, and I get the feeling she'll be in the kitchens." He adopted a slower pace to keep from leaving his older companion behind again. It was strange to think of Garam as older, but time was different for those without magic.

"And if she's not?"

Rune cast a grim smile over his shoulder. "Then at least they'll have some whiskey down there, eh?"

STRIKE

No matter how many times Ennil looked out the window, he couldn't get used to the view outside. Alwhen was fine enough, as far as cities went. It simply wasn't home.

"Your mother would like it here," he remarked as he clasped his hands behind his back and forced himself to be still. He didn't like waiting, especially when he knew things were happening without him. "She enjoyed traveling when we were young."

"I wouldn't have thought the island would allow for much travel." Vahn sat on the floor, handing wooden blocks to his daughter. The girl stacked them without skill, creating towers and fussing when they fell. Placid as ever, Vahn picked up the blocks and handed them to her over and over again without ever batting an eye.

Often, Ennil had wished his son had favored him. The fairhaired young man was mischievous but gentle, tender-hearted and tame. He'd never been cut out for the military. There was too much of Vivenne in him.

Ennil had wanted a ferocious boy, one strong enough to carry on the family name. He'd not been disappointed in the slender child he received instead, but frustrated. No matter how he tried, he couldn't change the boy's nature. And so the work fell to him. If their bloodline did successfully mix with the royal line, as Envesi promised it would, all would be well. Kifel had not been a strong ruler, but the Archmage had been strong enough for both of them. She had held the island together and torn it apart. While Ennil didn't care for Firal, he saw shades of her mother's strength and determination within her. A point in her favor, but favor wouldn't preserve House Tanrys.

"It didn't," Ennil said at last, watching a girl with a basket of laundry weave her way through the alleys below. "Though we still enjoyed it. She had favorite cities, and there were parts of the countryside that made her sigh over their beauty. But we never ventured into the Giftless lands. I think she would like it here."

"You could bring her," Vahn suggested.

The corners of Ennil's mouth twitched. His back was turned to his son, but the slight movement was betrayed by his reflection in the glass-paned window.

"You haven't told her, have you?"

"Your mother is a good woman, but not always understanding." Ennil closed his eyes and dispelled visions of his wife's face. He loved Vivenne, as he loved his son, but there were limits to what she would understand. She'd never been concerned with preservation of the Tanrys line, though she was proud to be part of it. Her priorities were different, that was all.

Vivenne's priorities were Vahnil and the child he played with, whom Vivenne had accepted as part of her family though she knew it was a lie.

"Maybe the problem is you won't take the time to explain things to her." Vahn didn't raise his voice, but it was as close to a challenge as Ennil had ever heard.

He offered his son a strained smile. "Marriage is a complicated thing, boy."

Shrugging, Vahn passed another block to the dark-haired girl. "Mine isn't."

Ennil almost sneered. "That's because you aren't in charge. No, don't be offended," he added before Vahn could speak. "Firal is the queen. No matter what I've done to ensure you have equal power, to make sure you can lead the kingdom when it needs you, a part of her will always know you only have that power through her. No matter how submissive she may be in private, she is and always will be the one in charge."

Vahn stared at him for a while, then lowered his eyes. "Perhaps that's the problem, then," he murmured.

Ennil twitched. "What?"

"You think someone has to be in control."

Irritation swelled within him, but Ennil stifled it and remained silent as he turned back to the window. Foolish child. Far too much of Vivenne in him. She shared those sort of utopian ideals, foolishly ignoring that without clear leaders, society failed. The simple fact of the matter was that people expected—and wanted—to be told what to do. The only path to progress came from the few who were willing and able to take the reins and drive a populace toward success.

"Someone will be," Ennil said after a time. "Regardless of what you think. If the position is open, then why not you?"

Vahn did not reply.

"Either way, Vivenne will know everything when the dust is settled. We're at the dawn of a change in the world. It's important we handle the situation with care. There have been enough missteps already." Ennil had avoided discussing the manner in which Lulu had come to their headquarters in Alwhen, though he thought Vahn might be more accepting—if not forgiving—now that he understood the motives behind the decision. It was easy to condemn something from the outside. It would be harder now that the boy saw the inner workings of their efforts.

"Missteps going back a long way, I'd say." Vahn glanced up and Ennil met his eyes.

He'd always had difficulty seeing any of himself in the boy's demeanor. Now, the way Vahn looked at him gave him pause. Perhaps it wasn't obvious, but there was a shrewdness in his mind Ennil had never been aware of before now.

"Pioneering something has that problem," Ennil said. "Carving your own path means making mistakes."

Vahn considered that for a while and sighed. "Do you ever worry your cause will ruin your life?"

Raising a brow, Ennil moved closer. Another block tower tumbled and the child whimpered. "Is that what you fear?"

"Don't you?" Vahn lifted his head and locked eyes with his father.

Ennil laid a hand on his son's shoulder, the closest he'd come to offering comfort. "Sometimes part of believing in something is being willing to take those risks."

Vahn bowed his head.

After a moment, Ennil withdrew his hand and laced his fingers behind his back once more. "If you're worried about Firal, don't be. She's a smart woman. The biggest obstacle we have to overcome is her relationship with her mother. Or the lack thereof, I suppose. It's not gone well, I know. We wouldn't be standing here if they were able to get along. But it's not too late for them to reach an understanding. Don't forget, Firal is a mage as well as a queen. The temple was her first home. She'll go to great lengths to see it defended."

It was a wonder the queen hadn't sent legions of her own mages in blue-trimmed white to defend the temple the moment their entourage had set foot in Kirban. Envesi had insisted they accompany the group, however short their visit had been. The Archmage claimed seeing Vahn among her mages would give the temple mages peace of mind. Ennil wasn't so sure it had helped. When she had offered to return them to the palace in Alwhen, he'd been eager to seize the opportunity and leave.

"And with that in mind, cooperation might be harder to reach than you realize. Remember that Envesi came close to destroying the temple when she tried to secede from Kifel's rule." Vahn opened his arms and Lulu climbed onto his lap, nestled into his chest and rubbed her eyes. He hugged the girl close and pressed a kiss to the top of her head.

Ennil tried not to sigh. Would that the girl were his granddaughter in more than name. With fortune, Firal and Vahnil's first child would be a son. The girl would likely take the throne, regardless. Just as well, as it would let the Tanrys family extricate themselves from the tangle of royalty and let them carry on as leaders of their House. The throne was certainly worth aspiring for, but if it came at risk of House Tanrys vanishing altogether, what use was it?

"Firal is a good queen," Ennil said at last, nodding as if to convince himself of his words. "She'll do what's best for her kingdom in the end."

Vahn carried the drowsing child to a nearby chair and sat, rocking the girl as he settled. "And if that means siding against Envesi?"

"She'll do what's best," Ennil repeated.

Or what she thought was best. He tried not to think of that, his eyes narrowing as he watched Lulu drift off to sleep with her round cheek squished against Vahn's chest.

If she didn't agree with their idea of what was best, would her mind change once she knew what Envesi really had to offer?

<hr>

ANAIDE MOVED like a frightened woodland creature, creeping down the hall a few steps at a time. She stopped frequently to look over her shoulder, as if she wasn't sure the others followed.

Firal found it irritating, but also unnerving.

The Master of Water could barely speak without tripping over her words, so shaken by whatever happened in the temple that it seemed a wonder she was on her feet. The woman trembled whenever she paused, and worried her hands as she led the way to the throne room.

At Firal's side, Ordin twisted his hand around the hilt of his sword. It was small, insignificant to most, but it was one of few outward signs of nervousness she'd learned to recognize in the man.

Kytenia followed close behind them, with Temar and Rikka at her heels. The mages were stone-faced. If Firal didn't know them as intimately as she did, she might have thought them indifferent. Instead, she knew they were bracing themselves for a problem, focusing their thoughts and energies in case it came to a fight. She didn't know what they could do if it came to that, but she appreciated they were willing to try.

Though Firal expected to find the former Archmage waiting before the throne when they emerged onto the walkway above the throne room, the room below was empty.

"She'll be along," Anaide whispered, as if afraid to speak out loud. "She will."

Firal sniffed and pretended to be unconcerned. "At least I'll be able to receive her from the throne." Though the matching seat beside hers—Vahn's place—would be uncomfortably empty.

She tried not to think about him. It was another worry she couldn't manage right now, not on top of everything else. She knew he and Lulu were together and she'd take that for comfort. Her daughter would be seen to and protected. Vahn was a good father. He'd lay down his life to keep the girl safe, and that was why she couldn't bear to think of what may have happened to him already.

Firal swept down the curved staircase behind the throne's dais, took her seat, and held her chin high. She'd barely seated herself before a ripple of energy on the other side of the throne room's doors made the fine hairs rise on the back of her neck.

Anaide scuttled forward, clutching her skirts. "Presenting," she began, pausing to clear her throat before she stammered on, "the A-Archmage of I-Ithilear."

Behind the throne, the mages made varying noises of displeasure and disapproval.

Firal only raised a brow.

Long moments crawled past before one of the doors opened and a figure swathed in white slid through. She moved casually but with an animal grace, and the sight of her made Firal's stomach turn.

Everything Rikka said was true. Envesi looked younger, more vital. Her snowy hair tumbled around her shoulders in a cascade of curls. She still painted her eyes with the markings of a Master, simple and utilitarian lines drawn outward from the corners toward her temples. But her eyes had changed, too vibrantly blue even for a mage, and the snakelike pupils made them seem devoid of feeling. Her clawed toes splayed against the plush blue carpet as she walked, and the white scales on her shins glittered with iridescent light. The skirt of her white silk dress was cut to show off her legs, as if proud of what she'd become. After everything Envesi had done to reject Rune, belittle him for what she made him, she was proud to be the same.

Firal tried to banish the man from her mind. He couldn't help her now. She'd been foolish to believe he could help at all. Still, a part of her yearned for his presence. His appearance that morning surprised her, as had his sudden change in temperament, and for a moment she regretted the way she'd spoken the night before. Despite everything, he was unshakable, a constant in a rapidly changing world. In her anger, she had robbed herself of the only stability she had left.

Envesi broke the silence. "How you've grown, child." She opened her arms as she approached the throne, though whether it was greeting or invitation, Firal wasn't sure. "Your daughter inherited all your finest features. A lovely girl, with a remarkable Gift. You should be proud."

"Where is my daughter?" Firal spoke coolly despite the rage that surged at the mention of her missing child.

"Safe, resting in my palace with her father and grandfather. They are quite comfortable, I assure you."

So Ennil had been captured as well. No surprise, since he'd been part of Vahn's party. But that, too, was something Firal could take as reassurance. Though the odd circumstances of Vahn's disappearance threw Ennil's allegiance into question, he was a clever politician and invested in his son's well-being. As long as Ennil was present, his protectiveness of his son would cascade over her daughter as well.

"Why are you here?" An edge crept into Firal's voice, in spite of her best efforts to remain calm.

Envesi appeared surprised by the question. "Why, to speak to you, of course. Why else would I have come all this way?"

"Perhaps you should have come to speak to me before invading the temple, which is beholden to me. A queen might take that as an act of war." Firal did not stir, but her hands, clasped in her lap, tightened until her fingers turned white.

"An invasion? Hardly. I wished to speak to your appointed Archmage, but she wasn't present." Envesi's eyes drifted to Kytenia behind the throne. "I intended to settle things with the mages first, but as things did not go according to plan, I may as well address you and let you deal with them as you will. You are, after all, the queen."

Firal snorted. "And you think I will have dealings with you? After you stole into my home, murdered my stewardess, and kidnapped my daughter? After you took my husband captive?"

Envesi paused her advance and her pleasant expression faltered. "I realize you have many reasons to resent me, child. I am the first to admit I have much to atone for, in regards to you."

"You have caused me nothing but pain." Firal's words grew frosty and she lifted her chin. She peered down her nose at the woman, grateful the dais put them on eye level even though she was seated. Others would have supplicated themselves before the throne. She expected no such thing from the former Archmage. "Each time you have stepped into my life has caused me suffering. Speaking to you at all is more than you deserve."

The snowy-haired woman sighed. "I am aware. Make no mistake, child, I appreciate your maturity in this. And I hope that in working together, you will come to realize your own value. That which, through my own shortcomings, I could never impart."

Firal almost laughed. "Why would I ever work with you?"

"Whether you like it or not, dear girl, we are family." Envesi inched forward again, one step at a time.

"You abandoned me as a child," Firal spat.

"Is that how you see it?"

Anger bubbled up anew, threatening to spill over. "How I see it?" Firal half rose from her throne. "How I *see* it? I grew up thinking I had no family! That my parents left me in the temple, never caring that I existed! And yet all that time, you were just on the other side of a door. What else am I supposed to think?"

"It isn't as it seems," Envesi said. "You don't know how I struggled."

Firal stood and glowered down at her. "You were the Archmage of Elenhiise. I find it hard to believe you suffered at all."

"Few of my choices were easy to make." Envesi stopped at the foot of the dais and met her eyes without hesitation. "When you are fighting to change the world, every action must be considered. Life in the temple was the best I could offer you. The safest option. Somewhere you would be looked after, cared for and trained. Somewhere you could grow up in a world shaped to the ideals I always hoped for."

"I grew up alone," Firal retorted. "I spent every day believing I was worthless and unwanted."

"Unwanted?" Envesi's face crumpled and Firal was startled to realize the woman was genuinely distressed by the suggestion. "After all my effort? You have no idea how difficult you were to conceive."

A crimson flush rose into Firal's cheeks.

"Did you think yourself an accident, girl? It took a year of effort before you were on your way. Your father was never an unpleasant man, but..." The former Archmage trailed off with a shudder. "I never connected with him in that way. But we all make sacrifices for what we desire."

The anger within her fizzled and Firal hesitated. She'd never spoken to her mother beyond the demands of formality. And though their dealings had been unpleasant, part of her was still snared in the woman's web, wishing for her words to be true. "You wanted to have me?" she asked, her voice barely above a murmur.

"Oh, dear child." Envesi stepped onto the dais and reached to cradle Firal's face in her scaly hands. "Of course I did. Never underestimate your importance. Your value. You were a vital part of my life."

Hot tears pricked her eyes, but Firal ignored them. "Why didn't you ever speak to me?"

"It was for the best," Envesi said. "Better that the Masters keep you safe. My work has always been dangerous, but your presence meant a great deal."

Firal bit her lip. A small flicker of hope rose within her. "Truly?"

"Of course." Envesi's snake-slitted eyes narrowed with her soft smile. "That way you could fulfill your purpose from behind the safety of the temple's walls, and I could continue my work."

Blinking twice, Firal tilted her head in her mother's grasp. "My purpose?"

The former Archmage beamed. "Forging a link between the temple and the royal family, sweet girl. Without you, I never could have secured Kifel's support."

Firal pulled away as the tiny flame of hope died. All her life, she'd never been anything more than a tool for people to make use of. It was foolish to think—even for a moment—she might have meant something else. Years of hurt formed storm clouds in her eyes, the sting of tears fading as cool anger chilled emotion into stony resolve.

"I am not here for your convenience." Firal's lip curled with distaste as she stepped backwards and squared her shoulders. Though Envesi stood several inches taller than she did, Firal had her throne behind her and her best mages at her back. She would not be intimidated. "If you think my only purpose is to give you easy access to Ilmenhith, then you're mistaken."

Envesi regarded her with surprise, though it was fast and fleeting. Her luminescent blue eyes narrowed and her mouth pinched with sour disapproval. "I offer you a chance for cooperation. Don't be foolish enough to think you can stand against me."

"Don't be arrogant enough to think you can offer me anything."

The former Archmage barked a laugh. "You think your pitiful temple can change anything on its own? Magic will rot, crumbling like char and ash in their hands!"

"Better decay than corruption," Firal replied dryly.

Envesi snarled and raised an arm to backhand her.

The blow never landed. A blast of energy lashed from behind the throne and flung the woman from the dais.

Shrieking in anger as she hit the floor, Envesi shot a glare full of hatred at her daughter. The air crackled with a swell of raw power, and the tainted Archmage's eyes darkened until they burned black.

FLIGHT

"Lord Daemon."

Rune hadn't gone far down the servant stairway before the call stopped him. He turned to look past a grumbling Garam, who lagged behind.

Tobias hurried down the staircase to join them, gripping his sword to keep it from knocking against the walls. Rune watched him with a frown. There was a hint of aggression in the way Tobias moved. Davan, the man's father, had been calm and stoic, erring on the gentle side. Tobias certainly looked like his father, but the longer Rune was around him, the less he thought them alike.

"Problem?" Garam asked. "Or did the queen decide one supervisor wouldn't be enough to manage him?"

"They went ahead. They're on the way to the throne room. I don't think they noticed me slipping away from the party. The mage from the temple said Envesi was coming to negotiate with Firal."

Rune spat a curse and pushed past Tobias to make for the top of the stairwell.

Garam caught the hem of his coat. "Where are you going?"

Shaking his head, Rune snatched his coat out of his friend's grasp. "Envesi doesn't negotiate."

Groaning, Garam hurried after him with Tobias close at his heels. "And what do you think you can do about it?"

Rune ignored the question. "Get to the throne room. Catch as many mages as you can on the way and send all of them there. Send servants for more." He didn't wait long enough for the men to protest. Instead, he sprinted on down the hall alone.

His quarters were close, but he cursed every second it took to retrieve his sword. Each instant was one he didn't know if he could spare, each echoing footstep in the silent palace corridors reminding him how devoid of power he was.

Garam's words needled him in the man's absence. What *could* he do? A sword was all but useless against a mage, but it was the only thing he had. That and a tiny sliver of hope they might have enough mages in the palace to let him draw enough power to match Envesi. He clung to that sliver as he ran, his heart already in his throat. Alone, the mages couldn't hope to stand against the Archmage.

A flurry of blue-trimmed white robes spun around the corner ahead and darted into the throne room before him. Had Garam and Tobias sent them, or were they answering someone else's call? He shook his head, dismissing the thought. It didn't matter. If Kytenia and the others from the council chamber were there, maybe he'd have enough power for a shield. That was all he could hope to do—shield until they found a way to escape. The mages could open a Gate without him, help Firal get somewhere safe.

That her safety was still his first thought was like an untended wound, raw and aching. She hated him. She wanted nothing to do with him. And yet, as energy surged in the throne room, the fear he might already be too late froze his heart.

He'd dodged the main walkway and emerged below the twin staircases that curved up to the second floor.

Firal stood before the throne. Kytenia, Rikka, and Temar

stood behind her, Rikka with her hand extended. Power still swirled from her fingertips, invisible but making his senses tingle.

Before them, the Archmage staggered back to her feet. She shrieked in rage and her eyes filled with the void black of pure power he'd seen only once before. Envesi raised her hand.

Surging past the mages, Rune threw himself between Firal and the former Archmage to strike the woman's arm from underneath. A shockwave of pure white energy fired from her fingers and lanced through the ceiling with a crash.

"Link!" he roared.

Envesi snarled and twisted away, her hand whipping up to aim another blast. Then she saw him, and she froze. "You," she breathed. "I thought they killed you."

"Sorry to disappoint." Rune spun his blade in hand and leveled its tip with her throat. His eyes darted away, searching for the mages. They clustered to the right of the throne. One of them pulled Firal to the side. A shift in the flows made his skin prickle, a familiar signal they were heeding his command.

A handful of mages joined the knot of power from somewhere behind him. Not enough, he noted with a grimace. There were no more mages present than the few he'd seen in the hallways.

Envesi's eyes narrowed, their impossible dark light fading. "What have you done?" she mused. "I didn't feel you here. How can you mask your Gift so efficiently?"

He felt her probe at him, a tendril of her energy coiling around him like a slimy eel. He drew from his own reserves and erected a shield to keep her from searching any deeper.

She made a small sound of surprise. "You've had a teacher."

"Many." He adjusted his grip on his sword and caught himself before his eyes wandered from her face. He couldn't allow himself to be surprised, no matter what had changed. No matter what she'd done.

Her lip curled in distaste. "No matter what they taught you, you can't believe you stand any chance against me."

Rune didn't reply, rooted in place between the Archmage and Firal with his sword ready.

Barking a laugh into the silence, Envesi raised her hand again. She drew flows from everywhere around her. "Move, boy. You're useful yet, but I've no need for the rest."

"Kytenia—" Rune started.

One of the mages behind the throne screamed and fell to the floor. Her eyes blistered and blackened in their sockets. Smoke poured from her mouth and nostrils as her body convulsed.

A wave of power emanated from Kytenia and the knot of mages. It came too late to heal her. The woman's presence winked out just before she crumbled to ash within her pristine white robes.

Rune spat a curse and lunged forward.

The Archmage moved, but not fast enough. The blade's edge sliced along her cheekbone and through her pointed ear. Envesi screeched and reeled back as she clapped a white-scaled hand to her face. Black blood dribbled on the shoulder of her white gown and bright crimson light flooded her serpentine eyes.

He twirled away in one step and brought his sword back around in the second.

Sparks burst around the blade as it struck an invisible barrier. Numbing quakes shot up his arms and yielded another curse. "Kyt!" He staggered back, shooting a glance over his shoulder. He dared no more than that, the air around him humming with energy as the Archmage called it again.

Already Kytenia's hands moved in a familiar pattern, the gestures most mages relied on to open Gates. But she stopped short of opening it and met his eyes with a panicked look.

They had nowhere to go. The temple, the Eldani cities, even the Grand College on the mainland—where could they go that Envesi couldn't follow?

Rune spun back just in time to duck a searing burst of energy shot from Envesi's palm. He grimaced as his knees hit the floor. Magic swelled everywhere, the flows as tangled as loose threads in the air. He dropped his shield and opened his senses to the full force of the magic around him. "Link!" he yelled again as he slid off the dais and sprinted a few steps away. Without a connection to the other mages, he was all but defenseless, but he still took a stance and readied his sword.

The mages couldn't move fast enough. A tentative stream of energy flowed toward him. Before he could grasp it, Envesi fired a second blast.

Unable to escape, Rune swung at it with his sword. Wild magic crackled like a lightning bolt as it struck the blade, skirted up its edge and streaked from its tip to shatter the stained glass windows overlooking the throne. A sound like thunder exploded through the palace, ringing in his ears and shaking him to the core. All across the dais, mages fell. Only he and Envesi remained standing.

Power pushed toward him again. This time, he caught hold of it. Pure, sweet magic rushed into him, stole his breath and bound him to the mages. "Give me lead!" He barely heard his own voice over the whine in his ears, but it tore from his throat so forcefully the others had to hear.

Several paces away, Firal climbed to her feet among shards of broken glass.

Rune's eyes flicked in her direction.

Envesi caught his line of sight and turned toward her.

No. A pang of terror drove his heart into his throat. He clawed at the magic the mages had offered. It lurched against his hold. It wasn't enough. It couldn't be. Desperate, he tore himself free of the connection and pushed outward with his own energy to snare whatever magic he could.

They caught.

Pure access to the flows hit him like a tidal wave. Pain blossomed in every inch of his body as the seal on his magic reacted. Slivers of glass tore through the scales on his feet as he bolted across the throne room to dive for Firal.

Another burst of energy came from behind him.

He pushed past the pain, reaching farther into the chaos than he ever had.

The sizzling, white-hot light of an opening Gate answered his call.

25

LANDING

THEY HIT THE GROUND AND ROLLED TWICE BEFORE FIRAL SEPARATED herself from the tangle of limbs. Rune came to a stop a short distance away and made it onto all fours before he emptied his stomach into the grass.

Firal tried to shut out the sound.

Garam strode forward from somewhere behind them to kneel at Rune's side and offer help. Rune waved him away and collapsed onto his side when his dry heaving subsided. Then he rolled onto his back, his face wrenched with pain. A streak of black blood marked his lip where he'd wiped a trickle from his nose.

"What was that?" Kytenia stumbled toward Firal with her arms spread, struggling to retain her balance.

Firal blinked at her and turned. All around her, people clambered to their feet. Rikka brushed dirt from her knees while behind her, Ordin helped Temar rise. The two other mages from the throne room—Kella and Asula, both court mages—stood together and stared at the ground, dazed.

Anaide was there too, though she sat on the grass and trembled so hard, Firal didn't think she could have found her feet if she wanted to.

281

None of them had been close enough to make it through that Gate.

"You must have a death wish." Garam scowled, but his hand rested on Rune's shoulder. As angry as he appeared, his tone was pure concern. "You're not supposed to be working with magic at all."

Rune grunted, one hand draped over his eyes. "Didn't have many options. Tobias?"

"He wasn't there. Said he had to get someone out of the palace, never even came close to the throne room." Garam surveyed the group and frowned. "What did you do?"

"Don't know." Rune stayed still, his voice strained. "Tends to happen to me under pressure."

"Gating, nothing unusual about it," Anaide said. Despite her trembling, she sounded calm. Her hands clasped in her lap and pressed down into her skirts to still her shakes. "Though I've never seen it used in quite that fashion before. We've always assumed that a Gate opening on top of a person would kill them."

Kytenia gave a humorless laugh. "And it might have, if they hadn't opened to exactly our sizes. Nearly ten Gates, all at once. If that's what you do under pressure, I'd be terrified to see what you can do when you're actually focused on your magic."

"You should be," Garam said. "It's a scary thing."

Rune only groaned.

Firal turned in a slow circle, trying to gain her bearings. Nothing about the landscape was familiar. Thick grass cushioned their landing spot, a small clearing where wildflowers in shades of yellow and white danced in the cool summer breeze. Trees in shapes she'd never seen before towered above them, the air fragrant and fresh and altogether too dry. There was no tropical humidity, the first clue that wherever they'd landed, it wasn't on the island. Her stomach turned. "Where are we?"

The others blinked and looked around as if just realizing they were outside the palace.

"Is this...?" Garam trailed off.

"The first place I thought of," Rune said. He gasped for breath as he pushed himself to sitting and pressed a hand to his head. Another thick, black droplet rolled free from his nose and he swiped it away with the side of his palm. "Somewhere she can't find us."

Kytenia moved to his side and offered a hand.

He shook his head, tried to rise, and bit off a curse. He drew up one clawed and scaly foot to inspect the bleeding cuts.

Chuckling quietly, Rikka knelt beside him. "Twice in one day? I'm starting to think you're dangerous to yourself," she murmured as she rested a hand against his leg. What she meant by that, Firal didn't know.

Kytenia touched his other leg and the two of them worked together to mend his injuries. Shards of glass pushed free of his feet and sprinkled the ground before him as his flesh repaired itself. From the looks of things, he was the only one hurt. A small blessing, but nothing compared to the new problems the morning had spawned.

"Envesi is alone in my palace." Firal's heart sank as the words left her mouth. She'd been the only thing standing between that woman and the people of Ilmenhith. Without her there, what would stop Envesi from assuming control? Firal had lost the temple only the day before. How could the loss of the entire island be so close behind?

"But you're alive," Anaide said with a shudder. "That's better than we can say for any of the loyal Masters from the temple, I'm sure."

"Alive and nowhere near the island! What good does it do me to be here? I don't even know where we are!" Tears filled her eyes and Firal blinked hard. Her family was on the island, far from where she could help them. Her people were suddenly leaderless, her palace controlled by the only living person she could say she despised. For the third time in her life, everything had fallen apart in a moment, and at the core of it was the same man.

"Somewhere safe," Rune said, his weary voice grating on Firal's nerves. He accepted a hand from Kytenia and Garam and leveraged himself to his feet. Despite the healing, he still grimaced. He tried to straighten, but it was clear he was weakened and exhausted. If he really had opened a Gate for every person present, it was no wonder.

Cold anger stirred in Firal's chest. He'd only just told them he was powerless. How could a man with no magic work such a feat?

Rune picked up his sword from the grass and turned to scan the clearing. The scabbard was gone, left behind in the throne room in Ilmenhith. He made a low sound of displeasure in his throat and rested the flat of the blade on his shoulder.

She eyed him dubiously as he turned eastward and started walking. Pain often lingered after healing, and he walked with a pronounced limp. "Where are you going?"

"Just come on," he said.

The others followed, even Asula and Kella, apparently having been shaken from their stupor.

Firal's eyes narrowed. She stood alone in the grass for a long time, the rest of the party shrinking into the horizon as they ventured toward who knew what. Swallowing her pride, she moved after them.

The wood was mature but well-kept, obviously manicured. Little scrub grew beneath the trees and even the grasses were not high enough to make walking difficult, for which Firal was grateful. Her blue silk gown was impractical for anything but mincing around the palace, and moving over hillocks of grass and wildflowers required her to hitch her skirts almost to her knees. Kytenia and Rikka fell back to help her, but even with their assistance, Firal lagged behind the rest of the group.

By the time they reached a hard-packed dirt avenue, sweat

made her ebony curls cling to her face and the back of her neck. Uncaring whether or not her dress survived, she dropped her skirts and breathed in relief. The rutted trails carved by carriage wheels and marred by hoof prints were just wide enough to walk single-file in either track. Rikka walked ahead of her, but Kytenia picked her way through the grasses by Firal's side. Deep worry marked Kytenia's face, her eyes distant with whatever troubling thoughts occupied her mind. Unlike her friend, Firal tried not to think at all.

Once they were on the road, it didn't take long for their destination to come into sight. Sprawling gardens surrounded a towering manor of pale stone. Ivy and clematis vines clustered with purple flowers crawled up its face, framing dark, diamond-paned windows to lend them a sleepy look. Despite the pleasant weather, the arched double doors at the front of the house were closed. Firal might have thought the house empty if not for the smoke drifting from one of the brick chimneys to coil lazily into the azure sky.

Something tingled at the edge of her senses as they approached, making her frown.

"Mages," Kytenia whispered beside her, frowning as well.

"You know this place?" Ordin peered up at the house, uneasy.

"No, I thought dumping us in a strange place would help keep us from being found," Rune replied sarcastically.

The captain scowled.

"We need to contact our allies and work out a plan as soon as possible," Rune continued, shifting the sword against his shoulder and looking up at the house. "There should be enough room for us to stay here while we figure things out."

"And you think these people will be willing to host us?" Ordin pressed, his hand clenching the hilt of his sword. He had good reason to worry, Firal realized; with them outside of Elenhiise, away from the rest of the guard, he became single-handedly responsible for her well-being.

"I hope," Rune replied.

Garam said nothing, but chuckled.

They moved past the trees and into the edge of the garden, where a sweet fragrance drifted on the breeze. A face appeared in the window as they approached, but vanished before Firal got more than a glimpse. Before they'd gone a dozen paces more, one of the carved oak doors opened.

A boy who couldn't have been older than fifteen bolted down the steps. He stumbled when he hit the ground and righted himself in the blink of an eye. "You're back!" he cried, throwing himself into Rune's chest to wrap him in a hug.

Rune staggered back a step before he found better footing and clapped the youth on the back.

The mages exchanged startled looks, but it wasn't until Firal crept closer that she saw what caused them.

The boy was barefoot. The claws on his three-toed, olive-scaled feet pushed into the dirt as he pressed into the hug with all his might.

Firal's stomach turned over, a sudden, nauseating wave of displeasure making heat rise in her ears. She drew a breath and straightened as she pushed down the white-hot ball of anger in her chest. It cooled to ice in her belly and left her limbs chilled.

A second figure appeared in the doorway, white skirts swirling as she hurried down the steps. Anaide let out a cry and Firal looked again. Her mouth fell open when she realized who it was.

"Brant's mercy," Alira gasped, hurrying across the garden and reaching over the boy to cup Rune's face in her hands. The woman's eyes filled with happy tears, pure relief on her face. "You're alive!"

"For the moment," Rune said, brushing her hands away. He turned toward the group behind him and hesitated.

Alira turned toward them, too, her brows darting upward in surprise. "Anaide? And who—"

"This is Archmage Kytenia of Kirban Temple," Garam

offered. He stepped forward and motioned to each of the people in the party. "Rikka, Master of Wind; Temar, Master of Ilmenhith, and her two mages; Ordin Straes, Captain of the Ilmenhith Royal Guard; and Her Majesty, Firal, Queen of Elenhiise."

At the sound of her name, the boy who stood with Rune straightened. He stared at her with wide, blue, snake-slitted eyes.

Rune planted a hand against the boy's head and shoved him away. "This is Rhyllyn. Seems you all remember Alira."

Rhyllyn stumbled back, rubbing his neck. "She's the *queen?*"

Rune shot him a warning look.

"What's happened? Why are they here?" Alira paused and turned back to Rune with a puzzled frown. "Why are *you* here?" Her eyes traveled to the crown that still rode on his brow.

"Don't tell her a thing!" Anaide snapped. "You weren't there, boy, but the rest of us know what sent her here. We'd best run, before she tattles to the very person we're hiding from." Though she glowered, the Master of Water hid behind the other mages. Firal felt like hiding, herself, but she stayed where she was and let the others talk.

"Alira is a trusted part of the Triad's council," Garam said, crossing his arms. "Considering you were jumping at Envesi's shadow just this morning, I think we have more reason to trust her than you."

Anaide made a quiet hissing sound and scowled in frustration. The other mages said nothing, but Kytenia and Temar exchanged troubled frowns.

Garam turned to Alira and went on as if nothing had transpired. "The temple was taken yesterday. The palace in Ilmenhith was, essentially, taken just now. It's a miracle we made it out." He gave Rune a sidewise glance, the corners of his mouth pulling down. He scratched the corners of his grayed beard as if the want to frown were an itch.

"Essentially," Rune agreed in a murmur. "I'm sure Envesi will have herself on the throne by sundown."

Alira's face darkened. "The witch. She should have burned with Melora. I should have figured it would only be a matter of time before she tried something like this."

"But there were mages in the palace." Rhyllyn hovered at Alira's side, his gaze wandering to the cluster of mages as he spoke. "How did she manage to beat all of you?"

"We should go inside," Rune said before anyone else could speak, starting toward the manor on his own.

"You expect me to stay in that woman's house?" Anaide cried, leveling a gnarled finger with Alira.

Ignoring her, Alira joined Garam and rested her hand on his arm in a diplomatic offer of assistance. He didn't reject her, and together they followed Rune toward the doors. Rhyllyn lingered behind, peering curiously at Firal.

She stared back, her face a stony mask despite the ill feeling the sight of him gave her.

The boy chanced a smile, then sprinted to the house.

"Do you wish to go in, Majesty?" Ordin asked beside her, his voice low.

Firal looked down at her dress and worried her lower lip with her teeth. She didn't. She didn't want to see what sort of life an exile had forged. She didn't want to see the teenage boy who wore Rune's scales and snakelike eyes, or the way his presence painted a clear picture of a life without her. It was jarring, awkward, and after a moment, she felt the heat of shame rising into her cheeks.

Was this how he felt? Stepping into Ilmenhith and finding a family built without him there?

"I would like to refresh myself," she said at last. Regardless of what she wanted, she had few options to choose from. "I am in need of a drink, perhaps food as well. We'll decide what to do after we've had a chance to rest." She picked up her skirts and attempted to look regal as she made her way toward the house. The mages clustered around her, providing a ragtag entourage, but at least it showed she was still in charge of something.

The interior of the manor startled her and, from the way Kytenia turned to look at her, she knew she wasn't alone.

Open staircases stood to either side of the entryway, leading to a railed space above that looked to be a parlor. A larger sitting room waited just ahead on the main floor, through an arching doorway that spanned the space between the stairways. The architecture was fine and showed hints of Ilmenhian influence, but that wasn't unusual. It was the color of things that surprised her.

Blue and silver banners hung from the railings, and the fine, dark wood furniture in the large sitting area was finished with blue upholstery. The furnishings were obviously made by craftsmen from Elenhiise.

It was as if someone had taken a slice of Ilmenhith and deposited it into this foreign place, and the familiarity made her heart ache.

Rune sighed as he made his way into the wide room before them and leaned his sword against the arm of one couch. "Another week, another adventure, eh, Garam?"

"Seems we were just here," the older man said. "Never thought we'd both be back here alive."

"I have to admit I wasn't sure of it, either." The smile Rune gave him was mirthless, but Garam still seemed amused.

"I suppose we'll be grateful," Garam said. "As grateful as I can be, that is. A few more years keeping your scaly backside alive might send me to an early grave."

Rune snorted and claimed a seat.

Alira escorted Garam to one of the couches and helped him sit. "Rhyllyn, would you fetch water and wine for our visitors?"

"Yes, ma'am," the boy murmured, giving Rune one wistful glance before he hurried out through a small door at the back of the room.

Firal crept into the comfortable-looking sitting room and took a seat on one of the couches. She sank deeper into the cushion than she expected. Nervously, she smoothed her skirts and folded her hands in her lap. She tried to look queenly, but her dress was torn and dirty, her hair disheveled, and she'd not worn her crown to the council meeting that morning, thinking it unnecessary for something so private. She regretted that choice. Of the two of them, Rune looked far more noble. His silver-embroidered coat seemed pristine, for all that he'd fought a free mage and tumbled in the dirt, and there was something to his bearing that made her feel as if she should shrink.

She hated it. No one had made her feel small after she'd taken the throne. She'd grown used to respect and deference, yet the power he exuded with the crown on his brow made it clear he was the sort of man who was meant to rule. And he had been, she reminded herself as Kytenia and Rikka sat alongside her. He'd been raised in the palace, not her. Once, Ilmenhith had expected him to be crowned king.

Ordin shifted on his feet beside her. He'd elected to remain standing beside Firal's couch. Even in the company of friends, he didn't relax. Firal couldn't imagine they were in worse danger here than in Ilmenhith, but he still stood with his blade's hilt in his sword hand, ready to draw at a moment's notice.

It wasn't until Firal turned to see where Temar had settled that she realized it was Anaide he watched, not their host. The woman cowered behind the couch and Temar, Asula, and Kella stood over her as if guarding a prisoner. Strange that neither paid any mind to Alira across the room, who was once exiled for treason. Then again, treason had been the reason behind Rune's death sentence, and he had just saved them all.

Too often in her life, it seemed the line between enemy and ally became blurred.

"You've done it again, haven't you?" Alira hastened to the couch where Rune sat alone.

He slumped in his seat, one scaly hand over his eyes. Firal had seen him after their landing, but hadn't noticed until that moment how profoundly unwell he looked.

Alira sat beside him, pressed one hand to his cheek and

rested the other on his shoulder. He barely twitched as the woman delved into his energy with her own. Gifted in healing as Firal was, her senses prickled with awareness of the deep inspection the other woman performed.

"How many times must we have this conversation?" Alira murmured. "You know you can't keep doing this. You'll kill yourself."

"And yet every time I almost kill myself, I can reach a little farther and do a little more afterward." He pushed her hands away.

"Well, the seal's still there," Alira said. "Just the same as ever. But your body's in a terrible state. Whatever you did, you'd best be mindful you don't do it again."

"That shouldn't be a problem," Rune replied dryly. "I don't know what it was in the first place."

Rhyllyn shuffled into the parlor with a tray of cups. Alira hurried to take it from him and set it on the low table. "You sit and speak with our guests," she said as she straightened and patted the young man's shoulder. "I'll fetch the drinks."

"Whiskey," Rune said.

"I'm sure that's the last thing you need," Alira intoned as she swept out of the room.

Rune growled and sank back into his couch.

The corners of Firal's mouth quirked. She shouldn't delight at him getting any sort of comeuppance, but Alira's answer came with such practiced ease that it seemed a response he got often. Firal's threads of resentment had grown brittle in his presence. It was easier for her to be angry if she focused on his shortcomings.

Rikka cleared her throat. "This is a lovely home, Rhyllyn."

The boy's head jerked up in surprise at being addressed, but he responded with a pleasant smile. "The nicest place I've ever lived, though I enjoyed the mage embassy, too. I'm just glad I won't have to live here alone." He tiptoed across the room to sit beside Garam on the couch nearest the entryway.

"Don't count on that just yet," Rune said, giving Firal a

withering stare. "It's harder for them to get a noose around my neck in the Triad, but not impossible."

"I wouldn't say that." Alira bustled back in with two pitchers, the corners of her mouth twisted with amusement. "You haven't seen the chaos your arrest started in the Royal City. Wine, Your Majesty? Or water?" She held up a pitcher and looked to Firal for an answer.

"Water, please." Firal didn't even blink when Ordin stepped forward. He took the fine silver cup from Alira's hand and tasted the drink before he passed it to Firal.

Rune lifted a brow at the display. "You trust me so little?"

"I am a queen." She raised the cup to her lips and met his gaze over the rim. "I'm at risk everywhere, it seems." Even in her own palace. Dismay stole up on her and quenched what little fire she had left.

"I wouldn't offer you refuge in my own home and then have you poisoned." His tone was flat and unamused.

Kytenia coughed into her own cup and lowered her eyes.

"*Your* home? How does a fugitive come to lordship in an allied country?" Anaide asked, her lips peeled back in mockery of a smile.

Rune shrugged and took a cup from Alira without looking at it. "Save a king's life a few times and you'd be surprised what opportunities open up to you." He took a sip and scowled into his cup. Evidently, he didn't appreciate the lack of alcohol.

"How noble." Anaide sneered.

"If not for him, Elenhiise wouldn't be our ally," Garam said. "If he hadn't been present when the proposal for contact was made, it would have been dismissed. The Triad owes a great deal to our trade agreements with the island. Vicamros I—our previous king—never forgot that."

"What reason would he have to aid us?" Temar asked.

Rune locked eyes with Firal, a cool intensity in his gaze. "I had reason enough."

Heat rose in her ears and she turned away.

There had been a time when every subtle shift in his posture or expression revealed his thoughts or feelings. Now when she looked at him and found herself caught in those violet eyes, she saw nothing. It bothered her more than it should.

Now and then she caught flickers of feeling, hints that there was still something familiar buried behind the barrier of ice that had grown during their separation. Then he looked at her like that, and though there was clarity and focus in his gaze, she saw nothing else. No heat, no passion, not even anger. As if he'd become nothing more than an empty vessel, moving and speaking with no hint of a soul inside.

For an instant, when she'd seen how placid and regal he looked as he sat swathed in Ilmenhith's colors with a crown on his brow, she'd regretted the way she'd spoken to him the night before. Now, just as quickly, she thought her words true again. With eyes that cold, how could he be anything but a monster?

"So, what do we do next?" Kytenia asked softly. Her voice was calm, though she had to be anything but. They'd only just begun to discuss how they'd regain the temple. Then they'd lost the whole island. "Does anyone have any suggestions? Some sort of plan?"

"We'll need to speak with Archmage Arrick as soon as possible." Rune reclined in his seat, swirling the contents of his cup. He took another sip and pulled a face. Water, no doubt. "The permanent Gates to Ilmenhith will need to be closed, and we'll need to have the college mages summoned from their embassies."

"That could take weeks," Garam said.

Rune shrugged. "Then we'd better hurry."

"Someone will need to speak to King Vicamros, as well." Alira started to say more, but closed her mouth instead. She took the water pitcher from the table and looked for cups to refill, though everyone had only just gotten their drinks. Firal cocked her head, curious what the woman had intended to say.

Garam nodded. "Might as well be us. He'll know it's serious if it's coming from two members of council."

"Three," Rune said, "along with an allied queen. This is her fight more than it is ours."

"Until it lands on our doorstep," Garam muttered.

"You're a member of the king's council, too?" Rikka asked.

"It took years for Cam to convince him." Rhyllyn grinned.

The mages looked at him with varying expressions of surprise. Rhyllyn bowed his head and coughed politely. "We were friends," he murmured. "When we were younger, I mean."

Garam gave him a stern frown. "I don't know if taking Rune straight back to the Royal City is the best idea."

Alira spread her hands and heaved a helpless sigh. "I don't see what choice we have. We can send someone ahead and clear the Gating parlor within the palace so that no one sees him, but you know how fast word will escape."

"Hard to say what that'll do." Garam rubbed his beard and stared at Rune, thoughtful.

"But it doesn't change that we need speed," Rune insisted.

"We'd best divide our efforts, then," Kytenia said. "We mages can speak with Arrick and get things underway there. The rest of you will go speak with King Vicamros."

"Are there enough of you present to open a Gate without Alira's help?" Firal didn't want to rely on the woman so soon, but as worn and frazzled as they already were, she couldn't imagine the six Elenhiise mages and herself were strong enough to manage on their own. Though they were court mages, Kella and Asula were not remarkably powerful. Firal herself was no better, technically only a mageling.

"We'll Gate you there," Rhyllyn volunteered. "We can manage on our own."

Firal eyed him suspiciously. She'd felt the wild note in the boy's presence, but he was young. In the temple, mages weren't taught how to bend the flows to open Gates on their own until they were ready to graduate to Master, though they were allowed to contribute before then. Even if Rhyllyn were as powerful as Rune had been before whatever ill fate ruined his magic, he couldn't be old enough to do that yet. Firal herself had been a special exception. Being queen, she'd been able to order the court mages to teach her what she wanted to know.

Rune nodded. "We'll take care of the Gates. Once you're in the college, you'll have hundreds more mages to help you get to the Royal City to join us. We'll plan to meet there for a formal council session, after we've had a chance to speak to Vicamros."

"How long will it take?" Firal asked bleakly. Every moment she was away from Elenhiise was torture.

"A few days, most likely," Garam said. "Even with Gates and messengers to hop through them, it'll take time to get word to the people who need to hear it."

The words cut like a knife. Firal slouched in her seat as the burden of despair settled over her shoulders.

"It's likely for the best," Alira said. "I can't imagine anyone wants to appear before Archmages and kings as we are. Except maybe you." Her blue eyes darted toward Rune.

He glowered back.

The mage continued, unruffled. "And it seems you've traveled enough, this morning. A short rest is best for everyone. We may have spare clothing upstairs. If our guests would like to come with me, I'll show them where the bath is and let them freshen up before we depart."

"That sounds magnificent." Kytenia's shoulders slumped with relief. She'd looked pristine in the white robe the court mages had provided for her when they landed, but even that was grimy after their trek through the woods.

Kella looked pleased at the offer and shared a quiet murmur with Asula before the pair of them stood. The two mages had been near silent, waiting and observing. Firal had never noticed how invisible the court mages made themselves in her presence. Now she felt a small stirring of embarrassment and guilt. These women had been in her service for decades. How could she know so little about them?

Shaking the thought from her head, Firal turned her eyes to Kytenia and cleared her throat. "I will stay here until the rest of you are settled."

Her friends gave her curious looks, but she ignored them.

"Very well," Kytenia said. She stood and Alira led her out of the parlor. The other mages were quick to follow.

"There's more than one bath if you want to get ready, Your Majesty." A patronizing tone colored Rune's words.

Firal shot him an icy look.

Rhyllyn's eyes darted between the two of them and he jumped to his feet. "I'll go pack."

Garam didn't even bother with an excuse; he simply removed himself from the parlor.

Ordin hesitated beside the couch.

"Leave us," Firal ordered.

The captain grimaced, but obeyed and made his way to the front door.

In the silence, she heard the steady ticking of a clock.

"You're welcome," Rune said. He poured his water into an abandoned cup and refilled his with wine.

Her brow furrowed. "For what?"

"The part where I saved your life."

"I didn't thank you."

"I know."

Falling quiet, Firal studied her cup. It was fine silver, another piece of an impressive life he'd cobbled together with the scraps she'd handed him. A landowner and lord, a councilor and politician, wealthy and apparently loved by the Triad's people— or respected, at the very least. His accomplishments made her uncomfortable, though she couldn't put a finger on why.

She drank, but the water did nothing for the dryness of her mouth. "How old is your son?"

Rune choked on his wine and covered his mouth. Dark

droplets fell from his chin, hit the carpet and hovered on its surface for long seconds before they soaked in. He coughed and cleared his airway with a grimace.

Firal stared without flinching.

Scowling, he wiped his chin with the back of his hand. "He's not my son."

That was not the response she'd expected. Her ears reddened and heat seeped into her cheeks.

"My brother," he added as explanation. He coughed again and had to clear his throat to continue. "Not blood, but accepted as if he were. They made him. Not like they made me, but close enough."

"They?" she repeated quietly.

"Envesi. And Melora. They forced Alira to help them. She thought it was wrong." He sipped his wine absently. "She fought Melora and won. Took Rhyllyn and ran. She brought him to me."

"Why?"

"She thought I would understand."

Silent, she turned the cup in her hands, her fingertips tracing the etchings.

Again he sank back into the upholstery and rested a hand over his eyes.

He carried an air of struggle, though tinged with the weight of responsibility. When first they'd met, so many years ago, he'd been vibrant and passionate, filled with ambition and vigor. The man in front of her now was worn and wearied, driven instead by some duty she didn't understand. A stark contrast to the man he'd been in Ilmenhith, too.

In the span of a night, he'd changed, and Firal couldn't understand how. Hints of his antagonistic behavior still floated on the surface, but so little of the fight he'd put up remained.

Rune exhaled. "What do you want?"

She blinked at the question. "Excuse me?"

"Well, we aren't alone for you to enjoy my company. What do

you want? Or did you just have the desire to criticize me for your mistaken ideas about Rhyllyn?"

Anger was quick to replace any embarrassment she might have felt. "Nothing I thought was unreasonable. Look at this." She waved a hand at the finely furnished room they sat in. "You expect me to think you never moved on?"

"It's none of your business if I did."

"And yet you'll walk into my palace, into my home, and think you're justified in anger that I have a family that doesn't include you?"

"That's different," Rune snapped, heat and venom in his voice.

She barked a laugh. "How is it different?"

"You willfully kept my child's existence from me!"

Firal threw up her hands. "Everything I've done was to keep her safe! The crown hadn't even touched my head before I found out. What was I supposed to do? Announce to the kingdom that I'd bedded their enemy and my child's father was the man they'd sought to hang?"

He snorted. "Not disregarding your vows within a week of me being gone would have been a start. I could have come back—"

"Well, you didn't," she interrupted. "And don't play that game with me. You think I'd believe you waited all this time?"

"I waited longer than you," he fired back, pushing himself up.

She had to fight to keep from rolling her eyes. "Here I thought for a moment you'd grown up and changed. You played an impressive part in council this morning, but you're still as petty and immature as ever."

Rune slammed his cup onto the table, rattling the rest of the dishes. "You're the one who sent everyone out so you could start a fight."

"All I did was ask a question." She tried to stay composed, though she felt like tearing out her hair. "With the sort of reputation you've apparently built for yourself, it's not an unreasonable assumption. I'm sure you have any number of women ready to fall into your bed."

"At least I didn't marry any of them!"

From the entryway, Ordin cleared his throat. "I don't mean to eavesdrop, but with the way the two of you are yelling, you're making it difficult not to."

Growling low in his throat, Rune seized his sword from where it rested against the couch and stalked out without another word.

The captain stepped aside to let him pass, his head bowed. Ordin looked uncomfortable. His silence made it worse.

"Wow," Rhyllyn said softly from the other end of the room. "You two really do fight all the time."

Firal stifled an unamused laugh. "Is that all the legacy we have to leave? Famous arguments?"

Rhyllyn crept into the parlor to gather the stray cups and pitchers onto the tray. "I wouldn't say they're famous. I mean, I only heard the tail end."

She squeezed her eyes closed.

"There's a room upstairs for you if you want to be alone," the boy offered. "Alira will get you some clean clothing."

"Probably for the best," she sighed. Her nerves still jangled. She struggled to soothe them. "I suppose I shouldn't meet your king like this."

He shrugged and picked up the tray. "Archmage Kytenia and her group are going soon, but Garam thinks it would be best if we send word to the king before we try to Gate to the Royal City. He definitely doesn't think it's a good idea for us to appear in the courtyard, so we'll need to make sure there's somewhere in the palace for us to meet in private. Alira mentioned the Gating parlor when everyone was in here, but that takes time to coordinate. It might be faster to get permission to Gate in somewhere else."

A wise choice, especially if Rune's arrest had caused as much trouble as Alira implied. "Very well." Firal didn't know what else to say.

"Yours is the last room in the north hall. I mean, left from the top of the stairs. Do you want me to take you?" He smiled shyly.

Now that she saw him up close, she realized there was no resemblance between the boy and Rune, save their scales and snakelike eyes. Even then, Rhyllyn's eyes were a rich cobalt, while his scales were a muddy olivine.

"I'll manage, thank you."

"All right. Just let me know if you need anything. The kitchen is that way. That's where I'll be." He nodded toward the rear doorway and reached for her cup with a smile.

She handed it over and lowered her eyes. "Did Garam say when we should expect word from the king?"

"No," Rhyllyn said, "but he expects we'll have permission to Gate into the palace by tomorrow."

Tomorrow. The words dragged her heart down as surely as an anchor. "I see. Thank you, Rhyllyn."

The boy nodded with another, more tentative smile, then disappeared through the doorway.

Silence fell around her like a shroud.

In the still, each tick of the clock she couldn't see struck like a death knell. Everyone else seemed calm, confident, but it took everything Firal had in her to keep from falling to the floor in tears.

She was half the world away from her kingdom, her husband, her child. A full day from any semblance of a plan, and alone, she was faced with the hard reality of how quickly things had changed. They'd landed on this side of the Gate no more than an hour before, but it was too late.

Ilmenhith had already fallen.

GLOSSARY

Affinity – One's natural inclination in magic. There are five major affinities: Earth, water, fire, wind, and life. These provide the primary source of power a mage can draw from and manipulate. While there are smaller subcategories affinities may fall into, granting specific talents in narrow fields, they are generally related to one of the five and, as result, only the five major affinities are recognized.

Aldaan – One of three provinces in the Triad.

Aldaanan *or* **Alda'anan** – A faction of free mages.

Alira – (*uh-LEER-ah*) – Former Master of the House of Fire, now part of the Triad's council. Rhyllyn's adoptive mother.

Alwhen – (*OWL-when*) – The capital of the eastern half of Elenhiise island, a region known as the Giftless Lands.

Anaide – (*uh-NAYD*) – Master of the House of Water.

Archmage – The leader of Kirban Temple, generally recognized as the leader of all mages.

Arrick Ortath – Current Headmaster and Archmage of the Grand College of Lore.

Balen – (*BAY-len*) – Master of the House of Fire.

Core – An underground city beneath the ruins, home of the Underlings.

Daemon – (*DAY-mun*) – Rune's previous name.

Davan - An officer among the Underlings. Was left in charge after Daemon's disappearance.

Edagan – (*ED-ah-gan*) – Master of the House of Earth.

Eldani – (*ell-DAN-ee*) – The only inhabitants of Ithilear who are known to be Gifted. Eldani are long-lived, due to their magic, and differ from humans only in their pointed ears. Diluted bloodlines are recognized by the reduced point of an Eldani's ear, which directly corresponds with their prowess as a mage.

Elenhiise – (*ELL-en-heese*) – A small island in the middle of the Lantaaran sea, generally used as a waypoint in trade between the region's northern and southern continents. The island is ruled by two factions, the Gifted Eldani and Giftless men.

Ennil – (*in-ill*) – Full name Ennil Tanrys. Former Captain of the Guard of Ilmenhith. Vahn's father.

Envesi – (*in-VESS-see*) – The former Archmage of Kirban Temple. Corrupted by her own power after granting herself free magic.

Eyrion Tolmarni – (*EAR-ee-on toll-MAR-nee*) – Previous Headmaster of the Grand College of Lore.

Filadiel – (*fil-LAD-ee-ell*) – Leader of the Aldaanan mages.

Firal – (*fur-ALL*) – Queen of Ilmenhith and the Eldani half of Elenhiise Island. Former green-rank mageling of Kirban Temple.

Flows – The natural ebb and flow of magic, which mages are able to seize and manipulate.

Garam – Full name Garam Kaith. Former Captain of the Royal City Guard, now part of the Triad's council. Sera's brother.

Gift – The ability to use magic.

House – A subsection of mages, ruled by a particular affinity. Mages within the House of Healing, Fire, etc. may take classes together, but their education is overseen by the Master of their House.

Ileara – (*ill-ee-ARE-ah*) – The second moon. The smaller of the two, Ileara is known as The Mother and is stationary in the sky. As it is only visible in the far western regions of the known world, such as the Westkings and the Chains of Raeldan, some residents of Elenhiise and the other eastern regions do not believe Ileara exists.

Ilmenhith – (*ill-men-HITH*) – The capital of the western half of Elenhiise island, which is under Eldani control.

Ithi – (*ith-EE*) – The first moon. The larger of the two, Ithi is known as The Soldier and circles Ithilear once per day. The thirteen months of the year are framed around Ithi's phases; its cycle is 28 days.

Ithilear – (*ith-ILL-ee-arr*) – The world. The name is derived from the two moons, Ithi and Ileara. In folklore, the moons are lovers. Ithi ventures forth to patrol and protect their child, Ithilear, while Ileara remains in one place to provide a stable home.

Kifel – (*kiff-EL*) – Full name Kifelethelas Penedhionn. The former Eldani king and ruler of the western half of Elenhiise island.

Kirban Temple – (*KER-ban*) – Founded by Archmage Envesi, Kirban Temple is the only school of magecraft on Elenhiise Island. A prestigious college sponsored by the Eldani crown and located near the southern edge of the ruins.

Kytenia – (*kit-teen-yah*) – Archmage of Kirban Temple and Firal's best friend.

Lore - One of three provinces in the Triad.

Lumia – (*loo-MEE-ah*) – Former Queen of the Underlings.

Lulu – Firal's daughter.

Mageling – A mage in training. Magelings are divided into five ranks before they graduate to Master and wear robes in corresponding colors. The five ranks are gray, lavender, yellow, green, and blue.

Marreli – (*mah-RELL-ee*) – A gray-rank mageling at Kirban Temple. Was one of Firal's friends.

Master – A mage recognized as skilled enough to wield magic without supervision. Masters outside the temple act as healers and scholars, and are in charge of scouting Gifted children to send for training. Masters who remain within the temple are generally teachers. Master mages are the only mages allowed to wear white. Court Masters and Masters of an affinity mark their eyes with black ink to distinguish their rank.

Medreal – (*mee-dree-al*) – Queen Firal's stewardess.

Melora – (*mel-LOR-ah*) – Deceased Master of the House of Wind.

Minna - An Underling woman who befriended Firal.

Nondar – (*non-DAR*) – Previously the Master of the House of Healing, later Archmage of Kirban Temple. Nondar was one of few recognized half-Eldani Masters and is unparalleled as a medic.

Ordin Straes – (*ore-DEN strays*) – Captain of Ilmenhith's guard.

Ran – Full name Lomithrandel. Another name for Rune.

Redoram – (*RED-or-AM*) – Full name Redoram Parthanus. Councilor in the Triad's Royal City.

Relythes – (*rell-uh-THEEZ*) – The Giftless King, ruler of Alwhen and the eastern half of Elenhiise island.

Rhyllyn – (*rill-in*) – Rune's adoptive brother. Like Rune, his physical body has been corrupted by wild magic, a change brought about by Envesi.

Ria – A gryphon messenger and amateur cartographer.

Rikka – (*RIK-kuh*) – Master of the House of Wind in Kirban Temple. One of Firal's friends.

Roberian – One of three provinces in the Triad.

Royal City – The capital of the Triad.

Ruins – A sprawling labyrinth in the center of the island. The ruins fall entirely on Eldani lands.

Rune - A free mage whose physical body is corrupted by his tainted magic. Previously the leader of the Underling faction on Elenhiise, now a soldier under King Vicamros II and part of the Triad's council.

Sera – Full name Sera Kaith. A mage in the Royal City and a scout for the guard. Garam's sister.

Shymin – (*SHY-min*) – Master of the House of Healing in Kirban Temple. One of Firal's friends and Kytenia's elder sister.

Temar – (*tim-MAR*) – Leader of Ilmenhith's court mages.

Tobias – Current leader of the Underlings.

Tren – Full name Tren Achos. Was Lumia's general.

Triad – An empire in the north, composed of three provinces—Aldaan, Lore, and Roberian—and ruled by King Vicamros II.

Underlings – Giftless people driven into the ruins by war, rumored to be monsters and believed to be legend.

Vahn – Full name Vahnil Tanrys. King of Elenhiise and husband to Firal.

Vicamros II – (*vi-CAM-rows*) – King of the Triad.

Vivenne – (*viv-INN*) – Full name Vivenne Tanrys. Vahn's mother. Ennil's wife.

www.ingramcontent.com/pod-product-compliance
Lightning Source LLC
Chambersburg PA
CBHW061556190726
48288CB00007B/2046